Random Harvest

James Hilton

"According to a British Official Report, bombs fell at Random."
—German Official Report

PART ONE

On the morning of the eleventh of November, 1937, precisely at eleven o'clock, some well-meaning busybody consulted his watch and loudly announced the hour, with the result that all of us in the dining-car felt constrained to put aside drinks and newspapers and spend the two minutes' silence in rather embarrassed stares at one another or out of the window. Not that anyone had intended disrespect—merely that in a fast-moving train we knew no rules for correct behaviour and would therefore rather not have behaved at all. Anyhow, it was during those tense uneasy seconds that I first took notice of the man opposite. Dark-haired, slim, and austerely good-looking, he was perhaps in his early or middle forties; he wore an air of prosperous distinction that fitted well with his neat but quiet standardized clothes. I could not guess whether he had originally moved in from a third-or a first-class compartment. Half a million Englishmen are like that. Their inconspicuous correctness makes almost a display of concealment.

As he looked out of the window I saw something happen to his eyes— a change from a glance to a gaze and then from a gaze to a glare, a sudden sharpening of focus, as when a person thinks he recognizes someone fleetingly in a crowd. Meanwhile a lurch of the train spilt coffee on the table between us, providing an excuse for apologies as soon as the two minutes were over; I got in with mine first, but by the time he turned to reply the focus was lost, his look of recognition unsure. Only the embarrassment remained, and to ease it I made some comment on the moorland scenery, which was indeed sombrely beautiful that morning, for overnight snow lay on the summits, and there was one of them, twin-domed, that seemed to keep pace with the train, moving over the intervening valley like a ghostly camel. "That's Mickle," I said, pointing to it.

Surprisingly he answered: "Do you know if there's a lake—quite a small lake—between the peaks?"

Two men at the table across the aisle then intervened with the instant garrulousness of those who overhear a question put to someone else. They were also, I think, moved by a common desire to talk down an emotional crisis, for the entire dining-car seemed suddenly full of chatter. One said there WAS such a lake, if you called it a lake, but it was really more of a swamp; and the other said there wasn't any kind of lake at all,

3

though after heavy rain it might be "a bit soggy" up there, and then the first man agreed that maybe that was so, and presently it turned out that though they were both Derbyshire men, neither had actually climbed Mickle since boyhood.

We listened politely to all this and thanked them, glad to let the matter drop. Nothing more was said till they left the train at Leicester; then I leaned across the table and said: "It doesn't pay to argue with local inhabitants, otherwise I'd have answered your question myself—because I was on top of Mickle yesterday."

A gleam reappeared in his eyes. "YOU were?"

"Yes, I'm one of those eccentric people who climb mountains for fun all the year round."

"So you saw the lake?"

"There wasn't a lake or a swamp or a sign of either."

"Ah..." And the gleam faded.

"You sound disappointed?"

"Well, no—hardly that. Maybe I was thinking of somewhere else. I'm afraid I've a bad memory."

"For mountains?"

"For names too. MICKLE, did you say it was?" He spoke the word as if he were trying the sound of it.

"That's the local name. It isn't important enough to be on maps."

He nodded and then, rather deliberately, held up a newspaper throughout a couple of English counties. The sight of soldiers marching along a Bedfordshire lane gave us our next exchange of remarks—something about Hitler, the European situation, chances of war, and so on. It led to my asking if he had served in the last war.

"Yes."

"Then there must be things you wish you HAD forgotten?"

"But I have—even THEM—to some extent." He added as if to deflect the subject from himself: "I imagine you were too young?"

"Too young for the last, but not for the next, the way things are going."

"Nobody will be either too young or too old for the next."

Meanwhile men's voices were uprising further along the car in talk of Ypres and Gallipoli; I called his attention and commented that thousands of other Englishmen were doubtless at that moment reminiscing about their war experiences. "If you've already forgotten yours, you're probably lucky."

"I didn't say I'd forgotten EVERYTHING."

He then told me a story which I shall summarize as follows: During the desperate months of trench warfare in France an English staff officer reasoned that if some spy whom the Germans had learned to trust were to give them false details about a big attack, it might have a better chance of success. The first step was to establish the good faith of such a spy, and this seemed only possible by allowing him, over a considerable period, to supply true information. Accordingly, during several weeks before the planned offensive, small raiding parties crawled across no-man's-land at night while German machine-gunners, having been duly tipped off as to time and place, slaughtered them with much precision. One of these doomed detachments was in charge of a youth who, after enlisting at the beginning of the war, had just begun his first spell in the front line. Quixotically eager to lead his men to storybook victory, he soon found that his less inspiring task was to accompany a few wounded and dying survivors into a shell-hole so close to the enemy trenches that he could pick up snatches of German conversation. Knowing the language fairly well, he connected something he heard with something he had previously overheard in his commanding officer's dugout; so that presently he was able to deduce the whole intrigue of plot and counterplot. It came to him as an additional shock as he lay there, half drowned in mud, delirious with the pain of a smashed leg, and sick with watching the far greater miseries of his companions. Before dawn a shell screamed over and burst a few yards away, killing the others and wounding him in the head so that he saw, heard, and could think no more.

"What happened to him afterwards?"

"Oh, he recovered pretty well—except for partial loss of memory... He's still alive. Of course, when you come to think about it logically, the whole thing was as justifiable as any other piece of wartime strategy. The primary aim is to frustrate the enemy's knavish tricks. Anything that does so is the thing to do, even if it seems a bit knavish itself."

"You say that defensively, as if you had to keep on convincing yourself about it."

"I wonder if you're right."

"I wonder if you're the survivor who's still alive?"

He hesitated a moment, then answered with an oblique smile: "I don't suppose you'd believe me even if I said no." I let it go at that, and after a pause he went on: "It's curious to reflect that one's death was planned by BOTH sides—it gives an extra flavour to the life one managed to sneak away with, as well as a certain irony to the mood in which one wears a decoration."

"So I should imagine."

I waited for him to make some further comment but he broke a long silence only to summon the waiter and order a whiskey-and-soda. "You'll have one with me?"

"No, thanks."

"You don't drink?"

"Not very often in the morning."

"Neither do I, as a rule. Matter of fact, I don't drink much at all."

I felt that these trivial exchanges were to cover an inner stress of mind he was trying to master. "Coming back to what you were saying," I coaxed, eventually, but he interrupted: "No, let's NOT come back to it—no use raking over these things. Besides, everybody's so bored with the last war and so scared of the next that it's almost become a social gaffe to bring up the matter at all."

"Except on one day of the year—which happens to be today. Then the taboos are lifted."

"Thanks to the rather theatrical device of the two minutes' silence?"

"Yes, and 'thanks' is right. Surely we English need some release from the tyranny of the stiff upper lip."

He smiled into his drink as the waiter set it before him. "So you think it does no harm— once a year?"

"On the contrary, I think it makes a very healthy purge of our normal —which is to say, our ABNORMAL—national inhibitions."

Another smile. "Maybe—if you like psycho-analyst's jargon."

"Evidently YOU don't."

"Sorry. If you're one of them, I apologize."

"No, I'm just interested in the subject, that's all."

"Ever studied it—seriously?"

I said I had, which was true, for I had written several papers on it for the Philosophical Society. He nodded, then read again for a few score miles. The train was travelling fast, and when next he looked up it was as if he realized that anything he still had to say must be hurried; we were already streaking past the long rows of suburban back gardens. He suddenly resumed, with a touch of his earlier eagerness: "All right then—listen to this —and don't laugh... it may be up your street... Sometimes I have a feeling of being—if it isn't too absurd to say such a thing— of being HALF SOMEBODY ELSE. Some casual little thing—a tune or a scent or a name in a newspaper or a look of something or somebody will remind me, just for a second—and yet I haven't time to get any grip of what it DOES remind me of—it's a sort of wisp of memory that can't be trapped before it fades away... For instance, when I saw that mountain this morning I felt I'd been there —I almost KNEW I'd been there... I could see that lake between the summits—why, I'd BATHED in it—there was a slab of rock jutting out like a diving-board—and the day I was there I fell asleep in the shade and woke up in the sun... but I suppose I've got to believe the whole thing never happened, just because you say there isn't a lake there at all... Does all this strike you as the most utter nonsense?"

"By no means. It's not an uncommon experience."

"Oh, it ISN'T?" He looked slightly dismayed, perhaps robbed of some comfort in finding himself not unique.

"Dunne says it's due to a half-remembered dream. You should read his book An Experiment with Time. He says—this, of course, is condensing his theory very crudely

—that dreams DO foretell the future, only by the time they come true, we've forgotten them—all except your elusive wisp of memory."

"So I once dreamed about that mountain?"

"Perhaps. It's an interesting theory even if it can't be proved. Anyhow, the feeling you have is quite a normal one."

"I don't feel that it IS altogether normal, the way I have it."

"You mean it's beginning to worry you?"

"Perhaps sometimes—in a way—yes." He added with a nervous smile: "But that's no reason why I should worry YOU. I can only plead this one-day-a-year excuse—the purging of the inhibitions, didn't you call it? Let's talk about something else—cricket— the Test Match... Wonder what will happen to England... ?"

"Somehow today that doesn't sound like cricket talk."

"I know. After the silence there ARE overtones... but all I really wanted to prove was that I'm not a complete lunatic."

"Most people have a spot of lunacy in them somewhere. It's excusable."

"Provided they don't inflict it on strangers."

"Why not, if you feel you want to?"

"I don't want to—not consciously."

"Unconsciously then. Which makes it worst of all. Not that in your case it sounds very serious."

"You don't think so? You don't think these—er— peculiarities of memory—are—er— anything to worry about?"

"Since you ask me, may I be perfectly frank?"

"Of course."

"I don't know what your work is, but isn't it possible you've been overdoing things lately—not enough rest—relaxation?"

"I don't need a psycho-analyst to tell me that. My doctor does— every time I see him."

"Then why not take his advice?"

"THIS is why." He pulled a small notebook from his vest pocket. "I happen to be in what is vaguely called public life—which means I'm on a sort of treadmill I can't get off until it stops—and it won't stop." He turned over the pages. "Just to show you—a sample day of my existence... Here, you can read it—it's typed." He added, as I took the book: "My secretary—very neat. SHE wouldn't let me forget anything."

"But she can't spell 'archaeological.'"

"Why does she have to?" He snatched the book back for scrutiny and I had the feeling he was glad of the excuse to do so and keep it. "Calderbury Archaeological and Historical Society?... Oh, they're my constituents— I have to show them round the House—guide-book stuff—an awful bore... that's this afternoon. This evening I have an Embassy reception; then tomorrow there's a board meeting, a lunch party, and in the evening I'm guest speaker at a dinner in Cambridge."

"Doesn't look as if there's anything you could cut except possibly tomorrow's lunch."

"I expect I'll do that, anyway—even though it's at my own house. There'll be a crowd of novelists and actors and titled people who'd think me surly because I wouldn't talk to them half as freely as I'm talking to you now."

I could believe it. So far he had made no move towards an exchange of names between us, and I guessed that, on his side, the anonymity had been not only an encouragement to talk, but a temptation to reveal himself almost to the point of self-exhibition. And there had been a certain impish exhilaration in the way he had allowed me to glance at his engagement book for just those few seconds, as if teasing me with clues to an identity he had neither wish nor intention to disclose. Men in whom reticence is a part of good form have fantastic ways of occasional escape, and I should have been the last to embarrass an interesting fellow traveller had he not added, as the train began braking into St. Pancras: "Well, it's been a pleasant chat. Some day—who knows?—we might run into each other again."

Spoken as if he sincerely half meant it, the remark merely emphasized the other half sense in which he did not mean it at all; and this, because I already liked him, irked me to the reply: "If it's the Swithin's Dinner tomorrow night we may as well introduce ourselves now as then, because I'll be there too. My name's Harrison. I'm on the Reception Committee."

"Oh, really?"

"And I don't know what your plans are, but after the show I'd be delighted if you'd come up to my rooms and have some coffee."

"Thanks," he muttered with sudden glumness, gathering up his newspapers and brief-case. Then I suppose he realized it would be pointless, as well as discourteous, to refuse the name which I should inevitably discover so soon. He saved it for a last unsmiling afterthought as he jumped to the platform. "My name's Rainier... Charles Rainier."

* * * * *

Rainier nodded rather coldly when I met him again the following day. In his evening clothes and with an impressive array of decorations he looked what he was—a guest of honour about to perform his duties with the touch of apathy that so effectively disguises the British technique of authority. Not necessarily an aristocratic technique. I had already looked him up in reference books and found that he was the son of a longish line of manufacturers—no blue blood, no title (I wondered how he had evaded that), a public school of the second rank, Parliamentary membership for a safe Conservative county. I had also mentioned his name to a few people I knew; the general impression was that he was rich and influential, and that I was lucky to have made such a chance

8

encounter. He did not, however, belong to the small group of well-known personalities recognizable by the man-in-the-street either in the flesh or in Low cartoons. On the contrary, he seemed neither to seek nor to attract the popular sort of publicity, nor yet to repel it so markedly as to get in reverse; it was as if he deliberately aimed at being nondescript. A journalist told me he would be difficult to build up as a newspaper hero because his personality was "centripetal" instead of "centrifugal"; I was not quite certain what this meant, but Who's Who was less subtle in confiding that his recreations were mountaineering and music.

On the whole I secured a fair amount of information without much real enlightenment; I hoped for more from a second meeting and travelled to Cambridge in a mood of considerable anticipation. It was the custom of the secretary and committee of the Swithin's Society to receive guests informally before dining in the College Hall; so we gathered first in the Combination Room, where we made introductions, drank sherry, and exchanged small talk. It is really hard to know what to say to distinguished people when you first meet them—that is, it is hard to think of talk small enough to be free from presumption. Rainier, for instance, had lately been in the financial news in connection with a proposed merger of cement companies, a difficult achievement for which negotiations were still proceeding; but it was impossible to say "How is your merger getting on?" as one might say "How are your chrysanthemums?" to a man whom you knew to be an enthusiastic gardener. Presently, to my relief, some other guests arrived whom I had to attend to, and it was perhaps a quarter of an hour before I saw him edging to me through the crowd. "Sorry," he began, "but I've got to let you down —awful toothache—where's the nearest dentist?" I hustled him out as inconspicuously as possible and at the door of the taxi received his promise to return to the dinner if he felt equal to it. Then I went back and explained to the company what had happened. Somehow it did not sound very convincing, and none of us really expected to see him again. But we did. An hour later he took the vacant place we had left at the High Table and was just in time to reply to the toast with one of the best after-dinner speeches I had ever heard. Maybe the escape from physical pain plus the Cambridge atmosphere, with its mingling of time-honoured formality and youthful high spirits, suited a mood in which he began with badinage about toothache and ended with a few graceful compliments to the College and University. Among other things I remember him recalling that during his undergraduate days he had had an ambition to live at Cambridge all his life, as a don of some sort (laughter), but exactly what sort he hadn't stayed long enough to decide (laughter), because fate had called him instead to be some sort of business-man politician, but even what sort of THAT he hadn't yet entirely made up his mind (more laughter)... "So because of this fundamental indecision, I still hope that some day I shall throw off the cares of too many enterprises and seek the tranquillity of a room overlooking a quadrangle and an oak that can be sported against the world." (Prolonged laughter in which the speaker joined.) After he had finished, we all cheered uproariously and then, relaxing, drank and argued and made a night of it in the best Swithin's tradition; when eventually the affair broke up, it was Rainier himself who asked if my invitation to coffee still held good.

"Why, of course—only I thought maybe after the dentist you'd feel —"

"My dear boy, don't ever try to imagine what my feelings are."

9

But he smiled in saying it, and I gathered he had forgiven not so much me as himself for having taken part in our train conversation. A few friends adjourned to my rooms near by, where we sat around and continued discussions informally. Again he charmed us by his talk, but even more by his easy manners and willingness to laugh and listen; long after most of the good-nights he still lingered chatting, listening, and smoking cigarette after cigarette. I didn't know then that he slept badly and liked to stay up late, that he enjoyed young company and jokes and midnight argument, that he had no snobbisms, and that public speaking left him either very dull and listless or very excitable and talkative, according to the audience. Towards three in the morning, when we found ourselves sole survivors, I suggested more coffee, and at that he sank into an armchair with a sigh of content and put his feet against the mantelpiece as if the place belonged to him— which, in a sense, it did, as to any Swithin's man since the reign of Elizabeth the Foundress. "I've been in these rooms before—often. Fellow with the disarming name of Pal had them in my time—'native of Asia or Africa not of European parentage,' as the University regulations so tactfully specify. High-caste Hindoo. Mathematician— genius in his own line—wonder what he's doing now?—probably distilling salt out of sea-water or lying down in front of trains or some other blind-alley behaviour. Used to say he felt algebra emotionally—told me once he couldn't read through the Binomial Theorem without tears coming into his eyes —the whole concept, he said, was so shatteringly beautiful... Wish I could have got into his world, somehow or other. And there are other worlds, too—wish sometimes I could get into any of them—out of my own."

"What's so wrong about your own?"

He laughed defensively. "Now there you've got me... Maybe, as you hinted yesterday, just a matter of overwork. But it's true enough that talking to all you young fellows tonight made me feel terribly ancient and envious."

"Not ENVIOUS, surely? It's we who are envious of you—because you've made a success of life. We're a pretty disillusioned crowd when we stop laughing—we know there won't be jobs for more than a minority of us unless a war comes to give all of us the kind of job we don't want."

He mused over his coffee for a moment and then continued: "Yes, that's true—and that's probably why I feel how different everything is here instead of how much the same— because my Cambridge days WERE different. The war was just over then, and our side had won, and we all of us thought that winning a great war ought to mean something, either towards making our lives a sort of well-deserved happy-ever-after—a long golden afternoon of declining effort and increasing reward—or else to give us chances to rebuild the world this way or that. It all depended whether one were tired or eager after the strain. Most of us were both —tired of the war and everything connected with it, eager to push ahead into something new. We soon stopped hating the Germans, and just as soon we began to laugh at the idea of anyone caring enough about the horrid past to ask us that famous question on the recruiting posters—'What did you do in the Great War?' But even the most cynical of us couldn't see ahead to a time when the only logical answer to that question would be another one—'WHICH Great War?'

"There was a room over a fish shop in Petty Cury where some of us met once a week to talk our heads off—we called ourselves the Heretics, but I can't remember anything said at those meetings half so well as I can remember the smell of fish coming up from the shop below. And J. M. Keynes was lecturing in the Art School, politely suggesting that Germany mightn't be able to pay off so many millions in reparations, or was it billions? — in those days one just thought of a number and stuck as many naughts as one fancied after it. And there were Holland Rose on Napoleon and Pigou on Diminishing Returns, and Bury still explaining the Decline and Fall of the Roman Empire, and one evening Pal and I—sounds sentimental, doesn't it, Pal and I?—lined up in a queue that stretched half-way round Trinity Great Court to hear a lecture by a fellow named Eddington about some new German fellow named Einstein who had a theory about light bending in the middle—that brought the house down, of course—roars of laughter—just as you heard tonight only more so—good clean undergraduate fun at its best. And behind us on the wall the portrait of Catholic Mary scowled down on this modern audience that scoffed at science no less than at religion. Heretics indeed—and laughing heretics! But my pal Pal didn't laugh—he was transfixed with a sort of ecstasy about the whole thing.

"I did a good deal of reading on the river, and also at the Orchard at Grantchester—you remember Rupert Brooke's poem? Brooke would be fifty today, if he'd lived—think of that... Still stands the clock at ten to three, but Rupert Brooke is late for tea—confined to his bed with rheumatism or something—that's what poets get for not dying young. The woman at the Orchard who served the teas remembered Brooke—she was a grand old chatterbox and once I got to know her she'd talk endlessly about undergraduates and professors past and present—many a yarn, I daresay, that I've forgotten since and that nobody else remembered even then... Trivial talk—just as trivial as the way I'm talking to you now. Nineteen-twenty, that was—Cambridge full of demobilized old-young men still wearing dyed officers' overcoats—British warms sent up to Perth and returned chocolate-brown—full of men still apt to go suddenly berserk in the middle of a rag and turn it into a riot, or start whimpering during a thunderstorm—after-effects of shell-shock, you know. Plenty of us had had that—including myself."

"As a result of the head injury you mentioned yesterday?"

"I suppose so."

"You had a pretty bad time?"

"No, I was one of the lucky ones—comparatively, that is. But when you're blown up, even if you're not physically smashed to bits..." He broke off awkwardly. "I'm sorry. It isn't Armistice Day any more. These confessions are out of place."

"Not at all. I'm interested. It's so hard for my generation to imagine what it was like."

"Don't worry—you'll learn soon enough."

"How long was it before you were rescued?"

"Haven't the faintest idea. I suppose I was unconscious."

"But you must have recovered consciousness later?"

"Presumably. I don't remember when or where or any of the details. But I've some reason to believe I was taken prisoner."

"Reason to believe? That's a guarded way of putting it."

"I know—but it happens to be just about all I can say. You see, I literally don't remember. From that moment of being knocked out my memory's a complete blank till years later when I found myself lying on a park seat in Liverpool."

"YEARS later?"

"Getting on for three years, but of course I didn't know that at first. And it was a wet day, as luck would have it." He smiled. "You don't find my story very plausible?"

"I might if you'd tell me the whole of it—without gaps."

"But there ARE gaps—that's just the trouble."

"What were you doing in Liverpool?"

"Once again, I haven't the faintest idea. I didn't even know it was Liverpool at first. The main thing was to know WHO I was—where and when were easy enough to find out later."

"Do you mean you'd been going by some other name until then?"

"Maybe. I suppose so. That's another of the things I don't know. It's as if... well, I've sometimes worked it out this way—there were different rooms in my mind, and as soon as the light came on in one it had to go out in the other."

"Well, what did you do when you realized who you were?"

"What anybody else would do. I went home. I felt in my pockets and found I had a small sum in cash, so I bought a new outfit of clothes, took a bath at a hotel, and then went to the railway station. It was as simple as that, because along with knowing my own name it had come to me without apparent effort that I lived at Stourton, that my father owned the Rainier Steelworks and all the other concerns, that we had a butler named Sheldon, and any other details I cared to recall. In fact I knew all about myself in a perfectly normal way up to the moment of that shell-burst near Arras in 1917."

"Your father must have got a very pleasant shock."

"He was too ill to be allowed it, but the family got one all right. Of course, since I'd been reported missing in the casualty lists, they'd long since given me up for dead."

"It's a very remarkable story."

"Remarkable's a well-chosen word. It doesn't give you away."

I thought for a moment; then I said: "But the Army authorities must have had some record of your coming back to England?"

"None—not under the name of Rainier."

"But wasn't there a disc or something you had to wear all the time on active service?"

"There was, but if you'd ever experienced levitation by high explosive you wouldn't put much faith in a bit of metal tied round your neck. It's quite possible there was nothing the Germans could identify me by when they took me prisoner."

"What makes you think you were ever in Germany at all?"

"Surely if I'd been dragged in by my own men they'd have known who I was?"

"H'm, yes, I suppose so."

He went on, after a pause: "I don't blame you at all if you don't believe a word of all this. And it's just as well you're the first person I've confided in for years—just as well for my reputation as a sober citizen." He laughed with self-protective cynicism. "It's been a conspiracy of events to make me talk like this—Armistice Day—our meeting on the train—and then something the dentist said tonight when I came out of his nitrous oxide."

"The dentist? What's he got to do with it?"

"He was making polite conversation while I spat blood. One of the things he said was, 'So you were a prisoner in Germany?' I asked him what gave him that idea, and he answered, 'Because I notice you have a tooth filled with a substitute metal German dentists were having to use during the latter part of the war'—apparently he'd come across other instances of it."

We were silent for a moment. I could hear the first stir of early morning traffic beginning along King's Parade. Rainier heard it too, and as at a signal rose to go. "A strange business, the war. The English told the Germans exactly where I was, so that the Germans could kill me... then the Germans did half kill me, patched me up, and saw that my teeth were properly cared for... after which the English gave me a medal for having displayed what they called 'conspicuous gallantry in the field.'" He fingered it on his lapel, adding: "I wear it at shows like this, along with the Most Noble Order of Something-or-Other which the Greeks gave me for arranging a loan on their currant crop in 1928." He began putting on his overcoat, heedless of my assurance that there was no hurry and that I often sat up till dawn myself. "Please don't bother to see me out —I'll take a bath at my hotel and be in time for the first train."

On his way across the room he paused at my shelves of books and asked what tripos I was taking.

"Economics. I took the first part of the History last year."

"Really? I did the same when I was here. But where does the psycho-analysis come in?"

"Oh, that's only a side-line."

"I see. Made any plans for when you go down?"

"I'd like to be a journalist."

He nodded, shaking hands at the door. "Well, I've got a few contacts in Fleet Street. Write to me when you're ready for a job—I might be able to do something for you."

* * * * *

Early the following year I took a Ph.D. and began looking around for the post which, it seemed to me then, ought to drop snugly into the lap of any bright young man who had written a two-hundred-page thesis on "The Influence of Voltaire on the English Laissez-Faire Economists." Cambridge had deemed this worthy of a doctorate; nobody in Fleet

Street, however, held it worth a regular job. I had a very small private income and could therefore afford to cadge snippets of highbrow reviewing from some of the more illustrious and penurious weeklies, reckoning myself well-paid if the books themselves were expensive and could be sold for more cash to Mr. Reeves of the Strand; but the newspaper world at that time was full of journalists out of work through amalgamations, and the chance of getting on the staffs of any of the big dailies was not encouraging. Of course I remembered Rainier's offer, but apart from my reluctance to bother him, he was abroad—in South America on some financial business. But by the time he returned I had been disappointed often enough to feel I should take him at his word. He replied instantly to my note, asking me to lunch the next day.

Thus I made my first trip to Kenmore. "Near the World's End pub," Rainier used to say, and it was the fashion among certain guests to pretend it was at some actual world's end if not beyond it—the world in this super-sophisticated sense being that part of London within normal taxi range. I went by bus, which puts you down at the corner of the road with only a hundred yards or so to walk. I had no idea how notable, not to say notorious, those Kenmore lunches were; indeed, since the invitation had come so promptly, I had beguiled myself with visions of an intimate foursome composed of host and hostess with perhaps a press magnate summoned especially to meet me. I did not know then that Mrs. Rainier gave lunches for ten or twelve people two or three times a week, enticing every temporary or permanent celebrity to meet other temporary or permanent celebrities at her house, and that these affairs were as frequently joked about as they were infrequently declined. She functioned, in fact, as a kind of liaison officer between Society and Bohemia, with a Maecenas glance at moneyless but personable young men; and though there is no kind of social service I would less willingly undertake myself, there are few that I respect more when competently performed by someone else.

Searching my memory for impressions of that first arrival, I find I cannot put Mrs. Rainier into the picture at all. She was there, she must have been; but she was so busy making introductions that she could not have given me more than a few words, and those completely unimportant. I came a little late and found myself ushered into a drawing-room full of initiates, all talking with great gusto, and all—so it seemed to me (quite baselessly, of course)—resentful of intrusion by a stranger who had neither written a banned novel nor flown somewhere and back in an incredibly short time. I say this because one of the guests HAD written such a novel, and another HAD made such a flight, and it was my fate to be seated between them while they talked either to their outside neighbours or across me to each other. There was an empty place at the head of the table, and presently I gathered from general conversation that Rainier often arrived late and sometimes not at all, so that he was never on any account waited for. I had already written off the whole affair as a rather profitless bore when the guests rose, murmured hasty good-byes, and dashed out to waiting cars and taxis. (Mrs. Rainier's lunches were always like that—one-fifteen sharp to two-fifteen sharp and not too much to drink, so that you did not kill your afternoon.) Just as I was following the crowd, a touch on my arm accompanied the whisper: "Stay a moment if you aren't in a hurry."

Mrs. Rainier led me a few paces back along the hall after the others had gone. "I didn't quite catch your name—"

14

"Harrison."

"Oh yes... You're a friend of Charles's—it's too bad he couldn't get here—he's so busy nowadays."

I murmured something vague, polite, and intended to be reassuring.

"It's a pity people who can fly half-way round the world haven't any manners," she went on, and I answered: "Well, I suppose there are quite a number of people who have manners and couldn't fly half-way round the world."

"But having manners is so much more important," she countered. "Tell me... what... er... I mean, are you a... let me see... HARRISON..."

I smiled—suddenly and rather incomprehensibly at ease with her. "You're trying to recall a Harrison who's written something, married somebody, or been somewhere," I said. "But it's a waste of time—I'm not THAT Harrison, even if he exists. I'm just—if I call myself anything—a journalist."

"Oh... then you must come again when we have really LITERARY parties," she replied, with an eagerness I thought charming though probably insincere. I promised I would, with equal eagerness, and every intention of avoiding her really LITERARY parties like the plague. Then I shook hands, left the house, and on the bus back to Fleet Street suddenly realized that it had been a very good lunch from one point of view. I had never tasted better eggs Mornay.

The next afternoon Rainier telephoned, profuse in apologies for his absence from the lunch, and though the matter could hardly have been important to him, I thought I detected a note of sincerity. "I gather you didn't have a very good time," he said, and before I could reply went on: "I'm not keen on the mob, either, but Helen's a born hostess—almost as good as an American—she can take in twenty new names all in a row and never make a mistake."

"She didn't take in mine. In fact it was pretty clear she didn't know me from Adam."

"My fault, I expect. Must have forgotten to tell her."

"So a perfect stranger could walk into your house and get a free lunch?"

"They're doing that all the time—though most of 'em have invitations... Look here, if you're not busy just now, why not come over to the House for tea?"

I said I would, and took the bus again to Chelsea. But at Kenmore the maid told me that Rainier hadn't been in since morning and never by any chance took tea at home; and just then, while we were arguing on the doorstep (I insisting I had been invited less than twenty minutes ago), Mrs. Rainier came up behind me and began to laugh. "He meant the House of Commons," she said, passing into the hall. "You'd better let my car take you there."

Extraordinary how stupid one can be when one would prefer to impress by being knowledgeable. I knew quite well that the House of Commons, along with the Stock Exchange and Christ Church, Oxford, was called "the House," yet somehow, when Rainier had used the phrase over the telephone, I could only think of Kenmore. Most of the way to Westminster in the almost aggressively unostentatious Daimler (so impersonal you could believe it part of an undertaker's fleet), I cursed my mistake as a poor recommendation for any kind of job. I had feared Rainier might be waiting for me, and was relieved when, after sending in my name, I had to kill time for half an hour before a policeman led me through devious passages to the Terrace, where Rainier greeted me warmly. But his appearance was slightly disconcerting; there was a twitch about his mouth and eyes as he spoke, and a general impression of intense nervous energy in desperate need of relaxation. During tea he talked about his South American trip, assuming far too modestly that I had read nothing about it in the papers. Presently the division bell rang and only as we hurried across the Smoking Room did he broach the matter I had really come about. "I inquired from a good many people after I got your letter, Harrison, but there doesn't seem to be a thing doing in Fleet Street just now."

"That was my own experience too."

"So I wondered if you'd care for a secretary's job until something else turns up?"

I hadn't really thought about such a thing, and maybe hesitation revealed my disappointment.

He said, patting my arm: "Well, think it over, anyway. I've had a girl up to now, but she's due to get married in a few weeks—time enough to show you the ropes... that is, of course, if you feel you'd like the job at all..."

* * * * *

So I became Rainier's secretary, and Miss Hobbs showed me the ropes. It had been flattery to call her a girl. She was thin, red-faced, middle-aged, and so worshipful of Rainier that no husband could hope to get more than a remnant of any emotion she was capable of; indeed, I felt that the chance of marriage was tempting her more because she feared it might be her last than because she was certain she wanted it. She hinted this much during our first meeting. "I almost feel I'm deserting HIM," she said, and the stress on "him" was revealing. Presently, showing me how she filed his correspondence, she added: "I'm so relieved he isn't going to have another LADY secretary. I'd be afraid of some awful kind of person coming here and—perhaps— INFLUENCING him."

I said I didn't imagine Rainier was the type to be influenced by that kind of woman.

"Oh, but you never know what kind of a woman will influence a man."

We went on inspecting the filing system. "The main thing is to see he doesn't forget his appointments. He doesn't do much of his correspondence here—he has another secretary at his City office. So it won't matter a great deal if you don't know shorthand and typewriting."

I said I did know shorthand and typewriting.

"Well, so much the better, of course. You'll find him wonderful to work with—at least _I_ always have, though of course we're more like old friends than employer and secretary. I call him Charles, you know, when we're alone together. And he always calls me Elsie, whether we're alone or not. We've been together now for nearly fifteen years, so it's really quite natural, don't you think?"

16

During the next few hours she gave me her own version of the entire Rainier ménage. "Of course the marriage never has been all it should be—I daresay you can imagine that. Mrs. Rainier isn't the right kind of wife for a man like Charles. He's so tired of all those parties she gives, especially the house-parties at Stourton—that's their big place in the country, you know... they have no children—that's another thing, because he'd love children, and I don't know why they don't have them, maybe there's a reason. When you've worked with him for a time you'll feel how restless he is—I do blame her for THAT—she doesn't give him a proper home—Kenmore's just a hotel with different guests every day. I do believe there's only one room he feels really comfortable in, and that's this one—with his poor little secretary slaving away while he smokes —and he shouldn't smoke either, so he's been told... D'you know, he often locks himself in when he wants to work, because the rest of the house is so full of Goyas and Epsteins and what not that people wander in and out of all the rooms as if it were a museum. Of course there really are priceless things in it—why not?—he gives her the money to spend, and I suppose she has taste—that is if you LIKE a house that's like a museum. I sometimes wonder if Charles does."

After a pause during which I made no comment she turned to the writing-desk. "Charles gets hundreds of letters from complete strangers —about one thing and another, you know. If they're abusive we take no notice—in fact, whatever they are, HE doesn't bother much about them, but I'll let you into a secret—something he doesn't suspect and never will unless you tell him, and I'm sure you won't—I always write a little note of thanks to anyone who sends a NICE letter... of course I write as if he'd dictated it... I really think a good secretary SHOULD do little things like that on her own, don't you?"

I said nothing.

"Really, if he were to ask me to stay, I believe I would, marriage or no marriage—I mean, it would be so hard to refuse him anything— but then, he's too fine and generous to ask—as soon as he knew about it he urged me not to delay my happiness on his account—just as if his own marriage had brought HIM happiness... Not that Charles would be an easy man to MAKE happy, even if he HAD got the right woman. But he isn't happy NOW—that I DO know—there's always a look in his eyes as if he were searching for something and couldn't find it."

For two or three days Miss Hobbs continued to show me the ropes; Rainier was away in Lancashire. During this time Mrs. Rainier gave several lunch parties to which I was not invited, though I was in the house at the time and was even privileged to give assistance to a foreign plenipotentiary who spoke little English and had strayed into the study in search of a humbler apartment. I could better understand after that why Rainier sometimes locked the door.

Then he returned, having wired me to meet his train at Euston. As soon as we had found a taxi and were driving out of the station he asked me how I'd been getting on, and added, without waiting for an answer: "I don't suppose you'll find it hard to be as good as your predecessor."

I said I should certainly hope to be.

"Then you've already found out a few of the things I've been putting up with?"

"Yes, but not why you HAVE put up with them, for so many years."

"Pure sentiment, plus the fact that I've always had a submerged sympathy with crazy people, and Elsie's crazy enough. She used to work at Stourton in my father's time, then she worked for my brother, and when he naturally wanted to get rid of her there was no one fool enough to take her but me. I made her my social secretary—because in those days I had no social life and it didn't matter. But after I married there were social things for her to do and she did them with a peculiar and fascinating idiocy. D'you know, I've found out she writes long letters to people I've never heard of and signs my name to them?... And by the way, did she tell you I'm not happy with my wife?"

"Well—er—"

"Don't believe it. My wife and I are the best of friends. I suppose she also hinted it was a marriage of convenience?"

I felt this was incriminating Miss Hobbs too much and was beginning a non-committal answer when he interrupted: "Well, THAT happens to be true. I married her because it seemed to me she'd be just the person to turn a tired business man into a thumping success. She WAS and she DID... Can you think of a better reason?"

"There's generally considered to be ONE better reason."

He switched the subject suddenly, pointing out of the window to a news placard that proclaimed, in letters a foot high: "Collapse of England." At that moment I felt that one thing Miss Hobbs had said about him WAS true —that look in his eyes as if he were searching for something and couldn't find it. He began to talk rapidly and nervously, apropos of the placard: "Odd to think of some foreigner translating without knowing it's only about cricket... it was something you said about that on a train that first made me want to know you better—but really, in a sense, it doesn't refer to cricket at all, but to how God-damned sure we are of ourselves—you can't imagine the same phrase in the streets of Paris or Berlin—it would begin panic or riots or something... Just think of it —'Débâcle de la France' or 'Untergang Deutschlands.'... Impossible... but here it means nothing because we don't believe it could ever happen—and that's not wishful thinking — it's neither wishing nor thinking, but a kind of inbreathed illusion... Reminds me of that last plenary session of the London Conference when it was quite clear there was to be no effective disarmament by anybody and we were all hard at work covering up the failure of civilization's last hope with a mess of smeary platitudes... Lord, how tired I was, listening to strings of words that meant nothing in any language and even less when you had to wait for an interpreter to turn 'em into two others... and all the time the dusty sunlight fell in slabs over the pink bald heads—godheads from the power entrusted to them and gargoyles from the way I hated 'em... and during all that morning, full of the trapped sunlight and the distant drone of traffic past the Cenotaph, there was only one clean eager thing that happened —young Drexel whispering to me during a tepid outburst of applause: 'See the old boy in the third row—fifth from the end— Armenia or Irak or some place... but did you ever see anybody more like Harry Tate?'... And by Jove, he WAS like Harry Tate, and Drexel and I lived on it for the rest of the session—lived on it and on our own pathetic fancy that foreigners were strange and at best amusing creatures, rather like music-hall comedians or one's French master at school—tolerable if they happen to be musicians or dancers or ice-cream sellers—but definitely to be snubbed if they venture on the really serious business of governing the world... Look—there's another!" It was a later placard, proclaiming in letters equally large, "England Now Without Hope." Rainier laughed. "Maybe some fussy archaeologist of the twenty-fifth century— a relative of Macaulay's sketching New Zealander—will dig this up from a rubbish-heap and say it establishes definite proof that we'd all been well warned in advance... Has my wife got a party tonight?"

"Yes."

"What sort of a crowd?"

"Mostly sporting and dramatic, I think."

"Then I'll dine and sleep at the Club. Borotra's the only dramatic sportsman I care about, and he probably won't come."

He put his head out of the cab window, giving the change of address, and also telling the man to drive more slowly. I could see he was nervously excited, and I was beginning to know by now that when he was in such a mood he talked a good deal in an attempt to race his thoughts—an attempt which usually failed, leaving a litter of unfinished sentences, mixed metaphors, and unpolished epigrams, with here and there some phrase worthy of one of his speeches, but flung off so carelessly that if the hearer did not catch it at the time Rainier himself could never recall it afterwards. I have tried to give an impression of this kind of talk, but even the most faithful reportage would miss a curious excitement of voice and gesture, the orchestration of some inner emotion turbulent under the surface. Nor, one felt, would such emotion wear out in fatigue, but rather increase to some extinguishing climax as an electric globe burns brighter before the final snapping of the filament. It was of this I felt suddenly afraid, and he noticed the anxious look I gave him.

"Sorry to be a chatterer like this, Harrison, but it's after a bout of public speech-making —I always feel I have to use up the words left over, or perhaps the words I couldn't use... I suppose you'd call me a rather good speaker?"

I said I certainly should.

"And you'd guess that it comes easily to me?"

"It always sounds like it."

He laughed. "That's what practice can do. I LOATHE speaking in public —I'm always secretly afraid I'm going to break down or stammer or something. Stammering especially... of course I never do... By the way, you remember that mountain in Derbyshire I thought I recognized?"

"Yes."

"The same sort of thing happened in Lancashire, only it wasn't quite so romantic. Just a house in a row. I was helping Nixon in the Browdley by-election—we held meetings at street corners, then Nixon dragged me round doing the shake-hands and baby-kissing stuff—that's the way his father got into the Gladstone Parliaments, so Nixon still does it. I admit I'm pretty cynical about elections—the very look of the voting results, with two rows of figures adding neatly up to a third one, gives me the same itch as a company balance-sheet, exact to the last penny... whose penny? Was there ever a penny?... My own majority in Lythamshire, for instance—precisely twelve—but who WERE the twelve? Twelve good men and true, maybe, or twelve drunken illiterates... ? Don't you sometimes feel how FALSE it all is, and how falsely reassuring—this nineteenth-century gloss of statistical accuracy, as if the flood tide of history could run in rivulets tidy enough for garden irrigation, safe enough for a million taps in suburban bathrooms... but when the storm does come, who'll give a damn if the rows of little figures still add up—who'll care if the sums are all wrong provided one man knows a right answer?"

"You were talking about a house."

"Oh yes... Just an ordinary four-room working-man's house—tens of thousands like it. A cold day, and as we stood waiting at the door I could see a great yellow glow of firelight behind the lace curtains of the parlour window. Nothing extraordinary in that, either, and yet... it's hard to describe the feelings I had, as if that house were waiting for me—a welcome—out of the wintry dusk and into the warm firelight... a welcome home."

His eyes were full of eagerness, and I said, trying to hasten his story before we reached the end of the journey: "Did the feeling disappear when a stranger answered the door?"

"I'm coming to that... There were three of us, Nixon, myself, and Ransome, the local party secretary, nice little man. We knocked and knocked and nobody came. Then I, saw Ransome fumbling in his pocket. 'Can't think where she is,' he said, 'but I expect she'll be back in a jiffy.' I realized then that it was HIS house, and that we were being invited in. He found a key, unlocked the door, and we entered. No lobby or hall—straight into the warmth and firelight. There was a kettle steaming on the hob, cups and saucers set out, plates of bread and butter. Everything spotlessly neat, furniture that shone, a clock ticking loudly somewhere. It was all so beautiful, this warm small room. The man kept talking about his wife—how proud she'd been at the thought of having two such men as Nixon and myself to tea in her home —such an honour—she'd never forget it—and how embarrassed she'd be when she came back and found us already there. 'I'll bet she's gone round the corner for a Dundee cake,' he laughed. But as time passed he began to be a bit embarrassed himself, and presently suggested having tea ourselves without waiting for his wife. So we did—I sat in a rocking-chair by the fireside, and the flames were still leaping up so brightly we didn't need any other light, even though it was quite dark outside by the time we left."

"So you never saw his wife at all?"

"No, she didn't come back in time... But that room—the feeling I had in it—of comfort, of being WANTED there... It's just another thing of the same kind. That part of my life —well, you remember what I told you at Cambridge."

"Why do you worry about it so much?"

"I wouldn't if it would leave me alone. But it keeps on teasing me— with clues. So what can I do?"

"I still say—more rest and less work."

He patted my arm. "It's good to know I can talk to you whenever I'm in this mood. Watson to my Sherlock, eh? Or perhaps that's not much of a compliment?"

"Not to yourself, anyhow. Watson was at least an HONEST idiot."

He smiled. "That must be the Higher Criticism. Of course you were born too late to feel as I did—Sherlock's in Baker Street, all's right with the world."

"Since we now realize that most things are wrong with the world— "

"I know—that was part of the illusion. I remember Sheldon taking me on a trip to London when I was six or seven years old... The first place I asked to see was Baker Street, and being a sympathetic fellow he didn't tell me that the stories were just stories. We walked gravely along the pavement one afternoon early in the century—a small boy and his father's butler—looking up at the tall houses with respectful hero worship. Distant thrones might totter, anarchists might throw bombs, a few lesser breeds might behave provokingly in odd corners of the world, but when all was said and done, there was nothing to fear while the stately Holmes of England, doped and dressing-gowned for action, readied his wits for the final count with Moriarty! And who the deuce WAS this Moriarty? Why, just a big-shot crook whom the honest idiot romanticized in order to build up his hero's reputation! Nothing but a middle-aged stoop-shouldered Raffles! And that, mind you, was the worst our fathers' world could imagine when it talked about Underground Forces and Powers of Evil!... Ah, well, happy days. You'd better keep the cab to go home in. Good night!"

* * * * *

I hadn't taken Rainier's problem very seriously till then. For one thing, loss of memory is normal. We all forget things, and are equally likely to be reminded of them long after we think they have been forgotten for good. Often, too, the reminder is faint enough to be no more than a clue which we fail to follow up because the matter does not seem important. The unusual part of Rainier's experience was that he DID think it important, so that from something merely puzzling it was already on the way to becoming an obsession.

Some part of his story could doubtless be verified, and I already felt enough curiosity to make the attempt. I said nothing to him, but the next time the chance occurred I led Miss Hobbs to talk in a general way about her employer's early life and career. She was more than willing—except for a continual tendency to drift into later and somewhat disparaging gossip about Mrs. Rainier. "Wasn't he in the war?" I began, putting the leading question that anyone might have asked.

"Oh yes. He got a medal—didn't you know that? And the strange thing was—they thought he was dead. So it was given post—post —"

"Posthumously."

"Yes, that's it. But you couldn't blame them, because after the attack he was reported missing and nothing was heard about him till—oh, it was years later, when he suddenly arrived home without any warning. And then it turned out he'd lost his memory."

"Seems to me the sort of story for headlines."

"You mean in the papers? Oh no, it was kept out—the family didn't want any publicity."

"That wouldn't have been enough reason for most of the journalists I know."

"Ah, but Sheldon arranged it."

"Sheldon?"

"He's the butler at Stourton. You haven't been to Stourton yet, have you?"

"No."

"It's really a marvellous place."

"Sheldon sounds a marvellous butler if he knows how to stop journalists from getting a good story and editors from printing it."

"Well, he IS rather marvellous, and I don't suppose there's much he doesn't know—not about the family, anyhow. He really rules Stourton —lives there all the year round, even during the winter when the family never go out of town. I really owe him a good deal— I was only just a local girl in those days, I used to do bookkeeping and secretarial work at the house, and that brought me into contact with Sheldon constantly." She added, rather coyly: "You know—or perhaps you don't know— how difficult it can be for a girl employed in a big house if the butler isn't all he should be."

I said I could imagine it.

"Sheldon was always a gentleman. Never a word—or a gesture— that anyone could object to."

I said nothing.

"And later, when Mr. Charles took over Stourton, Sheldon personally asked him if he could do anything for me, otherwise I don't suppose I'd be here."

"I see... But coming back to the time when Mr. Rainier—OUR Mr. Rainier, I mean— suddenly returned to Stourton. Were you working there then?"

"Not JUST then. It was Christmas and as old Mr. Rainier was ill they cancelled the usual parties and gave me a holiday. It was parties that always kept me busy—writing out invitations and place cards and things."

"What was Mr. Rainier like when he returned?"

"I didn't see him till a good while afterwards, but I do know there was a lot of trouble about it, one way and another—Sheldon would never tell us half that went on."

So there the trail ended; she didn't know much of what had actually happened; and since then a great many years had passed, old Mr. Rainier was dead, and probably the same fate had overtaken most of the personnel from whom any elucidating inquiries might have been made at the time. Perhaps there were traces somewhere, a dossier preserved in forgotten files, memoranda hidden away in official archives; but there seemed small chance of unearthing them, or even of finding if they existed at all.

"Quite a mystery," I commented. "Didn't Mr. Rainier himself ever try to solve it?"

"You mean, did he try to remember things?"

"Well, more than that—didn't he ever consult anybody— specialists, psycho-analysts, or anyone?"

"You don't know him, or you wouldn't ask that. The last thing he'd ever do is to go to anybody and tell them things about himself. The only person he ever did talk to was someone he'd known at Cambridge, some professor— Freeman, I think his name was."

"You mean DR. Freeman—THE Dr. Freeman?"

"Maybe he was a doctor."

"A tall white-haired man with a stoop?"

"Yes, that was him—he used to visit Charles a good deal before the marriage. You know him?"

"Slightly. Why not since the marriage?"

"He didn't like parties, and I don't think he liked Mrs. Rainier for beginning all that sort of life for Charles. She's very ambitious, you know. People say she'll make him Prime Minister before she's finished."

I laughed—having heard similar remarks myself, followed as a rule by some ribald comment on her party-giving technique. Miss Hobbs added: "Not that she isn't a good hostess—that I WILL say."

Since the point was raised, it seemed to me that Mrs. Rainier was TOO good, and that for this reason she might miss the secret English bull's-eye that can only be hit by guns sighted to a 97 or 98 per cent degree of accuracy. Anything more than that, even if achievable, is dangerous in England, because English people mistrust perfection, regarding it in manners as the stigma of foreigners, just as they suspect it in teeth to be the product of dentistry. All this, of course, I did not discuss with Miss Hobbs.

I saw Freeman a few days later. He had been a rather impressive figure at Cambridge, in my time as well as Rainier's, but had recently retired to live at Richmond with an unmarried sister. It was probably a lonely life, and he seemed glad to hear my voice on the telephone and to accept an invitation to dinner. I had known him fairly well, since he had long been president of the Philosophical Society and I in my last year its vice-president, and though he had written several standard works on psychology he was not psychologist enough to suspect an ulterior motive behind my apparent eagerness to look him up and talk over old times.

We met at Boulestin's that same evening.

After waiting patiently till the inevitable question as to what I was doing with myself nowadays, I said that I had become Rainier's secretary.

"Ah, Rainier—yes," he muttered, as if raking over memories. And he added, with a thin cackle: "Well, history won't repeat itself."

"How do you mean?"

"He married one of them."

"You mean MRS. Rainier? You mean she was his secretary before Miss Hobbs?"

"Oh, the Hobbs woman was with him all the time—a family heirloom. Must be forty now, if she's a day. What did she do at last— retire?"

"She's leaving to get married."

"Heavens—I never thought her turn would come. Who's the lucky man?... But I can answer that myself—Rainier is, to get rid of her."

"You know her then?"

"Hardly at all, I'm glad to say. But she used to write me the most ridiculous notes whenever Rainier made an appointment to see me. They were supposed to be from him, but I found out quite casually afterwards that she forged his name to 'em... ABSURD notes—it interested me, as a psychologist, that she should have thought them appropriate."

"But to come back to Mrs. Rainier—"

"Oh, she worked in his CITY office, I think. A different dynasty. These great magnates have platoons of secretaries."

"Queer Miss Hobbs never mentioned it. I should have thought it was something she'd have liked to drive home."

"On a point of psychology I think you're wrong. She'd prefer to conceal the fact that though they were both, so to say, equal at the starting-post, the other woman won."

"Maybe. I gather you know Rainier rather well?"

"I used to. You see, I began with the initial advantage of meeting him anonymously."

"I'm not quite clear what you mean."

He expanded over a further glass of brandy. "Rainier's a peculiar fellow. He has a curious fear of his own identity. He lets you get to know him best when he doesn't think you know who he is... It's an interesting kink, psychologically. I first met him through Werneth, who was his tutor at St. Swithin's. Apparently he told Werneth about—er— well, perhaps I ought not to discuss it, but it was something interesting to me—as a psychologist—but not particularly to Werneth, who was a mere historian." Again the cackle. "Anyhow, Werneth could only get his permission to pass it on to me by promising not to divulge his name, and on hearing what it was all about I was so interested that we actually arranged a meeting —again anonymously—I wasn't supposed to know who he was... But I'll let you into a, secret—Werneth HAD told me, privately, beforehand—unscrupulous fellow, Werneth. And then one morning several months later I couldn't find my bicycle outside the college gate after a lecture, but in its place was a similar model with the name 'Charles Rainier' on it. I made his mistake an excuse to call on him—and I must say —after the opening embarrassment—we very soon became friends." He added: "And now, of course, I know what you're going to ask me, but being less unscrupulous than Werneth I can't tell you."

"I don't think you need, because I already know about Rainier's—er —peculiarity. I suppose it WAS that."

"Suppose you tell me first of all what THAT is."

"The blank patch in his life that he can't remember."

"A rather inexact description."

"No doubt, and that's why I'd very much like to hear your own."

He smiled. "It was an unusual case—but I've heard of several similar ones. They're recorded, you know, in technical journals. Rainier had —if one might so put it—certain threads of recollection about the blank period, though they were so faint as to be almost non-existent at first. After he left Cambridge we didn't meet again for ten years—by that time the threads had become a little less faint. It was my aim, when I came to know Rainier again after the ten-year interval, to sort out those threads, to disentangle them— to expand them, as it were, into a complete corpus of memory."

"I understand. But you didn't succeed."

"Are you asking me that or telling me?"

"Both, in a way."

He said, smiling: "My expectation all along had been that his full memory would eventually return—a little bit here, a little bit there— till finally, like a key turning in a lock, or like the last few pieces of a jigsaw puzzle, the whole thing would slip into position. But I gather that it hasn't yet happened?"

"The bits are still being assembled, but nowhere near to completion."

"Tell me, Harrison, if I may ask the question—why are you taking such a keen interest in this matter? Hardly within the scope of secretarial duties... Or IS it?"

"I like him and I hate to see him bothered by it as he still is. That's the only reason."

"A good one."

"Now YOU tell ME something—have you any theories about the blank patch?"

"Theories? I can only guess it was a pretty bad time. He was injured, if I remember rightly, just above the left parietal bone of the..." He went off into a medical survey that conveyed nothing to me. "It was an injury that would require operative treatment— perhaps a series of operations. That's why it's perhaps a pity that he still bothers, as you say he does. Even if complete recollection were to return to him now, it would probably be only of pain, unhappiness, boredom."

"On the other hand, even such memories might be better than an increasing obsession about the loss of them?"

"Possibly."

We were silent for a time after that. Presently I said: "You know he was taken prisoner by the Germans?"

"Oh yes. But German or English—all hospitals are unhappy places, especially for a man who can't tell anyone who he is. I imagine the Germans treated him namelessly or by error under someone else's name, and eventually returned him to England under the same condition. Then there would be other hospitals in England, full of experiences nobody would wish to remember. There were a great many shell-shock and loss-of-memory cases that took years —some of them are still taking years, God help them. The whole thing happened so long ago I don't see how we can ever expect to know all the details. Tell me YOUR theory, if you have one."

"That's the trouble, I haven't."

"The real trouble, of course, is Mrs. Rainier."

Curious, the way people sooner or later led the talk to her. Freeman, reticent at first about a former friend, saw no reason now to conceal his opinion of a former friend's wife. "She's an unusual sort of woman, Harrison."

"Well, he's not so usual, either."

"They get on well together? Is that your impression?"

I answered guardedly: "I think she makes a good politician's wife."

"And I suppose, by the same token, you think he makes a good politician?"

"He has some of the attributes. Clever speaker and a good way with people."

"When he's in the mood. He isn't always... Did you ever hear about the Bridgelow Antiquarian Dinner?"

I shook my head.

"It was—oh, several years ago. He was supposed to be helping the candidate, and during the campaign we asked him to our annual beano— strictly non-party—just a semi-learned society, with the accent on the semi. I was president at the time, and Rainier was next to me at the table. Half-way through his speech, which began pretty well, there was a bit of a disturbance caused by old General Wych-Furlough fumbling in late and apologizing—his car had broken down or something. He talked rather loudly, like most deaf people, and of course it WAS annoying to a speaker, but the whole incident was over in a minute, most people would have passed it off. Rainier, however, seemed to freeze up suddenly, couldn't conceal the way he felt about it, finished his speech almost immediately and left the table rather sooner than he decently could. I went out with him for a moment, told him frankly I thought his behaviour had been rather childish—surely age and infirmity entitled people to some latitude—it wasn't as if there'd been any intentional discourtesy. He said then, in a rather panicky way: 'It wasn't that—it was something in the fellow himself— something chemical, maybe, in the way we react to each other.' I thought his explanation even more peculiar than his behaviour."

I checked myself from commenting, and Freeman, noticing it, said: "Go on —what was it you were going to ask?"

"I was just wondering—is it possible he had one of those submerged memories—of having met the General before?"

"I thought of that later on, but it didn't seem likely they could ever have met. He didn't even know the General's name. And if they HAD met before, I still can't think of any reason for antagonism—the old boy was just a fussy, simple-minded, stupid fellow with a distinguished military career and a repertoire of exceptionally dull stories about hunting."

"Was Mrs. Rainier at the dinner?"

"No, she wouldn't come to anything _I_ was president of—that's very certain." He added, as if glad to get back to the subject: "A strange woman. I'm not sure I altogether trust her—and that isn't because I don't particularly like her. It's something deeper. She always seems to me to be hiding something. I suppose it's part of my job to have these psychic feelings about people... You know about her famous parties?"

"Who doesn't? I've sampled them."

"Mind you, let's be fair. She's not a snob in the ordinary sense—I mean about birth or money. Of course it would be too ridiculous if she were —since she began with neither herself. But what exactly IS it that she goes for? Brains? Celebrity? Notoriety? I went to Kenmore once, and I must admit she plays the game loathsomely well. But all this relentless celebrity-hunting and party-giving doesn't make a home—and I'm damned if I know what it DOES make."

"Some people say it's made Rainier's career."

"I've heard that too—from people who don't like him. The people who don't like HER will tell you her methods have actually held him back. Still, I don't deny she's a good mate for a man of affairs. The real point is whether Rainier's life ought to be cluttered up with business and politics at all."

"What do you mean?"

"Simply that I've always considered him—abstractly—one of the rare spirits of our time, so that success of the kind he has attained and may yet attain becomes a detestable self-betrayal."

"So you think the marriage was a mistake?"

"Not at all, if he felt he had to have that sort of life."

"What other sort of life COULD he have had?"

"Out of my province to say. I'm talking about the QUALITY of the man, not his opportunities. I suppose it wasn't his fault his father left him a small industrial empire to look after—steelworks and newspapers and interlocking holding companies and what not—all more or less bankrupt, though people didn't know it at the time. Even the seat in Parliament was a sort of family inheritance he had to take over."

"Like Miss Hobbs?"

"Yes, like HER—just as idiotic but not so loyal. He only scraped in by twelve votes last time... But since you mention the Hobbs woman, let me assure you she's a modernistic jewel compared with the old butler they keep at Stourton... Sheldon, I think his name is."

"You don't like him either?"

Freeman shrugged. "It isn't that I mind his eccentric impertinences —Scottish servants are like that and one takes it from them— even Queen Victoria had to. What makes me really uncomfortable is the same feeling I have about Mrs. Rainier—that he's hiding something."

"Maybe they're hiding something together?"

His smile was of another kind and did not answer mine. "You haven't been to Stourton yet, have you? It's an amazing hiding-place for anything they've got to hide."

Miss Hobbs left during the week that followed and I settled down to the task of becoming her successor. It was not quite as simple as she had led me to believe. Rainier's interests were manifold; besides holding directorships of important companies he was a member of many societies and organizations —all this, of course, on top of his political work. I had plenty to do, and he expected it done quickly and efficiently. We had little chance to talk on other than business matters, and for the time he seemed to have dropped completely the preoccupation that had begun to interest me. One thing happened that I had not after Freeman's remarks anticipated: Mrs. Rainier invited me to another of her lunch parties. This time it was really LITERARY, as she had promised (Maurice Baring, Charles Morgan, Louis Bromfield, Henry Bernstein, Mrs. Belloc Lowndes, H. G. Wells, and a pale young man whose name I have forgotten who wrote highbrow detective novels whose names I have also forgotten), and despite initial misgivings I found the whole affair quite pleasant. Once more there was the empty chair for Rainier, if he should turn up, but he failed to, and nobody seemed surprised. Again also Mrs. Rainier asked me to stay a moment after the others had gone, but now the request was less remarkable, since I had work in the same house. "Can you spare time to look at my garden?" she said, leading me to the back of the hall where the French windows were open.

We sauntered across the lawn to a door in the high surrounding wall; unlocking it, she watched my face as I showed surprise, for within was a second garden, not much bigger than a large room, but so enclosed by trees and carpeted with flowers that one could hardly have believed it to exist in the middle of a London borough. "It's a secret," she confided. "I only show it to close friends—or to those who I hope are going to be."

I murmured something polite that might equally have referred to her last remark or to the garden itself.

"You see," she went on, "I never cared for Miss Hobbs. I don't think Charles did, either, but he was too kind to get rid of her. If she told you things against me, and I'm sure she did, just suspend judgment till you know me better."

I went on saying polite things.

"You and Charles first met on a train, didn't you?" She stooped to a vase. "One of those chance meetings—I've had them myself—when you tell all your secrets to a perfect stranger because you're certain you'll never meet him again... Something like that?"

I said guardedly: "I don't know about secrets, but we certainly found it easy to talk."

"And you like your work here?"

"Very much."

"I'm glad. It will be wonderful if you can really help Charles— apart from just office work. He needs the right sort of companionship sometimes—he has difficult moods, you know. Or perhaps you don't know —YET. Anyhow, the thing to do is not to take him too seriously when he has them." I waited for her to continue, knowing that she too was waiting for me; even if I were willing to suspend judgment I was also, like Freeman, unwilling to trust her completely. She suddenly smiled. "Well, now you know MY secret. Keep it for me." And she added, leading me back through the doorway: "THIS, I mean. It used to be the place where the gardener threw all the rubbish. I planned it myself—I do most of the work here still. Charles never looks in—hasn't time. Hasn't time for my lunches either —not that I mind that so much, but I do wish— sometimes— I'd find him sitting here—quietly—alone—like men you sometimes see outside their cottages in the country—at peace. He never is, you know."

I felt she would like to tell me something if I already knew enough to make it advisable, but she wasn't certain I did know, so she hesitated. I asked her why she thought he was never at peace.

"For one thing, he's so terribly overworked."

"Yes, I know, but apart from that?"

"Oh, well, it's hard for anyone to feel at peace these days. Don't you think so?"

"What about the men you sometimes see outside their cottages in the country?"

She smiled, suddenly on the defensive, sure now that I didn't know as much as she had half suspected, and for that reason anxious not to give me any further opening. "They're probably not really at peace at all—just too old and tired to worry about things any more." As we entered the house the social manner closed about her like the fall of a curtain. "Now that we're becoming friends you must come to Stourton for week-ends as soon as we open it up. There's a REAL secret garden there—I mean one that everybody knows about."

* * * * *

I hadn't expected Stourton to be quite so overwhelming. We drove there a few weeks later in four Daimlers—"like a high-speed funeral," said Rainier, who was in a macabre mood altogether; three of them packed with luggage and servants from Kenmore, the first one containing ourselves and an elegant young man named Woburn, who was coming to catalogue the Stourton library. Most guests would arrive the following day— perhaps twenty-odd: politicians, peers, actors, novelists, crack tennis-players, celebrities of all kinds. It was a warm morning and as we drove through Reading and Newbury the sun broke through the haze and kindled the full splendour of an English summer, with its ever-changing greens under a dappled sky.

Presently we turned off the main road and curved for a mile between high hedges; then suddenly, in a distant fold of the downs, a vision in cream-coloured stone broke through heavy parkland trees. Woburn, who had not seen it before, joined me in a little gasp of admiration. "You were intended to do that," said Rainier. "In fact the architect and road-builder conspired about it two hundred years ago. My brother Julian, who fancied himself as a phrase-maker, once called it 'a stucco prima donna making a stage entrance.' Now, you see, it goes out of sight." Intervening upland obscured the house for another mile or so until, at a new turn of the road, it reappeared so much more intimately that one could only give it a nod of respectful recognition. "But here we are again, and for the rest of the way we simply have to give it all the stars in Baedeker." We swooped into the final half-mile stretch that ended in a wide Palladian portico. "A house like this is like some kinds of women—too expensive even to cast off. Of course what you really pay for isn't the thing itself, but the illusion—the sense of ownership, the intangible Great I Am. Nowadays a bankrupt illusion —the farms don't pay, the hills that belong to me are just as free for anyone else to roam over, the whole idea of POSSESSING this place is just a legal fiction entitling me to pay bills. I think it would sooner possess me, if I'd let it... Hello, Sheldon."

Sheldon was waiting on the top step to welcome us. Neither plump nor cadaverous, obsequious nor pompous, he shook the hand that Rainier offered him, bowed to Mrs. Rainier, and gave Woburn and myself a faintly appraising scrutiny until Rainier made the introductions. Then he said: "Well, Mr. Harrison, if this is your first visit to Stourton it probably won't be your last. Mr. Rainier keeps his secretaries a long time." The remark struck me as rather offhandedly familiar as well as a somewhat gauche reminder of Mrs. Rainier's former position, but there was a general laugh, from which I gathered that Sheldon enjoyed privileges of this kind, perhaps on account of age. He was certainly a well-preserved antiquity, with an air of serene yet somehow guarded responsibility; in different clothes he might have looked a cabinet minister, in contradistinction to those cabinet ministers who, even in their own clothes, look like butlers.

By the time I had been shown to my room in the East Wing (Stourton, like every grand house of its period, had to have wings) the sun was almost down over the rim of the hills and the slow magic of a summer twilight was beginning to unfold; through my window the vista of formal gardens and distant skyline was entrancingly beautiful. I was admiring it as Rainier entered with Woburn, whom he had been showing round the library. "I hope you don't object to views," he said. "I know it's the latest artistic fad to consider them rather vulgar. I put in these large windows myself, against all the advice of architects who said this sort of house shouldn't have them. Otherwise, except for a few extra bathrooms, I haven't touched the place."

Behind the two of them stood Sheldon, announcing that our baths were ready; Rainier turned then and led us across the corridor into an extraordinary room of Moorish design embellished with fluted columns and Arabic gargoyles and a high domed ceiling. He watched our faces and seemed to derive a certain satisfaction. "My father built this," he explained, "as what he called an extra billiard-room. He made the bulk of his fortune during the Edwardian era, when the social hallmark was to have a billiard-room, and during the last year of the war, when money was coming in so fast he didn't know what to do with it, he conceived the idea of an EXTRA billiard-room as a symbol of utter superfluity... At least, that's the only theory I can imagine. I don't think a single game of billiards was ever played in it, and I turned it into a bathhouse without any feeling of impiety." We passed through the room, which was furnished with divans and sun-ray lamps, into a further apartment containing a row of small but quite modern cubicle bathrooms, three of which Sheldon was already preparing for our use. "There were only four bathrooms in the entire house before I made these," Rainier continued. "One was in the servants' quarters and Sheldon had actually paid for it out of his own pocket. That gives you some idea of the times, even as late as 1919." He added, after a pause and another glance at our faces: "And of my father too—I know that's what you're thinking. But it wasn't really niggardliness. He gave a great deal during his lifetime to the more orthodox charities. What he mostly suffered from were a few strikingly wrong notions. One of them was doubtless that servants didn't need bathrooms. Another was that he was really an English gentleman. And another was that the remaining saga of mankind would be largely a matter of tidying up the jungle and making the whole earth a well-administered English colony under a Liberal government. I think when the war ended he assumed that's what was going to be done to Germany."

"Maybe it should have been," said Woburn quietly. He had done little but smile until then, and I noticed Rainier give him a look of sharpened interest. Then we went into our respective cubicles, but the walls were only neck-high and conversation rose easily with the steam. I could hear Rainier and Woburn veering on to a political argument, while in my own cubicle Sheldon, arranging towels, saw me notice the slightly brown colour of the water as it filled the tub. "Won't harm you," he remarked. "We tell some of our guests it's due to mineral springs that are good for rheumatism, but as you're one of the family I'll let you into a family secret—IT'S JUST THE RUST IN THE PIPES."

He was going out chuckling when I retorted, quite without secondary meaning: "I hope all the family secrets are as innocent."

The chuckle ended sharply as he turned on me a look that evidently reassured him, for his mouth slanted into a slow smile as he resumed his exit. "I trust you will find them so, Mr. Harrison."

Meanwhile Rainier had come back to the subject of Stourton, and I heard him saying to Woburn: "My father bought it after it had bankrupted the Westondales, and the Westondales inherited it from ancestors who had built it out of profits from the African slave trade. This made my father's purchase almost appropriate, since my great-great-grandfather made his pile out of the first steam-driven cotton mills in Lancashire. You may imagine Stourton, therefore, peopled with the ghosts of Negroes and little children."

A short while later we dressed and dined in the vast room that would have seated fifty with ease, instead of our four selves. Mrs. Rainier, I noticed, was particularly gracious to Woburn, whom she probably felt to be shy in surroundings of such unaccustomed grandeur. There was talk of how he would set about the library-cataloguing job; most of the books, it appeared, had been taken over from the Westondales along with the house. "My father was not a great reader, but he had a curious knack of reading the right things. One day he read that some pine forests in Hampshire were supposed to be healthy to live amongst, so he promptly bought several hundred acres of them— on which part of Bournemouth now stands. Quite an interesting man, my father. He played the cornet, and he also cried over all Dickens's deathbed scenes —Little Nell and Paul Dombey, especially. He liked to have them read to him, for preference, and his favourite reader was an old governess of mine named Miss Ponsonby, who hated him and used to come out of one of those tearful séances muttering 'The old humbug!' But he WASN'T altogether a humbug—at least no more than most of us are. I'm not quite certain WHAT he was... Somebody ought to write a really good biography of him some day. He did have one written just before he died, but it was a commissioned job and made him into a not very convincing plaster saint—and, of course, it would be easy to write the other sort, showing him as a sinister capitalistic villain... But in between, somewhere, is probably the truth —if anyone thought it worth while to make the search."

"Why shouldn't Mr. Woburn try?" asked Mrs. Rainier.

"Not a bad idea, if he wants to. But let him finish the cataloguing first. Ever write anything, Woburn?"

"A few stories, Mr. Rainier. You read one of them—probably you've forgotten it—"

"Ah yes, of course. The one about the unfortunate Russian?"

Woburn nodded, and the somewhat mysterious reference was not explained. After coffee Mrs. Rainier said she was tired and would go to bed; Rainier mentioned letters he had to write; so there seemed nothing left for Woburn and me but to pass the evening together, somehow or other.

Sheldon suggested the library, ushering us into the fine sombre room with a touch of evident pride, and obligingly switching on a radio in time for the news summary of a Hitler speech delivered in Berlin earlier that day. We listened awhile, then Woburn snapped off the machine with a gesture— the meagre residuum of protest to which modern man has been reduced. "I hope there isn't a war this year," he remarked, as one hoping the weather would stay fine. "You see, as soon as I finish this job I have another with the Kurtzmayers—they have a big collection at Nice and I daresay I shall spend all the autumn there—unless," he added with a half-smile, "Mr. Hitler's plans interfere with mine." I smiled back with a touch of the uncomfortableness that afflicts me when some facetious travel-film commentator refers to "Mr. and Mrs. Hippopotamus" and waits for the laugh. I was thinking of this, and also wondering how a youngster like Woburn (at least ten years my junior) had managed to establish this cataloguing racket amongst the rich and eminent, when he disarmingly told me all about it. "It was the Rainiers who gave me an introduction to the Kurtzmayers— they've been rather good at putting things in my way."

I asked him how long he had known the Rainiers.

"Only a few months. And you?"

"About two years. I met him first—quite by accident—in a train."

"I met him first in a public library."

"By accident?"

"No, I had a job there and he came to see me. Mrs. Rainier sent him."

"MRS. Rainier?"

"Yes, I met her before him. It was her idea I should do the Stourton job —that's why she sent him to see me."

"I should have thought she'd have asked you to see him."

"So should I, but it seems he had a queer idea he wanted to see me first without either of us knowing who the other was, so that if he didn't like me the whole thing could be dropped."

"I see."

"Haven't you ever noticed that for all his glib speech and ease of manner he's really shy of meeting new people—in a rather odd way?"

I said perhaps I had, and asked him how his own meeting had happened.

"He didn't have far to come—the library was only just across the river in Lambeth. Of course I took him for just an ordinary visitor. He first of all asked at the counter if we had any illustrated books on English villages. It's the sort of vague request you fairly often get from people, so I picked a few books off the shelves and left him at a table with them. Presently he handed them back with a few words of thanks, and out of politeness I then asked if he'd found what he'd been looking for. He said, well, no, not exactly—he'd just thought the pictures and photographs in some illustrated book might happen to include one of a place he'd once seen but had forgotten the name of. They hadn't though, and it didn't matter."

"You must have thought it curious."

"Yes, but the really curious thing was that I'd just written a short story based on a similar idea. He seemed quite interested when I told him this and we talked on for a while—then finally he stared round rather vaguely and said, 'I'm supposed to see a man who works here called Woburn.' I said I was Woburn and he pretended to be surprised and pleased, but somehow I felt he had known all the time, though his pleasure seemed genuine. He then said his wife had talked about me and thought I might do some cataloguing, and of course he had to say then who he was. I told him I'd be very glad, and he said that was fine, he'd let me know; then he shook hands hurriedly and left."

"Did he let you know?"

"Not immediately. After a few weeks I wrote to him, because I really wanted the job if I could get it—I was only earning three pounds a week. Of course I'd found out all about him in the interval—about his Fleet Street interests—that's really why I sent him that short story I'd written, because I thought maybe he'd pass it on to one of his editors." Woburn smiled. "He returned it a few days later, without comment, but said I could begin the cataloguing any time I liked."

"Tell me about the story."

"Oh, it was nothing much—just a rather feeble yarn about a Russian soldier returning from the front after the Revolution."

"What happened to him?"

"Nothing exciting. He just roamed about the country trying to find where he lived."

"Had he—had he lost his memory?"

"No, he was just a simple fellow—couldn't read and write— all he could give was the name of the village and a description of it that might equally have applied to ten thousand other Russian villages. The government officials wouldn't bother with him, because he couldn't fill out the proper forms, so he just had to go on wandering vaguely about trying to find the place."

"And did he—eventually?"

"He was run over by a train and carried to a neighbouring village where he died without knowing that it actually was the one he'd been looking for... of course you might have guessed that."

"Having read Gogol and Chekhov, I think I might."

"I know, it was just an imitation. I haven't any real originality— only a technique. I suppose Rainier realized that. So I'd better stick to the catalogues."

It seemed to me a courageous, but also a rather desolate thing for a young writer to admit.

"Why not try the biography, if they give you the chance?"

"I might, but I doubt if it would work out. You can't be sure they'd really WANT anyone to be impartial. That's why it's an affectation of Rainier's to run down his ancestors. A sort of inverted snobbery put on to impress people because the direct kind isn't fashionable anymore... Mind you, I like him IMMENSELY."

"And her?"

"Oh, she's marvellous, isn't she? The way she can remember dozens of names when she introduces people..." I remembered Rainier had once commented on that too. But Woburn added: "Rather a mistake, though, in English life —never to make a mistake. Like knowing too much—such as the names of all the states in America. Stamps one as a bit of an outsider."

"You seem to have sized things up pretty well."

"Probably because I AM an outsider."

"So am I. So are most of the people who come here. So are half the names in Debrett. Come to think about it, that's one healthy symptom of English so-called society—its inside is full of outsiders."

"I suppose the Rainiers are outsiders—in a sense."

"Well, they haven't a title, but that makes no difference. Owning Stourton's almost a title in itself."

"Yes, it's a wonderful place. There's an odd atmosphere here, though, don't you think?"

"Do YOU think so?"

"You don't know everything, you don't know everything—that's what the place seems to say."

"Maybe those ghosts of Negroes and little children?"

"They haven't got any children, have they?"

"No."

"Did they ever have?"

"I don't know. One somehow doesn't get to know things like that."

"Do you think they're happy?"

Before I could attempt an answer we both turned sharply to see Sheldon carrying in a tray with siphon, glasses, and whiskey decanter. "I thought perhaps you two gentlemen might like to help yourselves, either now or later." Without offering to serve us he placed the tray on a table and walked out of the room, pausing at the door to deliver a quizzical good-night.

We returned the salutation and then, as soon as the door closed, looked at each other rather uneasily. "I didn't hear him come in," said Woburn, after a pause. "He didn't knock."

"Good servants don't—except at bedroom doors."

"Oh? I don't know things like that. My mother never had a servant."

"Now who's being an inverted snob? My mother had ONE servant, whom we called the skivvy. That sets us both pretty equal so far as Stourton's concerned."

"You probably went to a good school, though."

I mentioned the name of my school and agreed that it was generally considered fairly good. "As good as Netherton, which is where Rainier went. Anyhow, from a social angle, the main thing is the accent—which you and I both seem to have. Nobody's going to ask us where we picked it up."

"I don't mind if they do. I was at a board school up to the age of twelve —then I won a scholarship to a suburban grammar school. I took a London degree last year, working in the evenings. I never try to conceal the truth."

"CONCEAL it? I should think you'd boast about it."

"I suppose that's really what I AM doing. Will you have a drink?"

"Yes, please."

He began to mix them and presently, while working off a certain embarrassment, added: "How does that fellow Sheldon strike you?"

I said I thought he was the kind of person one could avoid a decision about by calling him a character. "Maybe the keeper of the family skeleton," I added.

"No—because if there were one, Rainier would take a perverse delight in dragging it out of the cupboard for everyone to stare at."

We laughed and agreed that that might well be so.

It was past eleven before we yawned our way upstairs. When I reached my room I found it full of cool air and moonlight; in the vagrant play of moving curtain shadows I did not at first see Rainier sitting by the window in an armchair. He spoke as I approached: "Don't let me scare you—I'm only admiring your view. It's exactly the same as mine, so that isn't much of an excuse... How did you and Woburn get along?"

"Quite well. I like him. An intelligent young fellow."

"Spoken with all the superiority of thirty to twenty?"

"No, I don't think so. I DO like him, anyhow."

"He's my wife's protégé. She wants to see him get on in the world—made me root him out of a municipal library to do this card- indexing job... Yes, he might go far, as they say, if there's anywhere far to go these days."

"That's the trouble, and he probably realizes it as much as we do."

"Well, we can't change the world for him, but it's nice to have him around —company for Helen, if nothing else. I like him too, for that matter. I like most boys of his age— and of your age. Wish I had an army of 'em."

"What would you do with an army of them?"

"Something better, I hope, than have them catalogue books or write biographies of my ancestors." He read my thoughts enough to continue: "I daresay you're rather surprised at my lack of enthusiasm for the family tree. That may be because I didn't have a very satisfactory home life. When I was a small boy my father was just something distant and booming and Olympian —a bit of a bully in the house, or at least a bit of a Bultitude (if you remember your Vice-Versa)—all of which made it fortunate for the family that he wasn't much in the home at all. My mother died when I was ten."

"But you liked HER?"

"I loved her very dearly. She was a delicate, soft-voiced, kind-hearted, sunny-minded, but rather helpless woman—but then most women would have been helpless against my father. HE loved her, I've no doubt, in his own possessive way. Perhaps a less loving and more thoughtful husband would have sent her to a warmer climate during the winters, but my father wasn't thoughtful—at best his thoughtlessness became comradely, as when he insisted on taking her for brisk walks over the hills on January days. It was a cherished saying of his that fresh air would blow the cobwebs out of your lungs. It also blew the life out of my mother's lungs, for it was after one of those terrible walks, during which she gasped and panted while my father shouted Whitmanesque

36

encouragement, that she called in Sanderstead, our local doctor, who diagnosed t.b. My father was appalled from that moment and spent a small fortune on all kinds of cures, but it was too late—she died within the year, and my father, I have since felt, promptly did something about her in his mind that corresponded to winding up or writing off or some other operation that happens even in the best financial circles."

He suddenly stood up and moved to the open window, staring out as if facing something that challenged him. "Those are the hills where he made her walk. You can see the line of them against the sky." Then he turned abruptly and said he was sure I was tired and would want to go to bed.

I assured him I wasn't sleepy at all.

"But you came in yawning."

"Maybe, but I'm wide-awake now. The breeze is so fresh... You must have hated your father."

He answered slowly: "Yes, I suppose I did. Freud would say so, anyhow. But of course when I was a boy and even up to my undergraduate days people only admitted the politer emotions."

"The war changed all that."

"Yes, indeed, and so many other things too."

He was silent for a moment; then I went on: "You once told me about a certain day, sometime after the war ended, when you found yourself on a park seat in Liverpool."

"When did I tell you that?" He controlled a momentary alarm, then added with a smile: "Ah yes, I remember—in your rooms at St. Swithin's. I'm always garrulous after public speeches... Well, if I told you, you know. That's how it was. And don't ask me about anything BEFORE the park seat because I can't answer."

"But how about AFTER the park seat?"

He seemed relieved. "AFTER? Oh I can stand any amount of cross- examination there —I'm on safe ground from about noon on December 27, 1919."

"I wish you'd begin your story there, then, and bring it up to date."

"But there IS no story—except my life story."

"That's what I'd like to hear."

"How I Made Good? From Park Seat to Parliament?"

"If you like to call it that."

He laughed. "It's mostly a lot of sordid business details and family squabbles. You don't know the family, either."

"All the same, I wish you'd tell me. The effort of setting it all out might even help you towards the other memory—if you're still anxious for it."

I could see the response to that in his eyes as he entered the light again.

"So you really think memory's like an athlete—keep it in training —take it for cross-country runs? H'm, might be something in the idea. When do we start?"

"Now, if you're not too sleepy. I'm not... Go back to that park seat in Liverpool."

"But I told you about that once."

"Tell me again. And then go on."

So he began, and as it makes a fairly long story, it goes better in the third person.

PART TWO

He found himself lying on that park seat. He had opened his eyes to see clouds and drenched trees, and to feel the drops splashing on his face. After a while his position began to seem more and more odd, so he raised himself to a sitting angle, and was immediately aware of sodden clothes, stiff limbs, a terrific headache, and a man stooping over him. His first thought was that he must have been drunk the night before, but he soon rejected it, partly because he could not remember the night before at all, partly because he somehow did not think he was the sort of young man to have had that sort of night, but chiefly because of a growing interest in what the man stooping over him was saying. It was a kind of muttered chorus—"That's right, mister—take it easy. Didn't 'ardly touch yer—it was the wet roadway, you sort o' slipped. Cheer up, mister, no bones broke—you'll be all right—wouldn't leave you 'ere, I wouldn't, if I didn't know you'd be all right..."

Presently, suggested by the muttered chorus and supported by the fact that his clothes were not only sopping wet but also muddied and torn, another hypothesis occurred to him—that he had been run down by a car whose driver had brought him into the park and was now leaving him there.

But WHERE? His brain refused an answer, and when pressed offered a jumble of memories connected only with war—shell-fire for headaches, a smashed leg for stiffness, no-man's-land for all the mud and rain in the world.

He stood up, feeling dizzy, swayed and almost fell. The man had gone, was now nowhere to be seen. Then he noticed he had been lying down on sheets of newspaper. He stooped to peel one off the seat, hoping it might afford some clue, but the top of the page that would have contained a name and date was an unreadable mush, and the rest was rapidly softening under the heavy rain. He peered at it, nevertheless, searching for some helpful word or phrase before the final disintegration. Most of the letterpress seemed to be news about floods and flood damage—rescues from swollen rivers, people stranded in upper floors, rowboats in streets, and so on.

Then suddenly his eyes caught a paragraph headed "Rainier Still in Germany"—one of those mock-cheerful items that tired sub-editors put in to fill an odd corner—something about soaked holiday crowds taking comfort from the thought that somebody somewhere was faring even worse.

Now it is curious how one's own name, or the name of one's home, or a word like "cancer," will sometimes leap out of a page as if it were printed in red ink. It was like that for the young man as he staggered through the deserted park towards a gate he could see in the distance. Rainier Still in Germany —Rainier Still in Germany. It was a challenge, something he had to answer; and the answer came. "IMPOSSIBLE—I'm HERE, reading a newspaper, and the newspaper's in English—therefore this can't be Germany."

Presently he passed through the park gate into a busy thoroughfare. A tram came along, mud-splashed to its upper windows and sluicing swathes of water from the rails to the gutters. It was difficult to see through the spray of mud and rain, but on the side of the tram as it passed by he could just read the inscription—"Liverpool City Corporation."

He walked along by the high railings till the park came to an end and shops began. Meanwhile he had been feeling in his pockets, finding money —coins and several treasury notes, amounting in all to over four pounds. Reaching a newsagent's shop he went inside and asked for a paper.

"Post or Courier, sir?"

"Doesn't matter."

A paper was handed over. "Looks like you've had a fall, sir? Terribly slippery after all this rain... Like me to give you a bit of a brush?"

"Er... thanks."

"Why, you're wet through—if I was you I'd get home and to bed as quick as I could. Like me to get you a cab?"

"No, that wouldn't help. I don't live here. But if there's a tailor nearabouts—"

"Two doors ahead, sir. He'll fix you up. Say I sent you."

"Thanks."

He walked out, glancing at the paper as he did so. He saw that the date was December 27, 1919.

So now he knew three important things: Who, Where, and When.

Two hours later Charles Rainier was in a train to London. He had had a hot bath and a meal; his clothes did not fit well, but were dry; and after a lightning headache-cure across a chemist's counter he felt somewhat drowsily relieved.

Beside him were several more newspapers and magazines. As it was the end of December, some contained résumés of the events of 1919; and these at first he had found very astonishing. Biggest of all surprises was to find that the war had been over for more than a year and had ended in complete victory for the Allies; this was surprising because his last recollected idea on the subject had been that the Allies were just as likely to lose. But that dated back to a certain night in 1917 when he lay in a shell-hole near Arras, half delirious with the pain of a smashed leg, watching shell after shell dig other holes round about him, until finally one came that seemed to connect by a long dark throbbing corridor with his headache that morning.

Charles arrived in London towards dusk, in time to catch the last train that would get him to Stourton that night. The train was late in reaching Fiveoaks, which is the station for Stourton, and three miles away from it, as anyone knows who has ever received a letter on Stourton notepaper. From Fiveoaks he walked, because all the cabs were taken before he reached the station yard, and also because he hoped the cold air might clear that still-surviving headache. He was glad they were putting out the lamps as he gave up his ticket at the barrier, so that the collector did not recognize him.

He realized that his return was bound to come as a shock, and he hardly knew what reason he could give anyone for his long and peculiar absence; he hardly knew yet what reason he could give himself. He was puzzled, too, by an absence of joy in his heart at the prospect of home and familiar faces; more than by any excitement he was possessed by a deep and unutterable numbness of spirit, a numbness so far without pain yet full of the hint of pain withdrawn and waiting.

Presently he turned off the main road. He remembered that turn, and the curve of the secondary road over the hill to the point where suddenly, in daylight, the visitor caught his first glimpse of the house. Often, as a boy, he had met such visitors at Fiveoaks, hoping that when they reached that particular point of the drive they would not be so immersed in conversation as to miss the view.

Now when he came to the view there was nothing to see, nothing to hear but an owl hooting, nothing to feel but the raw air blowing from the uplands.

He was glad he had sent no wire to tell them of his arrival. He had refrained because he felt the shock might be greater that way than if he were to see Sheldon first, and also because he hardly knew how much or how little to say in a wire; but now he perceived another advantage in not having sent any message—it preserved for a few extra minutes the curious half-way comfortableness of being alive only in the first person singular.

Towards midnight he reached the wrought-iron gates of the main entrance; they were closed and locked, of course, but there was a glow in one of the adjacent windows, and as he approached the small square-built lodge a gap in a curtain revealed a lighted Christmas tree. Odd, because he remembered Parsloe as a tight-fisted bachelor unlikely to spend money on that sort of thing—unless, of course, he had married in the interval; but that was odder still to contemplate—Parsloe married!

It was not Parsloe, however, who opened the door to his persistent ringing, but a half-dressed stranger—middle-aged, suspicious, challenging.

"Well, young man?"

"I'd like to go up to the house, if you'll let me through."

"We don't admit anyone, not without you give your name and business."

"I know, but you see..." He hesitated, realizing the difficulties ahead —his story, told cold with no corroborations, would sound sheerly incredible. Eventually he added, rather weakly: "If Parsloe were here, he'd know me."

"Maybe he would, but he ain't here—having been dead these fifteen months. You'd better be off, sir, dragging people out of bed at this hour."

The "sir" was some progress anyway; a social acknowledgment that, drunk or sober, honest or fraudulent, at least one had the right accent.

"Perhaps I could see Sheldon, then—"

"You can't disturb Mr. Sheldon either—especially now."

"You mean there's a party?" (Of course there would be—there were always big parties at Stourton through Christmas and New Year.)

Suddenly the question: "You wouldn't be Dr. Astley, by any chance?"

Charles was about to ask who Dr. Astley was when he thought better of it and replied hastily, perhaps too hastily: "Yes, that's who I am."

But the lodge-keeper was still suspicious. Moving over to a telephone just inside the door, he wound up the instrument, listened, then began muttering something inaudible. Afterwards he turned to beckon Charles inside. "Mr. Sheldon says he'd like a word with you first, sir."

"Certainly. I'll be glad of one with him, too."

Good old Sheldon—taking no chances. The voice at the other end was impersonally wary. "Dr. Astley? Have you come alone?"

No need to say anything but: "Sheldon, it isn't Dr. Astley—whoever he is. It's Charles— you know, CHARLES."

"CHARLES?"

"Charles who was... Oh, God, I don't want to have to go into all that, but remember the Left-Handed Room?... THAT Charles."

"Mr. Charles?"

"Yes—Yes!"

Long pause. Then: "I'll—I'll come along—immediately —if—if you'll wait there—for me."

"Good—but first of all say something to this fellow—he thinks I'm a fake. Don't tell him anything—just say it's all right."

He handed the receiver to the lodge-keeper, who took it, listened a moment, then hung up with more puzzlement than satisfaction. "Well, sir, you'd better wait here, seeing as how Mr. Sheldon says so."

"Thanks. And please understand that I don't blame you in the least. One can't be too careful."

Somewhat mollified, the man brought forward a chair, then accepted a cigarette that Charles proffered. "Marsh is my name, sir. If you're a friend of the family, you'll know of course there's no parties this year on account of old Mr. Rainier being ill."

"ILL? No, I—er—I didn't know that."

41

"That's why I thought you might be Dr. Astley. He's a London doctor they're expecting."

"But what about Sanderstead?"

"Dr. Sanderstead wanted to consult with Dr. Astley, sir."

"Sounds serious."

"Yes, sir, I'm afraid so. Of course he's an old man, getting to be. It's his heart."

"Where's the family?"

"They're all here, sir, except Mrs. Jill and Mr. Julian."

"Where are they?"

"On their way back from abroad, I think, sir."

Strange to be edging one's way into such realizations. The sick man was his father, and yet, somehow, the springs of his emotion were dried up, could offer nothing in response to the news but an intensification of that feeling of numbness. He went on smoking thoughtfully. Really, when he came to think of it, Sheldon was the person he came nearest to any warm desire to see... Marsh continued after a pause: "I could get you a nip of something, sir, if you wanted. It'll take Mr. Sheldon twenty minutes at least to come down —all the cars are locked up, and it's a good mile to walk."

(As if he didn't know it was a good mile to walk!) He answered: "That's not a bad idea."

Marsh went to an adjoining room and came back with two stiff drinks. "Thought you looked a bit pale, sir, that's why I suggested it."

"DO I look pale?"

"Just a bit, sir. Or maybe it's the light."

Charles walked over to a near-by mirror and stood for a moment examining himself. Yes—there was a queer look; one could call it pallor, for want of an exacter word. Actually, he felt overwhelmingly tired, tired after the long and troubled journey, tired after that knock on the head in the early morning, tired after something else that was difficult— impossible—to analyse. He sipped the whiskey and relaxed as he felt it warming him. "By the way, Marsh—it's some time since I was here last... any particular changes? You told me of one of them just now, for instance—Parsloe dead. Anything else?"

"You mean among the staff, sir? I've only been here fifteen months."

"Well, the staff or—oh, anything." He hardly liked to ask direct questions.

"There's been a few changes in the house, sir—maybe you'll notice. Mr. Rainier pulled down the old billiard-room and built two new ones."

"TWO new billiard-rooms? Good God!"

"Well, one of them isn't much used. There's just a table in it, in case anyone wants to play. And of course since Mr. Rainier took ill—"

"He's been ill a long time?"

"Six months, sir, just about. Sort of gradual, it's been..."

And so on; so that when, eventually, the knock came at the door and Marsh opened it, recognition was silent, tight-lipped, almost wordless till they were alone together. Just "Hello, Sheldon"—and "Good evening!"

Leaving Marsh more puzzled than before, they turned into the darkness of the long curving drive. Out of earshot Charles stopped a moment, feeling for the other's hand and shaking it rather clumsily.

"Sorry to be sentimental, Sheldon, but that's how glad I am to see you. Matter of fact, it's too dark to see you, but I've a feeling you look exactly the same."

"I—I can't quite collect myself yet, Mr. Charles—but —I—I'd like to be the first to—to congratulate you!"

"Thanks—though I don't know whether congratulation's quite the word."

"It's so—extraordinary—to have you back with us. I can hardly believe it—"

"Neither can I, Sheldon, so don't press me for details. All I can tell you is that I was in Liverpool this morning—and don't ask why Liverpool, because I don't know any more than you. But I had some money as well as the devil of a headache from having been run down by a car, maybe... that's all the evidence, so help me God. Before that I can't remember a thing since —since all sorts of things I don't WANT to remember—the war —lying between the lines with shells bursting... years ago, I realize. There's a sort of dark corridor between then and this morning—don't ask me about that, either. What you and I've got to decide now is how to go about the job of reintroducing me, as it were... Any ideas?"

"If you'll give me a little time, Mr. Charles—I'm still rather —"

"I know—bumfoozled is the word old Sarah used to use."

"Fancy you remembering that."

"What's happened to her?"

"She's still living in the village. Of course she's very feeble."

"Poor old girl... And too bad about Parsloe—how did that happen?"

"Pneumonia after the flu. Very sudden. We had quite an epidemic about a year ago."

"The new man seems all right."

"Marsh? Oh yes. Used to be one of the gardeners."

"Don't remember him... God, what are we gossiping like this for?"

"Just what I was thinking, sir, because there ARE more important things I must tell you about. I'm afraid you'll find the house in a rather disturbed condition—"

43

"I know. I realize I couldn't have turned up at a more awkward moment —in some ways. Much rather have come when it's quiet—nobody here—"

"You mean the family?"

"Well, yes—bit of a problem, how to let them know."

"We have to face it, sir."

"THEY have to face it, you mean."

"Naturally they'll be delighted to see you once they get over the— the surprise."

"The surprise of finding I'm still alive?"

"Well, after such an interval, and with no news—"

"I know. For God's sake don't think I'm blaming anybody."

"May I say, sir, speaking for myself—"

"I know, I know, and I'm grateful—think it was marvellous the way you kept your head in front of Marsh. Of course he'll have to know soon, like everybody else, but I was glad you postponed the—er—the sensation. Funny... when I wanted to say something over the telephone that would make you know I was genuine and yet wouldn't mean a thing to him, the only thing I could think of was the Left-Handed Room—remember how we used to call it that because the door opened the other way?"

"You remember those days very clearly, sir."

"So clearly it's like—like head-lamps along a road on a dark night. TOO clearly, that is —everything a bit out of focus. It'll all come right, I daresay."

"I hope so, sir."

"Well, let's not talk about it... We've got this other problem to settle, and my suggestion is what we always used to say when we were kids— leave it to Sheldon."

"I was about to suggest that too."

"Well, go ahead—any way you like. And in the meantime if you'll find me a bedroom that's a bit off the map I'll get a good night's sleep before making my bow at the breakfast table."

"I'm afraid—er—Mr. Rainier doesn't come down to breakfast nowadays."

"I know, Marsh said he was ill. I'm sorry. You'd better go easy when you tell him—the shock, I mean." He caught Sheldon's glance and interpreted it. "Don't worry about me, Sheldon—I know you're thinking I'm not behaving according to formula, but I can't help it—I'm too dead tired to face any reunions tonight."

After a pause Sheldon answered: "I doubt if there IS any formula for what you must be feeling, Mr. Charles. I could give you a bed in my own apartments if that would suit."

"Excellent... Thank heaven something's settled... Been having decent weather here lately?"

"Fairly, sir, for the time of the year. I noticed the barometer's rising."

"Good. It was raining in Liverpool this morning."

He slept a heavy troubled sleep, full of dreams he could not clarify, but which left him vaguely restless, unsatisfied. December sunlight waked him by pouring on to his bed; he stared round, wondering where he was, then remembering. But he could not recognize the room—somewhere in the servants' wing, he supposed, and he confirmed this by leaning up to the window. The central block of Stourton faced him grandly across the courtyard —there was the terrace, the big curving windows of the dining-room, the East Wing with its corner turret. The spectacle found and fitted into a groove of his mind—somehow like seeing a well-known place and deciding it was reasonably like its picture postcards... He was still musing when Sheldon came in with a tray.

"Good morning, Mr. Charles. I brought you some tea."

"Thanks."

"The barometer's still rising. Did you sleep well?"

"Pretty well. What time is it?"

"Eight o'clock. The family usually begin to come down about nine, but perhaps this morning—we stayed up rather late, you see... on the other hand, they may be anxious..."

"I understand. You can't ever be certain how people will react, can you?"

"No, sir."

"You should have brought an extra cup for yourself. Sit down and tell me all about it. What time did YOU go to bed? You look fagged out."

"To tell you the truth, I haven't been to bed at all. There were so many things to do—I had to talk to Dr. Sanderstead—and then your clothes—you'd hardly wish to wear them again, I think."

"No?"

"I took the liberty of borrowing a suit from Mr. Chetwynd—"

"Look here, never mind about all that—let's have first things first. You told them all?"

"Not your father, sir—but I told the others."

"How did they take it?"

"They were naturally surprised—in fact they could hardly believe me at first."

"And then?"

"Well, I suppose they DID believe me—eventually. They expect to see you at breakfast."

"Good... but you say you haven't yet told my father?"

"That was why I went to see Dr. Sanderstead—to ask his advice."

"Ah yes, of course. You always think of the sensible things, Sheldon."

"He was rather troubled about the danger of giving the old gentleman a shock—he says he'd like to have a talk with you about it first."

"All right, if he says so."

"I also took the liberty of telephoning to Mr. Truslove."

"Truslove?"

"It seemed to me that—er—he ought to be informed also, as soon as possible."

"Well, maybe that's sensible too, though it hadn't occured to me... How about a bath?"

"Already waiting for you—if you'll follow me."

"What about the servants, if I meet any of them?"

"They don't know yet, except Wilson and Lucas—I shall call the others together during the morning and tell them. And Mr. Truslove will be here for lunch—along with Dr. Sanderstead and Dr. Astley from London."

By that time they were at the door of the bathroom. "Quite elegant, Sheldon—new since I was here, isn't it?"

"Yes, sir."

"From which I gather the family income remains—er—not so bad?"

A wrinkled smile. "Like the barometer, sir—still rising..."

He bathed, smoked a cigarette, and put on the clothes Sheldon had laid out for him. Brown tweeds—Chet had always favoured them, and they fitted pretty well—as children he and Chet could generally wear each other's suits. And a Netherton tie—trust Sheldon to think of details. NETHERTON; and a whole cloud of memories assailed him suddenly: strapping on cricket pads in front of the pavilion; strawberries and cream in the tuckshop; the sunlight slanting into the chapel during Sunday services; hot cocoa steaming over the study gas-ring in wintertime; the smell of mud and human bodies in a Rugby scrum... Netherton. And then Cambridge. And then the cadet school. And then France. And then... the full stop... He controlled himself, leading his thoughts back from the barrier, gently insinuating them into the immediate future. He found he could best do this by adopting a note of sardonic self-urging: come along—trousers, waistcoat, tie, shoes, coat—button up for the great family reunion. "All aboard for the Skylark"— which set him recollecting holidays with his mother as a small boy—never with his father; his father had always been too busy. They used to rent a house at Brighton, in Regency Square, taking servants with them—Miss Ponsonby and a maid named Florrie, and every morning they would walk along the front not quite as far as Portslade, turning back so inevitably that Portslade became for him a sort of mysterious place beyond human access—until, one afternoon while his mother was having a nap, he escaped from the house and reached Portslade a dauntless but somewhat disappointed explorer.

"I hope the clothes will do for the time being, Mr. Charles."

"Fine—just a bit loose in front. Chet must be putting on weight."

"I'll have a talk with Mr. Masters sometime today. He has your old measurements, but it might be safer to have him visit you again."

"Much safer, I'm sure. You think I've changed a lot, Sheldon?"

"Not in appearance, sir. You look very fit."

"And yet there IS a difference?"

"In your manner, perhaps. But that's natural. It's a nervous strain one can well understand after all you've been through."

"I'd understand it better if I knew what I HAVE been through. But never mind that. Time for breakfast."

He walked across the courtyard, entering the house from the terrace. No one had yet appeared; the usual new-lit fire was burning, the usual blue flames distilling a whiff of methylated spirit from under the copper dishes. The Morning Post and Times on the little table. A cat on the hearthrug —a new cat, who looked up indifferently and then resumed a comprehensive toilet. Wilson was standing by the dishes, trying hard to behave as if the return of a long-lost son were one of the ordinary events of an English household.

"Good morning, Mr. Charles."

"Morning, Wilson."

"What can I get you, sir? Some kedgeree—or ham and eggs— kipper—kidneys—"

"Suppose I have a look."

He eased a little of his embarrassment by the act of serving himself. He knew Wilson must be staring at him all the time. As he carried his plate back to the table he said: "Well, it's good to be back." It was a remark without meaning—a tribute to a convention that did not perfectly fit, like Chetwynd's clothes, but would do for the time being.

"Yes, indeed, sir. Very glad to see you again."

"Thanks." And he opened The Times, the dry and crinkly pages engaging another memory. "You still warm the paper in front of the fire, Wilson?"

"Yes, sir. I always had to when Mr. Rainier used to come down—it's got to be a sort of habit, I suppose."

"Queer how one always associates big things with little things. I get the whole picture of my childhood from the smell of toasted printer's ink."

"Yes, sir."

He ate his ham and eggs, scanning the inside news page. Trouble in Europe —the usual Balkan mix-up. Trouble in Ireland, and that was usual too —British officers assassinated. Not much of a paper after the holiday —never was. The usual chatty leader about Christmas, full of Latin quotations and schoolmasterly facetiousness—dear old Times. A long letter from somebody advocating simplified spelling—God, were they still at that? Now that the war was over, it seemed both reassuring and somehow disappointing that England had picked up so many old threads and was weaving them into the same pattern.

Then Chetwynd, eldest of the brothers, began the procession.

"Hello, old chap, how are you?"

(What a thing to say! But still, what else?)

(Miss Ponsonby, his old governess, had once adjured him: When people say "How are you?" the correct answer is "How are YOU?" If you tell them how you are, you show yourself a person of inferior breeding... "But suppose, Miss Ponsonby," he had once asked, "you really WANT to know how somebody else is, mustn't they ever tell you?")

However, he answered: "Hello, Chet. How are YOU?"

"Want you to meet my wife, Lydia... Lydia... this is Charlie."

An oversized good-looking woman with small, rather hostile eyes.

And then Julia, plumper than when he had seen her last, but still the same leathery scarecrow—red-complexioned, full of stiff outdoor heartiness.

"Hel-LO, Charles! Sheldon told us ALL about it, and it's just too wonderful. I can't TELL you how—"

But then, as he kissed her, the fire went out like a damp match and they neither of them knew what to say to each other. He and Chet almost collided in their eagerness to serve her with food; Chet beat him to it; he slipped back into his chair.

"Kidneys, Julia?"

"Only scrambled eggs, please, Chet."

"Not even a little piece of bacon?"

"No, really, Chet."

"Any news of Father this morning?"

"I saw one of the nurses as I came down—she said he'd had a fairly good night and was about the same."

"Oh, good... Quite sure about the bacon, Julia?"

"Quite sure."

"Charles, what about you while I'm here? You don't seem to have much on your plate."

"Nothing more for me, thanks."

"Well, must be my turn then, and I don't mind admitting I'm hungry. Thrilling events always take me that way... Too bad Father's ill—we'd have had a party or something to celebrate."

"I'm sorry he's ill, but not for that reason, I assure you."

"No? Well..." Chet came to the table with his plate, having deliberately delayed at the sideboard till he heard the voices of others approaching. Now he looked up as if in surprise. "Morning, George... Morning, Bridget..."

George, a nervous smile on his plump moustached face; Bridget, the youngest of the family, sweet and shy, always ready to smile if you looked at her or she thought you were likely to look at her. George's wife Vera, and Julia's husband... an introduction necessary here—"Charles, this is Dick Fontwell"—"Ahdedoo, ahdedoo"—a tall, long-nosed fellow who threw all his embarrassment into a fierce handshake.

Breakfast at Stourton was a hard meal at the best of times, only mitigated by ramparts of newspapers and unwritten permission to be as morose as one wished. But this morning they all felt that such normal behaviour must be reversed—everybody had to talk and go on talking. Charles guessed that they were all feeling as uncomfortable as he, with the additional drawback of having had less sleep. During the interchange of meaningless remarks about the weather, the news in the paper, Christmas, and so on, he meditated a little speech which he presently made to them when Wilson had left to bring in more coffee.

He began, clearing his throat to secure an audience: "Er... I really do feel I owe you all sorts of explanations, but the fact is, this whole business of coming back here is in many ways as big a mystery to me as it must be to you—I suppose loss of memory's like that —but what I DO want to tell you is that in spite of all the mystery I'm a perfectly normal person so far as everyday things are concerned—I'm not ill, you don't have to be afraid of me or treat me with any special consideration... So just carry on here as usual —I'm anxious not to cause any additional upset at a moment when we're all of us bound to be upset anyhow."

He hoped that was a helpful thing to have said, but for a moment after he had finished speaking he caught some of their eyes and wondered if it had been wise to say anything at all. Then Bridget leaned over and touched his hand.

"That's all right, Charles."

Chet called out huskily from the far end of the table: "Quite understand, old chap. We're all more pleased than we can say, God bless. Of course with the old man being ill we can't exactly kill the fatted calf, but—but —"

"I'll consider it killed," he interrupted, just as Wilson arrived with more coffee. They all smiled or laughed, and the situation seemed eased.

Dr. Sanderstead had been expected for lunch, but he arrived a good deal earlier, along with Dr. Astley. Sanderstead was a wordy, elderly, fairly efficient general practitioner who could still make a good living out of his private patients, leaving a more efficient junior partner to take care of the rest. He had been the Stourton doctor ever since the family were children. Accompanied by the London heart specialist, whose herringbone tweeds for a country visit were almost too formally informal, he spent over an hour in the sickroom, after which Astley left and gave him a chance to talk to Charles alone.

They shook hands gravely, then at the doctor's suggestion began walking in the garden. Five minutes were occupied by a see-saw of congratulations, expressions of pleasure, thanks, and acknowledgments. Charles became more and more silent as these proceeded, eventually leading to a blank pause which Sanderstead broke by exclaiming: "Don't be afraid I'm going to ask you questions—none of my business, anyhow. Sheldon told me all that you told him—it's a very peculiar case, and I know very little about such things. There are some who claim to, and if you wished to consult— "

"At the moment, no."

"Well, I don't blame you—get settled down first, not a bad idea. All the same, though, if ever you want—"

"That's very kind of you, but I'd rather you tell me something about my father."

"I was coming to that. I'm afraid he's quite ill."

They walked on a little way in silence; then Sanderstead continued: "I'm sure the first thing you wished to do on coming back to us in this—er —remarkable way was to see him, and for that reason I'm grateful to you for deferring the matter at my request."

Charles did not think there was any particular cause for gratitude. He said: "Tell me frankly how things are."

"That's what I want to talk to you about. In a man of his age, and suffering from his complaint, complete recovery can't exactly be counted on —but we can all hope for some partial improvement that will enable him to—to—face a situation which will undoubtedly give him a great deal of pleasure once the initial shock has been—er— overcome."

Charles was beginning to feel irritated. "You don't have to break things gently with ME, Sanderstead. What you're hinting at, I take it, is that my father shouldn't learn of my existence till he's a good deal better than he is at present."

"Well—er—perhaps—"

"To save you the trouble of arguing the point, I may as well tell you I entirely agree and I'm willing to wait as long as you think fit."

"I don't know how to express my appreciation—"

"You don't have to. Naturally I'd like to see my father, but if you say he's not well enough, that settles it. After all this time I daresay we can both wait a bit longer."

They did not talk much after that. Charles was aware he had rumpled the doctor's feelings by not living up to the conventional pattern of a dutiful son; but he began to feel increasingly that he could not live up to any conventional pattern, still less could he be "himself," whatever that was; all he could do was to cover his inner numbness with a façade of slightly cynical objectivity. It was the only attitude that didn't seem a complete misfit.

A further problem arose later in the morning, but Sheldon broached it, and somehow he found it easier to talk to HIM.

"Dr. Sanderstead tells me you've agreed to his suggestion that for the time being—"

"Yes, I agreed."

"I'm afraid that opens up another matter, sir. Now that the servants know —which of course is inevitable—I don't see how we can prevent the story from leaking out."

"I don't suppose you can, nor do I see why you should. I'm not breaking any local by-laws by being alive, am I?"

"It isn't that, Mr. Charles, but your father sometimes asks to see a paper, and I'm afraid that once the story gets around it'll attract quite a considerable amount of attention."

"Headlines, you mean?"

"Yes, sir."

"I wouldn't like that for my own sake, let alone my father's."

"It would doubtless be very unpleasant. A young man from the Daily Post was on the telephone just now."

"ALREADY? Well, if they think they're going to make a national hero of me, they're damn well mistaken. I won't see ANYBODY."

"I'm afraid that might not help, sir. It's their job to get the news and they usually manage it somehow or other."

"Well, what do you suggest?"

"I was thinking that if somebody were to explain the matter personally on the telephone, giving the facts and using Mr. Rainier's state of health as ground for the request—"

"You mean get in touch with all the editors?"

"No, not the editors, sir—the owners. You see, Mr. Rainier has a large newspaper interest himself, and that makes for a certain—"

"Owns a paper, does he? I never knew that."

"It was acquired since your time, sir. The Evening Record."

"Well, if you think it'll do any good, let's try. Who do you think should do the talking—George or Chet? Better Chet, I'd say."

"Well, yes, Mr. Chetwynd would perhaps explain it more convincingly than Mr. George. But what I really had in mind—"

"Yes?"

"Lord Borrell has stayed here several times, sir—bringing his valet, a very intelligent man named Jackson. So I thought perhaps if I were to telephone Jackson—"

An hour later Chet came up to Charles with a beaming smile.

"Everything fixed, old boy. Sheldon wangled it through Borrell of the International Press—there won't be a word anywhere. Censorship at source. Borrell was puzzled at first, but eventually he said he'd pass the word round. All of which saves me a job, God bless."

So the story, which became one for curious gossip throughout the local countryside as well as in many a London club, was never hinted at by Fleet Street. The only real difficulty was with the editor of the Stourton and District Advertiser, a man of independent mind who did not see why he should not offer as news an item of local interest that was undoubtedly true and did not libel anybody. A personal visit by Chetwynd to the landlord of the premises in which the Advertiser housed its printing plant was necessary before the whole matter could be satisfactorily cleared up.

Charles spent the morning in a wearying and, he knew, rather foolish attempt to play down the congratulations. Every servant who had known him from earlier days sought him out to say a few halting, but demonstrably sincere words. It rather surprised as well as pleased him to realize that he had been remembered so well; but the continual smiling and handshaking became a bore. There were new faces too, recent additions to the Stourton staff, whom he caught staring at him round corners and from doorways. They all knew his story by now and wished to see the hero of it; the whole thing was doubtless more exciting than a novel because more personal in their lives, something to save up for relatives when they wrote the weekly letter or took their next day off.

Once, on his way through the house, he passed the room on the first floor where his father lay ill. It was closed, of course, but the door of an adjoining room was open, and through it he could see two young nurses chatting volubly over cups of tea. They stared as he went by, and from that he knew that they too had heard and were excited over the news.

When he appeared at lunch, he found Sanderstead and Truslove in the midst of what was evidently a sharp argument. Truslove was the family solicitor, a sallow sharp-faced man in his late fifties. During the little hiatus of deferential how-d'ye-dos and handshaking, the doctor and the lawyer continued to glare at each other as if eager to make an end of the truce. It came as soon as Charles said: "Don't let me interrupt your talk."

"What I was saying, Mr. Charles," resumed Truslove, eager for an ally, "is that the problem has a legal as well as a medical side. Naturally one would prefer to spare your father any kind of shock, but can we be certain that he himself would wish to be spared —when the alternatives are what they are?"

"All I can say," Sanderstead growled, "is that in his present state a shock might kill him."

"But we have Mr. Charles to think about," urged Truslove; which made Charles interject: "Oh, for heaven's sake don't bother about ME."

"Very natural of you to say that, Mr. Charles, but as a lawyer I'm bound to take a somewhat stricter viewpoint. There's the question of the WILL." He spoke the word reverentially, allowing it to sink in before continuing: "None of us should forget that we're dealing with an estate of very considerable value. We should bear in mind what would be your father's wishes if he were to know that you were so—so happily restored to us."

"We should also bear in mind that he's a very sick man," retorted Sanderstead.

"Precisely—and all the more reason that his desire, which I am sure would be to make certain adjustment necessary for the fair and equal division—"

Charles drummed his fingers on the table. "I get your point, Truslove, but I'm really not interested in that side of it."

"But it's my duty, Mr. Charles—my duty to your father and to the family quite as much as to you. If I feel morally sure that a client of mine —"

Sanderstead interrupted: "If changing his will is what you're thinking about, he could no more do that than address a board meeting! And that's apart from the question of shock!"

"Isn't it possible that a shock caused by good news might give him sudden strength—just enough to do what he would feel at once to be necessary?"

"Thanks for the interesting theory, Truslove. When you want any advice about law, just come to ME."

Charles intervened with a slightly acid smile. "I don't know why you two should quarrel. You may be right, either of you—but suppose I claim the casting vote? I don't want to see my father if there's any chance the shock might be bad for him, and I don't give a damn whether I'm in or out of his will... Now are you both satisfied?"

But of course they were not, and throughout lunch, which was a heavy affair with nobody quite knowing what to talk about, he was aware that the two men were engrossed in meditations of further argument.

During the afternoon he tried for a little quiet in the library, but Chet found him there and seemed anxious to express HIS point of view. "You see, old chap, I can understand how Truslove feels. Legally you're—well, I won't say DEAD exactly—but not normally alive. He's bound to look at things from that angle. What I mean is, if anything were to happen to the old man—let's hope it won't, but you never can tell—you wouldn't get a look in. Now that's not fair to you, especially as there's plenty for everybody, God bless. That's why I think Truslove's right—surely there must be a way of breaking good news gently—Sheldon, for instance—"

"Yes, we all think of Sheldon in emergencies. But I do hope, Chet, you won't press the matter. Truslove tells me there'll be no difficulty about my resuming the income we all had from Mother—"

"But good God, man, you can't live on five hundred a year!"

"Oh, I don't know. Quite a number of people seem to manage on it."

"But—my dear chap—WHERE? What would you DO?"

"Don't know exactly. But I daresay I should find something."

"Of course if you fancied a salaried job in one of the firms—"

"I rather feel that most jobs in firms wouldn't appeal to me."

"You wouldn't have to take it very seriously."

"Then it would probably appeal to me even less... But we don't have to decide it now, do we?"

"No, of course not. Have a drink?"

"No, thanks."

"I think I will. Tell you the truth, all this is just about wearing me down. Gave me an appetite at first, but now I feel sort of—"

"You mean all the fuss connected with my return?"

"Oh, not YOUR fault, old chap. After all, what else could you do? But you know what families are like—and wives. Argue a man off his head."

"But what could there have been any argument about?"

"Well, Truslove and Sanderstead—like cat and dog all day. Personally, as I told you, I back Truslove—but Lydia—well, she's never seen you before—she can't help feeling there's something a bit fishy about it—and of course, old chap, you must admit you haven't explained everything down to the last detail."

"I'm aware of that. If the last detail were available, I should be very glad to know it myself."

"Don't misunderstand me, though. Far more things in heaven and earth than —than something or other—know what I mean? I accept your statement ABSOLUTELY."

"But I haven't made any statement."

"Well, at breakfast you did—you said you were all right— NORMAL, I mean. And I'm prepared to take your word for it whatever anyone else thinks."

"Meaning that your wife believes I'm a fake?"

"A fake or else... Well, if she does, she's wrong, that's all I can tell her."

"I hope you won't bother to."

"Nice of you to put it that way, but still... Sure you won't have a drink?"

"No, thanks."

"Cheerio, then. God bless..."

By evening he had decided to leave. It was not that anyone had been unkind to him—quite the contrary, but he felt that he was causing a disturbance, and the disturbance disturbed him just as much as the others. He had given Truslove and Sanderstead his decision; it merely irritated him that they continued to wrangle. "The fact is, Sheldon, my remaining here is just an added complication at the moment, affording no pleasure either to myself or anyone else—so I'll just fold my tent and silently steal away. But I won't go far and I'll leave you my address so that you can get in touch with me if there's any need—if, for instance, Sanderstead decides my father's well enough to see me. Don't tell Truslove where I am—I don't want any messages from HIM—and as for what you say to the others, I simply leave it to you, except that I'd rather they didn't take my departure as a sign of either disgust or—er—abdication... Perhaps you could think of something casual enough? And while I'm in Brighton I'll warm your heart by buying a few good suits of clothes."

"BRIGHTON, sir?"

"Yes, I always did like Brighton. I'll be all right alone—don't worry. If you could pack a bag for me, and get hold of a little pocket-money from the family vault or archives or wherever it's kept—I suppose the hardest thing is to find any spare cash in a rich man's house..."

"I can advance it, sir, with pleasure."

"Good... and put a few books in the bag, some of my old college books if you can find them."

"Maybe you oughtn't to overtax your mind, sir?"

"On the contrary, I feel rather inclined to treat my mind as one does a clock when it won't go—give it a shake-up and see what happens... Oh, and one other thing—I'd prefer to have the car drive me to Scoresby for the train. I'm so tired of shaking hands with people, and most of the station staff at Fiveoaks—"

"I understand." Sheldon hesitated a moment and then said: "You really ARE going to Brighton? I mean, you're not—er—thinking of— er—"

Charles laughed. "Not a bit of it, Sheldon. Put detectives on me if you like. And to show you it's all open and aboveboard, you can send a wire booking a room for me at the Berners Hotel."

"BERNERS? I don't think that's one of the—"

"I know, but I looked it up in the back of the railway guide and it's in Regency Square— where my mother and Miss Ponsonby used to rent a house for the summer when I was a small boy."

So much for sentiment; actually when he got there he found the Berners Hotel in Regency Square not quite comfortable enough, and moved to a better one the next day, notifying Sheldon of the change. It teased him to realize that though he did not care for grandeur and did not insist on luxury, he yet inclined to a certain standard in hotels—a standard above that of the clothes in which he had arrived at Stourton. He wished he hadn't told the Liverpool tailor to throw away his original torn and rain-sodden suit; it might have afforded some clue to the mystery. He pondered over it intermittently, but the effort merely tired him and brought nearer to the surface an always submerged sadness, that sense of bewildering, pain-drenched loss. He was afraid of that, and found relief in recollecting earlier clear-seen days of childhood and boyhood, the pre-war years during which he had grown up to be—as Miss Ponsonby would have said (only a governess could say such a thing outright)—an English gentleman.

Sheldon had packed a few books, chosen almost at random; a further selection, more carefully made, arrived from Stourton two days later. They included several he remembered studying in preparation for Cambridge— Stubbs's Constitutional History of England, Bryce's Holy Roman Empire, Gibbon's Decline and Fall. Good meaty reading, a little tough in places, suitable for whole mornings on the Promenade in one of the glass shelters; equally suitable for wet days in the hotel lounge. One morning, walking along the cliffs towards Rottingdean, he met an elderly man with a dog; interest in a wreck on the beach below drew them into a conversation which presently veered to books and politics. For three successive mornings afterwards he took the same walk, met the same man, and continued the same conversation, each time more interestingly; but on the fourth morning the man didn't appear, nor on any subsequent morning when Charles took the same walk. He didn't particularly mind; indeed, it almost comforted him to think of such mutual contacts as possible without the foolish establishment of names and identities.

Sheldon wrote to him regularly, giving him news of Stourton, but there wasn't much to relate: Mr. Rainier kept about the same; Sanderstead and Truslove were still quarrelling; while the family chafed more restively, finding Stourton rather dull to do nothing in, and wondering how long they must wait before they could decently decide to return to their respective homes. Not, of course, that they wanted the old man to die, but they clearly felt they shouldn't have been sent for so soon; on top of which Charles's return had somehow disturbed their equilibrium, for if there is one thing more mentally upsetting to a family than death, it must be (on account of its rarity) resurrection. All of which Charles either deduced from or read between the lines of Sheldon's direct reportage of facts—such as that Truslove had had an unsatisfactory interview with Dr. Astley, that Chet's wife was no longer on speaking terms with Bridget, that Chet had taken to spending most of his time practising shots in the billiard-room, that the local vicar had paid a discreet visit hoping to see Charles, and that the weather was still fine, but the barometer beginning to fall.

One morning at breakfast, while he was in the midst of reading Sheldon's latest assurance that things were still about the same, a page-boy brought a wire informing him at a glance that things were no longer the same at all. His father had died suddenly a few hours before.

He packed his bag and left for Stourton by the next train, arriving at Fiveoaks towards late afternoon. There he acknowledged the greetings of several of the station staff (noting with relief that the sensation value of his own existence had considerably diminished), and hurried into the waiting car. This time the skies were darkening as the moment of the "view" appeared, but the great house still made its bow impressively.

Sheldon was waiting at the open door to receive him; within the house, in the deliberately half-lit hall, Chet stood holding a whiskey and soda.

"Hello, old chap. Had a good time? Sheldon says you've been dosing yourself with sea air—don't blame you... Turned chilly these last few hours—what about a drink?"

Charles said he would have one, so Chet marched him into the dining-room, where the liquor was kept. "You know, I once went to see a man in London —somewhere in Campden Hill, I think it was—sort of artist's studio—but the chap had built a regular bar, like a pub, at one end of his dining-room—awfully good idea, don't you think?... Well, God bless."

Charles asked for details of his father's death and received them; then, alone, he went upstairs and entered the room where the old man lay. The numbness in his heart almost stirred; he touched the dead hand, feeling a little dead himself as he did so. Then he went downstairs to meet the others of the family, among them three recent arrivals, Jill with Kitty, and Julian. Jill was a heavily built, smartly dressed woman in her late forties, the eldest of the family and the widow of a civil servant who had left her with a daughter by an earlier marriage of his own. Kitty was fourteen and generally described, even by those who did not dislike her, as "a bit of a handful." Julian, back from Cannes, where he had been spending the winter, gave Charles a languid salutation and a remark evidently well prepared in advance. "How charming to see you again, Charles! I understand that when you regained your memory you found yourself in Liverpool on a wet day! Your only consolation must have been that it wasn't Manchester!"

Epigrams of this kind had established Julian's reputation as the family wit, but they lacked spontaneity and his opening remark in any conversation was generally on a level, however disputable, to which he did not afterwards attain. In appearance he was tall, lean, and handsome in a rather saturnine, over-elegant way; he lived most of his life in fashionable resorts where he played a little tennis, indulged in little friendships, and painted little pictures of scenery which his friends said were "not so bad."

So now they were all gathered together, the Rainier family, in descending order of age, as follows: Jill, Chetwynd, George, Julia, Charles, Julian, and Bridget. It was a stale family joke to say that they were seven. Like many families who have dispersed, they found conversation hard except in exchanges of news about their own affairs—troubles with servants, new houses, business squabbles, and so on. During the difficult interval between death and the funeral it was Sheldon who took control like some well-built machine slipping into a particularly silent but effective gear. Charles was grateful for this, and especially, too, that Sheldon had arranged a quiet room for him, his old turret room, in which he could rest and read a good deal of the time. He was aware that all the family viewed him with curiosity and some with suspicion, and that intimacy with any of them would probably lead to questions about himself that he could not answer.

A minor but on the whole welcome diversion was caused by the revelation that during the last twelve months of his life old Mr. Rainier had been having his biography written. The author was a young and unknown man named Seabury, who had apparently made a business of persuading rich men that posterity would regret the absence of any definitive story of their lives. Rainier, usually a shrewd detector of flattery, had in this case succumbed, so that the book had been commissioned, a sum paid to Seabury there and then, and a further sum promised "on completion" and "if approved." When the old man's state of health became serious, Seabury had evidently begun to fear for the balance of his payment, and so had hurried his manuscript into final shape, hoping perhaps to impress the assembled relatives by a certain fulsomeness of treatment that might be considered additionally appropriate in the circumstances.

The manuscript, neatly typed and with a covering letter, was brought to Stourton by special messenger on the evening before the funeral; Sheldon accepted it and placed it on the hall table; Charles, passing by an hour later, opened it at random. He happened to light on a description of Cowderton, where the Rainier steelworks were situated, and read:—

But what has been sacrificed in the sylvan peace of its surroundings has been gained in the town's prevalent atmosphere of optimism and prosperity; and for these gifts, connected so visibly with the firm of Rainier, Cowderton must thank the dreams of a lad who was himself born in the heart of rural England.

Charles smiled slightly and did not read any more. He felt that the book, if it were all in such a vein, would probably have pleased his father, while at the same time affording him the additional pleasure of not being taken in by it.

Others of the family, however, got hold of the manuscript and read enough of it to decide it was rather good, though of course they had to be a little patronizing about a mere writer, especially an unknown one, while at the same time nourishing the secret wonderment of all healthy-minded Philistines that the act of writing can be protracted throughout three hundred pages. But the manuscript's chief value lay in its usefulness as a subject for conversation during the rather hard-going lunch-party that assembled towards half-past two the following afternoon. Those who had just seen old Mr. Rainier's remains lowered into their final resting-place in Stourton Churchyard were relaxing after the strain of the ordeal while steeling themselves for another— the reading of the will; and there, at the table, with all the secrets in his pocket, sat Truslove, somehow larger now than life, munching saddle of mutton in full awareness that his moment was about to arrive, and striking the exact professional balance between serious-mindedness and good-humour— prepared to respond to a joke if one were offered, or to commiserate with a tear if one were let fall.

It seemed to be a family convention—unwritten, unspoken, even in a sense not consciously thought about—that Sheldon was one of them at such moments, and that as soon as the other servants had left the dining-room his own remaining presence need impose no censorship. Chetwynd had been talking business optimism with Truslove. "What we've got to do now, old chap, is to plan for peace as efficiently as we planned for war, because there's going to be no limit to what British industry can do in the future — why, only during the last few weeks one of our war factories turned to making motor-cycles—we're snowed under with orders already, simply can't cope with them." This was vaguely pleasant news to the family, though business was always tiresome— and yet, what else was there to talk about? Then somebody thought of the biography, and George asked Sheldon his opinion of it.

"I looked it over, sir, and it seemed quite respectably written."

"Respectably—or respectfully?" put in Julian, staking out his epigram rather faster than usual.

"Both, I think, sir."

Sheldon smiled, and then all of them, except Charles, began to laugh, as if suddenly realizing that there was no reason why they shouldn't. In the midst of the laughter Chetwynd glanced across the table and caught a ready eye. "How about an adjournment to the library, Truslove?"

Half an hour later the secrets were known, and there was nothing very startling about them. The bulk of Henry Rainier's fortune, amounting after payment of death duties to over one million eight hundred thousand pounds, was divided equally between six of the children enumerated by name, except that Chetwynd, because of seniority and closer contacts with the industrial firms, took over a few additional controlling interests. Stourton was also left to him, as well as the town house in London. A few heirlooms went to various members of the family; there were bequests to servants and a few small gifts to charity. Charles, of course, was not mentioned.

The whole revelation was so unspectacular that when Truslove had folded up the will and replaced it in his pocket there was a general feeling of relief and anticlimax. Any faint fears the family might have entertained (and there always are such faint fears where money is concerned) could now be disbanded; they were all going to stay comfortably rich for the rest of their lives —even richer than most of them had anticipated.

Sheldon had not been present during the actual will-reading, but when he next entered Chetwynd was the first to address him, almost jauntily: "Well, Sheldon, he remembered you. You get a thousand."

"That was very generous of Mr. Rainier."

"And if you take my advice you'll put it back in the firm— wonderful chance to double or treble it... However, we can discuss that later. By the way, I'm taking it for granted you'll stay with me here?"

"I shall be very pleased to do so, Mr. Chetwynd."

Chet, it was clear, was already seeing himself an Industrial Magnate, Master of Stourton, and Supreme Arbiter of Family Affairs. There was a touch of childishness in his attitude that prevented it from being wholly unpleasant. Having made his gesture, he now turned to Truslove, whose eye still watchfully waited. "Now, old chap, before we close the meeting, I think you've something else to say."

Truslove rose, cleared his throat, and began by remarking that it was perhaps appropriate at such a moment to turn from a sad event to one which, by being almost contemporaneous, had undoubtedly served to balance pleasure against pain, gain against loss. Indeed, had the late Mr. Rainier been permitted to learn of it, who knows but what... However, they knew his views about THAT, and the differences that had arisen between himself and Dr. Sanderstead; death had put an end to them, so it was perhaps unnecessary to refer to them again. What he did feel was undoubtedly what they all felt —a desire to welcome Mr. Charles to their midst and to assure him of their unbounded joy at the extraordinary good fortune that had befallen him. "We don't pretend to understand exactly how it happened, Mr. Charles, but a very famous hymn informs us that God moves in a mysterious way." A little titter all around the room. "And if our congratulations may have seemed either belated or lacking in expression, I am sure you will make allowances at this troubled time."

Charles bowed slightly. He did not think their congratulations either belated or lacking in expression—indeed, his chief complaint was that there had been so many of them so many times repeated.

The lawyer continued: "Now I come to a matter nearer to my own province, and one that I must deal with directly and briefly. It has seemed both to Mr. Chetwynd, as the future head of the family concerns, and to myself, as representing in some sense the wishes which I feel would have been those of the late Mr. Rainier, a man whom it was my privilege to know for over forty years, and whose probable intentions I can therefore speak of with some justification..."

And so on. What had happened, clearly, was that Truslove, having lost his battle with the doctors, had talked the family into an equity settlement —each of them agreeing to sacrifice a seventh part of his or her bequest in order that Charles should acquire an equal share. Dressed up in legal jargon, and with a good deal of smooth talk about "justice" and "common fairness," the matter took ten minutes to enunciate, during which time Charles sat back in his chair, glancing first at one face and then at another, feeling that nothing could have been less enthusiastic than (except for Chet's and Bridget's) their occasional smiles of approval. Chet was expansive, like Santa Claus basking in an expected popularity; Bridget was sweet and ready with a smile, as always. But the others were grimly resigned to doing their duty in the most trying possible circumstances—each of them saying goodbye to forty thousand pounds with a glassy determination and a stiff upper lip. They were like boys at a good English school curbing their natural inclinations in favour of what had been successfully represented to them as "the thing to do." Truslove must have given them a headmasterly pi-jaw, explaining just where their duty lay and how inevitably they must make up their minds to perform it; Chet had probably backed him up out of sheer grandiloquence—"Damn it all, we MUST give the fellow a square deal"; begun under such auspices the campaign could not have failed. But when Charles looked at George, and Julia, and Jill, and Julian, and Lydia, he knew they were all desperately compelling themselves to swallow something unpleasant and get it over; which gave him a key to the mood in which he felt most of them regarded him: he was just a piece of bad luck, like the income tax or a horse that comes in last.

Suddenly he found himself on his feet and addressing them; it was almost as if he heard his own voice, spoken by another person. "I'm sure I thank you all very much, and you too, Truslove. The proposal you've outlined is extremely generous—TOO generous, in fact. I'm a person of simple tastes—I need very little to live comfortably on—in fact the small income I already have is ample. So I'm afraid I can't accept your offer, though I do once again thank you for making it."

He looked round their faces again, noting the sudden amazement and relief in the eyes of some of them—especially Chet's wife, Lydia. Clearly they had never contemplated the possibility of his refusing. That began to amuse him, and then he wondered whether his refusal had not been partly motivated by a curiosity to see how they would take it. He really hadn't any definite inclination, either to have the money or not; but his lack of desire for it himself was certainly not balanced by any particular wish that they should be enriched.

Truslove and Chetwynd were on their feet with an instant chorus of objections. Truslove's were doubtless sincere—after all, he had nothing to lose. But Chet—was it possible that HIS protests were waging sham war against an imperceptible hope that had dawned in him, a hope quite shamelessly reflected in the eyes of his wife? Was he seeking to employ just a featherweight too little persuasion to succeed? Charles did not believe that Chet would have attempted this balancing act if left to himself, but there was Lydia by his side, and he was undoubtedly afraid of her. Nevertheless he kept up the protesting, and Charles kept up the refusal; the whole family then began to argue about it, with more vehement generosity now that they felt the issue was already decided; but they made the mistake of keeping it up too long, for Charles suddenly grew tired and exclaimed: "All right then, if you all insist, I'll agree to take it."

Truslove beamed on what he imagined to be his own victory; Chet, after a second's hesitation, came across the room and shook Charles by the hand. "Fine, old chap... Now we're all set and Truslove can do the rest." But the others could only stare in renewed astonishment as they forced deadly smiles into the supervening silence.

There were papers they all had to sign; then Charles escaped upstairs. His room was the one he had slept in as a boy, though it had since been refurnished more opulently; it expanded at one corner into a sort of turret, windowed for three-fourths of the circle, and from this viewpoint the vista of gardens and skyline was beautiful even towards dusk on a gray day. He was staring at it when Kitty entered. "Oh, Uncle Charles, I MUST show you this —it's in today's Times..." She held out the paper, folded at the column of obituary appreciations. The item she pointed to ended as follows: —

A lifelong individualist, there was never any wavering in his political and economic outlook, while his contributions to the cause of Free Trade, both financially and by utterance, were continual and ungrudging. A man whose character more easily won him the respect of his foes than the applause of the multitude, he rightly concentrated on an industrial rather than a political career, and though his representation of West Lythamshire in the Conservative interest had been in the strictest sense uneventful, his influence behind the political scene was never entirely withdrawn, nor did his advice go long unsought.

"Uncle Charles, what does it mean?"

"It's just something—that somebody's written."

"But I can't understand it—at least, I can understand some of the words, but they don't seem to mean anything. It's about HIM, isn't it?"

He answered then, forgetting whom he was addressing: "It's a charming letter about my father from a man who probably knew him slightly and disliked him intensely."

"Why did he dislike him?"

He tried to undo the remark. "Stupid of me to say that—maybe he didn't dislike him at all... Run along—haven't you had tea?"

When he had been her age there had been a schoolroom high tea, with Miss Ponsonby dispensing bread and jam and cakes.

"They're serving it now on the terrace. Aren't you coming down?"

Self-possessed little thing; not quite spoilt yet.

"I'll probably miss tea today."

"Don't you feel well?"

"Oh, I'm all right."

"Did it upset you, going to the funeral?"

"Funerals are always rather upsetting."

She still stood by, as if she wanted to be friendly. Suddenly she said: "Julian's very funny, isn't he?"

"Yes, he's quite the humorist of the family."

"He's going back to Cannes tonight."

"Oh, is he?"

"Do you mind if I smoke a cigarette?"

"A cigarette? Well—"

"I do smoke, you know—most of the girls at Kirby do as soon as they get into the sixth." She had taken a cigarette out of her bag and was already lighting it. "You don't mind, do you?"

"Not particularly."

"I knew you wouldn't. You don't give a damn about anything."

"Do they also say 'damn' in the sixth?"

"No—that's what Mother said to Uncle Chet about you."

"I see... Well..."

"But I've got to stay here now till I finish it... Don't you think Sheldon's rather marvellous?"

"Not only rather, but quite."

"I think he's the one who really ought to write a book about Grandfather."

"Not a bad idea—why don't you tell him?"

"I did, but he only smiled. He's so nice to everybody, isn't he? We had a wonderful Christmas party here last year, before Grandfather was ill— we had charades and one of them was his name—SHELL, you know, and then DONE—but of course everybody guessed it—it was far too easy. Then we had Buffalo—BUFF, the colour, and then a Frenchman answering the telephone—and then the whole word BUFFALO in America... No, it wasn't Christmas, it was New Year, because Bridget and I had an argument about who had the darkest hair to let the New Year in with... but I did it."

"You would, I'm sure."

"Will Uncle Chet have any New Year's party this year?"

"I shouldn't think so... Here's an ash-tray."

62

"What I really came for was to say good-bye. Mother wants to get away this evening." She held out her hand.

"Good-bye, Kitty—nice of you to come up."

He led her to the door. Then:—

"Uncle Charles, is it true you don't remember a thing that's happened to you for over two years?"

"Perfectly true."

"But how marvellous. Then ANYTHING might have happened to you?"

He laughed at that and patted her on the shoulder. "Yes, and forgetfulness may have its points. For instance, I daresay you'd rather I forgot that you smoked a cigarette—or don't you mind?"

"Perhaps I'm like you—I don't give a damn," she answered, scampering out of the room. "Good-bye, Uncle Charles!"

When she had gone he decided he had behaved pretty badly, encouraging her to smoke and swear; there was some imp of mischief in him that drove him to such things, except that "imp" and "mischief" were far too cheerful words for it.

Dinner, a little later, proved another difficult meal. Julian, Jill, and Kitty had already left; others were planning a departure the following day. Julia and her husband had agreed to stay over the New Year, "helping" Chet and Lydia. Lydia said: "Jill and Julian were anxious to say good-bye to you, Charles, but they felt you mightn't want to be disturbed, especially as Kitty said you weren't coming down for tea."

He smiled and said he perfectly understood. Chet talked business again with Truslove, who was staying the night; Chet also drank too much and said that British business was headed for the biggest boom in history, by Jove, always provided the government would keep off their backs. Which led to politics and the family constituency of West Lythamshire: "I'm no politician, old chap, but still if the local association were to make the suggestion... of course it's too early yet even to think of it."

But Chet evidently WAS thinking of it, readying himself for the doing of his duty, wherever it might lead him.

The following morning, when George and his wife had left immediately after breakfast, taking Bridget with them, Charles suddenly decided to return to London with Truslove, who had a car. They drove away together, amidst noisy farewells from Chet and a few quiet words from Sheldon as the latter stowed away the bags.

"Do you propose to stay in London, Mr. Charles?"

"I'll let you know, Sheldon. I'll be all right, anyway."

"I hope so."

During the journey through Reading and Maidenhead he told Truslove he had been quite sincere in his original refusal of the equity settlement, and had only agreed to it because it was what the family said they wanted, so if they now cared to go back on the decision; it would still be all right with him.

Truslove, of course, replied that that was out of the question. "In fact, Mr. Charles, you seem to have given this matter far too little thought. A quarter of a million pounds is not to be treated lightly."

"That's just the point. I don't know HOW to treat it."

Truslove assured him, entirely without irony, that there would be no trouble attaching to the inheritance. "The bulk of it's invested in shares of the company—you'll merely receive the regular dividends."

"That leads me to what I wanted to say. I'd rather not be connected with the family business at all. I'm not a business man. If I HAVE to have the money, I'd like to sell the shares immediately and invest the proceeds in government stock."

"But, Mr. Charles, I—I really don't advise—"

"Why not? Isn't it possible to do that?"

"POSSIBLE, of course—the shares command a very ready market. But I couldn't ADVISE it—not as things are."

"That's odd—I always thought you lawyers had a passion for government stocks. Aren't they supposed to be safer than anything else? What about consols?"

Truslove seemed disturbed at the prospect of having to assess the relative merits of consols and Rainier ordinaries. "Naturally I've nothing against government securities—no one CAN have, and I should be the first to advise such prudence in investment, but for... well, perhaps I may let you into a secret—of course the whole matter's very technical and hasn't been settled yet, but it was on the cards when your father passed away and I think events will go forward a little quicker now... it's a question of refloating the entire group of Rainier companies on terms that would of course be very favourable to present holders. I can't give you any details, but you'll realize why it would be unwise to dispose of anything at the present moment."

"Still, I'd rather you sell. I'm not interested in speculation and share movements. I really mean what I say, so don't wait for me to change my mind."

"Of course if you give me direct instructions, I can't refuse. But you realize that, in addition to any question of capital value, the income from government stocks will be very much less?"

"I don't mind that, either. I'll probably live very well on a fraction of it. Matter of fact, you might as well know my plans. I'm going to Cambridge."

"Cambridge?"

"I was going to go there, you know, when war broke out—I'd already taken the entrance examination. Not a bad idea to go on where you left off, especially if you can't think of anything else to do."

* * * * *

His rooms at St. Swithin's overlooked the river and the Backs, and from the first January day when he settled in, he felt peace surrounding him. It was not that he himself was at peace—often the contrary; but he always felt the rooms and the college weighing WITH him, as it were, in the silent pressures of his mind. His rooms were rather austerely furnished when he took possession; he made them less so by books, pictures, and a couple of easy-chairs, yet they still remained—as Herring, his gyp, remarked —a READING gentleman's rooms. After half a century of experience as a college servant, Herring counted himself fortunate whenever a newcomer to his staircase entered that category.

Charles had visited Cambridge for a week during his last term at Netherton; he had then put up in back-street lodgings while taking the Little-go, which had left him no time to make acquaintances or get much impression of the place except that he thought he was going to like it. He was glad of this now, for it meant that no one remembered him and that his past life was neither known nor inquired about. To be a younger son of a rich industrialist counted for nothing among dons and fellow undergraduates; that he had served in the war merely placed him among the vast majority; and that he made few friends and liked to be left alone was, after all, the not unusual characteristic of reading gentlemen.

He told his Senior Tutor, a harassed little man named Bragg, that he would like to take history; and a further interview with Werneth, the history don, decided him to try for the tripos instead of an ordinary degree. So he acquired the necessary books, began to attend recommended lectures, and dined in Hall for the required nights each week— which is about all a Cambridge life need consist of structurally, until the scaffolding is removed later and one sees how much else there must have been.

Sheldon sent him news from Stourton fairly often, generally to say there wasn't any news. Still reading, however, between the lines, Charles gathered that Chet and Lydia were failing to evolve a well-controlled household, and that Sheldon was less comfortable than in the earlier days of despotism. Truslove also wrote, reporting progress in his own sphere; transfers of property took time, and it was March before the lawyer could notify him that he no longer possessed any financial interest in the Rainier enterprises. The shares had been sold for seventy shillings (fifteen more than the price at Christmas), and the purchaser had been none other than Chetwynd, who had apparently been glad to add to his own already large holding. Truslove added that he regarded the price as satisfactory, though he still thought the sale unwise in view of a probably much higher price eventually.

Charles wrote back that he was perfectly satisfied, and that if his "unwise" action had been the means of obliging Chet, so much the better. Just about then came the Easter vacation; he did not visit Stourton or see any of the family, but spent the three weeks in an unplanned trip around northern France, visiting Chartres, Lisieux, Caen, and Rouen. Returning to London the day before the Cambridge summer term began, he bought an evening paper at Victoria Station and glanced through what had come to be the almost usual news of famine and revolution somewhere or other on the Continent; not till late at night, in his hotel room, did he happen to notice a headline on the financial page —"Rainier's Still Soaring: Reported Terms of Bonus." He read that the shares had topped five pounds and that there was talk of an issue of new stock to existing shareholders in the proportion of two for one. It wasn't all very clear to him, for he never studied the financial columns and did not understand their jargon; but he realized that, from the point of view of immediate profit, Truslove and Chet had been right, and he himself wrong; which didn't trouble him at all. He was almost glad for his own sake, as well as Chet's, for he would have had no use for the extra money, whereas Chet enjoyed both spending and the chance to say "I told you so, old chap." In fact he felt so entirely unregretful about what had happened that he sent both Chet and Truslove short notes of congratulation.

The next day he went to Cambridge and completely lost track of financial news amidst the many more interesting pursuits of term-time. He still did not make friends easily, but he joined the "Heretics" and sometimes attended the weekly debating sessions over the fish shop in Petty Cury; he also came to know the occupant of the rooms next to his on the same staircase—a high-caste Hindoo named Pal who was a mathematician and perhaps also a genius. Pal claimed to feel numerals emotionally and to find them as recognizable as human faces; Charles took him first as an oddity, then as a personality, later as a friend. He formed a habit of having coffee in Pal's rooms once or twice a week.

As summer came, he did most of his reading on the river, generally on the Upper Cam at Grantchester, and sometimes he would portage the canoe across the roadway to the deep tranquil reach beyond the Old Mill. One morning, having done this, he turned to the right, along a tributary; the going was difficult, for he had to slide over sunken logs and push away branches that trailed in the water, but after an arduous yard-by-yard struggle he was suddenly able to paddle into a dark pool overhung with willows; and there, as he rested, a feeling of discovery came over him, as if it were the Congo or the Amazon instead of a little English stream; he felt strangely happy and stayed there all day till it was time to return for tea at the Orchard, which was the Grantchester resort patronized by undergraduates. He was on friendly terms with the old lady there who served strawberries and cream under the apple trees, and when he showed his scratched arms and said where he had been, she answered very casually: "Oh, you must have been up the Bourne —Rupert Brooke used to say how beautiful it was there—HE got his arms scratched too." Somehow the whole incident, with its hint of something seen by no human eye between Brooke's and his own (highly unlikely, but tempting to contemplate), gave him a curious pleasure which he felt he would spoil by ever going there again; so he never did.

He got on well with lecturers and tutors, and soon acquired one of those intangible reputations, breathed in whispers across High Tables, that rest on anything except past achievement; he lived retiringly and took hardly any part in University activities, yet it had already become expected that he would do well. Werneth had even consented to his taking the first part of the history tripos in July—after two terms of preparation for an examination for which most students took three, and some even six. "But you have a good background of knowledge," he told Charles, adding with a smile: "And also a good memory."

On an impulse he could not check quickly enough Charles answered: "It's odd you should compliment me on my memory, because—" And then he told Werneth about his war injury, and the strange gap of years which he had christened in his own mind the Dark Corridor.

Werneth listened with an abstract attention beyond the range of mere inquisitiveness. After the brief account was finished, he tore a sheet of paper from a pad on his desk and drew a large rectangle. "Not exactly my province, as a historian, but nevertheless quite a teasing problem, Rainier. Your life, from what you say, appears to be divided into three parts— like Caesar's Gaul?"

"Or like Regent Street," Charles interjected, beginning to be amused.

"Or like a Victorian novel," capped Werneth, delightedly.

"Or like an artichoke," recapped Charles.

That put them both in a highly agreeable mood. "Let us call the parts A, B, and C," resumed Werneth, drawing verticals across the rectangle and lettering the segments. "A is your life before the war injury; B is your life between that injury and the moment in Liverpool last December 27 when, according to your statement, you suddenly remembered your name and identity; C is your life since then. Now it is demonstrably true that during Period C —that is to say, at the present time—you enjoy a normally clear recollection of both Period C and Period A, but not of Period B. Am I right?"

"Perfectly."

"And it must also be inferentially clear that during Period B you could not have had any recollection at all of Period A?"

"Naturally not."

"Thank you... There's only one thing more I should like to ask—and that is if I might send this diagram to my friend Dr. Freeman, of St. Jude's, along with a brief résumé of the facts which it illustrates?"

When Charles hesitated before replying Werneth added: "I won't mention your name if you'd prefer not."

Charles then consented. The matter was not referred to at his next meeting with Werneth, but some weeks later the history don asked Charles to stay behind after a lecture. "As I expected, my friend Freeman found my notes on your case extremely teasing. In fact he'd very much like to meet you if you haven't any objection. You probably know his reputation as a philosopher and psychologist."

Again Charles was reluctant, and again consented on the understanding that his name was not to be divulged; so the curious meeting took place in Werneth's rooms. The eminent authority talked to Charles for over an hour in a completely detached and anonymous way, stating as his opinion that Period B would probably return, though there could be no certainty about it or prophecy as to the time required. Charles had several further interviews with Freeman, and began to take a certain pleasure in consulting an expert thus obliquely; he thought it typical of the amenities of Cambridge civilization that such a plan could have been worked out to suit him. At the same time he came to like Freeman personally, so that when his own identity became later revealed through an accident, it did not bother him much.

Charles took a First Class in the first part of the history tripos, which was quite a brilliant achievement in the circumstances. After consultations with Bragg and Werneth, he decided to switch over to economics during the following year—an effective piece of specialization, for he had already gone a certain way in economic history. He was increasingly interested in the background of knowledge and theory behind the lives of men, and the astounding clumsiness of world behaviour compared with the powers of the planning mind. To use Werneth's favourite word, he found the paradox teasing.

During the Long Vacation he stayed in Cambridge, putting in mornings and evenings of study interspersed with afternoons on the river or walks to Granchester through the meadows; he liked Cambridge during vacation time —the quieter streets, the air of perpetual Sunday, the August sunlight bleaching the blinds in many a shop that would not pull them up until term-time. Most of the bookshops remained open, however, and there were a few good concerts. The two months passed very quickly.

Sheldon wrote to him every week, but with no news except of domestic trouble at Stourton—an outbreak of petty thefts due (Charles could judge) to Chet's refusal to back up Sheldon in some earlier trouble with one of the gardeners. Now that it was too late, Chet seemed to be handling the matter rather unfortunately, dealing out wholesale dismissals to servants who had given years of service, and leaving a staff both too small and too disgruntled to work well. Chet also wrote, giving his side of the question, casting doubts on Sheldon's efficiency, and asking how Charles, as one of the family, would feel about selling the place. Charles replied instantly that Chet should sell by all means; Stourton was far too big for any modern uses, and family sentiment should not weigh against common sense. Chet did not reply to that, but a few weeks later, at Cambridge, Charles heard from Truslove that Stourton was on the market, but wouldn't be easy to sell "in these days."

Then one Saturday, returning to his rooms from a lecture, he found Kitty sprawled on a sofa and Herring teetering doubtfully in the pantry. "Hello, Uncle Charles," she cried loudly, and then added in a whisper: "That's for HIS benefit. He didn't believe me—I could see that."

"But why didn't you tell me you were coming?" Charles began, trying to infuse a note of mild pleasure into his astonishment.

"Because you'd probably have told me not to," she answered promptly.

He admitted he probably would, and then asked why she HAD come.

"It's my birthday."

"Is it? But—well, many happy returns—but—"

"Uncle Chet promised me a big party at Stourton, but he cancelled it at the last moment because he said Aunt Lydia wasn't very well, and as I'd already got leave of absence from Kirby I didn't feel I could WASTE the week-end."

"But you're not intending to stay here for the whole week-end, are you?"

"Oh yes, I've taken a room at the Bull. Surprising what a girl can do by herself these days."

"But if they find out—at Kirby—"

"That I've been visiting one uncle instead of another? Will it matter? And I don't really care if they DO find out—I'm tired of school anyway. I'd like to go to Newnham."

"Anything wrong with Somerville at Oxford?"

"Oh, how you'd loathe to have me anywhere around, wouldn't you?"

He began to laugh and suggested taking her to lunch.

"Can't I have lunch here—in the college?"

"No."

"Well, that's better than the little German at our school who pretends to be French and gives us art lessons—he gets in an awful temper and then says, 'In one word I vill not have it.'"

They lunched at Buol's, in King's Parade, and afterwards he said: "Now, young lady, having invited yourself here, you'll have to take the consequences. My usual way of spending an afternoon is to punt up the river, and I don't care how dull you find it, it's either that or off you go on your own."

"But I don't mind at all—I can punt awfully well."

"You won't get the chance—I'LL do the punting."

But she lazed quite happily during the hour-long journey, chatting all the time about school, life, the family, herself, and himself. "It's made a great difference, you passing that examination, Uncle Charles. I believe the family had an idea you were a bit queer till you did that—now they still think you're queer, but a marvel too. You've quite pushed Uncle Julian off the shelf as the one in the family with brains."

He made no comment; the effort of digging the pole in and out of the river-bed gave him an easy excuse for silence. He didn't dislike Kitty, indeed there were certain qualities in her—or perhaps there was only one quality—that definitely attracted him.

She went on: "Of course the family don't really RESPECT brains— they just have a scared feeling that brains might come in handy some day."

"What makes you say that?"

"Oh, I don't know—just the general atmosphere before Mother went away. She's at Cannes, you know—staying with Uncle Julian."

They had tea at the Orchard and then returned to her hotel for dinner. "I'm glad you're showing up with me here," she said, as they entered the lobby, he in cap and gown as prescribed by University regulations for all undergraduates after dark. "It lets them know I'm respectable even if I AM only fifteen... By the way, how old are YOU?"

"Twenty-six."

"Do you FEEL twenty-six?"

"Sometimes I feel ninety-six—so I try not to bother about how I feel."

"Are you HAPPY?"

"Oh, happy enough."

"Can you remember ever being TERRIBLY happy?"

He pondered. "Once when I was a small boy and Sheldon visited us at Brighton for some reason, and HE took me for a walk along the Promenade instead of Miss Ponsonby." He laughed. "Such a thrill."

She laughed also. "And I was happiest once when I'd had a toothache and it began to stop. Before it FINISHED stopping. I really enjoyed the last bit of the pain."

"Morbid creature."

"But pain is part of love, isn't it?"

He was studying the menu. "At the moment I'm rather more concerned with the question of steak versus lamb chops."

"You WOULD say that, but you don't really mean it... Oh, and another time I was happy was Armistice Night, at school. So wonderful, to think the war was all over, wasn't it? Like waking up on end-of-term morning and realizing it's really come. But somehow everything's been a bit of a let-down since, don't you think? I mean, if you stop now and say to yourself, the war's over, the war's over, it can't keep on making you happy as it did that first night, can it?"

"I've practically decided on steak. What about you?"

"Uncle Charles, are you sorry I came here to see you?"

"Well, I'm a little puzzled about what to do with you tomorrow."

"I'd like to do whatever you were going to do."

"That's well meant, but I don't think it would work. I intended to read most of the day and go to a concert in the afternoon."

"I'd love the concert."

"I don't expect you would. Beethoven Quartets make no attempt to be popular."

"Neither do you, Uncle Charles, but _I_ don't mind."

He smiled, appreciating the repartee whilst resolute to make no concessions throughout the rest of the evening and the following day; he would teach her to play truant from school and fasten herself on him like that. After a long and, he hoped, exhausting walk on Sunday morning, he took her to the concert in the afternoon, and in the evening saw her off on the train with much relief and a touch of wry amusement.

"Uncle Charles, you've been so SWEET to me."

"I haven't been aware of it."

"Would you really mind if I were to come to Newnham?"

"It isn't in my power to stop you. But don't imagine you'd see much of me —the Newnham rules wouldn't allow it, for one thing."

"Do you think Newnham would be good for me?"

"Another question is would you be good for Newnham?"

"Won't you be serious a moment? I wish you'd write to Mother and tell her it would be good for me."

"Oh, I don't know that I could do that. It's for her and you to decide."

"She says she doesn't think she can afford it these days."

"Not AFFORD it? Surely—" But that, after all, wasn't his business either. If Jill thought she could afford expensive cruises and winterings abroad, and yet decided to economize on her daughter's education— well, it still remained outside his province.

The girl added, as the train came in: "It's because trade's not so good, or something. I think that's really why Uncle Chet cancelled my party, not because of Aunt Lydia." She mimicked Chet as she added: "Time for economies, old chap."

"I don't think you really know anything about it. After all, a party wouldn't cost—"

"I know, but Uncle Chet wouldn't think of that. There's nobody worse than a scared optimist." She gave him a look, then added: "I suppose you think I heard somebody say that? Well, I didn't—I thought it out myself. I'm not the fool you think I am."

"I don't think you're a fool at all. But I don't see how you can know much about financial matters."

"Oh, can't I? Uncle Chet used to rave so much about Rainier shares whenever I saw him that I and a lot of other girls at Kirby clubbed together and bought some. We look at the price every morning."

He said sternly: "I think you're very foolish. You and your friends should have something better to spend your time on—and perhaps your money, too... Good-bye."

The train was moving. "Good-bye, Uncle Charles."

Returning to St. Swithin's in the mellow October twilight he pondered on that phrase "in these days." Truslove had used it in connection with the possible sale of Stourton, and now Jill also, about the expense of sending Kitty to college. Always popular as an excuse for action or inaction, and uttered by Englishmen in 1918 and 1919 with a hint of victorious pride, it had lately—during 1920—turned downwards from the highest notes. There was nothing gloomy yet, nothing in the nature of a dirge; just an allegro simmering down to andante among business men and stockbrokers. Trade, of course, had been so outrageously and preposterously good that there was nothing for the curve to do except flatten; the wild boom on the markets could not continue indefinitely. Charles looked up Rainier shares in The Times when he got back to his rooms; he found they stood at four pounds after having been higher—which, allowing for the bonus, really meant that the shares he had sold to Chet for seventy shillings were now more than twice the price. Chet shouldn't worry—and yet, according to Kitty, he WAS worrying—doubtless because there had been a small fall from the peak. Her comment had been shrewd—nobody like a scared optimist.

The next morning at breakfast his thoughts were enough on the subject for him to glance at the later financial news, which informed him by headline that Rainier's had announced an interim dividend of 10 per cent, as against 15 the previous year. It seemed to him good enough, and nothing for anyone to worry about, but by evening as he walked along Petty Cury the newsboys were carrying placards, "Slump on 'Change" and "Rainier Jolts Markets." He found that the reduced dividend had tipped over prices rather as an extra brick on a child's toy tower will send half of it toppling. Rainier's had fallen thirty shillings during the day's trading, and other leading shares proportionately. It had been something that sensational journalism delighted to call a "Black Monday."

Still he did not think there was anything much to worry about. The theoretical study of economics was far removed from the practical guesswork of Throgmorton Street, and his reading of Marshall and Pigou had given him no insight into the psychology of speculation. For a week afterwards he ignored the financial pages, being temperamentally as well as personally disinterested in them; not till he received an alarming letter from Sheldon did he search the financial lists again to discover that in the interval Rainier ordinaries had continued their fall from two pounds ten to seventeen shillings. And even then his first thought was a severely logical one— that they were either worth more than that, or else had never been worth the higher prices at all.

Sheldon wrote that Chet was terribly worried, had been having long consultations with bank and Stock Exchange people, and had stayed all night in his City office on several occasions. Charles could not understand that; what had bank or Stock Exchange people got to do with the firm? Surely the Rainier business was principally carried on at Cowderton and other places, not in the City of London; and as for the falling price of the shares, what did it matter what the price of something was, if you didn't have either to buy or to sell? He replied to Sheldon somewhat on these lines, half wishing he could write a similar note to Chet, but as Chet had not approached him, he did not care to offer comment or advice.

But towards the beginning of December a letter from Chet did arrive; and it was, when one reached the last page, an appeal for a loan. He didn't say how much, but no sum, it appeared, would be either too small or too great; he left the choice to Charles with a touch of his vague expansiveness, assuring him that it was a merely temporary convenience and would soon be repaid. Charles was puzzled, unable to imagine how much Chet needed—surely it couldn't be a small sum, a few hundreds, and if it were a matter of thousands, what could he possibly want it for? He felt he had a right to inquire, and did so. Back came a franker, longer, and much more desperate appeal, again saving its pith until the last page, wherein Chet admitted he had been speculating heavily in the shares of the firm, borrowing from banks in order to do so. At first the result had been highly successful; his own constant buying on a rising market had given him huge profits, and with those (uncashed, of course) as security he had borrowed and purchased more. Then the inevitable had happened. Chet didn't put it in this way; he seemed to think that a conjunction of bad trade, falling share prices, and a request by the bank for him to begin repayment of loans was some malign coincidence instead of a series of causes and effects. If only Charles could help him out with ten or twelve thousand—he'd pay interest, let's call it a short-term investment, old chap, the badness of trade could only be exceptional, Rainier shares were destined to far higher levels eventually —hadn't they once been "talked" to twenty pounds? And Chet added that he hated making such a request, and only did so because there was much more at stake than his own personal affairs; Rainier's was a family concern, there were Julian and Jill and Bridget and Julia and all the others to think about. If he threw his own shares on the market, it would make for a further fall in the price, and that would be bad for the firm itself and so affect the stability of the family property and livelihood.

The letter arrived on a Friday; Charles answered it that same evening, enclosing a cheque for as large a round figure as he happened to have on hand, and promising more in a few days. But by the following morning the affairs of Rainier's had already broken out of the financial columns and were invading the news pages of all the daily papers. Apparently the shares had crashed in the "Street" after the Stock Exchange closed the previous evening, the final price being a very nominal half-crown. Accompanying the collapse were wild rumours—some of them, according to a discreet reporter, "of a serious nature."

That sent him to Bragg to ask for leave of absence; he then wired Sheldon and left immediately for Stourton, reaching the house in the late afternoon. From the cars outside he guessed there was a family conclave before Sheldon told him who had arrived. He found them assembled in the library, already in the midst of stormy argument. Bridget, who was near the door, said "Hello, Charlie," but the others were too preoccupied to hear this, even to see him at first. It was curious to note the utter disintegration of formal manners in face of such a crisis; to watch a favoured few, long accustomed to regard the family business as a rock of ages cleft for them, suddenly contemplating phenomena so normal in most people's lives—the uncertainties of the future. Charles stayed close to the door, reluctant to intervene; so far as he could make out, the family had been heckling Chet for some time, for his temper was considerably frayed, and at one question he suddenly lost it and shouted: "Look here, I'm not going to shoulder the blame for everything! You were all damned glad to leave things in my hands as long as you thought they were going well—"

"As long as we thought you knew what you were up to—we never guessed you were monkeying like this—"

"God damn it, Jill—what did YOU ever do except draw dividends and spend 'em on Riviera gigolos?"

"How DARE you say that!"

"Well, if you can suggest there's been anything crooked in the way I've —"

Jill was on the verge of hysteria. "I know my life isn't stuffy and narrow-minded like yours—but did I have to travel all the way here just to be insulted? Julian knows what a lie it is—he LIVES there —he's been at Cannes all the season except when we went to Aix for a month—Julian, I appeal to you—are you going to stay here and allow things like this to be said—JULIAN—"

George interposed feebly: "Steady now, steady—both of you."

73

Julia said, with cold common sense: "I think we might as well stick to the point, which isn't Jill's morals, but our money."

Jill was still screaming: "Julian can tell you—JULIAN— "

Everybody stared at Julian, who couldn't think of a sufficiently clever remark and was consequently silent. Meanwhile Chet's anger rose to white heat. "Look at ME—don't look at Julian! _I_ haven't had a decent sleep for weeks, while you've all been gallivanting about in Cannes or Aix or God knows where! LOOK at me! I've put on ten years—that's what they say at the office!" And he added, pathetically: "To say nothing of it giving Lydia a breakdown."

It was also pathetic that he should have asked them to look at him, for his claim was a clear exaggeration; he certainly looked tired—perhaps also in need of a Turkish bath and a shave; but his hair had failed to turn white after any number of sleepless nights. He was still expansive, even in self-pity. Charles felt suddenly sorry for him, as much because as in spite of this.

Julian, having now thought of something, intervened in his sly, high-pitched voice: "I'm afraid it wasn't your looks we were all relying on, Chet..."

Then Julia, glancing towards the door, spotted Charles. "Ah, here's the mystery man arrived! Hello, darling! How wise you were to sell Rainier's at three pounds ten and buy War Loan, you shrewd man! Come to gloat over us?"

It was the interpretation Charles had feared. He stepped forward, nodded slightly to the general assembly. "You're quite wrong, Julia... How are you, Chet?"

Chet, on the verge of tears after his outburst, put out his hand rather as a dog extends an interceding paw; he murmured abjectly: "Hello, old chap —God bless. Caught us all at a bad moment... And thanks for your letter—damn nice of you, but I'm afraid it's a bit late—a sort of tide in the affairs of men, you know—"

Charles, not fully aware what Chet was talking about, answered for want of anything else to say: "I should have come earlier, but I just missed a train."

"You missed Chet's news, too," Jill cried, still half-hysterical. "Such SPLENDID news! I've been travelling all night to hear it—so has Julian—would somebody mind repeating it for Charles's benefit?"

"I'LL tell him," Julia interrupted, venomously. "We're all on the rocks, and Chet's just the most wonderful financier in the world!"

"Except," added Julian, "a certain undergraduate who thoughtfully added a quarter of a million to Chet's bank loan by demanding cash."

Charles swung round on him. "What on earth do you mean by that?"

"Well, you sold your stuff to Chet, didn't you?"

"He wanted to buy—I didn't ask him to."

"But he paid you in cash."

"Naturally—what else?"

"Well, where d'you suppose he found the cash? In his pocket?"

"You mean he had to borrow from the bank to pay me?" Charles then turned on Chet. "Is this true?"

"'Fraid it is, Charlie. After all, you WANTED the cash."

"Well, YOU wanted the shares."

"Wasn't exactly that I wanted 'em, old chap, but I had to take 'em."

"But—I don't see that—surely I could have sold them to someone else?"

"Not at that price. You try dumping sixty thousand on the market and see what happens. I had to take 'em to keep the price firm. Isn't that right, Truslove?"

Charles peered beyond the faces; Truslove was standing in the shadows, fingering the embroidery at the back of a chair; leaning forward he answered: "That was your motive, undoubtedly, Mr. Chetwynd. But I think we can hardly blame Mr. Charles for—"

"Is it a matter for blaming anybody?" Charles interrupted, with tightened lips. "I can only say that I—I—"

And then he stopped. What COULD he say? That he was sorry? That had he known Chet was having to borrow he would have insisted on selling in the market? That if he could have forecast a crisis like this, he would have held on to his shares, just to be one of the family in adversity? None of these things was true, except the first. He said, lamely: "I feel at a disadvantage —not having known of these things before."

"Well, whose fault was that?" Jill shouted at him.

"My own, I'm perfectly well aware. I took no interest in them."

"It doesn't cost you anything to admit it now, does it?"

There was such bitterness in her voice that he stared with astonishment. "I—I don't know what you mean, Jill."

"Oh, don't put on that Cambridge air—we're not all fools! And we haven't all got queer memories either! If you want my opinion, you can have it—you're morally liable to return that cash—"

Truslove stepped forward with unexpected sprightliness. "I must say I consider that a most unfair and prejudiced remark—"

Jill screamed on: "I said MORALLY, Truslove, not LEGALLY! Isn't that the way you argued us all into the equity settlement with Charles after Father died? We didn't HAVE to do it then! He doesn't HAVE to do it now! But what he OUGHT is another matter!"

Nobody said anything to that, but Julian stroked his chin thoughtfully, while Julia stared across at Jill with darkly shining eyes. It was as if the family were at last converging on a more satisfying emotion than that of blaming Chet, who, after all, was only one of themselves. But Charles was different. He took in their various glances, accepting—

even had he never done so before—the position of utter outsider. His own glance hardened as he answered quietly: "I'm still rather hazy about what's happened. Can't I talk to somebody:—alone, for preference, and without all this shouting? How about you, Chet?... Or you, Julian?" Chet shifted weakly; Julian did not stir. "Truslove, then?"

The room was silent as he and the lawyer passed through the French windows on to the terrace. They did not speak till they were well away from the house, half-way to the new and expensive tennis-courts that Chet had had installed just before he decided to sell Stourton if he could. Truslove began by saying how distressed he was at such a scene, as well as at the events leading up to it; in all his experience with the family, over forty years... Charles cut him short. "I don't think this is an occasion for sentiment, Truslove."

"But perhaps, Mr. Charles, you'll allow me to say that I warned Mr. Chetwynd a great many times during recent months, but in vain—he fancied he had the Midas touch—there was no arguing with him... I only wish he had more of your own level-headedness."

"No compliments either, please. I want facts, that's all. First, is the firm bankrupt?"

"That's hard to say, Mr. Charles. Many a firm would be bankrupt if its creditors all jumped at the same moment, and that's just what often happens when things begin to go wrong. I daresay the firm's still making profits, but there are loans of various kinds and if they're called in just now, as they may be with the shares down to half a crown—"

"Is that a fair price for what they're worth?"

"Well, there again it's hard to say—always hard to separate price from worth."

"What will happen if the loans are called in?"

"The company will have to look for new money—if it can find any."

"And if it can't?"

"Then, of course, there'd be nothing for it but a receivership, or at any rate some sort of arrangement with creditors."

"May I ask you, though you needn't answer if you don't want—did Chet speculate with any of the firm's money?"

"Again, it's hard to draw a line between speculation and legitimate business practice. Mr. Chetwynd bought rather large quantities of raw materials, thinking prices would continue to rise. In that he made the same mistake as a great many very shrewd and reputable people."

"Will HE be forced into bankruptcy?"

"A good deal depends on what happens to the firm. If it weathers the storm the bank would probably give him a chance—subject, of course, to mortgaging Stourton and cutting down personal expenses to the bone. That applies to the others also."

"I see... Now may I ask you one final question? You were saying just now that the firm will need new money. You know how much I have myself. Would such a sum be any use in weathering the storm, as you put it?"

"That also is hard to say, Mr. Charles. I hardly care to advise you in —"

"I'm not asking for advice. I want to know how much the firm needs, so that I can judge whether it's even possible for me to save the situation at all."

"I—I can't say, Mr. Charles. The whole matter's very complicated. We should have to see accountants, and find out certain things from the banks —it's quite impossible for me to make an estimate offhand."

"Well, thanks for telling me all you can. Perhaps we could return by the side gate—I'd like to escape any more of the family wrangle if it's still in progress..."

He drove away from Stourton an hour later, without seeing the family again; but he left a note for Chet with Sheldon, saying he would get in touch within a day or two. After a dash across London he was just in time to catch the last train from Liverpool Street and be in his rooms at St. Swithin's by midnight. He had already decided to help if his help could do any vital amount of good. He couldn't exactly say why he had come to this decision; it certainly wasn't any sense of the moral obligation that Jill had tried to thrust on him. And he didn't think it could be any sentimental feeling about the family, whom (except for Chet and Bridget) he didn't particularly like, and whose decline to the status of those who had to earn their own living would not wring from him a tear. If sentiment touched him at all it was more for Sheldon and other servants whom he knew, as well as for the thousands of Rainier employees whom he didn't know, but whom he could imagine in their little houses sleeping peacefully without knowledge that their future was being shaped by one man's decision in a Cambridge college room. That aspect of the thing was fantastic, but it was true, nevertheless. But perhaps strongest of all the arguments was the fact that the money didn't matter to him; even the income from it was more than he could ever spend; if he could put it to some act, however debatable, at least it would not be useless, as it was and always would be in his possession. For his own personal future had already begun to mould itself; he would probably stay at Cambridge after obtaining a degree. Werneth had once hinted at a fellowship, and if this should happen, he would be enabled to live frugally but quite comfortably on his own earnings.

End of term came a couple of days later; he returned to London and took a room at a hotel. Having conveyed his conditional decision to Chet and to Truslove, he had now only to discover if his money had any chance to perform the necessary miracle. This meant interviews in City offices with bank officials and chartered accountants, long scrutinies of balance-sheets and many wearisome hours in the Rainier Building, demanding documents and statements that took so long to unearth and were frequently so confusing that he soon realized how far Chet's slackness had percolated downwards into all departments.

One of the accountants took him aside after an interview. "It's no business of mine, Mr. Rainier, but I know something of the situation and what you're thinking of doing, and my advice to you would be to keep out of it —don't send good money after bad!"

77

"Thanks for the tip," Charles answered, with no other comment.

During the next two weeks it became a matter of some absorption to him to discover exactly what Chet had been up to. So far he hadn't detected any actual crookedness—only the grossest negligence and the most preposterous—well, EXPANSIVENESS was perhaps again the word. Chet had not only bought shares at absurd prices and in absurd quantities; he had done the same with office desks, with electric lamps, even with pen nibs. A small change, apparently fancied by him, in the firm's style of notepaper heading had condemned enormous stacks of the original kind to waste-paper. An ugly marble mantelpiece in Chet's private office had cost six hundred pounds. And so far as Charles could judge from his somewhat anomalous position of privileged outsider, every department was staffed by well-paid sycophants whose most pressing daily task was to convince their immediate superior that they were indispensable.

By Christmas Charles had almost reached the same opinion as the accountant —that it would be folly to send good money after bad. Even a total repayment of loans would not alone suffice to lift the firm from the trough of depression into which the entire trade of the country was rapidly sinking; nothing could save an enterprise of such complexity but completely centralized and economical control. Without that a cash loan could only stave off the inevitable for a few months.

On one of those oddly unbusinesslike days between Christmas and the New Year he lunched with Chet and Truslove in Chet's office and told them this. "I must be frank, Chet. I've spent a fortnight looking into every corner I could find, and I'm not much of an optimist as a result. It isn't only new MONEY that the firm needs, it's new—well, new other things."

Chet nodded with an air of magnanimous comprehension. "You're probably right, old chap. How about a new boss? Suppose I were to swap round with George on the board?" Charles smiled gently. "I know my faults," Chet ran on. "I'm a fair-weather pilot—good when everything's on the up-and-up. Nobody can act and think bigger when times are right for it. But these days you want a chap who can act and think SMALL. That's what put George in my mind."

Charles was quite willing to subscribe to a theory that left Chet holding all the laurels, but he felt he had to say more. "I'm afraid it isn't just a matter of changing the pilot. You've got to change a good deal of the ship. And you also may have to change the voyage—or perhaps even lie up in harbour for a time and make no voyages at all."

"Just a figure of speech, old chap—don't press it too far."

"All right, I won't... but take this lunch as an example. Although I'm a guest, you'll perhaps forgive me for saying it's a pretty bad lunch. And I know where it comes from —the canteen, as they call it, downstairs. And I've seen the prices on the menu, so I know your canteen is either badly managed or a swindle or both."

"Well, maybe—but surely it's not so important—"

"It's one thing with another. The whole place wants reorganizing from top to bottom, and I can't exactly see George as the new broom."

"Well, let's assume you're right—but the more urgent issue still remains. The banks don't give a damn whether the canteen serves good food or not. They just won't wait for their money. What do YOU say, Truslove?"

Truslove temporized as usual. "I think we owe Mr. Charles a deep debt of gratitude for devoting two weeks of his Christmas vacation to making this inquiry. I'm sure everything he has said is very valuable."

"But some of his cash would be more valuable still—don't we agree, old chap?"

"That, I understand, is why Mr. Charles has met us here—to give us his decision."

Both of them looked to Charles, who answered, rather hesitantly: "I was hoping you'd see what I'm driving at without forcing me to a direct reply. In my opinion a loan or even a gift wouldn't help unless you completely reorganize the firm. That's all I can say."

"You mean your answer's a definite 'no'?"

"If you insist on putting it that way, but you've heard my reasons."

"Well, I'm damned." Chet stared gloomily at the tablecloth for a moment, while the waitress came in with coffee. Transferring his stare to the cup, he suddenly turned on her with a vehemence that almost made her drop the tray. "Call this COFFEE? Take it back and bring something worth drinking. And what's the cause of the rotten meals we get here? Send up the canteen manager to my office afterwards... and let me look at your hands! Why... damn it, I won't have this sort of thing—get your week's wages and don't come here again!"

Throughout all this Truslove and Charles had looked on uncomfortably. As soon as the girl, too startled and upset to make any reply, had left the room, Charles said quietly: "I'm not sure that was very fair of you, Chet. She wasn't responsible."

"What more can I do? Her hands—you should have seen them."

"Yes, yes... I daresay."

There was a long silence. Then Chet exploded:—

"Well, have I done anything WRONG? You talk about reorganization— what do you MEAN by it? If it isn't just a word, TELL me. Unless it's merely that you haven't got the courage to say outright that you're not going to risk your precious cash. I'd respect you more for saying that than for hiding behind all this reorganization pi-jaw."

("Pi-jaw"—that was the word they used at Netherton for interviews with the head master. It stirred in him a little instant pity for Chet.)

"I'm not hiding behind anything."

"You mean you'd lend the money if we DID reorganize?"

Charles was silent a moment; Chet went on: "That's a fair question, isn't it, Truslove? Let him answer, then we'll know where we stand. Let's have a straight 'yes' or 'no,' for God's sake."

"Very well, then... probably I would."

Chet beamed. "Fine, old chap. I take back any aspersions, God bless. NOW all you've got to tell us is what you'd call reorganizing. What have I got to do? Or what's anybody got to do? And for that matter, who's got to be the fellow to do it?"

"I—I can't easily answer those questions, Chet. I'm not a business expert. It's hardly possible for me to suggest a new board, new managers, new heads of departments—all out of the blue—in a couple of minutes."

"You think we ought to have new ones—all of them?"

"I do."

"You mean you've seen enough during these last two weeks to get an idea who's not pulling his weight?"

"To some extent, yes."

Then Chet, beaming again, played his trump card. "Well, all I've got to say, old chap, is —come here and do the job yourself." He kept on beaming throughout their stare of immediate astonishment. "Why not? Lend the money, then come and look after it. What could give you a better safeguard? You say you're not a business man, but you know enough to have found out what's wrong—that's a good deal of the way to knowing what's right. Truslove, arrange a board meeting or whatever there has to be and get it all fixed up. I'll resign, and then—"

Charles got up from the table and strode to the window, interrupting as he stared over the City rooftops. "But I don't WANT such a job—can't you understand that? I've got my work at Cambridge—"

"You could go back there afterwards—putting things straight mightn't take you more than a few weeks, once you got down to it."

"But I've no desire to get down to it!"

"Then it's damnably selfish of you! Worse than that, it's nothing but hypocrisy the way you've led us on into thinking you'd help us! First you make terms for getting us all out of a hole—then we agree to the terms—then you go back on them—"

"But I never made such terms! I never hinted at tackling a job like this myself! I don't even know that I could do it, anyhow."

Chet shrugged his shoulder, turning round to the lawyer. "Well, that's his second 'no'—I suppose we'll just have to let the little tick go back to his study books."

("Tick"—the worst term of Netherton opprobrium, and one that Charles had never used, even at school, because he had always considered it childish.) Afterwards, walking disconsolately along Cheapside and through Paternoster Row to Ludgate Hill and his hotel in the Strand, he felt he had considerably bungled the entire interview. He should have said "no" from the first; then there would have had to be only one "no."

Charles took over control of the Rainier firms in January 1921. To do so he obtained a term's leave of absence from St. Swithin's, smiling at the tense in Bragg's remark: "You would have done very well here, you know."

"WOULD have? I still intend to."

"Well, we shall see, we shall see."

He practically lived in Chet's office in Old Broad Street—no longer Chet's, of course, but he refused to put his own name on the door. At a special board meeting he had been appointed managing director with the consent of the bank creditors, to whom he had turned over his own government securities. The bank men doubtless smiled over the arrangement, since it was one by which they could not possibly lose; while the family, faced with even a thousand-to-one chance, grabbed it gladly if not gratefully. They could not get it out of their minds that Charles was somehow taking advantage of them, instead of they of him; but if (as Kitty had said) they had ever had a scared feeling that brains might come in handy some day, this was undoubtedly the day. The scared feeling developed until they actually believed in him a little, but without reasoned conviction and certainly without affection —rather as if he were some kind of astrologer whose abracadabra might, after all, perform some miracle of market manipulation. That, of course, was their only criterion of success; and it so happened that the mere closing of bear accounts sent up the price of Rainier shares from half a crown to six shillings within a month of his taking control, a rise that considerably helped his prestige though he made no attempt to claim any. Less popular was his early insistence on economies in their personal lives, but after one or two suggestions had been badly taken, he contented himself with sending each member of the family a personal note, merely conveying advance information that the preference dividend that year would not be paid. (The preference shares were all held by the family.) Expected protests came in the form of a personal visit from Chet, telephone calls from Jill, Julia, and George, and a strong letter from Julian in Cannes. He took no notice of any of them, his only concession being an offer to Jill to pay for Kitty's college education, if she still wanted one.

Kitty came to his office to thank him. "Sweet of you, Uncle Charles. But of course you don't mind my going to Newnham now you're not at St. Swithin's —isn't that it?"

"Not altogether. Besides, I hope I'll be back there soon."

"You mean you haven't taken on this as a life-work?"

"Good heavens, no!"

"I hear you're dismissing everybody."

"Not EVERYBODY."

"And nobody wants to buy Stourton."

"That doesn't surprise me."

"Where do you live?"

"In a little apartment near the British Museum."

"How appropriate! Can I visit you there?"

"You wouldn't find me in. I work late most evenings."

"Won't you take me to lunch?"

"I was just going to ask you. But there's no TAKING—we have it here—on my desk. And it's pretty bad—though not so bad as it used to be."

She chattered on about her personal affairs, the new and smaller house Jill and she had had to move into—a little suburban villa at Hendon, with only one maid—"and there's a house further along the road where a little man kisses his wife on the doorstep every morning at three minutes past eight and comes running past our house to catch the eight-seven— just like you read about in the comic papers."

"I'm glad you live so near a station. It must be very convenient."

"I know—you think I'm a snob."

"Not exactly."

"Then what?"

"I'm not quite certain."

"You mean you haven't made up your mind?"

"That would be too flattering to your sense of importance."

"I believe you DO think about me, sometimes."

"Obviously—that's why it occurred to me you might go to college."

"Uncle Charles... what's going to happen to everybody... whether they go to college or not?"

"I don't think I know what you mean."

"I get terribly upset thinking about it sometimes. The little man who runs for the train every day—I'm not really a snob about him, I think he's wonderful, and it's beautiful the way you can always tell the time by him, and the way he always catches the train—at least I hope he does, in case somebody like you goes round his firm dismissing everyone who's late... Oh, but what's going to happen, Uncle Charles—eventually?"

"You mean will he stop running?"

"Yes, or will the train stop running, or will he stop kissing his wife, or will you stop being able to dismiss people?—I don't know, it all seems so fragile—the least touch—"

"I've had that feeling."

"Oh, you HAVE?" Then pleadingly: "Don't make a joke about too much to drink, or lobster for supper. Please don't make a joke."

"I wasn't going to. There isn't any joke."

She said sombrely: "I know that too, and I'm only seventeen."

A tap came at the door and a young man entered with a sheaf of papers. When he had gone Charles scanned them through, then apologized perfunctorily for having done so. "But you see, Kitty, I'm terribly busy."

"Perhaps I'd better leave you to it then?"

"If you wouldn't mind." He smiled, escorting her to the door and saying as she left him: "I'm really glad you're going to Newnham. Write to me when you're there and tell me what it's like."

Then he went back to his desk. The papers included a list of names, over a hundred, of employees who would have to go that week. He glanced down the list, initialed his approval of it, and passed on to another job.

(But what would happen to them? And yet, on the other hand, what else could he do?)

By Easter he had made economies everywhere, yet the continuing malaise of trade kept up a tragic pace. There were few positive signs that his job could be regarded as approaching an end, and it was small satisfaction to know that without his efforts the whole concern would have already foundered like a waterlogged ship. As it was, the pumps were just a few gallons ahead of the still-encroaching ocean. Even the very energies he devoted to the task, his frequent feelings of thanklessness and exasperation, fought for a continuance of effort; he was giving the job so much that he had to give it more, because "if you work hard enough at something, it begins to make itself part of you, even though you hate it and the part isn't real." He wrote that in a letter to Kitty, explaining why he would have to postpone returning to Cambridge for another term. He found he could write to her more freely than he could talk to her, and more freely than he could talk to anyone except Sheldon.

He was still at his desk in the Rainier office when Kitty left Newnham in 1924. The desk was the same, one of Chet's fantastic purchases that were really more economical to keep and use than to sell in exchange; but the office was different—no longer opulent in Old Broad Street within a few yards of the Stock Exchange, but tucked away in an old shabby building off St. Mary Axe. Convenient, though—within easy reach of Mark Lane Station, and near enough to the river to get the smell of the tide and an occasional whiff of tobacco from the big bonding warehouses.

Much had happened since 1921. He had pulled Rainier's out of the depths into shallow water; there had even, during the second half of 1923 and first few months of 1924, been a few definite pointers to dry land. The preference dividend was now being paid again, while the ordinary shares, dividendless and without sign of any, stood at twelve shillings and were occasionally given a run up to sixteen or seventeen. Chet had a continuing order with a broker to sell a couple of thousand at the higher figure and buy back at the lower; it was the only speculation Charles would allow, but Chet derived a good deal of pleasure from it, imagining himself a titan of finance whenever he made the price of a new car. Chet still lived at Stourton, though part of the place was closed up; it was really cheaper to live in a house one couldn't sell than rent another.

The rest of the family had had to make similar economies, but the real pressure had been relaxed by the resumption of the preference dividend, and they were all comfortably off by any standards except those of the really rich. Jill could afford once more her cruises and flirtations, with no handicaps to the latter except advancing middle age and none to the former save an increasing difficulty in finding new places to cruise to. Julia and her husband lived in Cheltenham, playing golf and breeding Sealyhams; George and Vera preferred town life and had taken a newly built maisonnette in Hampstead. Julian was at Cannes, doing nothing in particular with his usual slightly sinister elegance; once or twice a year he turned up in London, took Charles for lunch to the Reform Club, and worked off a few well-polished epigrams. Bridget had married an officer in an Irish regiment and lived in a suburb of Belfast. She had had one child, a boy, and was expecting another. With George's girl and Julia's boy and girl, this made a problematical five as against seven of the previous generation, unless (as Chet put it) Charles hurried up. They were not, however, at all anxious for Charles to hurry up; and as both Lydia and Jill were past the age when any amount of hurry might be expected to yield result, and as Vera was sickly and Julia (so she boasted) had nothing to do with her husband any more, the ratio really depended on Bridget—plus, of course, an outside chance from Charles. Nobody even considered Julian in such a connection.

Much more, though, had happened between 1921 and 1924. The ancient Irish problem had apparently been settled; a conference at Washington had arranged limitation of naval armaments between England, Japan, France, and the United States; someone had almost climbed Everest; the German mark had collapsed and French troops had entered the Ruhr; Mussolini was rebuilding Italy and had already bombarded Corfu; there had been an earthquake in Japan, there had almost been another war with Turkey, there was still a war in Morocco, and there was going to be an exhibition at Wembley.

By 1924 Charles also had changed a little. It was not so much that he looked older— rather that he seemed to have reached the beginnings of a certain agelessness that might last indefinitely. He kept himself fit with careful living and week-ends by the sea; faithful to memories, he had bought a small house in Portslade that was not too expensive to keep up in addition to his London apartment—no longer the one near the British Museum, but a service flat in Smith Square. He worked long office hours, and had to make frequent journeys to Rainier factories throughout England; there were certain hotels where he always stayed, and to the staffs of these he was satisfyingly known as the kind of man who gave no trouble, drank little, tipped generously but not lavishly, and always appeared to be wearing the same perfectly neat but nondescript suit of clothes. The fact that he was head of the Rainier firm merely added, if it added at all, to the respect they would have felt for such a man in any case.

In 1924 Charles was thirty and Kitty nineteen. She had done well at Newnham, obtaining a second in the men's tripos examination, but of course she could not take a degree. On the day that she finally left the college she went direct from Liverpool Street Station to the Rainier offices, hoping Charles might be free for lunch; he was out, but found her still waiting in his private room on his return during the late afternoon.

"Oh, Uncle Charles, did you mind? I felt I must call—I feel so sad, I don't know what to do with my life—I've said good-bye to so many people there seems nobody left in the world but you!"

He laughed and telephoned for tea. "I'm glad I never had the experience of leaving Cambridge knowing it would be for good. It was only going to be for a term, and then two terms, and then a year..."

"And what now? Don't say you've given it up altogether."

"It must have given me up, anyway."

"But that's so awful to think of. You fitted Cambridge life, somehow. Remember that day I came from Kirby and waited in your rooms at St. Swithin's —just like this, except that the chair was more comfortable?"

"I don't hold with too comfortable chairs in offices."

"But you DO remember that day?"

"Yes—and so does Herring, I'm sure."

"God, I always thought it was a shame to drag you from what you wanted to do to run a business, but I must say you've done it pretty well—even Mother admits that, but I'll tell you something that'll amuse you— just because YOU'VE done it she thinks it couldn't have been so very hard and probably other people could have done it just as well."

"Probably they could. Anyhow, if it releases your mother from any embarrassment of gratitude, it's a thought worth thinking. Where is she now, by the way?"

"Somewhere in mid-Mediterranean, drinking cocktails. Chet asked me down to Stourton for the week-end. Why don't you come?"

"To be quite frank, because when I do go there, I'm usually bored."

"You mightn't be if I were there too."

He laughed and said he'd think about it, and after thinking about it several times during the next twenty-four hours he rang up Chet and said he was coming. Chet was delighted. Apparently Kitty was in the same room with him when the conversation took place, because he heard her excited voice in the background, then a scuffle to grab the instrument, and finally a torrent of enthusiasm which he cut short by asking to speak to Chet again.

He enjoyed himself at Stourton that week-end, and his lack of boredom was not entirely due to Kitty, for there was another guest, a man who had travelled in China and was interesting to listen to if difficult to talk to —a division of labour which suited Charles; and there were also local people, agreeable enough, who played tennis in the afternoons and stayed to dinner. Actually he did not see much of Kitty, who seemed generally to be surrounded by handsome young men in white flannels, and when chances came to join her group he did not do so. He wondered why he did not, and with a touch of quizzical self-scrutiny was prepared to diagnose even a twinge of jealousy; he would really have liked to, just for the chance to laugh at himself, but honestly he could not. Naturally the girl liked people of her own age; but there was another sense in which he had to realize now how old as well as young she was; those youths treated her with such obvious worship, it would not be fair for him to come along with his usual offhand badinage as to a child, and so deflate her adult prestige. And yet that was the only way he knew HOW to treat her—casually, unsparingly, never very politely. Perhaps that made up the chief reason he kept out of her way.

As soon as the dinner guests had left on the Sunday evening, he began to make his own farewells, for he intended to drive off early in the morning to reach his office by nine. Leaving Chet, Lydia, and Kitty in the drawing-room, he sidestepped into the library for something to read in bed. It was a superb July night; he did not feel sleepy, yet he knew he must sleep—he had a busy day tomorrow. One of the library windows was open to admit the warm breeze; there was a full moon, and the illumination, tricked by flapping curtains, played over the books like something alive and restless. He was fumbling along the wall for a switch when he heard a sound behind him. "Uncle Charles—don't put on any lights." He turned round, startled. She went on: "Why have you been avoiding me? And don't say you haven't."

"Of course I won't. I have. I know I have. And this is why. I can tell you very clearly, because I've been thinking it out myself."

He made his point about her age, and the young men, and his own offhand manner. When he had finished she said: "It's TOO clear, too INGENIOUS."

"But don't you think one's subconscious mind does work ingeniously?"

"Maybe yours does. I'll bet it would."

"You see, Kitty, you're no longer a child."

"Oh, God—for YOU to tell me that!"

Suddenly the wind dropped, the curtains ceased flapping, the moonlight seemed to focus in a stilled and breathless glare upon her face. It was not exactly a beautiful face, but he knew at that moment it held something for him, touched a chord somewhere, very distantly. He said, smiling: "I'll try to practise company manners for a future occasion."

"No, NEVER do that. Be yourself—as you were in all those letters. And if you'd rather have the Cambridge life than run the firm, then give it up—before it's too late!"

"NOW what are you talking about?"

"You—YOU—because I'm always thinking about you. You're not happy—you're not REAL! But those letters you wrote were real— when you felt crushed and hopeless and things had gone wrong all day, and you used to sit in your office when everyone had gone home and type them yourself, with all the mistakes... I suppose I'm being sentimental. The little college girl, treasuring letters from the beloved uncle who saved the family from ruin... But haven't you FINISHED that yet? Haven't you done enough for us? You pulled the firm through the worst years—now trade's improving, Chet says, so NOW'S your time to get free! Don't you realize that? You still hanker after the other kind of life, don't you —study, books, all that sort of thing? When I came in just now and saw you in the moonlight peering along the shelves I could have cried."

"I don't see why. I was only looking for the lights and hoping there was a detective novel I hadn't read."

"But—but don't you want—Cambridge—any more?"

"I wonder, sometimes, if I do... To grow old in a cultured groove, each year knowing more and more about less and less, as they say about those specialist dons, till at last one's mental equipment becomes an infinitely long and narrow strip leading nowhere in particular—"

"Like the Polish Corridor!"

He laughed. "How do you think of such things?"

"My subconscious—like yours—ingenious. But never mind that —what DO you want to do?"

"You talk as if I'd been complaining. Far from it. I'm quite satisfied to go on doing what I am."

"Managing the firm, increasing the dividends, refloating the companies, a regular Knight of the Prospectus, Saviour of the Mites of Widows and Orphans —"

"Now you're being sarcastic."

"Can't you think of anything you've ever wanted passionately and still —would like?"

He said after a pause: "Yes, I can, but it's rather trivial. When I was at school I had a great ambition to paddle down the Danube in a canoe, but my father didn't approve of the idea and wouldn't let me have the money for it."

"Oh, but that's not trivial—it's wonderful. And you can afford it now all right."

"The money, perhaps, but not the time."

"You ought to MAKE the time."

He laughed. "If I can steal a quiet fortnight at Portslade I'll be lucky this year." He took her arm and led her towards the door. "And now, I'm afraid, since I have to leave so early in the morning—"

"I know. You want to look for a book." She suddenly took his hand and pressed it over the switch. "Good night, Uncle Charles."

As he went back to the shelves he heard her footsteps fading through the house—no longer a child, that was true, but she still scampered like one. He searched for a while without finding anything he wanted to read.

Nineteen twenty-five was another improving year, the year of Locarno, the false dawn. It was a year perhaps typical of the twenties in its wishful optimism backed by no growth of overtaking realism; another sixpence off the income tax, another attempt to harness a vague shape of things to come with the even vaguer shapes of things that had been. For the public would not yet look squarely into that evil face (publishers were still refusing "war books") and few also were those who feared the spectre might return. The England hoped for by the majority of Englishmen was a harking back to certain frugalities of the past (lower and lower income tax, smaller and smaller government expenditure) in order to enjoy more and more the pleasures of the present; the Europe they dreamed of was a continent in which everybody placidly "saw reason," while cultivating summer schools, youth hostels, and peasant-costume festivals in the best tradition of Hampstead Garden Suburb; in exchange for which the City would make loans, trade would thus be encouraged, and taxes fall still further. Mixed up with this almost mystic materialism was the eager, frightened idealism of the Labour Party (both the eagerness and the fright came to a head a year later, in the General Strike); the spread of the belief that the League of Nations never would be much good but was probably better than nothing, a belief that effectively converted Geneva into a bore and anyone who talked too much about it into a nuisance. Meanwhile a vast and paralysing absence of hostility gripped Englishmen from top to bottom of the social scale, not a toleration on principle but a muteness through indifference; they were not AGAINST the League of Nations, they were not AGAINST Russia, they were not AGAINST disarmament, or the Treaty of Versailles, or the revision of the Treaty of Versailles, or the working classes, or Mussolini—who had, after all, made the Italian trains run on time. Their favourite gesture was to give credit to an opponent ("You'll find a good many of those Labour chaps are quite decent fellows"); their favourite conclusion to an argument the opinion that, "Ah, well, these things'll probably right themselves in time."

And amidst such gestures and opinions the post-war England took physical shape and permitted itself limited expression. By 1925 the main features were apparent: arterial roads along which the speculative builder was permitted to put up his £600 houses and re-create the problem the roads themselves had been designed to solve; the week-end trek to the coasts and country through the bottle-necks of Croydon and Maidenhead; the blossoming of the huge motor coach, and the mushrooming of outer suburbs until London almost began where the sprawling coast towns left off—while in bookshops and theatres the rage was for Michael Arlen and Noel Coward, two men whose deft orchestrations of nerves without emotions, cynicism without satire, achieved a success that must have increased even their own disillusionment.

In this same year 1925 Rainier's made a profit that could have paid a small dividend on the ordinary shares; but Charles chose not to do so, despite appeals and protests from the family. And in that same year Lydia died of pneumonia, and Bridget had another baby, and Kitty got herself engaged to a young man named Walter Haversham, who preached Communism at London street corners and had been to Russia. For six months she was swept by an enthusiasm which considerably shocked the family, but somehow did not especially disturb Charles. He saw her once carrying a pictorial banner with Wal (they called him Wal) in a May Day procession; when he met her some weeks later he chaffed her gently about it, saying that workmen on banners always had enormous fists, whether for fraternization or for assault and battery he could never be quite certain— maybe both. He smiled as he said it, but she suddenly flew into a rage, accusing him of being a coward who took refuge in cynicism from the serious issues of the world. "And don't tell me I've lost my sense of humour. I have—I KNOW I have. There isn't any room for humour in the world as it is today. And it's that English sense of humour, which everybody boasts about, that really prevents things from being done."

"You're probably right. But think of all the things that are better left undone."

"The day will come when men may be KILLED for laughing."

"And that will also be the day when men laugh at killing."

She went out of his office, banging the door. He did not see her again for several months—till after the General Strike in 1926. One day she rang him up on the telephone. "Uncle Charles, may I come and talk to you?"

"Of course." He was about to add an invitation to lunch when the receiver was banged down at the other end. Two minutes later she came bounding into his office.

"I rang up from just outside. I thought you might not want to see me after our last meeting."

"I don't think I should ever not want to see you. What's been happening to you all this while?"

"Not much. But I've got my sense of humour back."

"Where's Wal?"

"He's gone to Russia—for good. You know, I really ADMIRE him. He has the courage of what he believes, he's going to become a Russian citizen if they let him. He wanted me to go with him—as his wife, but I just couldn't. I'm weak—I couldn't live in a little cubicle and learn a new language and wear rough clothes—I'd die of misery, even if I really loved him—which I'm beginning to doubt, now that he's gone. I saw him off at Tilbury and felt awful, and then I went into a little pub near the docks and a fellow was standing in the doorway, playing a mandolin and singing with his mouth all crooked,—you know the way they do,— and inside the bar there was a workman sitting over a glass of beer and looking up at the other man with a funny sort of adoring expression, same as you see people looking up at the Madonna in Catholic pictures, and presently he said to me, quite casual, as if he'd known me for years—'Gawd, I wish I could do that'... and I wanted to laugh and cry together. I know I'll never leave England as long as I live, so here I am—and Wal's in Moscow."

Nineteen twenty-six went by, the year of the General Strike, and Germany's admission to the League of Nations; of an Imperial Conference and trouble in Shanghai; of large Socialist gains in municipal polls throughout England, and of Hitler's climb towards power in Germany. Trade remained good; the stock market pushed up Rainier's to twenty-five shillings in anticipation of a dividend which Charles again declined to pay. Nineteen twenty-seven brought riots in Vienna and executions in Russia; while for once Englishmen found themselves suddenly and astonishingly AGAINST something—they were against the Revised Prayer Book, proposed by the Church Assembly and sent to the House of Commons to be voted on, according to the curious English custom by which a political majority decides the dogmatic beliefs of a religious minority. And during the next year, 1928, the House of Commons again turned down the Revised Prayer Book, as if it tremendously mattered. But this flurry of against-ness was soon exhausted, and Englishmen, including Members of Parliament, resumed their benevolence towards most things that continued to happen throughout the world.

And in that same year 1928 Bridget had another baby, her fourth, and Kitty got herself engaged again, to a young man named Roland Turner, who had advanced ideas about the "cinema," and was understood to be working on a scenario or something or other that he hoped to sell for a fabulous price to somebody or other, but was otherwise romantically out of a job— romantically, because he wasn't eligible for the dole yet managed to run a car.

"And I suppose if he DID draw the dole and COULDN'T run a car, that would be prosaic?" Charles queried, when she told him.

"You still think I'm a snob, don't you? But I'm not—it isn't that at all—I'm just lost in amazement, because he always dresses well and goes to the best restaurants, and has a sweet little studio off Ebury Street —I don't know WHERE he gets the money from, but I do wish you could find him something to do."

"But I don't want any scenarios today, thank you."

"Not THAT, of course, but he can do all kinds of other things— write and paint, for instance—he does marvellous frescoes, at least they say the one he did was marvellous, but most of it came off during the damp weather... He can paint machinery, too."

"Unfortunately we don't paint our machinery."

"Pictures of machinery, I mean—he did one for an exhibition, symbolizing something— but I'm sure he could do a serious one, if you wanted it. Don't you ever have illustrated catalogues?"

Charles smiled. "Suppose you bring him to lunch?"

They met at the Savoy Grill; Roland Turner proved to be rather tall and thin ("lissom" was almost the word); his clothes were impeccable, with just a faintly artistic note in his silk bow tie; his manners were perfect and his choices of food delicate; even his talk was sufficiently intelligent and modulated to what Charles felt to be an exactly determined mean between independence and obsequiousness in the presence of Big Business. Immediately after coffee the youth mentioned an afternoon appointment and decorously bowed himself out, leaving Kitty and Charles together.

Laughing, she said: "He's got no appointment, he's just being tactful —giving me a chance to do the Don't-you-think-he's-wonderful stuff." She paused for a few seconds, then added: "Well, DON'T you?"

"He's a very personable young man, and if you like him, that's the main thing."

"PERSONABLE? What exactly do you mean by that?"

"Attractive."

"Are you sure it's not something nice to say about someone you don't care for?"

"Not at all. I like him all right, and if there's anything he could do that I wanted done, I'd be glad to give him the job."

"He was wondering about Stourton—do you think I could take him down there to see Uncle Chet?"

"With what in mind?"

"You're so suspicious, aren't you? Well, he has ideas about landscape gardening... Of course he knows Chet and you aren't my real uncles."

"I don't see how he knows that, unless you told him, and I don't see that it matters, anyway."

"I had to tell him—indirectly. You see, Mother discovered him first of all—in Mentone. He was staying with somebody there and they danced a lot—Mother and him, I mean. I think she rather fell for him, because when he came on to London she had him to stay at the house, with me as a sort of chaperon. We weren't attracted at all in the beginning, but I began to be awfully sorry for him when I saw how bored he was with Mother. He has nice feelings, you know—I don't think he'd have found it easy to switch over if she'd REALLY been my mother."

"I'm afraid the point is too subtle for me to grasp."

"Well—like The Vortex, you know... Of course Mother was furious."

"The whole situation must have amused you a good deal."

"Well, it had its funny side... Of course his friends don't like me —they never thought he'd pick up a girl."

"Are you in love with him?"

"Yes, I think I am... By the way, he's having an exhibition of paintings at the Coventry Galleries—you WILL come, won't you, and buy something?"

He promised he would, and went to the private view the following week. He didn't think much of the pictures, but his private view of Roland Turner was worth the journey —that suave young man, again impeccably dressed, saying the impeccably correct things about his own paintings to patrons who greeted him as they walked around, striking another exactly determined mean, Charles felt—this time between modesty and self-esteem. To please Kitty he bought a picture for five guineas—a view of an English country house as Botticelli might have painted it if he had painted English country houses rather badly.

"It's really very odd, Mr. Rainier," said the young man, as Kitty proudly stuck the red star on the corner of the canvas, "but you've chosen the best thing I've ever done!"

"Very odd indeed," Charles answered, "because I know almost nothing about painting."

Afterwards he took them both to dinner at Kettner's, encouraging them in a rather vulgar way to choose all the expensive items—caviare and quail and plenty of champagne. Of course the young man was a poseur, but half-way through the meal he became aware that he himself was posing just as artificially as the Philistine industrialist and champagne uncle. When Turner talked about Stourton (Kitty had evidently taken him there) and how wonderful it was to own such a place, Charles answered: "Oh, it's an awfully white elephant, really. The house is uneconomical and the farms don't pay. If it were nearer London my brother could carve it up into building plots, but as it's only England's green and pleasant land nobody wants it and nobody can afford it and nobody will pay a decent price for anything that grows on it."

"But it's a privilege, all the same, to keep up these old family possessions."

"It isn't an old family possession—at least not of OUR family. My father bought it cheap because the other family couldn't afford it."

"Well, he must have admired the place or he wouldn't have wanted to buy it at any price."

"Oh, I don't know. He liked buying things cheap. He once bought a shipload of diseased sharkskins because they were cheap and he thought he could make a profit."

"And did he?"

"You bet he did."

"A business man, then?"

"Yes—like myself. But rather more successful because he had a better eye for a bargain and also because he lived most of his life during a rising market."

Turner gave a somewhat puzzled sigh. "Well, well, I suppose that's the system."

"Except in Russia," Kitty interposed. Then brightly: "Roland's been to Russia too." She must have been remembering Wal.

With a slight awakening of interest as he also remembered Wal, Charles said: "Oh, indeed? And what made YOU go there, Mr. Turner?"

"I wanted to see what it was like."

"And what WAS it like?"

The young man smiled defensively. "I don't think I could answer that in a single sentence."

"Many people do. They say it's all marvellous or else it's all horrible."

"I didn't see all of it, Mr. Rainier, and I didn't think what I did see was either."

"So you don't believe in the coming Revolution?"

"I daresay it's coming, but I don't particularly believe in it." And he added, with a gulp of champagne: "Just as you, Mr. Rainier, don't particularly believe in capitalism, though you go on trying to make it work."

"I wonder if that's true."

"The fact is, Mr. Rainier—perhaps we can both admit it after a few drinks—we neither of us believe in a damn thing."

Afterwards Charles regretted the conversation and his own pose throughout it, but he remained vaguely troubled whenever he thought of Roland Turner and Kitty; he slightly disapproved of that young man, and felt avuncular in so doing. He did not see them again that year, for they were abroad most of the time, and he himself had many other things to worry about. By April of 1929 he was so exhausted from overwork that, after settling an especially troublesome labour dispute at the Cowderton works, he went to Switzerland for a holiday, despite the fact that it was not a good time of the year— past the snow season, and before the end of the thaw. He stayed at Interlaken, in an almost empty hotel, and while he was there a letter came from Kitty, forwarded from an address in Provence through London. He wondered what she was doing in Provence until he read that she was with Roland Turner, who was engaged in painting a portrait of an Indian rajah. "He's a very fat rajah," she reported, "and he's given Roland five hundred pounds to go on with, which I expect will be all he'll get out of it, because the picture gets less and less like the rajah every sitting." Charles replied from Interlaken, expressing pleasure that her fiancé had found such profitable employment—to which he could not help adding that the fee was much higher than the Rainier firm could ever have paid for catalogue illustrations. Two days later came a wire from Avignon: COMING TO INTERLAKEN DON'T GO AWAY EXPECT ME TEN TOMORROW MORNING.

During the intervening day he wondered at the possible cause of her visit, though capricious changes of plan were really nothing to wonder at where Kitty was concerned; the theory he considered likeliest was that the portrait commission had fallen through, and that she and Roland had decided to touch him, as it were, for a Swiss holiday. (He had already discovered, from other sources, that Turner's never-failing affluence was bound up with his never- failing debts and geared by his skill and charm in cadging.) He did not mind, particularly; after all, he could always go back to London if the situation became tiresome.

It was a cold bright day when he waited on the Interlaken platform. There was still a litter of shovelled snow in the gutters and against the railings, and the train came in white-roofed from fresh falls in the Simplon-Lötschberg. She was dressed in a long mackintosh with a little fur hat, like a fez, and as she jumped from the train before it quite stopped, it was as if something in his heart jumped also before it quite stopped.

"Oh, Uncle Charles, I'm so happy—I was afraid you'd take fright and leave before I got here! It seems ages since I saw you. How ARE you?"

"I'm fine." (Breaking Miss Ponsonby's old rule.) "And it IS ages since you saw me— nearly a year. Where's Roland?"

"Not with me. I've left him. Take me somewhere for a drink—there was no diner on the train."

In a deserted restaurant-café opposite the station she told him more about it. "I found myself getting SILLY—saying silly things to all his silly crowd—there's a regular colony of them wherever he goes. But more than that—after all, I don't mind so much saying silly things myself, but it got to the point where I didn't notice when things THEY said were silly. Softening of the brain—" She tapped her head. "I simply HAD to take it in time. And I felt sorry for the poor old rajah. He was pretty awful to look at, but at least he knew what's what with women —which is more than most of Roland's friends do."

"So I rather imagined."

"Of course YOU really fixed it—that night at Kettner's."

"_I_ fixed it?"

"I could see you didn't like him."

"On the contrary, I think I began to like him then—just slightly —and for the first time. He has his wits about him."

"He'd better have—they're what he lives by. But it's no good denying it—you DON'T like him. I could feel that."

"Well, I'm not as keen on him as you are."

"WERE."

"Oh, is it WERE? Well, in that case there couldn't be a better reason for breaking off the engagement."

"But it never pleased you to think of me marrying him. Did it now?"

"Why should that matter to you?"

"Because it DOES matter! I can't bear to do things you don't want, except when you don't want them to my face—like forcing myself on you here, I don't mind THAT—" She suddenly lowered her head into her hands and looked up a few seconds later with eyes streaming. "Can't you see you've spoilt me for other men?"

"But, my dear—that's ridiculous!"

She went on: "I'm not asking for anything. I can go back by the next train if you'd prefer it. I'll probably marry someone eventually and be quite happy, but it'll have to be a man whom you like fairly well, and who doesn't sneer because you do an honest job of work instead of battening on rich people."

"Battening on poor people is more in my line—according to your former fiancé."

"Poor Wal—I often wonder what's happened to him—I really liked him more than Roland... By the way, I saw the papers—you've been having strikes at Cowderton, haven't you? Was it very serious?"

"While it lasted. That's really why I came out here—for a rest."

"Oh God, why don't you give the whole thing up? You've got enough money, haven't you?"

"For what?"

"To live on, for the rest of your life, at about a thousand a year."

"Depends on several things—how long I live, how much a thousand a year will continue to be worth, and how long people will pay me anything at all for not working... But that's not the whole point, in any case."

"You mean you WANT to stay with the firm? It's still a game, as you said in one of those letters—a game you want to win even if it isn't worth playing? Haven't you won enough?... Or maybe it's more than a game now —it's become the life-work?"

He smiled. "Perhaps it's somewhere between the two—more than a game, but not quite a life-work yet. You know, when I first took over the job it was with all kinds of reluctance—because I'd been more or less jockeyed into it by the family crying out to be saved. Well, that was the idea, originally—to save 'em and then be off quick, before they needed more saving. Rainier's was just something that kept the family going, and I didn't respect it enormously for that. But then, when I began to look into things personally, I found it kept a good many other families going. Over three thousand, to be precise."

"I see. Responsibility. Uncle Atlas."

"You can laugh at me if you like, provided you believe me sincere. I'm not a sentimentalist. I don't call the firm the House of Rainier, or myself a Captain of Industry, or any of that nonsense. But there IS a responsibility, no use denying it, in owning a three-thousand-family business. If I can contrive a little security for those people—"

"But there ISN'T any security—as you said yourself when I asked you about your thousand a year. It's an illusion put up by banks and insurance companies and lawyers and building societies and everybody who goes without what he wants today because he thinks he'll enjoy it more later on. Supposing some day we all find out there isn't any 'later on'?"

"Then, my dear, will come Wal's revolution."

"And we shall all make a grab for what we can get?"

"Provided there IS anything to get by then. If the whole thing's an illusion, then the rewards may fade equally."

"Then you try to comfort those three thousand families by encouraging them to believe in a future that doesn't exist?"

"They don't believe in it. Every street-corner speaker warns them not to at the top of his voice. What I DO comfort them with, since you put it that way, is enough of a regular wage to buy food and pay their rent and smoke cigarettes and go to the local cinema. That keeps them satisfied to go on waiting."

"For the big grab?"

"Or for the discovery that there isn't anything left to grab."

"Which makes you one degree more cynical than they are. They don't believe in the security they accept because they're looking to the revolution, but YOU don't believe in either the security of the present or the revolution of the future!"

"Your other ex-fiancé put it even more simply, my dear, when he said I didn't believe in a damn thing."

"Well, don't you?"

"That's what I've been asking myself very carefully and for a long time, and I still can't find an answer."

"Probably because you've been asking it TOO long and TOO carefully. The answer to that sort of question ought to FLY out—like a child when he's asked what he wants for his birthday—he always knows instantly without having to think—either a bicycle or a toy-train or something... Oh, I'm quite happy again now. I don't miss Roland a bit. Just talking to you freely like this makes the difference, though you don't talk to ME freely —there always seems a brake on—I can hardly believe you once sent me those letters."

"Curious—I don't remember much about them. If you kept any, I'd like to—"

"Oh, no, NEVER! That would be a really awful thing to do! And of course I know why you were so free in THEM—because you thought I was too young to understand. I was only the vehicle—the letter-box, so to speak —where you posted them to another address."

A gleam came into his eyes. "What on earth are you talking about?"

"Well, what more could I have been in those days? Letters to a schoolgirl... Of course I was crazy about you—always have been ever since that time at Stourton when I came up to your room and smoked a cigarette. Remember?... It might be fun if you loved me now—we'd have a good deal in common. I sometimes wonder why you don't."

"In my slow and careful way I've been wondering that too—ever since you stepped off the train."

"Well, why don't you—just to be curious?"

"I haven't said I don't."

"Oh NO!"

"Would it be so very incredible?"

"It would be FANTASTIC!"

"Then it IS fantastic."

"Darling, you don't mean—" She seized his hand across the table. "You're not saying it just to be kind?"

"I don't feel a bit kind. I fed—well, let's stick to fantastic."

"But I—I—I don't know what else to say for the moment."

"You don't have to say anything."

They sat in silence, his hand changing places over hers. A train entered the station opposite; the tick of its electric engine was like a clock measuring the seconds. Presently she said: "There's the oddest thing in my mind for us to do—if it's all real and not a dream. Let's go down the Danube in a canoe, as you always wanted."

"Yes, we'll do that. And up the Amazon too, if you like." His face was very pale. "I'll take a year off—from the firm and the City and the three thousand families and everything else. Let someone else have his turn..."

Back at his hotel that night he could hardly believe in the changed future; it was almost as if he had been another person during the day and was now perusing with amazement a report of what had happened to someone else. He was not regretful—far from it—but a little bemused at so many decisions made all at once, somewhat startled that they must all have been his own, yet ready to accept them with a loyalty that might well become more enthusiastic when he had had a chance to think them over.

At breakfast he compared notes and found that her emotions had been similar only as far as a doubt as to whether he could really have meant what he said enough to go on meaning it; he assured her laughingly that he had and did, and immediately happiness blazed across the rolls and honey between them as they planned the trivial details of the day. The future was still fantastic to talk about, even to think about, and they agreed for the time being not to give themselves the even heavier task of explaining it to others. No one expected him in London before the end of the month (the Rainier board meeting was on the thirtieth), and no one knew she was not still in Provence, except Roland and his crowd, who did not count. Jill was in the Aegean, cruising among the antiquities but taking (one suspected) very little notice of them. He and Kitty could have at least two weeks in Switzerland before returning to announce the astonishing news to the family and to the world. Of course they could send the news by letter, but somehow to pull the lever that would release all the commotion even at a distance required a certain fortitude; they decided to enjoy those two weeks first of all.

And so began an interlude that might have been in another world, and almost was. They stayed for the first week in Interlaken, making it a centre for mountain trips into the high Oberland. The weather improved after the last big snowfall of the year; the sun dried the drenched meadows, so that they were able to walk by the lakeside to Giessbach, and up the Lauterbrunnen Valley as far as the lower slopes of the Roththal. It was pleasant to see the industrious Swiss polishing up their ballrooms and cocktail bars and funicular railways in readiness for what was to come; but pleasanter still to tramp along the cleared roadways in face of the sun and snow. During the second week they discovered the hotel on the two-mile-high Jungfraujoch, where there was nothing to do but talk and absorb the physical atmosphere of being above and beyond the earth. They liked it enough to stay there till the last day before the necessary return to England.

That last day came, and with it the descent to natural levels—a curious deflation of mood that was easy to interpret as sadness at leaving a place where they had been so happy. Throughout the long rail journey through Berne and Basle to Boulogne the mood persisted—seemed impossible to shake off, being perhaps a physical effect of the changed altitude, they both agreed. They reached London amidst driving rain and had dinner in a restaurant near Victoria Station, saying all the time and over and over again how wonderful it had been in Switzerland and how sorry they were to have returned. The Rainier board meeting was four days away, and it was understood that no announcement of future plans should be hinted at to anyone until then.

The board meeting came, and with it all the commotion. He had not guessed how considerable it would be. He had suspected that the family would not be altogether pleased, but he hadn't realized they would have so many reasons for being displeased. He soon found that they regarded his year's absence from Rainier's as a form of abdication amounting almost to desertion— in spite of the fact that they had long been jealous of what they called his "domineering" over the firm's affairs. Then also, those who had hoped their children would inherit his personal fortune strongly resented his marriage to anybody at all; he hadn't anticipated that, even remotely. And finally, all except Jill (and in one sense even including Jill) were manifestly and desperately jealous of his choice. Only Chet seemed to have any genuine tolerance of the idea—a tolerance not quite reaching the point of enthusiasm. He had so long joked about the need for Charles to "hurry up" that now Charles WAS hurrying up he could not withhold somewhat rueful good wishes.

The party at Stourton to celebrate the engagement was not a successful affair.

Then, in June, quite suddenly, Chet died after a heart attack, and plans for the marriage in July were postponed till autumn; it would have been impossible, in any event, to leave England during all the legal complications that ensued.

The marriage was finally fixed for October. Charles took Kitty to dine at Kettner's again one night in late September, and for some reason the same mood came upon them as during the journey back from Switzerland five months before. She suggested that, on his side, it was due to news in the evening paper—a big stock-market crash in New York, with inevitable repercussions in London.

He was too honest with her to accept that as a reason. "I'm not a speculator. Rainier's dropped five shillings today, I notice, but it doesn't affect me or the firm—they can go down ten times as much before it'll begin to worry me. Matter of fact, everything's been pushed too high lately, especially in America. I could make a lot of money now if I backed my opinion."

"What opinion?"

"That the fall will go much further."

"How would you make money by backing your opinion?"

"Selling short, as they call it. That means—"

"I know—I learnt all about it at Kirby when we used to gamble in Rainier shares. Remember?"

"You must have lost everything."

"Nearly everything. About thirty-two pounds all together." She laughed. "Well, why DON'T you sell short?"

"I will, if it amuses you. But I'd have no other reason."

"Yes, do it—to amuse me. Please, Charles."

"Then there's two things I have to do at the office tomorrow morning." He took out his notebook and made a pretence of writing something down. "Sell short to amuse Kitty. Also get Miss Hanslett to send out the wedding invitations."

"Who's Miss Hanslett?"

"My new secretary. You saw her last time you called."

"Oh, that quiet girl?"

"I suppose she's quiet. I certainly wouldn't want her to be noisy."

"Darling, how soon can we leave—afterwards?"

"You mean for our world tour? Maybe next month. It'll be too late for the Danube, though, this year. We'd better do the Amazon first. Or the Nile."

"No, not the Nile—Jill's there."

"What's she doing?"

"Looking at the tombs, I suppose, and having a good time."

But the laugh they rallied themselves into failed to shift the mood that made him, as soon as dinner was over, confess that he felt tired and would prefer an early night in bed. He dropped her at Jill's new house in St. John's Wood, where she was living with a cook-housekeeper, and kept the taxi for his own journey to Smith Square. But his apartment seemed so inexplicably cheerless that after a drink and an attempt to feel sleepy, he called another cab and drove round the West End till he found a film that looked tolerable enough for whiling away the rest of the evening. He stayed in the cinema less than an hour, his restlessness increasing all the time, so that at last he walked out and paced up and down the thronged pavements till past midnight, longing suddenly for the sun and snow of the Jungfraujoch, yet knowing that it was only a mirage of what he would still long for if by some miracle he were to be transplanted there.

Usually when he could not sleep he was quite satisfied to stay up reading, often until dawn; but that night he felt he would be far too restless to concentrate on any book, so he bought tablets and took several on his return to Smith Square. They gave him a heavy unrefreshing sleep, from which he woke about noon to find a pencilled letter from Kitty at his bedside. It had been delivered by hand early that morning, and contained, in effect, the breaking of their engagement and an announcement that she was leaving immediately to join her stepmother in Luxor.

PART THREE

The first gray smudge was peering over the hills and it seemed that we both saw it together.

"Well, we've talked all night—and for the second time. Aren't you sleepy yet?"

"No... You were telling me about that letter, the one Kitty left for you. Didn't it give any reasons?"

"Plenty. But I really think we'd better go to bed if we're to be in any decent condition tomorrow. The crowd will soon be on us, worse luck."

"Then why do you have them here?"

"That's part of another story. Well, I must have a nightcap, even if it IS morning. Have one with me?"

99

We went down to the library, feeling our way in the dim dawn shadows without switching on any of the house lights. Meanwhile he continued: "I'd show you that letter if I had it here, but it's locked up in my safe in the City. I admit I'm sentimental about it —a little puzzled also. It's the last word I ever had from her, except picture postcards from all kinds of places. What happened to her afterwards is what she said would happen— except that it didn't last for long. She married a man she met in Egypt —she was quite happy—and he was a man I liked when I met him, but I didn't meet him till after she was dead. He had plantations in the F.M.S. and she went out with him there and died of malaria within six months."

He bent over the decanter, his shape and movements ghostly against the gray pallor from the windows. The moon had gone down, and it was darker than at midnight.

"And then?" I said.

He handed me a drink and raised his own.

"The rest," he declaimed half-mockingly, "is a simple saga of success. I flung myself into business with renewed but disciplined abandon: I sold short and made more money out of the slump than I'd ever done out of ordinary trading; I accepted directorships in other companies and became what they call 'a figure in the City'—I even assumed the burden of two other family heritages, by taking over Stourton and by allowing myself to stand for my father's old Parliamentary seat of West Lythamshire. And a few years later, my affairs having more than survived the storms of 1931 and the doldrums of 1932, I married a lady who had become quite indispensable to me in this struggle for fresh fame and fortune—Miss Hanslett, the quiet girl. That again turned out to be an astonishing success. You never know what these quiet girls can do. From being quiet, she became one of the busiest and cleverest of London's hostesses—and the miracle is, she's STILL quiet —you'd hardly know the machine's running at all."

"So different from Miss Hobbs—but that, I suppose, is because you chose her yourself."

"Or else SHE chose HERSELF. She was just a girl in the general office first of all, until one evening I was working late and she invaded my private office to ask outright if she could work for me personally. Said she knew the other girl was leaving and she was certain she'd be better than anyone else. After that I simply had to give her either the sack or the job."

"Anyhow, YOU made the right choice there."

He laughed. "Oh yes, and I soon knew it. She was everything she promised. I've nothing but praise for her. I'd never have made so much money or acquired such style in after-dinner oratory but for her. She's intensely loyal, tremendously ambitious for me, and personally charming. I love her more than most men love their wives. She's guided my career—in fact she's almost made a personally conducted tour of it. I never do anything, in politics or business, without seeking her advice. She runs Stourton and Kenmore like a pair of clocks—she doesn't care if I'm in or out to lunch or dinner, or if I go to India or South America for six months or merely to Brighton for a week-end. She's everything a man like me could wish for in a wife—always provided—" He paused and took a drink, then added: "Always provided he's completely satisfied to be a man like me."

"And aren't you?"

He took my arm. "Let's save up something for another night. I'm going to bed, and after all this, I really think I shall sleep. Tell Sheldon not to wake me till the guests begin to arrive."

The guests began to arrive in groups during the following afternoon, but I did not see Rainier till tea-time, when he appeared on the terrace to greet the assembly; and from then throughout the week-end I had no chance to talk with him alone. Nor with Woburn either, for that young man, after initial shyness, turned into a considerable social success. Observing him from time to time I felt there was a certain scientific detachment in his obvious effort to make good at his first fashionable house-party (he had told me it was his first, and that he had never mixed in that class of society before); it was as if he were exploring himself, discovering his own powers; experimenting with the careless flatteries, the insincere attentions that make up the small change of such occasions; finding that he could do it just as well as people born to it, perhaps even a little better after practice. He was clearly a very adaptable and cool-headed young man, and the whole party was a good deal pleasanter for his being always at hand to pass interesting conversational cues, to make up a bridge four, to play a not offensively good game of tennis, and to dance with otherwise unpartnered matrons. One could almost read in his face the question, too wondering to be smug: Is this all there is to it?

Mrs. Rainier was the perfect hostess as usual, and I should have been lost in admiration at everything she did had it not been a repetition on a larger scale of what she habitually did at Kenmore. All, in fact, was as gay and brilliant and smooth-running as usual, but something else was not QUITE as usual—and I don't know how to describe it except as a faint suspicion that the world was already swollen with destiny and that Stourton was no longer the world—a whiff of misgiving too delicate to analyse, as when, in the ballroom of an ocean liner, some change of tempo in the engines far below communicates itself to the revellers for a phantom second and then is lost behind the rhythms of the orchestra.

The simile was Rainier's as we drove back to London on Monday evening, leaving Woburn and Mrs. Rainier at Stourton. Within a few weeks the same misgiving, many times magnified, had become a headline commonplace; trenches were being dug in the London parks; the curve of the September crisis rose to its monstrous peak. Rainier lived at his Club during those fateful days and we were both kept busy at all hours transcribing reports, telephoning officials, and listening to the latest radio bulletins. Diplomatic machinery had swung into the feverish gear of guesswork and divination: Was Hitler bluffing? What sort of country was this new Germany? Would Russia support the Czechs? When would the bombers come over? Every chatterer could claim an audience; journalists back from Europe were heard more eagerly than ambassadors; the fact that all seemed to depend on the workings of one abnormal human mind gave every amateur psychologist an equal chance with politicians and crystal-gazers. And behind this mystery came fear, fear of a kind that had brought earlier peoples to their knees before eclipses and comets—fear of the unknown, based on an awareness that the known was no longer impregnable. The utter destruction of civilization, which had seemed a fantastic thing to our grandfathers, had become a commonplace of schoolboys' essays, village debating societies, and after-dinner small talk; for the first time in human history a sophisticated society faced its own extinction not theoretically in the future, but by physical death perhaps tomorrow. There was a dreadful acceptance of doom in all our eyes as we sat around, in restaurants and at conference tables and beside innumerable radios, listening and talking and drinking, the only three things to do that one could go on doing—paralysed as we were into a belief that it was too late to act, and clinging to a last desperate hope that somehow the negation of an act might serve as well.

That negation was performed, if performed is the word; talking, listening, and drinking then merged into a sigh of exhausted relief, and only a few Cassandra voices, among whom was Rainier's, murmured that no miracle had really happened at all. But national hysteria urged that it had, and that one must not say otherwise, even if it hadn't. Anyhow, the crisis passed, the rains of autumn soaked into half-dug trenches, and as the days shortened and darkened the Kenmore lamplight glowed again in the faces of diseuses and diplomats—Sir Somebody This and the Maharanee of That, the successful novelist and the Wimbledon winner, delegates from somewhere-or-other to the something-or-other conference, as well as visiting Americans who thought they were experiencing a real pea-souper fog because the sun of a November midday had turned red over the roofs.

I went to a good many of those lunches, and somehow, I don't remember exactly when, it became a recognized thing that I should have a place at all of them unless my duties with Rainier called me elsewhere.

Often they did. Many days during that strange, almost somnambulist winter of 1938-1939 I sat in the Gallery of the House of Commons, listening to dull debates and hearing Big Ben chime the quarters till I saw Rainier get up and push his way through the swing doors with that casualness which is among the specialties of House procedure —a form of self-removal that implies neither rudeness nor even indifference to the speech in progress. Then he would dictate letters in a Committee Room, or order tea, or we might stroll along the usually empty Terrace, watching the last spears of sunset fade from the windows of St. Thomas's Hospital, or staring over the parapet at a train of coal barges on their way upstream. It was at such moments that I came to know him most intimately, and to feel, more from his presence than from words, that the years he no longer talked about were still haunting; that he was still, as two women had said, vainly searching for something and never at rest. Yet outwardly, and to others, there were few signs of it. Indeed, the disfavour into which he fell as a result of his attitude towards official policy seemed to come rather as a release than as a suppression. It was not that he blamed the government for what had happened at Munich; such blame, he said, when history assessed it, would doubtless be spread over many years and many personages, of which the men of 1938 were but last in a tragic line. He did, however, blame those who had stepped out of panic only to sink back into hypnosis. "These are the last days," he said to me once. "We are like people in a trance—even those of us who can see the danger ahead can do nothing to avert it—like the dream in which you drive a car towards a precipice and your foot is over the brake but you have no physical power to press down. We should be arming now, if we had sense,—arming day and night and seven days of the week,—for if the Munich pact had any value at all it was not as a promise of peace to come, but as a last-minute chance to prepare for the final struggle. And we are doing NOTHING— caught in the net of self-delusion and self-congratulation. We don't realize the skill and magnitude of the conspiracy—the attempt to reverse, by lightning strokes, the whole civilized verdict of two thousand years."

Such talk, during the winter of 1938-1939, was heresy in a country that permitted heresy, but could not regard it as in good taste. People began to remark, in advance of any argument about him, that they LIKED Rainier— this also was a bad sign in a society where likings are rarely expressed except by way of fair-minded prelude to disparagement. And one reflected that there had always been something against his chances of attaining high office —something expressed by his political enemies when they praised him as "brilliant," and by his political friends when they doubted if he were altogether "safe." Such doubts were now running high.

In the City, however, safety and brilliance were not held as incompatibles by gatherings of grateful shareholders at annual meetings in the Rainier Building. Here also it was my duty to accompany him, handing out appropriate documents and keeping his memory jogged against forgetfulness of such things as—"You will be glad to know that during the past year we have opened a new factory at West Bromwich where we are now manufacturing a model especially designed for the Colonies." He made such announcements with a solemnity in which only I, perhaps, detected any ironic note; similarly there seemed to me a touch of disdain in his bent for handling complicated masses of figures, a touch that did not detract from the enormous confidence reposed in him by enriched but usually mystified investors. Nor was that confidence misplaced. Once I said to him: "Leaving sentiment out of it, you haven't done so badly. You saved the family inheritance, you rescued the money of hundreds of outsiders, and you kept intact the jobs of a whole army of workpeople. You did, in fact, everything you set out to do."

"There's only one thing more important," he answered, "and that is, after you've done what you set out to do, to feel that it's been worth doing."

That was the day when he took me down to the sub-basement of the Rainier Building to show me the result of certain constructional work that had been in progress there for several weeks. "I've allowed it to be supposed that these are new storage vaults," he told me, as we entered the first of a series of empty catacombs, "but actually I had another thought in mind —and one that it would be too bad to thrust on a group of happy dividend collectors. But the fact is—and entirely at my own personal expense—I've made this place bombproof. So you see, SOMETHING'S been worth doing." He walked me round like an estate agent. "Comfort, as well as safety,—there's an independent heating plant,—because it's no good saving people from high explosive just to have them die of influenza. And another reason—the greatest man of the twentieth century may have to be born in a place like this, so let's make it as decent as we can for him. A steel and concrete Manger—sixty feet below ground... that's why I've had to keep it a big secret, because you couldn't expect the investing public to swallow THAT."

But we liked the City—"the City of Meticulous Nonsense," he called it once, after an annual meeting at which somebody had used the adjective in praise of his own attention to the firm's affairs. "METICULOUS," he echoed, afterwards, "really meaning TIMID —and how right that it should nowadays be used as a compliment, since so many of the most complimented people nowadays deserve it! Meticulous little people attending meticulous meetings, passing meticulous votes of thanks for meticulous behaviour!"

One rainy Saturday we waited several minutes while the homeward rush-hour crowd swarmed in front of the car, taking no notice of the horn until a man, just an ordinary mackintoshed fellow with (I remember) a piece of garden trellis under his arm, called out: "'Ere, give the bloke a chawnce!"— whereat the crowd, heeding just as casually as they had been heedless before, made way for us to pass. There was no resentment in their faces because we had an expensive car or because we kept them waiting a few seconds longer in the rain, no social significance in the appeal to give the bloke a chance, no indication of who the bloke was—I or Rainier or the chauffeur. The very absence of all these things was English, Rainier said—something offhand but good-humoured, free but obedient, careless but never heartless.

"But tell that," he added, "to the Indians in Amritsar, to the Chinese who read the notice in a Shanghai park, 'No Dogs or Chinese Allowed,' to the tribesmen in Irak, to the peasant in County Cork, to the..." But then he laughed. "God, how we're hated! It isn't so much because we really deserve it. Even at the bottom of the charge-sheet I could quote Santayana's remark that the world never had sweeter masters. SWEET—a curious adjective —and yet there IS a sweetness in the English character, something that's almost perfect when it's just ripe—like an apple out of an English orchard. No, we're not hated altogether by logic. It's more because the world is TIRED of us—BORED with us—sickened by a taste that to some already seems oversweet and hypocritical, to others sour and stale. I suppose the world grew tired of the Romans like that, till at last the barbarians were excused for barbarism more readily than the Caesars were forgiven for being tough. There come such moments in the lives of nations, as of persons, when they just can't do anything right, and the world turns on them with the awful ferocity of a first-night audience rejecting, not so much a play it doesn't want, as a playwright it doesn't want any more... But wait till they've experienced the supplanters—if we are supplanted. A time may come when a cowed and brutalized world may look back on the period of English domination as one of the golden ages of history..."

I remember that afternoon particularly because as we were waiting for the traffic lights in Whitehall we saw Nixon at the kerbside vainly signalling a taxi and Rainier had the car stopped to offer him a lift. Bound for Victoria to catch a train, he chattered all the time during the short drive, finally and quite casually remarking: "Oh, you remember that fellow Ransome who took us to tea at his house in Browdley that day when his wife wasn't there?"

Rainier looked up sharply.

"Rather sad business," Nixon continued. "She'd gone out to buy a cake, as Ransome thought—must have been hurrying back, because she was carrying it as she ran into the bus... killed instantly... poor chap was in a terrible state, so I heard. Only been married about a year."

We drove on in silence after dropping Nixon in the station yard; Rainier's face was strained, tense, as if he had suffered a personal blow. Half-way to Kenmore he tapped on the window and ordered the chauffeur to turn and drive back. "Let's hear somebody play the piano," he said. "That's the best cure for the mood I'm in."

We drove to the West End, while I searched the Telegraph for recital announcements. The only one I could find was of the first and only appearance in London of Casimir

Navoida, who would give a mixed programme of Beethoven, Chopin, Brahms, and Ravel at the Selsdon Hall. I had never heard of Navoida, and the fact that Rainier hadn't either lent no optimism to my expectations. We found a photograph on the rain-sodden posters outside the Hall—the conventionally sombre, heavy-lidded profile brooding over the keys. That too was not encouraging, nor was the obviously "paper" audience of only a few score. Nor, for that matter, were the explanatory notes in the printed programme—composed, Rainier grimly suggested, by some schoolgirl in a mood of bibulous Schwärmerei. With less distaste we read a paragraph about the performer, though even that was vague enough—merely mentioning a Continental reputation, tuition under Leschetizky (misspelt), a prix-de-somewhere, and an ancient press-agent anecdote beginning—"One morning, at the So-and-so Conservatoire..." Then the door at the rear of the platform opened and this fellow Navoida walked to the piano, gave a hinge-like bow to half-hearted applause, and began. He did not look much like his photograph, though a description could not have omitted the same points —the gloomy profile, wrinkled nape, and upflung hair. We listened with tolerance, soon aware that his playing was not exactly bad. When the interval came I noticed a woman in the seat beyond Rainier's fumbling for a dropped programme; presently he stooped and retrieved it for her. She thanked him with a foreign accent and added: "You think he plays well?"

Rainier answered: "He might be good if he weren't out of practice."

"You are a critic?"

"Only to myself."

"You are not on one of the newspapers?"

"Oh dear, no."

She seemed both relieved and disappointed. "I thought you might be. I suppose they ARE here."

Rainier looked round and included me in the conversation by saying: "Notice anybody? _I_ don't... I'm afraid Saturday afternoon's a bad time in London."

Then Navoida came on again and played the Chopin group. At the next interval she said: "You are quite right. He is out of practice. He played cards till four this morning."

Rainier laughed. "Stupid of him, surely?"

"Oh, he doesn't care. He lost much money, also. If only people would realize that he CAN play so much better than this—"

"Why SHOULD they? If he chooses to drink and gamble the night before a concert—"

"Oh no, not DRINK. He NEVER drinks."

"No?"

"But gambling is in his blood. It is in the blood of all the Navoidas. If he travels by autobus he will bet on how many people get in at each stop."

Rainier looked slightly interested. "How do you know all this about him?"

She had just time to reply, as the piano began again: "I am his wife."

I could judge that throughout the Brahms Sonata Rainier was feeling somewhat embarrassed at having discussed the pianist so frankly, but when the next interval came she gave him no time to apologize. "Oh, I could KILL him for being so bad! The foolish boy... Maybe it was a mistake to come to England at all."

Rainier answered: "Oh, no need to feel that. But your husband's concert agent ought to have chosen a better day for a first appearance. Londoners like to get away to the country at week-ends."

"Even when it rains?"

"My goodness, we never bother about rain."

"Ach, yes, your London climate... when it is not rain, it is fog... I understand."

I winked at him, apropos of this foreign belief that English weather is the worst in the world; it is not, Rainier had once said, but the convention is useful in that it enables an Englishman to appear modest by conceding something that, whether true or false, is of little consequence. All the time that Madame Navoida was bemoaning London rain and fog I was glancing at her sideways and judging her to be forty-five or so—younger, at any rate in looks, than her husband. The light in the concert hall was not particularly kind, and her make-up had either been put on hurriedly or else had got blurred by raindrops; her eyes were brown and rather small, but her forehead had a generous width that somehow compensated; it was an interesting face.

During the Ravel I whispered this to Rainier and received his reply: "I don't give a damn about her face. And I don't give a damn about this Ravel either. I only know she amuses me and I'm more cheerful than I was an hour ago..."

For the next few minutes I heard the two of them in whispered conversation; then he turned to me. "They're Hungarians, but she lived for a long time in Singapore—hence the English. She also speaks French and German—besides, of course, Hungarian. Writes poetry in all four, so she'd have you believe. Also worships Romance with a capital R. Reads Dekobra and D' Annunzio, but prefers Dekobra—so do I, for that matter... Altogether rather like a female spy in a magazine story—every minute I expect her to say 'Hein' and produce a bundle of stolen treaties out of her corsage. And she says such delicious things—like—'Ach, your English climate—' and that bit about gambling being in the blood of all the Navoidas... I'm trying to think of something half as good as what she'll say next—remember that game we used to play?"

That was one of the fooleries we would sometimes indulge in during our morning car journeys to the City. There was a certain newspaper shop at a street corner in Pimlico, and outside it, every Tuesday, appeared a picture poster advertising that week's issue of a publication called Judy's Paper; and this poster always showed an evening-clothed couple in some highly dramatic situation, captioned by such a sentence as "He refused her a ring" or "She lied to save him." Most Tuesdays, before we reached the shop, Rainier and I would try to invent something even triter than what we should presently discover, but we never succeeded, so hard is it for the sophisticated mind to think in the natural idiom of the ingenuous. But it made an amusing diversion, for all that.

After further whispering he turned to me excitedly. "She's SAID it! I KNEW she would! She's just told me that we English are so COLD!" At that moment Navoida finished the Ravel and Rainier was able to answer her amidst the applause. I heard him say: "Madame, we are NOT cold—it's merely that we have to be warmed up, especially on wet Saturdays. So I beg you to make allowances for us during the rest of your stay here."

"We are leaving tomorrow."

"So soon?"

"Casimir has a concert in Ostend on Wednesday."

"You'd better take care of him there. It's a great place for gambling."

"Oh, that will be all right. We shall go to the Casino and have champagne and Casimir will be lucky—he always is at roulette. It is cards he is no good at—especially poker." (She pronounced it "pokker.") "When I saw him playing poker with some Americans at the hotel last night, I knew he would be a bad boy today."

"I thought you said he didn't drink?"

"Only champagne. But of course it is so expensive in England. When we were in Singapore we drank nothing but Heidsieck all the time. A bottle every meal. It prevented him from being dysenteric."

"Probably it also prevented him from being Paderewski."

"You mean it is not good for him? But consider—if it pleases him, is he not entitled to it? What is the life of a concert artist nowadays? Nobody cares—there is no musical life as it used to be—in Berlin, in Leipzig, in Wien. Only in America they pay an artist well, but I do not want him to go there again."

"Why not?"

She whispered something in Rainier's ear and then added: "Of course I forgave him afterwards. He was faithful according to his fashion."

Rainier let out a shout of sheer glee. "What's that? WHAT?"

She repeated the sentence. "Do you not know the poem by one of your English poets, Ernest Dowson?" And she began to recite the whole thing from beginning to end, while Casimir, in whom I was beginning to feel a deeper interest after these varied revelations, appeared on the platform to play the Chopin "Black Key Study" as an encore, muffing the final octaves and finishing on a triumphantly wrong note in the bass. "Perhaps you would now like to meet him?" she concluded.

So we trooped round to the little room at the back of the platform where a few mournfully mackintoshed women were loitering while the pianist scrawled his signature across their programmes in a mood of equal mournfulness. The entrance of Madame Navoida brought a touch of life to these proceedings, and I noticed then a certain vital quality that made her still an attractive woman, despite sagging lines and the bizarre make-up. As soon as the autograph-seekers left she approached Casimir as one making a stage entrance, kissed him resoundingly on both cheeks, and cried: "Casimir, mon cher, tu étais magnifique!" Then, for a moment, she gabbled something incomprehensible and turned to Rainier. "He speaks Hungarian best. I have to tell him he is wonderful now, but soon I shall tell him he was awful— ATROCIOUS! Poor boy, he is always tired after a concert—please excuse him. He says he has a headache."

Rainier answered: "That's too bad! I was about to suggest that you both had dinner with us somewhere—that is, if you had nothing else to do."

Her face lit up. "Oh, but we should be ENCHANTED! It is so kind of you. I am sure his headache will get better. But there is one thing I must tell you beforehand—he will not dress. Not even a smoking. Only for the casinos where they will not admit him otherwise—and then he curses all the time. So if you do not mind—"

"Not at all. We probably wouldn't dress ourselves, anyway."

"Then he will be delighted." She turned to her husband. "Casimir, this is —" And of course another turn. "But I do not know your name?"

I had guessed it would come to that, and I remembered that moment on Armistice Day when all Rainier's pleasure had disappeared at the enforced disclosure of his identity. I wondered if it would be different with foreigners to whom his name would almost certainly be unknown.

But he answered, with a sort of gleeful solemnity: "Lord Frederic Verisopht—and this"—with a bow to me—"is Sir Mulberry Hawk..."

Having arranged to meet them at seven at Poldini's we spent the interval at Rainier's club, where his spirits soared fantastically. When I reminded him of an engagement to speak that evening at the Annual Dinner of the Gladstone Society he told me to wire them a cancellation on account of urgent political business. "That's all very well," I answered, "but then somebody will see us dining at Poldini's with a couple who look like a rather seedy croupier and a soubrette out of a pre-war musical comedy."

He laughed. "Not if we do what nobody else does nowadays—engage a private room."

"And what was the idea of introducing me as Sir Somebody or other?"

"To find out whether she reads Dickens. YOU evidently don't... Well, that was PARTLY the reason. The other was to give her a thrill. I'm sure titles do. Poldini's will too—it's got that air of having seen better and more romantic days. I rarely go there, so the waiters don't know me, and I've never been in one of their private rooms since my uncle took me when I was twelve years old. That's a story in itself. I don't think I ever told you about him—he was a charming and very shortsighted archdeacon, and the only one out of my large collection of uncles whom I really liked. He liked me too, I think—we often used to spend a day together. One evening during the Christmas holidays, we felt hungry after a matinée of Jack and the Beanstalk, so as we were walking to the nearest Underground station he said, 'Let's go in here for a snack'—and it was Poldini's. I think he mistook it for some sort of cheap but respectable tea-shop—anyhow, we walked in, all among the pretty ladies and the young men-about-town; we were the cynosure of every eye, as novelists in those days used to write —because it wasn't at all the kind of place a Church of England dignitary would normally take his schoolboy nephew to, and my uncle, with his white hair and flashing eyes (the drops he had to put in them made them flash), must have looked rather like Hall Caine's Christian about to create a disturbance... Anyhow, old Poldini,—he's dead now,—scenting something funny about us, pretended all his tables were booked and asked if we'd mind dining upstairs—so up we went, my uncle blinking his way aloft without a word of protest, and presently Poldini showed us into a cosy little room furnished in blue and gold, with a very thick carpet and a convenient chaise-longue against the wall and gilt cupids swarming in a suggestive manner all over the ceiling—in fact, Poldini took charge of us completely, recommending à la carte dishes and serving them himself, and as the meal progressed my uncle grew more and more surprised and delighted—still under the impression it was an A.B.C. or some such place; and when the bill came I snatched it up and said I'd stand treat, and he said, 'My boy, that's very generous of you'—and by God, it was, for it took all the money he'd just given me as a Christmas present. But I never let him know, and to the end of his life he always used to tell people he'd never enjoyed a better meal than at that eating-house off the Strand... EATING-HOUSE, mind you!" He took a long breath and added: "So that's where we'll dine tonight—among the ghosts of the past—a couple of milords entertaining the toast of the town—and rather battered toast, if you'll pardon two bad puns at once."

When I look back on that evening I remember chiefly, of course, the incident that crowned it; but I can see now that the entire masquerade was somehow Rainier's last and rather preposterous effort to tease a way into self-knowledge, and that the climax, though completely accidental, was yet a fitting end to the attempt. I realized also, even if never before, how near he was to some catastrophic breakdown—partly from overwork, but chiefly from the fret of things that could not be forgotten because they had never been remembered. And all that day, ever since meeting Nixon, the fret had strengthened behind an increasing randomness of acts and words.

We drove to Poldini's through the rain, and were glad to find the place reasonably unchanged—still with its private rooms upstairs, little used by a generation that no longer needs such an apparatus of seduction, and therefore slightly melancholy until gardenias and ice-buckets revived a more festive spirit. Then, with some commotion, the Navoidas arrived, the pianist rather pale and glum in a long overcoat with an astrakhan collar, and Madame very florid and voluble with heavy gold bangles and ancient but good-quality furs, obviously bewitched (but by no means ill-at-ease) at the prospect of dining intimately with English nobility. We soon discovered that both of them were equally accomplished champagne-bibbers, but whereas Madame grew livelier and gayer with every glass, her husband sank after the first half-dozen into a settled gloom from which he could only stir himself at intervals to murmur to the waiter a demand for "trouts"—for there had been some confusion over his order, due perhaps to the waiter's reluctance to believe that anyone in 1939 would ask for truites bleues in addition to Beluga caviare, steak tartare, and English rosbif. But all that too, and to Rainier's feverish delight, was in the halcyon tradition—the age of monstrous dinners and fashionable appendicitis, the one most often the result of the others.

Presently, after the popping of the fourth magnum, Madame grew sentimental and talked of her romantic adventures in all parts of the world—a recital garnished with copious quotations from the poets, of whom she knew so many in various languages that I began to think it really must be a passion with her quite as genuine as that for Heidsieck; she liked amorous poetry best, and there was something perhaps a little

109

charming in the way she obviously did not know which was too hackneyed to quote, so that from a worn-out tag of Shakespeare she would swerve into a line from Emily Brontë or Beddoes. A few words she wrongly pronounced or did not understand; she would then ask us to correct her, quite simply and with an absence of self-consciousness that made almost piquant her theatrical gestures and overstudied rhythms. Suddenly I realized, in the mood of half-maudlin pity that comes after a few drinks yet is none the less percipient, that she was a sadly disappointed woman, getting little out of later life that she really craved for, without a home, a wanderer between hotels and casinos, listening to the same old Brahms and Beethoven in half-empty concert halls, tied for the rest of her days to a flabby maestro, yet alive in her illusion that the world was still gay and chivalrous as a novelette.

After Rainier had called for more cognac he asked if she had any ideas for spending the rest of the evening, because he'd be glad to go on to a show if she fancied any particular play. She answered, with enthusiasm: "Oh yes, it is so kind of you—there is one place I have always wanted to go because I have heard so much about it—your famous old English music-hall!"

Rainier said how unfortunate that was, because the famous old English music-hall no longer existed; there were only assortments of vaudeville turns and dance bands.

"Then perhaps we could go to see Berty Lowe."

"Berty Lowe?"

"A man at the hotel told me this morning he was acting in London somewhere, and I should like to see him because I once knew an Englishman in Budapest who used to do imitations of him. He always said Berty Lowe was the greatest comedian of the famous old English music-hall."

Rainier had asked the waiter for an evening paper and was now glancing down the list. "Yes, he used to be quite funny, but I haven't heard of him in London for years—he's a bit passé, you know... well, he's not at the Coliseum or the Holborn Empire... that rather limits the possibilities... wait a minute, though—'Berty Lowe in Salute the Flag Twice Nightly at the Banford Hippodrome'—"

She clapped her hands ecstatically. "Oh, I should love to go there!"

"But it's miles away in the suburbs—" he was beginning, but suddenly then I could see the mere caprice of the idea seize hold of him; to drive out to Banford to see Berty Lowe at the local Hippodrome was in the right key of fantasy for such an evening. He handed me the paper. "They call it a riot of rip-roaring rib-tickling—doesn't that sound awful? Wish you'd ring 'em up and book a box for four at the second house."

"Salute the Flag," echoed Madame, with hands clasped. "Oh, I know I am going to love it if it is about soldiers. The Englishman I knew in Budapest was a soldier. It was during the war, but he wasn't interned at first, because the Hungarians always liked the English, but when he began to send me flowers every day with little notes hidden in them— written in English, of course—the police arrested him for espionage, but when they translated the notes—oh, mon dieu, you should have seen their faces—and HIS—and MINE—because, you see, he was crazily in love with me—CRAZILY—not a bit like an Englishman! Oh, how I wish I had made them give me back those notes... Casimir, of course, was mad with jealousy."

Casimir, no longer capable of being mad with jealousy, looked up as a dog will on hearing his name mentioned, then shook his head with a bemused belch over his unfinished crêpes Suzette.

I went out to telephone.

An hour later we were sitting on four very uncomfortable cane chairs as the curtain rose on Salute the Flag. It had been a mistake, I could see, to have engaged a box; the orchestra seats would have been much more comfortable, and further away from certain plush hangings which, on being merely touched, shook out clouds of dubious-looking dust. I gathered from the way we were escorted to our seats, and also from the fact that the other boxes were empty, that our arrival had created a little stir; it would be odd, I thought, but perhaps not absolutely catastrophic, if some member of the audience were to recognize Rainier. However, no one did, despite the fact that some of the actors played at us outrageously—even, by the end of the show, making jokes about "the gentleman in the box who's fast asleep." It was true; Casimir was fast asleep. Madame awakened him several times, but he slumped forward again almost immediately; soon she gave it up as a bad job.

As for the play, it had been (I guessed) an originally serious melodrama on a wartime theme, dating probably from 1914 or 1915; its villains had then been Germans of impossible villainy and its heroes English soldiers of equally impossible saintliness. A quarter of a century of lucrative adaptation, however, had merged both the villainy and the saintliness into a common mood of broad comedy burlesque; such patriotic speeches as remained were spoken now only to be laughed at, while the hero's first appearance was in the always comic uniform of a scoutmaster.

But Madame was puzzled. During the intermission she said: "I cannot understand why they laugh at some of the lines. When the recruiting sergeant made that speech about the British Empire, what was funny about it?"

"It's just our English sense of humour," Rainier explained. "We think recruiting sergeants ARE funny. We think long speeches are also funny. The British Empire has its funny side too. So put them all together and you can't help making an Englishman laugh."

"But it was a PATRIOTIC speech!"

"Englishmen think them the funniest of all."

"But in Austria, if anyone laughed at a patriotic speech there would be a riot and the man would be arrested."

"That just proves something I have long suspected—that Austria isn't England."

"You know Austria?"

"I once spent a few days in Vienna on business."

111

"Ah, you should have stayed longer and gone to the Semmering and then to Pressburg down the Danube in a steamboat."

"Curious you should mention it, but that was one of my boyhood ambitions. But in a canoe, not a steamboat."

"Oh, but that would be more wonderful still! Why did you not do it?"

"Because when I first wanted to, I hadn't enough money—then later, when I had enough money, I hadn't the time... and today, whatever I have, there isn't any Austria."

"Ah, yes, it is so sad. But let us not think about it—see, the curtain rises!"

She said that so much like a musical-comedy cue that I almost expected to see her jump down to the stage and begin a song. However, Salute the Flag was doubtless better entertainment. It continued to be equally hilarious during its second half, though Berty Lowe, as the heavily moustached German general, was actually less funny than some of the smaller parts; there was one especially that had the audience holding their sides— when an English subaltern entered his colonel's tent (the colonel being a German spy in disguise) to exclaim, between chattering teeth and amidst paroxysms of stammering —"The enemy advances—give the order to attack, or, by heaven, sir, I will myself!" As a rule I do not care for jokes based on any physical defect, but I must admit that this particular player brought the house down by some of the most ludicrous facial contortions I have ever seen —the whole episode being topped by the final gag of a door-knob coming off and rolling across the stage when he banged his exit.

It was difficult to keep up or down to such a level, but the play romped on with a good deal of vulgar gusto until the last scene, evidently the dramatic high-spot of the original play, when the heroine, threatened by the villain with a revolver, cried: "You cannot fire on helpless womankind!" —whereat another woman, of suggestive male appearance and elephantine proportions, invaded the stage from the wings brandishing weapons of all kinds from tomahawk to Mills bomb. Crude, undoubtedly; but the Banford audience loved it, and were still laughing throughout the perfunctory finale in which all the cast rushed on to the stage to chase off the villain and line up for a closing chorus.

As we left the theatre I saw that Rainier's mood had changed. He almost bundled Madame and her husband into the car, and spoke very little during the ride back to London; she chattered to me for a while, but Rainier's moods had a queer way of enforcing their atmosphere upon others, and she also was somewhat subdued by the time we reached their hotel in Russell Square and set the two of them down on the pavement.

"Good-bye, my lord," she said to Rainier, evidently remembering her manners but not the name. But she remembered mine. "Good-bye, Sir Hawk."

Casimir nodded grumpily as she took his arm to help him up the hotel steps. The last we saw was her effort to get him through the revolving door. It should have been funny, but perhaps we had had enough laughter for one evening; it wasn't funny, therefore, it was somehow rather sad.

"Of course she's ruined him," Rainier commented, as we drove away towards Chelsea.

"What makes you think that?"

"His playing. I could tell he was good once."

"Well, he's ruined her too. She can't get much fun out of life, watching over him wherever they go. Incidentally, I think she was rather shocked by our rough island humour."

"Probably it was too unsanitary and not sexy enough for her."

"And then that fellow's stammer. I suppose on the Vienna stage you couldn't have an officer stammering—only a private."

"God, yes—that stammer... they kept it in—and the door-knob coming off as well... But the gag at the end was new."

"Sounds as if you've seen the show before."

He was thoughtful. "Yes, I think I have."

"Not surprising. It's been played up and down everywhere for years."

"But more than that—more than SEEING it before—I—I —" He turned to me with a curious abrupt eagerness. "Do you mind if we drive around for a while before going home?"

"Of course not... But what's happened? You look—" I stopped, but he cut in sharply: "Yes, TELL me—what's the matter with me— HOW do I look?"

I said, meeting his eyes and speaking with as little excitement as I could: "You look as you did when I first saw you staring at a mountain because you thought you recognized it—through the train windows that Armistice Day."

"ARMISTICE DAY," he repeated. Then he added, quietly, almost casually: "I was in hospital... I mean on that first Armistice Day—the first one of all. The REAL one." He suddenly clutched my sleeve. "Yes, I remember —I was at Melbury!"

I said nothing, anxious not to break any thread of recollection he was about to unravel, and afraid of the tension in my voice were I to speak at all.

"There were so many hospitals," he went on. "I was at Sennelager first —then Hanover. Then they exchanged the shell-shock and t.b. cases through Switzerland. So back home —Birmingham for a time—then Hastings—and another place near Manchester... then Melbury. That was the last of them... I'd like to go to Melbury."

I still couldn't answer; I was afraid of breaking some kind of spell. He seemed to read this into my silence, for he went on, in a kindly voice: "Do you mind? Or are you very tired?"

"No, I'm not tired." My voice was all right, but I was still apprehensive, and more so than ever when I realized he wanted to go to Melbury that very night, immediately. I added something about Hanson being probably tired, even if we weren't—after all he'd driven us to Banford and back, and to ask him now to make another excursion into the distant suburbs...

"Yes, of course—glad you thought of it." He was always considerate to servants. "We'll drop him here and send him home by taxi. Then I'll drive —or perhaps you'd better if you think I've had too much to drink." He was already reaching for the speaking-tube, and had given the new instructions before I could think of anything else to say at all, much less frame an objection. Hanson pulled up at the kerb, showing no more curiosity than a good servant should. But it was still pouring with rain, and he must have thought it odd to choose such a night for a pleasure drive.

Rainier moved next to me in the chauffeur's seat; as I drove off he said he hoped I knew the way.

"Through Stepney and Stratford, isn't it?"

"Don't ask me—I've never been there since—since the morning I left."

"You remember it was a MORNING?"

He turned to me excitedly. "Did I say morning? Yes, it WAS... and if I can only SEE the place again—"

"You won't see much tonight, I'm afraid."

"I didn't see much last time, either—it was too foggy. God— that's something else... Just let me talk on anyhow. Don't feel you have to answer—I know it's hard to drive these juggernauts on a wet night —why does my wife always buy such monsters?—and we have four of them."

"Nothing to stop you buying a small car yourself if you wanted."

"But I'm not interested in buying cars."

I laughed and said: "Well, you can't have it both ways. If you're not interested in cars, you can't blame Mrs. Rainier for buying the kind she thinks is suitable for a rich man who isn't interested in cars."

"True, true..." The side issue had lowered the tension.

We drove through the almost deserted City, past Aldgate and along the wide, brilliant, rococo Mile End Road. It was midnight as we crossed Bow Bridge, five minutes past as we reached the fork of the road in Stratford Broadway; I had to drive slowly because of the slippery tram-rails. Once I stopped to inquire from some men drinking at a coffee-stall; they waved us on into the deepening hinterland of the suburbs. The slums here lost their sinister picturesqueness, became more and more drably respectable: long vistas of lamplit roads, with here and there a block of elementary schools rising like a fortress over the rooftops, and at every shopping centre the same names in a different order— Woolworth, Maypole, Sainsbury, Home and Colonial, Lyons. We passed an old-fashioned church with a new-fashioned sign outside it, proclaiming the subject of next Sunday's sermon—"Why Does God Permit War?"—and that set Rainier improvising on the kind of sermon it would be—"very cheerful and chummy, proving that God isn't such a bad sort when you get to know Him"; and then abruptly, in the tangential way so characteristic when he was inwardly excited, he talked again of his favourite uncle the archdeacon. "HE never preached a sermon on 'Why Does God Permit War?' To begin with, I don't suppose he ever thought about it, and if he had, he'd probably have answered 'Why shouldn't He?' He took it for granted that the Deity minded His own business, and that 'God's in His Heaven' was just Browning's way of putting it. All this craze for bringing Him down to earth and appealing to Him at every turn would have struck my uncle as weak-kneed as well as in appallingly bad taste. And yet, in his way, and on the outskirts of Cheltenham, he lived an almost saintly life. He would never kill insects that strayed into the house, but would trap them in match-boxes and set them free in the garden. He approved of hunting, though, and thought the smearing of a girl's face with fox blood after her first ride to hounds was a rather charming custom. All in all, I don't suppose he was any more inconsistent than the modern parson who tries to combine Saint Francis, Lenin, and Freud into one all-embracing muddle."

We drove on through Leytonstone; there the tram-lines ended and we could put on a little speed. It was just after one o'clock when we reached the market square in the centre of Melbury; I pulled up and looked to him for further instructions. He was peering through the window and after a moment I wound the window down on my side. The rain had increased to the dimensions of a storm, and a solitary policeman sheltering under a shop awning called out to us: "Looking for somewhere?"

Rainier turned at the sound of the stranger's voice.

"Yes, the hospital," he answered. "Where's the hospital?"

"You mean the new one or the old one, sir?"

"The old one, I think." Then in a sudden rush: "It's on a hill—has big gates and a high wall all round it."

The policeman looked puzzled. "That don't sound much like either of 'em." Then, as I was about to thank him and drive off, he came towards the car, leaned in, and said, with a glance across me to Rainier: "You wouldn't be meanin' the ASYLUM, would you, sir?"

PART FOUR

He was so tired of stammering out to a succession of doctors all he knew about himself that eventually he jotted it down on a single sheet of notepaper for them to refer to at will. He had recently been transferred to Melbury from another military hospital, and the change had somewhat upset him, because it meant beginning everything all over again—contacts with new doctors, nurses, and patients, the effort to find another corner of existence where people would presently leave him alone. Besides, he didn't like the place—it was too big, too crowded, and altogether too permanent-looking. Overworked psychiatrists gave him treatments that were supposed to have done well in similar cases, but perhaps it was part of his own case that he didn't feel any similar cases existed, though he admitted there were many worse ones; he also felt that the doctors—grand fellows all of them, he had no specific complaints—aimed at raising a statistical average of success rather than his own individual cure.

That particular morning in November he began the regulation mile along the cinder paths, glad that the fog had kept most of his fellow victims indoors. Only alone did his various symptoms ever approach vanishing point, and amidst the fog this sense of aloneness was intensified so reassuringly that as he continued to walk he began to feel a curious vacuum of sensation that might almost be called contentment. Walking was part of the encouraged regimen at Melbury; extensive grounds surrounded by a fifteen-foot spiked wall permitted it, while an army greatcoat kept the cold air from penetrating his thinnish hospital uniform.

Suddenly, as he neared the main entrance where the name had been painted over (though it was still readable in burnt letters on brooms and garden tools—"Property of the So-and-so County Asylum")—suddenly, as the heavily scrolled ironwork of the gates loomed through the fog, a siren screamed across the emptiness beyond—a factory siren, already familiar at certain hours, but this was not one of them, nor did the sound stay on the single level note, but began soaring up and down in wild flurries. A few seconds later another siren chimed in, and then a third; by that time he was near enough to the gates to see two uniformed porters rush hatless out of the lodge, shouting excitedly as they raced up the shrouded driveway. For the moment—and he realized it without any answering excitement—there was no one left on guard, no one to stop him as he passed through the lodge into the outer world, no one to notice him as he walked down the lane towards the town. Behind his mute acceptance of things done to him, there was a slow-burning inclination to do things for himself, an inclination fanned now into the faint beginnings of initiative; but they were only faint, he had no will for any struggle, and if anyone ran after him to say "Come back" he would go back.

Nobody ran after him. The lane turned into the main road at the tram terminus; a small crowd was already gathering there in groups, chattering, laughing, greeting each newcomer with eager questions. Nor had the sirens stopped; they were louder now, and joined by tram bells, train whistles, a strange awakening murmur out of the distance. He walked on, still downhill, edging into the roadway to avoid people, glad that the fog was thickening as he descended. Soon he was aware of some approaching vortex of commotion, of crowds ahead that might cover all the roadway and envelop him completely; he felt as well as heard them, and a nagging pinpoint of uneasiness expanded until, to relieve it even momentarily, he turned into a shop at the corner of a street.

The inside was dark, as he had hoped, revealing only vague shapes of counter, shelves, and merchandise; it seemed to be a small neglected general store, smelling of its own shabbiness. The opening door had tinkled a bell, and presently, as his eyes grew used to the dimness, he saw an old woman watching from behind the counter—thin-faced, gray-haired, rather baleful. He tried to ask for cigarettes and began to stammer. He always did when he talked to others, though he could chatter to himself without much trouble—that was one of the points he had noted for the doctors, though he suspected they didn't believe him, and of course it was something he couldn't prove. Just now, with all the extra excitement, his stammer was worse than ever—not a mere tongue-tie, but a nervous tic that convulsed his entire head and face. He stood there, trembling and straining for speech, at last managing to explode a word; the woman said nothing in answer, but after a long scrutiny began sidling away. He relaxed when she had gone, hoping she would just return with the cigarettes and not oblige him to say more, wondering if she would think it odd if he stayed to smoke one of them in the shop. Anyhow, it was good to be alone again. Then suddenly he realized he was not alone. A girl had entered, or else had been there all the time and he hadn't noticed; she too was waiting at the counter, but now she turned to him and began urgently whispering. "She's gone to fetch somebody —she knows where you're from."

He stared hard, trying to isolate her face from the surrounding shadows.

"You ARE, aren't you?"

He nodded.

"She knows you're not supposed to be out."

He nodded again.

"Not that I'd blame anybody for anything today. The war's over—you know that? Isn't it wonderful... ? And you certainly don't LOOK as if you'd do any harm." She smiled to soften the phrase.

He shook his head and smiled back.

"Well, if you HAVE given them the slip, I wouldn't stay here, old boy, that's all."

He smiled again, a little bewildered; somebody was talking to him normally, casually, yet personally too. It was a pleasant experience, he wished it could go on longer, but then he heard the old woman's footsteps returning from some inner room behind the shop; with a final smile he summoned enough energy to walk away. A few seconds later he stood on the pavement, blinking to the light, aware of the prevalent atmosphere as something pungent, an air he could not breathe, a spice too hot for his palate. Shouts were now merging into a steady sequence of cheers, and through the pale fog he saw a tram approach, clanging continuously as it discharged a load of yelling school-children. He turned away from the clamour into a side street where two rows of small houses reached upwards like flying buttresses astride a hill; presently he came to a house with a dingy brass plate outside —"H. T. Sheldrake, Teacher of Music." He spoke the name, Sheldrake, to himself—he always tested names like this, hoping that some day one of them would fit snugly into an empty groove in his mind. No, not Sheldrake. There was the sound of a piano playing scales; he listened, calming himself somewhat, till the playing stopped and shrill voices began. That made him move on up the hill, but he felt tired after a short distance and held to a railing for support. Just then the same girl caught up with him.

"What's the matter?"

He smiled.

"I followed you. Thought you looked a bit off-colour."

He shook his head valiantly, observing her now for the first time. She was dressed in a long mackintosh and a little fur hat, like a fez, under which brown straight hair framed a face of such friendly eagerness that he suddenly felt it did not matter if she saw and heard his struggles for speech; rather that than have her think him worse than he was. He wanted to say: You should see some of the other fellows up there—what's wrong with me is NOTHING—just a stammer and not being able to remember things.

117

While he was planning to say all this she took his arm. "Lean on me if you like. And talk or not, whichever you want. Don't be nervous."

After that he decided to say merely that he was not really ill, but only tired after walking further than usual; he began bracing himself to make the effort, smiling beforehand to console her for the ordeal of watching and listening. Then a curious thing happened; it was like taking a rush at a door to break through when all the time the door was neither locked nor even latched. He just opened his mouth and found that he could speak. Not perfectly, of course, but almost as easily as if he were talking to himself. It made him gasp with an astonishment so overwhelming that for the moment he expected her to share it.

"Did you hear THAT? I wasn't so bad THEN, was I?"

"Of course you weren't. Didn't I tell you not to be nervous?"

"But you don't know what a job I have, as a rule."

"Oh yes, I do. I heard you in the shop. But that old woman would scare anybody. Where d'you want to go?"

"I don't know."

"Well, this street doesn't lead anywhere."

"I was just—walking."

"But weren't you trying to get away?"

"Not—not exactly. I hadn't any real plans. I just came out because —well, because there was nobody at the gate."

"Do they look after you all right?"

"Oh yes."

"I've heard they're a bit rough with some."

"Not with me."

"All the same, you don't really LIKE the place?"

"Not—not very much."

"Then you oughtn't to be in it, surely?"

"There's nowhere else, until I get all right again."

"How can you get all right again when you're not happy in a place?"

He had often asked himself the same question, but he answered, parrying the idea: "Perhaps I wouldn't be very happy anywhere—just now."

"But the war's over—doesn't that make any difference?" She came near to abrupt tears, then dashed a hand to her eyes and began to laugh. "Silly, that's what I am—everybody's gone silly today. Seems an awful morning to end the war on, doesn't it?—I mean, you'd almost think the sun ought to shine—blue skies—like a picture..." She almost cried again. "Shall we stroll down?"

She gripped his arm as they slowly descended the hill. His walk was pretty good, and he was suddenly proud of it—just the faintest shuffle, nobody would notice. When they reached the piano-teacher's house he hesitated. "I'd rather not get mixed up with the crowd—if you don't mind."

"Righto—we'll keep well away." She added: "So you don't like crowds?"

"Not very much."

"Or hospitals?"

He smiled and shook his head.

"Well, that's fine. If I keep on trying I'll really get to know you."

They both laughed; then she said: "There's a place where we could get some hot coffee, if you like THAT."

The Coronation Café was a cheap little place along the Bockley Road, patronized mostly by tramway men on duty who stopped their vehicles outside and dashed in with empty jugs, leaving them to be filled in readiness for the return trip. All day long these swift visitations continued, with barely time for an exchange of words across the counter. But today, the eleventh of November, 1918, drivers and conductors chatted boisterously as if they were in no hurry at all, and passed cheery remarks to the couple who sat at the marble-topped table in the window alcove. They could see the man was a soldier by his greatcoat, and it was a good day for saying cheery things to soldiers. "Wonder 'ow long it'll take to git the rest of you boys 'ome, mate?"... "Maybe they'll march 'em to Berlin now and shoot the Old Kaiser."... "Seems queer to 'ave the war end up like this—right on the dot, as you might say."... "Wouldn't surprise me if it's just a rumour, like them Russians comin' through."... "But it's all in the papers, see —it sez the Germans 'ave signed a what's-a-name—means PEACE, don't it?" All this and much else in snatches of news and comment. The proprietor always answered: "You're right there, mister"—"That's just what I always said meself," or, if the remark had been especially emphatic: "You 'it the nail straight on the 'ead that time, mister." Towards noon the fog grew very thick indeed and drivers reported crowds still increasing at the busy centres; workpeople had been sent home from offices and factories, as well as children from all the schools. Then the trams stopped running, impeded by fog and crowds equally, and as there were no more customers at the Coronation Café the proprietor set to work behind his counter, polishing a large tea-urn till it glowed in the gloom like a copper sun. Presently he came over to the table. He was a little man, pale-faced, bald, with watery eyes and a drooping moustache.

"Wouldn't you two like a bite o' somethin'?"

The girl looked to her companion, saw him frame a word and then begin to struggle with it; she intervened quickly: "Sounds a good idea. What have you got?"

"Eggs, that's about all. 'Ow d'yer like 'em—soft or 'ard?"

Again she looked across the table before answering. "Oh, middling'll do."

119

"That's the ticket. That's 'ow I like 'em meself. And two more coffees?"

"Righto."

"Keep yer warmed-up a day like this. War's over, they say, but anybody can die of pewmonia."

"That's a fact, so bring those coffees quick."

He went away chuckling; then the girl leaned across the table and said: "Don't look so scared. He won't bite."

"I know. But I'm always like that with strangers—at first. And besides—I don't think I've enough money."

"Well, who cares about that? I have."

"But—"

"Now don't start being the gentleman. You were telling me about yourself when that fellow came up. Go on with the story." He stared at her rather blankly till she added: "Unless you'd rather not. Your mind's on something else, I can see."

"I'd just noticed that sign outside." He pointed through the window to a board overhanging the pavement above the café doorway—the words "Good Pull-Up for Carmen" were dimly readable through the fog. "CARMEN," he muttered. "That gives me something—why, yes... MELBA."

"MELBA? Oh, you mean the opera?" She began to laugh. "And Melba gives me peaches. What IS this—a game?"

"Sort of. I have to keep on doing it, one of the doctors says—part of his treatment. You see, I've lost my memory about certain things. It's like being blind and having to feel around for shapes and sizes."

"I'm terribly sorry. I didn't realize, or I wouldn't have laughed."

"Oh, that's all right—I'd rather you laugh. I wish everybody would laugh... Now what was it you were asking me before?"

"Well, I was wondering why you had to be in a hospital at all, but now of course I understand."

"Yes—till I get thoroughly better. I daresay I will— eventually."

"And then your memory'll come back?"

"That's what they think."

"But in the meantime what are you going to do?"

"Just wait around till it happens, I suppose."

"Isn't there some way of tracing any of your relatives and friends? Advertising for them, or something like that?"

"They've tried. Some people did come to see me at the hospital once, but —I wasn't their son."

"I'll bet they were disappointed. You'd make a nice son for somebody."

"Well, _I_ was disappointed too. I'd like to have belonged to them— to have had a home somewhere."

He then gave her some of the facts he had written out for the doctors —that he had been blown up by a shell during 1917, and that when he recovered consciousness he was in a German hospital somewhere, unidentified and unidentifiable. Later there had been an exchange of wounded and shell-shocked prisoners through Switzerland, and by this means the problem had been passed on to the English—but with no more success. He had been a pretty bad case at first, with loss of speech and muscular co-ordination, but those things had gradually returned—perhaps the memory would follow later. Altogether he had spent over a year in various hospitals, of which he liked the one at Melbury least of all. "Mind you," he added, seizing the chance to say what he thought of saying before, "I'm miles better than some of the others. You'd think so too if you saw them."

"And that's why YOU shouldn't see them at all. Doesn't exactly help you, does it?"

"No, but I suppose all the hospitals are so crowded—there's no chance to separate us properly."

The proprietor, coming up with the coffee and eggs, saw them break off their conversation suddenly. "Gettin' a bit dark in 'ere—I'll give yer a light," he murmured, to satisfy a dawning curiosity. Standing on a bench he pulled the chain under a single incandescent burner in the middle of the ceiling; it sent a pale greenish glow over their faces. He stared at them both. "You don't look so chirpy, mite. Feelin' bad?"

"He's just tired, that's all." And then, to get the fellow out: "Bring a packet of cigarettes, will you?"

When he had gone she leaned across. "That's what you were trying to ask for in the shop, wasn't it?"

"Yes, but I didn't really need them."

"Oh, come, I know what you need more than you do yourself. Don't be scared of that little chap—he means all right."

The proprietor returned to their table with the cigarettes. "Looks to me as if 'e might 'ave the flu, miss. Lots o' flu abart 'ere. Dyin' like flies, they was, up at the 'orspital a few weeks ago."

When he had gone again she comforted: "There now, don't worry. If you don't like it here, let's eat and then we'll be off."

"It isn't that I don't like it, only—only I'd rather them not come after me, that's all."

"Why should they?"

"He mentioned the hospital. He knows I'm from there, just as you did when you first saw me. It's in my face—the way I look at people. I haven't a chance—even if I knew where to go. They come round the wards every night at six. If I get back by then there'll be no trouble."

"You really mean to go back?"

"There's nothing else to do." He smiled wanly. "You've been very kind to bring me here."

"Oh, don't talk like that."

"But you have. I'm grateful. Maybe I'll be more satisfied now, because I shall know I'm not really well enough to be on my own—YET."

They ate in silence for a few moments after that; then she went up to the counter and paid the bill. "One and tenpence, miss. Can't make it any more or I would. An' if I were you, I'd get your pal 'ome pretty quick. 'E don't look as if 'e ought to be aht, an' that's a fact."

A moment later the fog was curling round them in swathes, fanning the sound of cheers over distant invisible roofs. She took his arm again as they walked to the next corner, then turned through quiet residential roads away from the centre of the town. But at one place jubilant householders were dancing round a bonfire, and to avoid passing through the blaze of light they made a second detour, along alleys that twisted more and more confusingly till, with a sudden rush of sound, they were back in the main street, caught in a madder, wilder throng. Already the war had been over for several hours, and the first shock of exultation was yielding to a hysteria that disguised an anticlimax. The war was over... but now what? The dead were still dead; no miracle of human signature could restore limbs and sight and sanity; the grinding hardships of those four years could not be wiped out by a headline. Emotions were numb, were to remain half-numbed for a decade, and relief that might have eased them could come no nearer than a fret to the nerves. A few things were done, symbolically; men climbed street-lamps to tear away the shades that had darkened them since the first air raids in human history; shop windows suddenly blazed out with new globes in long-empty sockets. The traffic centre at Melbury was like a hundred others in and around London that day; the crowds, the noise, the light, the fog. Beyond a certain limit of expression there was nothing to say, nothing much even to do; yet the urge to say and to do was self-torturing. So, as the day and the night wore on, throngs were swayed by sharp caprices—hoisting shoulder-high some chance-passing soldier on leave, smashing the windows of tradesmen rumoured to have profiteered, making a fire of hoardings that proclaimed slogans for winning the now-extinct war, booing the harassed police who tried to keep such fires in check. From cheers to jeers, from applause to anger, were but a finger touch of difference in the play of events on taut nerves.

Presently a girl summoning help for a soldier in hospital uniform who had fainted provided a new thrill—compassion; within a few seconds the crowd was entirely swept by it, pressing in on the two donors with cries of pity, indignation, and advice to do this and that.

"Give 'im air! Keep back there! Pick 'im up and carry 'im inside—I got some whiskey—give the poor chap a nip... No, 'e shouldn't 'ave no alco'ol, not without a doctor... Phone the 'orspital, they'll send an amberlance... Christ, I wouldn't let 'im go there if 'e was my boy— they kill 'em, that's what they do up there."

Presently a few men carried the soldier from the pavement into a grocery, whose owner nervously unbarred his front door to repeated knockings. Inside the shop the stream of advice would have continued indefinitely, but for the girl, who kept saying she would take him home.

"Better 'ave a doctor first, miss."

"I'll get a doctor when he's home."

"Where's 'e live?"

"Not far away."

"Wounded badly, was 'e?"

"No, he's all right—just fainted, that's all. See, he's coming round now—if I can get him home—"

"Your 'usband, lidy?"

"That make any difference?"

"Come to think of it, I seem to 'ave seen your face before."

"Maybe you have, old boy, but that doesn't mean I'll stand any of your lip. Come on now, and give me a hand. If I could get a cab—"

"Not much chance o' that, miss, not on a night like this."

But the shopkeeper, anxious to get them all off his premises, whispered to her, while the others were still arguing the point: "I've got a van and my son'll drive you. Think your friend can walk to it?"

"Oh yes, I'm certain he can. Let's try."

It proved to be a large van, smelling of miscellaneous foods and soaps; its driver was a thin youth who easily made room for them on the front seat. After he had inched his way out of the yard he lit a cigarette and began proudly: "You ain't supposed to drive these vans till you're eighteen, but Dad don't tell nobody. Where to, miss?"

"D'you know the Owl—the other side of Bockley?"

"You bet I do. Biffer's place?"

"That's it. But stop in the lane just before you get there."

"Right you are. Won't arf be a journey though, in this fog. 'Ow's the patient?"

"Fine. You keep your eye on the road."

123

"That's all right. I could drive round 'ere blindfold. Aren't you on at the Empire this week?"

"If there's any show at all. They said there wouldn't be tonight."

"I saw the show in Bockley last week. Jolly good."

"Think so? I thought it was rotten. Look where you're driving."

"Sorry."

"Good of you to take us, anyhow, even if we do get killed on the way."

"Don't mention it. Be in the army meself next year."

"Not now the war's over, will you?"

"Won't they 'ave me because of that?" He looked puzzled and rather disappointed.

"Maybe they will—if you live that long."

"Pretty quick, ain't you, miss? Reminds me of that scene you 'ad in the play, when you kept tellin' orf that fat old gent with the moustaches. I could 'ave larfed."

"Why the devil didn't you then? You were supposed to."

"My dad'll stare when I tell 'im it was Paula Ridgeway. 'E didn't recognize you. Went to the show same as I did, only 'e don't see so well lately."

They drove on, slowly, gropingly, chattering meanwhile, avoiding the main streets as far as possible, and especially the road junctions and shopping centres where crowds were likely. Melbury and Bockley were adjacent suburbs, completely built over in a crisscross of residential roads that afforded an infinity of routes; but once beyond Bockley the rows of identical houses came to an end with the abruptness of an army halted, and the wider highways narrowed and twisted into lanes. They pulled up eventually at the side of a hedge.

"'Ere y'are, miss. The Owl's just rahnd the corner. Sure I can't tike yer no further?"

"This'll do fine. We can walk now."

He helped them out. "Sure you know where y'are?"

"Yes—and thanks." She was fishing in her bag for a coin when he stopped her. "No, miss—you send me a signed picture of yourself, that's what I'd rather 'ave... 'Is nibs feelin' better? That's good. Well, it's bin a pleasure. Good luck to both of you. Good night, miss."

She waved to him and he drove off, leaving them alone.

"Where are we going?"

"Home—at least it'll do for one."

"But—I—I have to get back to the hospital!"

"We'll see about that tomorrow."

"But this place—I don't understand—"

"It's the Owl Hotel if you like the word. Call it a pub to be on the safe side. I know the landlord."

"Will he mind?"

"The odds are he won't even know, old boy, not in the state he'll be in tonight."

She guided him a little way along the lane, then through a side gate into a garden where the shapes of trees loomed up at regular intervals. "Lovely here when the summer comes—they serve teas and there's a view."

"What name was it he called you?"

"Paula Ridgeway. It's not my real name, though. What's yours?"

"Smith—but that's not real either."

"You don't remember your real name?"

He shook his head.

"Well, Smith's good enough. Come on, Smithy."

As they found their way along a path, the silent blanket of fog was pierced by a murmur and then by a paleness ahead, the two presently merging into a vague impression of the Owl on this night of November the eleventh, 1918. A two-storied, ivy-clustered, steep-roofed building, ablaze with light from every downstairs room, and already packed with shouting celebrants of victory; a friendly pub, traditional without being self-consciously old-world. Established in the forties, when neighbouring Bockley was a small country town, it had kept its character throughout an age that had seen the vast obliterating spread of the suburbs and the advent of motor traffic; it had kept, too, the sacred partitions between "private" and "public" bars —divisions rooted in the mythology of London life, and still acceptable because they no longer signify any snobbish separation, but merely an etiquette of occasion, dress, and a penny difference in the price of a pint of beer. Even the end of a great war could not shatter this etiquette; but with the sacred partitions still between, the patrons of both bars found community in songs that were roared in unison above the shouting and laughter and clatter of glasses. They were not especially patriotic songs; most were from the music-halls of the nineties, a few were catchy hits from the recent West End revues. But by far the most popular of all was "Knees Up, Mother Brown," a roaring chorus that set the whole crowd stamping into the beer-soaked sawdust.

On the threshold of the Owl Smith felt a renewal of nervousness, especially as the girl's entry was the signal for shouts of welcome from within. She pushed him into a chair in an unlighted corner of the lobby. "Stay there, Smithy—I won't be long." A group of men pressed out of the bar towards her, dragging her back with them; he could hear their greetings, and her own in answer. He sat there, waiting, trying to collect his thoughts, to come to terms with the strange sequence of events that had brought him to a noisy public-house in company with a girl who was something on the stage. A few people passed without noticing him; that was reassuring, but he suspected it was only because they were drunk. He decided that if anyone spoke to him he would pretend to be drunk also, and with the safeguarding decision once made the waiting became easier. He watched the door into the bar, expecting her to emerge amidst a corresponding roar of farewells, but when she did come, it was quietly, silently, and from another direction. "I managed to get away, old boy, and believe me it wasn't easy. Come on—let's go before they find us."

She led him through another door close by, and up a back staircase to the first floor, turning along a corridor flanked by many rooms; she opened one of them and put a match to a gas-jet just inside. It showed up a square simple apartment, containing an iron bed and heavy Victorian furniture. He stared around, then began to protest: "But how can I stay here? I can't afford——"

"Listen, Smithy—the war stopped this morning. If that's possible, anything else ought to be. And you've got to stay somewhere." She began to laugh. "You're safe here—nobody's going to bother you. I told you I know the man who runs this place—Biffer Briggs—used to be a prize-fighter, but don't let that frighten you... It's cold, though—wish there was a fire."

She suddenly knelt at his feet and began to unlace his boots. Again he protested.

"Well, you MUST take your boots off—that's only civil, on a clean bed. I'll come up again soon and bring you some tea."

He took off his boots as soon as she had gone, but the effort tired him more than he could have imagined. The day's strains and stresses had utterly exhausted him, in fact; he almost wished he were back at the hospital, because that at least promised the likelihood of a known routine, whereas here, in this strange place... but he fell asleep amidst his uneasiness. When he woke he saw her standing in front of him, carrying a cup of tea. She placed the cup on the side table, then fixed the blankets here and there to cover him more warmly. She was about to tiptoe away when he reached out his hand in a wordless gesture of thanks.

"Awake, Smithy?"

"Have I been asleep?"

"I should think you have. Four solid hours, and this is the third cup of tea I've made for you, just in case... God, I'm tired—tell you what, old boy, I've had just about enough of it downstairs."

"It's late, I suppose."

"One A.M. and they're still hard at it."

"Do you live here?"

"Not me—I just know the Biffer, that's all. I reckon EVERYBODY'S living here tonight, though. Hope the noise won't keep you awake— it'll probably go on till morning."

"I shan't mind."

"You sleep well?"

"Sometimes."

"Lie awake thinking about things?"

"Sometimes."

"About who you are and all that?"

"Sometimes."

Her voice softened with curiosity as she looked down at him. "Drink it up, Smithy. What does it feel like—to think of the time before— before you can remember?"

"Like trying to remember before I was born."

She gave his hand an answering touch. "Well, you're born again now. So's everybody. So's the whole world. That's the way to look at it. That's why there's all this singing and shouting. That's why I'm drunk."

"Are you?"

"Well, not really with drinks, though I have had a few. It's just the thought of it all being over—I've seen so many nice boys like yourself, having a good time one week and then by the next... Oh, well, mustn't talk about THAT—better not talk any more about anything; you're too sleepy, and so am I. How about making a bit of room?"

Without undressing, except to slip off her shoes, she lifted the blankets and lay down beside him. He felt her nearness slowly, luxuriously, a relaxation of every nerve. "Tell you what, old boy, I'm just like a mother tonight, so cuddle up close as you like and keep warm... Good night, Smithy."

"Good night."

"And Paula's the name, in case you've forgotten that as well."

But he felt no need to answer, except by a deeper tranquillity he drew from her, feeling that she was offering it. The crowd were still singing "Knees Up, Mother Brown" in the bars below. It sounded new to him, both words and tune, and he wondered if it were something else he had forgotten. He did not know that no one anywhere had heard it before—that in some curious telepathic way it sprang up all over London on Armistice Night, in countless squares and streets and pubs; the living improvisation of a race to whom victory had come, not with the trumpet notes of a Siegfried, but as a common earth touch—a warm bawdy link with the mobs of the past, the other victorious Englands of Dickens, Shakespeare, Chaucer.

Presently, as he lay listening, he fell asleep in her arms.

In the morning he had a temperature of 103. He didn't know it; all he felt was a warm, almost cosy ache of all his limbs, as well as a trance-like vagueness of mind. She didn't know it either, but his flushed face and incoherent speech made her telephone for a doctor. A majority of the other occupants of the Owl on that first morning of Peace were also flushed and incoherent, though from a different cause. The Biffer himself, sprawling, dishevelled, and half undressed, snored loudly on a sofa in the little room behind the private bar; Frank, the bar-tender, boastful of never having touched a drop,

127

languished in sober but melancholy stupor on the bench in the public bar, watching the maids sweep sawdust and broken glasses into heaps. Other persons, including a second bar-tender, a waiter, and several dilatory patrons who had either declined or been unable to go home, were not only fast asleep in various rooms and corridors, but likely to remain so till many more hours were past. It had been a night in the history of the Owl, as of the world.

The only doctor who heeded the call proved, on arrival, to be extremely bad-tempered. As she met him in the lobby he took a sharp look round, eyeing distastefully the prostrate figures visible through doorways. "Daresay you know how busy I am—three Bockley doctors down with the flu— I'm trying to do the work of five men myself, so I hope you haven't brought me here for nothing. I know Briggs—known him for years—he drinks too much and I've told him he'll die of it—what more can I do? A man has a right to die as well as live the way he chooses—anyhow, a doctor can't stop him." By this time she had led him upstairs and into the bedroom. He walked across to the bed, took one look, and swung round angrily. "What's the idea? Who is he?"

"He's been a soldier. He's ill."

"But I thought it was Briggs... You had no right to drag me out here —who ARE you?"

"A friend of the Biffer—like yourself."

"Well, I've no time for new cases."

"But he's ILL. Can't you see that?"

"How much did he drink?"

"Nothing. It isn't that."

"How do you know?"

"I was with him."

"You're his wife?"

"No."

"Well, what IS he to you? And what's he doing here? You call me away from my regular patients—you tell me it's urgent—I hurry here because Briggs is an old friend—" But by this time he had drawn back the blankets. "Why, God bless my soul, the man's in his uniform..."

"I told you—he's been a soldier."

"He's still a soldier—he belongs to a hospital."

"Aren't you going to help him at all?"

"Can't interfere in a military case—all I can do is notify the authorities. What's the fellow's name?... Ah, here it is—"

"But he's TERRIBLY ill."

"He'll be sent for."

"But you can't leave him like this!"

"You don't need to instruct me in my duty."

Smith half heard all this as he lay on the bed, his mind tremulous with fever and his body drenched in perspiration; he heard the door close and then saw her face coming towards him out of a mist.

"I bungled that, Smithy. I'm afraid the old boy's gone back to tell 'em you're here."

He smiled. He didn't care. She seemed to read that in his face. She went on: "Yes, you think it doesn't matter, you'd just as soon go back—but WOULD you, when you once got there? You don't really WANT to be in a hospital again... Or DO you?"

He smiled again, more faintly. He was too ill to speak.

"Well, if you die, it'll be pretty hard to explain you being here, but if you weren't going to die I wouldn't be so pleased at having let you go. So you'd just better stay here and not die, Smithy."

He kept smiling as if the whole thing increasingly amused him.

Thus it happened that when, towards twilight, the doctor revisited the Owl, striding into the lobby in an even greater hurry and temper than before, she met him there with answers rehearsed and ready.

"Well, young lady, I've made arrangements about that man. The Melbury Hospital will send an ambulance this evening."

"But he's gone!"

"WHAT?"

She repeated: "He's gone."

The doctor flushed and seemed on the verge of an outburst, then suddenly began to cough. She thought he looked rather ill himself. When he could regain breath he said more quietly: "You'd better do some explaining. Where has he gone? How did he get away?"

She offered him a chair. "Maybe he wasn't so ill. Perhaps he was just drunk, as you said."

"Nonsense! He's a shell-shock case, if you know what that is—has delusions that people are against him. Men like that can be dangerous— might have a crazy fit or something." He began to cough again. "Now come on, don't waste any more of my time. Tell me where he is."

She was facing him steadily when all at once his coughing became worse; he struggled with it for a while and then gasped: "Where's Briggs? Let me talk to HIM about this."

"He's out."

129

"Well, I'll call again later when I've finished my round." He seemed to have a renewal of both energy and anger as he stalked out of the room, for he shouted from the doorway: "It's all a pack of lies you've been telling —I know that much!"

But he did not call back later when he had finished his round. In fact he never did finish his round. He collapsed over the wheel of his car half an hour later, summoning just enough final strength to pull up by the roadside. It was a lonely road and they did not find him till he was dead. The flu of 1918 was like that.

Later in the evening a military ambulance drove up to the Owl and drove away again after a few minutes. The Biffer was emphatic in his assurance that there must have been some mistake—nobody on his premises was ill. But he called the driver and the two attendants into the private bar and hospitably stood them drinks.

The flu had other victims: Biffer Briggs himself, Frank the bar-tender, Annie the maid; they recovered. But an old man named Tom who for decades had odd-jobbed in the Owl garden died quietly, like ten millions more throughout Europe; indeed the war during all its years had not taken so many. But because the larger claims were made without horror they were surrendered without concern, and the Owl was far less perturbed when three-fourths of its occupants were ill and near to death than on a night some months before when a German air raider had dropped a solitary bomb in a meadow miles away.

Meanwhile Lloyd George was organizing his khaki election; the world grew loud with promises; the ex-Kaiser was to be hanged; the losers must pay the whole cost of the war; the armies of the victors were all to come home and find work waiting for them; the new world was to be one of peace and plenty for Englishmen. Among all the promises a few things were real and immediate: a vote for the women, and gratuities to the men as they put off their uniforms—sums in cash that ranged from the field-marshal's fortune to the private soldier's pittance. The morning these were announced Paula took the newspaper upstairs along with the breakfast tray, but said nothing till she was holding a thermometer to the light. "Well, Smithy, you're down to nearly normal, so I reckon I can tell you the other good news—the government owes you some money." She read him the details and added: "So stop worrying—you'll be able to pay for everything soon."

"But in the meantime?"

"NOW what's bothering you?"

"I hate to seem inquisitive, but—I mean—you—you probably aren't so well off as—as to be able to afford—to help me—"

"Darling, I'm not well off at all, but helping you isn't bankrupting me, either. And why should you hate to seem inquisitive?"

She sat on the bed waving the thermometer happily. "I'm afraid you're too much of a gentleman, old boy. After all, you don't know WHAT you are, do you? Maybe you're a lord or an earl or something. Can't you remember going to Eton? You talked a good bit lately while you were in a delirium, but it was all war stuff—not very helpful. You've been pretty bad, incidentally —know that? This morning's the first time you've dropped

130

below a hundred." She poured out a cup of tea. "All the others caught it too— good job _I_ didn't."

"You've been living here?"

"Living and life-saving. The flu closed the theatre so I'd have had nothing else to do, anyway."

"I still don't see how you can afford to help me like this."

"Darling, I'll let you into a secret—I'm not paying for your room, but if it makes you feel better, you can turn over anything you like as soon as the government gives you the money."

"That's another trouble. I can't be demobilized till I'm officially discharged from hospital."

"Well, hurry up and get better, then they'll discharge you quick enough."

"But—in the meantime—don't you see?—I can't HIDE —like this—in somebody else's house!"

"But you don't have to hide. I've talked to the Biffer about you already."

"You mean he knows I'm here—and where I come from?"

"Yes, and he doesn't mind. Doesn't give a damn, in fact. I knew I could fix it."

"But—why does he think you're doing all this for me?"

"Well, why do YOU think I am?" She laughed. "It's just a hobby of mine. Now listen to this—it's the Biffer's idea, not mine. He says for the time being—when you've got over this flu and are strong enough —why don't you do a bit in the garden same as old Tom used to? If you LIKE, that is. Might be good for you to have a quiet job in the fresh air —you wouldn't have to talk to people much. And it's lovely here when the summer comes."

Something flicked against his memory. "You said that once before."

"Did I?"

"The night we came here—as we walked through the garden in the fog. You said—'It's lovely here when the summer comes.'"

"Well, it certainly is, but I don't remember saying it. And you're the one who's supposed to forget things!"

"That's why I'm always trying to remember them—things that have happened before."

The Biffer's not minding was a mild way of expressing his willingness to co-operate. He was, in truth, delighted to join in any outwitting of authority, which he visualized as the same malign power that had placed so many restrictions on his wartime management of the Owl. Jovial, obese, and somewhat thick-witted after the hundreds of collisions his skull had withstood in years gone by, he remained the product of an early education that had taught him to read printed words with difficulty and to believe them with ease; so

131

that he did indeed believe the things he could read with least difficulty—which included the sporting pages of the daily papers, Old Moore's predictions, and "powerful articles" by the more down-writing journalists of the day. He had a few fierce hatreds (for such things as red tape, government interference, and Mrs. Grundy) and a few equally fierce affections, such as for Horatio Bottomley, "good old Teddy" (meaning the late King Edward the Seventh), and Oxford in the Boat Race. He took pride in the oft-repeated claim that "there ain't a more gentlemanly House than the Owl in all London," and that it should shelter a victim of the things he most hated added zest to a naturally generous impulse. "Pack of Burercratic busybodies," he exclaimed, during his first meeting with the victim. "Just let 'em come 'ere, that's all. I've still got strength to give 'em what I gave the Gunner!" What he had given the Gunner (at Shoreditch on May 17, 1902) was a straight left in the fourteenth round—this being the peak of his career, and one which, in money and fame, he had never afterwards approached. But he had bought the Owl with the money, and the fame, carefully husbanded too, had survived pretty well within a ten-mile radius of his own brass-bound beer engines.

So Smith began to work in the garden of the Owl; and in the meantime President Wilson crossed the Atlantic to be cheered as a new Messiah in the streets of London, Rome, and Paris; English, French, and American troops held the Rhine bridgeheads; the first trains crept again through the defiles of the Brenner; and in the great cities of central and eastern Europe revolution and famine stalked together.

It was the Biffer's second-favourite boast that from the garden of the Owl you could see "the Palace" on a clear day—the Alexandra Palace, that was, seven miles west across the Lea Valley; in the other direction the trees of Epping Forest made a darkly etched panorama that grew brown, and then suddenly green, as spring advanced. There was only preparatory gardening to be done until that time, but then the grass grew long in a single week and a line of daffodils flowered in every window-box. Hardly anyone visited the garden during the daytime, and by evening, when a few already preferred to take their drinks out of doors, Smith was in bed and asleep, except on Sundays, when Paula would generally pay a visit if her show were playing in or near London.

Of course he knew she didn't come to see him only, but chiefly the Biffer and the crowd in the bar, who all seemed to be her friends and greeted her with vociferous cordiality; naturally she spent a good deal of the time with them, and it wasn't easy to get away for a solitary chat with a semi-invalid. She managed it, though, as a rule, meeting him in the garden and walking with him along the Forest paths as far as the big beech trees. He enjoyed such walks, because it was dark and he still shrank from meeting people; but he also shrank from the thought that he might be dragging her away from much livelier company in the bar. He tried to tell her this.

"Don't you worry, Smithy. I won't let you bore me."

"But you have such a good time with the crowd."

"I know—that's because I like people. Can't help it. But don't think so little of yourself —you're included. Gives me plenty of fun to see you getting better like this, week by week."

"Yes, I think I AM getting better."

"You only THINK you are?"

"I still don't like to talk to people, though." He tried to explain. "It isn't so much fear of them as a sort of uneasiness—as if I really oughtn't to be alive, and everybody knows it and wonders why I still am. I know that's foolish, but it isn't enough to know—I've got to FEEL, before I can free myself."

"You will, Smithy. You'll suddenly feel you're free as air one of these days."

"If I do, I'll have you to thank—chiefly. You've given me so much of your time."

"Oh God, don't start being grateful. Listen, I'll tell you something. If you oughtn't to be here, neither should I, and I wouldn't be, but for luck. A house I was living in was hit by a bomb—I was asleep in one room and two people were killed in the next. I wasn't going to tell you that— thought it might upset you to be reminded of the war, but now maybe it'll cheer you up to think we're both like that. They did their best to finish us off, Smithy, but we managed to trick 'em somehow or other. That's the way to feel, and it's easier now the war's over and there's a future."

"I'd like to feel that, if I could."

"You will. You'll go on getting better, and then one night I'll see you in the front row of the stalls, watching the show."

"Yes, I'd like to see you act."

"Oh, don't come for that reason. I don't act—I'm just a comic."

"I WILL come, when I'm better."

"That's a promise, now!"

There wasn't only the question of his reluctance to meet strangers. Any prospective employer, no matter how sympathetic, would ask for details of his history, his army discharge papers and so on, and if it came out that he'd escaped from a mental hospital, the authorities would certainly send him back there, at least for tests and observation, and if he WERE sent back, even for a short time, he felt terribly certain he would get worse again. There was nothing for it but to stay where he was and be thankful for such a sanctuary; it was really an astounding piece of good fortune ever to have found it. So he stayed, pottering about the Owl garden and gradually returning to the world of ordinary awareness. There came a day when he could open a newspaper and face whatever catastrophe the turn of a page might reveal; another day when he could pick up an exciting novel without perilously identifying himself with one or other of the characters. He was recovering.

Sometimes while he was busy in the garden the landlord, puffing and sweating in his shirt-sleeves, would bring out a couple of pints of beer. He took a naïve, childlike interest in his protégé. "Easy does it, mate—don't work your head off. Seen the paper? They 'aven't 'anged the old Kaiser yet, but it looks like they'll do for this chap Landru — supposed to have murdered twenty women—what d'you think of that?"

Smith didn't have to answer much, because the Biffer was always glad to talk, especially about his favourite diversion, which was a word competition in a well-known weekly paper. He usually sent in several entries; they consisted of some supposedly apt comment on a selected phrase. The prize-winning comment generally had wit, or at least a double meaning; but the Biffer could never grasp that, and his hard-wrought efforts were invariably trite, and just as invariably failed to score. But every night in the private bar he would discuss them with his regular customers, and in the daytime he was glad enough to add the new gardener to his list of consultants. The latter, encouraged to take a rest from work and study the weekly contest, soon developed an inkling of what might stand a chance, and from time to time made suggestions that the Biffer dutifully incorporated into his own efforts. Suddenly one of them won a prize of a hundred pounds, and never since his epic fight with the Gunner had anything happened to give the Biffer a greater feeling of elation. His first response was to insist on an equal split, paid over there and then in five-pound notes, for he believed (more truly than he realized) that the gardener's emendation might have helped. But that was not all. In the Owl bar that same evening, under stress of many drinks and congratulations, he could not withhold credit as well as cash from his collaborator. "Quiet well-spoken sort of chap—stammers a bit—been shell-shocked in the war. Matter of fact, they 'ad 'im locked up in that big guv'ment hospital at Melbury till the poor chap got away. I reckon that's a fine joke on them guv'ment busybodies—a feller they make out is off 'is chump goes and thinks up something that wins a hundred quid!" And the more the Biffer contemplated this extremely ironic circumstance, the more he repeated and elaborated it over a period of several hours and before changing audiences.

A few evenings later Smith was tidying up in the greenhouse; but it was a Sunday and there had not been much to do. It was hardly time for Paula to come yet, even if she did come; he knew she was at Selchester that week —perhaps it was too far away. The uncertainty as to whether she would come or not made a curious little fret inside him; it didn't matter so much if she wasn't coming provided he hadn't looked forward to it in advance. That brought him to a realization of how much he did look forward to her visits. Of course, now that he was getting better he didn't expect to see her so much; she had been kind while he was ill, he mustn't trade on that. And another thing was curious —his memory of the night she had brought him to the Owl, every word she had said, little intimacies of physical presence, details that swung like lamps amidst the background of fever and delirium. He could hardly believe that certain things had happened at all, that she had so comforted him throughout that long night of Armistice. There had been no other nights like that, there never would be, neither in his life nor in the world's. He could not expect it; and it was natural that their relationship, begun in such a wild vacuum of despair and ecstasy, should by now have become a more normal one.

Suddenly the greenhouse door opened and she stood there in the sunlight, breathless. "Oh, Smithy, you've got to go—immediately! Drop those things and don't stay here a moment longer. I'll pack your bag—I'll find where everything is—meet me in the Forest by the beech trees in half an hour! But go NOW—don't waste any time—"

"But what's the matter? What on earth's happened?"

"Two men from Melbury Hospital talking to Biffer in the bar. They've come for you."

"For ME?" He stared at her, bewildered at first, then enraged and indignant. "They want to take me BACK? They STILL want to get me?"

She ran to him, holding him, trying to stop his cries. "Don't shout —and don't argue— just go as I tell you!" She pulled him out of the greenhouse and across the garden to the side gate. "Wait for me— you know where—I shan't be long."

They met again, under the trees. He was calmer; he had waited, smoking cigarettes and thinking things out. The day had been hot and pockets of warm air lingered amidst the fast-cooling shades. The Forest was very beautiful, and something in him was beginning to respond to beauty, as to anger and indignation also. He sprang to eagerness as he saw her approach, carrying bags and parcels. They stood still for a moment, while she regained her breath. "It's all right—nobody saw you—we're safe so far. The men have gone—the Biffer got mad and said he'd give 'em what he gave the Gunner." She laughed. "But of course that wouldn't help—they've got the law on their side—the law and the doctors... I didn't say much to Biffer. He means well, but as soon as he's had a few drinks he tells all he knows, which isn't much as a rule, but it's too much just now. So he'd better not know about us till he finds out."

"US?"

"Well, of course. We're going together, aren't we?"

"But how can—I mean—"

"Are you being the little gentleman again?"

"It's not that, but isn't it time—"

"Listen, Smithy, I'm only trying to help you—"

"I know that, but it's time I began helping myself."

"What a moment to think of it!"

"It isn't that I'm not grateful, but—"

"I know, you feel independent. Well, go on your own then, but where will it take you? You haven't an idea. One place is as good as another, what's wrong with Selchester then? I'm there for the week and after I've gone you can do as you like... You've got those ten fivers in your pocket, haven't you?"

"Yes."

"Then hand over half to me."

He did so, willingly and seriously; she took them with a laugh. "Thanks, Smithy—you'll feel better now."

They reached Selchester late at night, after a confused journey by various trains and buses; but all the way he had been aware of a barrier rising between them, so that at Selchester Station she summoned a cab and did not suggest that he accompany her. "You'll be all right, Smithy—the town's full of pubs and lodgings—I reckon you'd rather choose one yourself. I lodge with the company, of course. Well, good night— you're safe here if you look after yourself, and you will, won't you?" She leaned up and gave him a sudden kiss—the first she had ever given him, but he knew it meant less than her hand touch the first time they had met. "Good night, old boy," she repeated.

"Good night, Paula."

When her cab turned the corner and he was left alone with the crowd of strangers in the station yard, he felt suddenly, hopelessly lost. It was a sensation of sheer panic for the moment, but he conquered it—as if he had seen a loathed insect and shudderingly ground it with his heel. He walked into a near-by hotel and engaged a cheap room under the name of Smith. They gave him a very small attic with dormer windows and a view over the railway goods yard; throughout the night he kept waking up with a start whenever express trains screamed by, but somehow he did not mind that kind of panic; it was the inner kind that paralysed him—or rather, could not quite paralyse him any more, since he had fought it, alone and so terribly, after she had gone. How comforting, as well as fearful, that word ALONE was; he wanted aloneness, because it was the hardest training ground for the kind of strength he also wanted; and yet, once he had that strength, he knew he would not wish to be alone. And he knew, too, that his feeling for Paula was no longer an eagerness to submit, like a child; but something positive, strong enough to demand equality, if there were ever to be any further relationship between them at all. He knew there probably could not be. That warm outpouring pity had saved his life, but he could only keep his life from now on by refusing it. Lying awake that night in the Station Hotel, he made up his mind that he would not try to see her in Selchester that week; she would be busy, no doubt, with rehearsals and performances; and he, too, ought to be busy—looking for a job if the town offered any, and if not, deciding where else to go.

For five days he walked about Selchester alone. He visited the Cathedral, sat for hours in the Close under the trees, spent an afternoon in a very dull municipal museum, watched the trains in and out of the railway station, read the papers in the free library. None of these pursuits involved conversation, and—except to waitresses and the maid at the hotel—he did not utter a word for anyone to hear. Sometimes, however, during walks in the surrounding country, he talked to himself a little—not from eccentricity, but to reassure himself of the power of speech. There were a few factories also that he scouted around, wondering if he should ask for a job, but sooner or later he always found a door with a notice "No Hands Wanted." He knew that subconsciously he was glad, because he still feared the ordeal of cross- examination by strangers.

One rainy afternoon he sat in the refreshment room at the railway station, drinking a third cup of tea that he did not want and staring at an old magazine that he was not reading. Curious how one had to simulate some normal activity or purpose in life, even if one hadn't one, or especially if one had a secret one; in a town café he could not have stayed so long without attracting attention, but at the station it was merely supposed he was waiting for a train. Trains were things people waited hours for; one did not, unless one were peculiar, wait hours for a desire to clarify itself. But that was what HE was waiting for. It was Saturday; he had been in Selchester almost a week. He had a definite desire to go to the theatre and see the show, but he could not decide until he felt certain what his desire signified. If it were weakness, an urge to go back on his pledge to himself, he would not give way; he could endure plenty more of the aloneness, it would not break him. But, on the other hand, supposing it were not weakness but strength— supposing it meant that he could now walk into a theatre as normally as into a library or museum, could face the crowd and the lights and the excitement without a qualm?

He had walked past the theatre several times and had judged the kind of show it was from bills and photographs; nothing very uplifting, but probably good entertainment, and it would be interesting to see what she was capable of. Thus, he made his desire seem casual, normal, almost unimportant, until suddenly he decided he was strong and not weak enough to go. He got up and walked briskly to the counter to pay for the tea. "Gettin' tired of waitin'?" remarked the girl, with mild interest. "The Winton train's late today."

"Yes," he said, smiling. "I think I'll get a breath of fresh air."

He left the station and walked through the rain to the centre of the city, feeling more and more confident.

It was an odd thing, this loss of memory; he could not remember personal things about himself, yet he had a background of experience that gave him a certain maturity of judgment. He had probably been to many theatres before, just as he had probably been to schools and received a decent education. There were things he knew that he could only have picked up from school books, other things that he could only have learned from some forgotten event. It was as if his memory existed, but was submerged; as if he could lower a net and drag something up, but only blindfold, haphazardly, without the power of selection. He could not stare into the past; he could only grope. But by some kind of queer compensation, his eyes for the present were preternaturally bright; like a child's eyes, naïve, ingenuous, questioning.

In such a mood he sat in the third row at the first house of the Selchester Hippodrome that night and looked upon a show called Salute the Flag, described on the programme as "a stirring heart-gripping drama, pulsating with patriotism and lit by flashes of sparkling comedy." Actually it was a hangover from wartime, having begun in 1914 as a straight melodrama with no comedy at all, but with many rousing speeches that audiences in those days had liked to cheer. Then, as the war progressed and the popular mood changed from that of Rupert Brooke to that of Horatio Bottomley, the patriotic harangues were shortened to make room for the writing in of a comic part, which speedily became such a success that by 1918 the show had developed into a series of clowning episodes behind which the dramatic structure of what had once been a very bad play appeared only intermittently. Nobody knew the authorship of the original, or of any of the later accretions; successive actors had added a gag here and a gag there; every now and then the show became too long, and the parts left out were naturally those that elicited neither laughs nor cheers, no matter how essential they were to the original plot. But nobody minded that—least of all the audiences who paid their ninepences and shillings in the few remaining small-town English theatres that had so far escaped conversion into cinema houses. Salute the Flag had certainly helped to preserve the very existence of such a minority; it had also made a great deal of money for a great many people. Probably, in the aggregate, it had been more profitable than many a better-known and well-advertised West End success.

Smith found it endurable, even before the moment when Paula appeared. Her part in the play was trivial, that of an impudent girl at a hotel desk who got people's bedrooms mixed up, but in one of the other scenes she stepped out of the part for a few impersonations in front of the drop-curtain; he thought them pretty good, not from any definite competence to judge, but because of the warm vitality that came over the

137

footlights with them, her own rich personality, full of giving—even to a twice-nightly audience. Evidently the audience too were aware of this, for they cheered uproariously, despite the likelihood that few had seen the originals, which included Gerald du Maurier, Gladys Cooper, Mrs. Pat Campbell, and the ex-Kaiser. They cheered so much that she came on again to give an impression of a society woman telephoning her lover, all smiles and simperings, in the midst of grumbling at her maid, all scowls and snarls— a bit of broad unsubtle farce that demanded, however, a sure technique of changed accents and facial expressions. She did not appear again till the final scene in the last act, when the heroine, a nurse, unfolded a huge and rather dirty flag in front of her, and with the words "You kennot fahr on helpless womankind" defied the villain, who wore the uniform of a German army officer, until such time as the entire rest of the company rushed on to the stage to hustle him off under arrest and to bring down the curtain with the singing of a patriotic chorus. Smith was half-way down the aisle on his way out of the theatre when an usher touched him on the arm. "Excuse me, sir, one of the artists would like you to go behind, if you'd care to. She says you'd know who it was."

He hesitated a moment, then answered: "Why, of course."

"This way, sir."

He was led back towards the stage, stooping under the brass rail into the orchestra, stepping warily amidst music-stands and instruments, then stooping again to descend a narrow staircase leading under the stage into an arena of ropes and canvas. The usher piloted him beyond all this into a corridor lined by doors; on one of them he tapped. "The gentleman's here, miss." A moment's pause. "I expect she's dressing, sir—you'll excuse me, I've got to get back."

Again, after the usher had left him, he felt the beginnings of panic, but it was different now—an excitement that he fought only as much as he wanted to fight it. And the door opened before he could either yield or conquer to any extent.

"Oh, Smithy—Smithy—you kept your promise!"

She dragged him into the room with both hands and closed the door. It was a shabby little dressing-room, with one fierce light over a mirrored table littered with paints and cosmetics; playbills and an old calendar on the wall; clothes thrown across a chair; a mixture of smells— grease-paint, burnt hair, cigarettes, cheap perfume, lysol. She wore a dressing-gown over the skimpy costume in which she was soon to appear again.

"I didn't see you till the end—glad I didn't—I'd have been so excited I'd have ruined the show."

He said, smiling: "I enjoyed it very much—especially your part."

"Oh no, Smithy, you don't have to say things like that... Tell me how you are! Better, I can see—or you wouldn't be here. But what have you been doing with yourself all week?"

"Oh, just looking around. Have to find some sort of a job, you know."

"Any luck?"

"Not so far. I somehow don't feel Selchester's a very good place to try."

"We're going on to Rochby next week. More chance in a place like that, maybe."

"I daresay I'll get something somewhere."

"And you FEEL better?"

"Oh yes—fine."

The call-boy shouted through the door, "Five minutes, miss."

"That means I've only got five minutes." She paused, then laughed. "I do say intelligent things, don't I?"

He laughed also. "They keep you pretty busy—two shows a night."

"Yes, but this is Saturday, thank heaven. You'd be surprised what a rest Sunday is, even if you spend most of it in trains."

"You leave in the morning?"

"Ten o'clock."

"But it isn't far."

"About three hours. We have a long wait at Bletchley. Somehow that always happens. I seem to have spent days of my life waiting at Bletchley."

"I don't think I know Bletchley."

"Well, you haven't missed much. There's nothing outside the station except a pub that never seems to be open. Oh God, what are we talking about Bletchley for?... I've got some money of yours, you know that? Or did you forget?"

"No, but—"

"Well, I'd better give it back since I'm off in the morning." She began to fumble in her dress. "I carry it about with me—doesn't do to leave fivers lying loose."

"Oh, but you mustn't—"

"Well, you don't think I'm going to KEEP it, do you?"

"I—I—never thought about it, but—"

"DID you think I was going to keep it?"

"Well—I don't know—it would have been quite fair— after all, you'd done so much—"

"Listen, you little gentleman—I kept it because I thought I'd have to help you again, and I thought you'd feel better if I was spending your own money! But now you ARE better, thank God, and you don't need my help, so here you are!" She pushed the notes into his pocket. "I've got to go on again in two minutes, so don't make me angry! You'll need that cash if you're looking for a job... What sort are you looking for?"

"Any kind, really—"

"Outdoor or indoor?"

139

"I'm not particular about that, provided—well, you know some of the difficulties—"

"You're scared they'll ask you too many questions? What you'd really like is for someone to stop you in the street and say—'I don't know who you are, or what you've been, and I don't care either, but if you want a job, come with me.' Isn't that the idea?"

He laughed. "Yes, that's exactly the idea, if anyone would."

"You wouldn't mind what the job turned out to be, though?"

"I think I could do anything that I'd have even the faintest chance of getting."

"Figures? Keeping books?"

"Oh yes."

"A bit of talk now and again—even to strangers—in that charming way you have?"

"I wouldn't CHOOSE that sort of job, but of course—"

"You mean you're still bothered about meeting people?"

He hesitated. She went on: "Well, leave that out. What about a bit of carpentry mixed up with the bookkeeping?"

"Why carpentry?"

"Why not?... Back at the intelligent conversation, aren't we?" The call-boy knocked again. "Well... I suppose it's got to be good-bye till we meet again—unless you want to see the show through twice— you'd be a fool if you did."

"Perhaps I could meet you somewhere afterwards?"

"We always have supper together on Saturday nights—all the company, I mean—it's a sort of regular custom, wherever we are. Of course I could take you as my guest, but there'd be a crowd of strangers." Abruptly her manner changed. "Smithy, would you really come?"

"Do you WANT me to come?"

"_I_ wouldn't mind a bit, it's what YOU want that matters. You're free as air now— that's how you always hoped to be. And they can be a rowdy gang sometimes. So please yourself, I'm not inviting you anywhere any more... but if you ARE coming, say so now, then I can tell them."

He felt suddenly bold, challenging, almost truculent. "I'll come, and I don't care how rowdy they are."

She flashed him a smile as she slipped off the dressing-gown and put final touches to her make-up. "Number 19, Enderby Road—that's near the cattle market—about eleven-thirty. You don't need to hang around here for me—just go straight to the house at the time. I'll come sharp —ahead of the others. See you then."

The rain had stopped; he took a long walk in the washed evening air, then sat on a seat in the Cathedral Close and smoked cigarettes till the chime of eleven. He could not quell his nervousness at the thought of meeting so many strange people for the sort of evening party that was a weekly custom of theirs—that in itself made him an outsider. He half wished he hadn't said he would go, and it occurred to him that of course he didn't have to —if he failed to turn up, that would be the end of it. But the reflection, though tantalizing up to a point, had the stinging afterthought that he would then not see her again.

Enderby Road was a quiet cul-de-sac of Edwardian houses, most of them let to boarders; Number 19 looked no different from the others, but had a gas lamp outside the front gate. He waited there, watching for her after the Cathedral clock chimed the half-hour; it was comforting to reflect that nobody knew him yet—he was just an anonymous man standing under a lamp-post. Presently she turned the corner, her walk breaking into a scamper as she saw him. "On time, Smithy—I mean YOU are, I'M not. But I hurried to be ahead of the others—I didn't even stop to clean off the make-up."

She led him into the house. "Wait in the hall while I go up and finish."

He waited about ten minutes; the hall was dark and smelt of floor polish with an added flavour—which he took practically the entire time to detect—of pickled walnuts. Near him stood a bamboo hall-stand overloaded with hats and coats; the staircase disappeared upwards into the gloom with thin strips of brass outlining the ascent. Voices came from a downstairs room. He wondered what he should say if anyone came out of one of the rooms and accosted him, but when the thing happened it turned out to be no problem at all; the voices stopped, a thin old man with a high domed forehead suddenly emerged through one of the doors, collided with him, murmured "Pardon," and disappeared along the passage. After a moment, he returned, collided again, murmured "Pardon" again, and re-entered the room. Then the voices were resumed.

Soon after that she came down the stairs two at a time, to whisper excitedly: "Now I'm ready."

They entered the room, in which—despite the voices—there was only one person, the thin old dome-headed man; he was sitting at the dining-table with a large book open before him, propped against the cruet. The domed head rose over the book as from behind a rampart.

"Mr. Lanvin—this is Mr. Smith."

"A pleasure to meet you, my dear sir." He smiled, but did not offer to shake hands. Then he closed the book slowly, and Smith could see it was a Braille edition. Somehow that gave him peculiar confidence; Lanvin could not SEE him, could only judge him by his voice; so for the time being he had only one thing to concentrate on.

Lanvin was placing the book exactly in its place on a shelf; it was clear he knew by touch and feeling every inch of the geography of the room. "So you are to join the weekly celebration, Mr. Smith?"

"That seems to be the idea. I hope you don't mind."

"Mind? I'm a guest like yourself, though I've been one before. I warn you —they're a noisy lot—though no noisier than I used to be in my young days. If they weary you later on, come over and talk to me."

Smith said he certainly would, and Mr. Lanvin began to talk about Shakespeare. It seemed he had been reading The Merchant of Venice, taking the various parts in various voices. "I used to be quite a good Shylock, though I say it myself—and of course it's a fine acting part, and the trial scene has wonderful moments. But taking it all in all, you know, it's a bad play—a bad play. Why do they always choose it for school use? The pound of flesh—gruesome. The Jewish villain—disgustingly anti-Semitic. And a woman lawyer—stark feminism... Oh, a bad play, my dear sir. You're not a schoolmaster, by any chance?"

"I'm afraid not."

"Because if you were, I should like to... but never mind that. Since my eyes compelled me to retire from the stage I've spent a great deal of my time reading, and do you know, the Braille system gives one a really new insight into literature. You see, you can't skip —you have to read every word, and that gives you time to think for yourself, to criticize, to revalue —"

Meanwhile the door had reopened and a heavily built, red-faced, pouchy-eyed man stood in the entrance, waiting till he was quite sure he had been seen before stepping further into the room. Eventually he did so, exclaiming: "Paula, my angel, so THIS is the friend you spoke of?"

She completed the introduction; the red-faced man's name was Borley. He lost no time in dominating the scene. "Fine to have you with us, old chap." And then, dropping his voice to an almost secret parenthesis and leaning over the table with the gesture of one about to unveil something: "I don't know if you've ever noticed, but the food in English boarding-houses is always in inverse proportion to the size of the cruet. The larger the cruet, that is, the worse the food. Now this is a perfectly ENORMOUS cruet." He gave it a highly dramatic long-range scrutiny. "You'd think it ought to light up or play music or something—it's really more like a municipal bandstand than a receptacle for Mrs. Gregory's stale condiments."

Just late enough to miss these remarks the landlady entered with a trayful of small meat pies. Smith had to be introduced to her also, and it was Mr. Borley who made haste to do this. "Mrs. Gregory, I was just remarking on the quality of your food, and I perceive from yonder succulent morsels that all I have said will soon be amply demonstrated!" Whereupon Mr. Borley delivered a portentous wink all round the room while Mrs. Gregory bounced the tray on the table without much response. She looked so completely indifferent to the bogus compliment that Mr. Borley's joke was somewhat dulled. "Glad to serve you all," she muttered. "I do my best, as the saying goes—consequently is, I keep my reg'lars."

"You not only keep us, Mrs. Gregory, but WE keep YOU—and proud to do it!"

She shuffled out of the room, leaving Mr. Borley to proffer the dish of pies with an air of controlled distaste. "Well, the risk's yours, Smithy. Don't mind if I call you Smithy, do you? That's what SHE calls you."

Rather to his surprise, after all this, Smith found the pies excellent. He said so to Mr. Borley, adding that he was even hungry enough to have another.

"Right you are, then—and fortified by your example I'll even try one myself." Mr. Borley then began eating and hardly stopped throughout the entire rest of the evening. He added, with his mouth full: "But if you're a hungry man, God help you at Mrs. Beagle's!"

Smith did not see how the food at Mrs. Beagle's, whoever and wherever she was, could be any concern of his, but he had no time to explore the point because another member of the party had just arrived—a young man in tweeds, puffing at a pipe, almost like a magazine advertisement of either the tweeds or the pipe; he had a pink, over-handsome, rather weak face to which only premature dissipation had begun to lend some interest. Once again Mr. Borley officiated at the introduction, and while he was still performing two other persons entered, one a pale thin girl with a large nose and spotty complexion, the other an elderly silver-haired man of such profoundly sorrowful appearance that the beholder could not keep back a first response of sympathy. Mr. Borley had to summon all his technical powers to hold attention against such competition, but he did his best by shouting the further introductions.

The silver-haired man smiled and bowed, while the girl marched on Smith, delivered a crunching handshake, strode to the window, stared out for a moment as if deeply meditating, then swung round with husky intensity. "Oh, Mr. Smith, hasn't it been a wonderful day? I'm SURE you're a rain-lover like me!"

Smith felt somewhat cheered by a feeling that in this encounter all the others were standing round to see fair play, especially when the tweedy youth nudged him in the ribs. "Don't worry about her—she's always like that. Why Tommy married her nobody can imagine—not even Tommy any more... can you, Tommy?"

Here a sharp-nosed, jockey-sized man with bloodshot blue eyes and straw-coloured hair came across the room to be introduced, shook hands wordlessly and continued to do so while he glanced around with concentrated expressionlessness. Presently, turning his eyes on Smith, he whispered: "What made you first take an interest in slumming?" He went on, before Smith could think of any reply: "We're just a low vulgar crowd. Rogues and vagabonds, they called us in Shakespeare's time—am I right, Lanvin? We have no homes, we live in dingy lodging-houses in every middle-sized town in England, we know which landlady counts the potatoes, which theatre's full of fleas, and which has a roof that leaks on the stage when it rains. None of your high-class West End stuff for us—we lure the coppers, the orange peel, and the monkey-nuts, and we spend our one-day-a-week holiday chewing stale sandwiches in Sunday trains."

Mrs. Gregory then came in with what was evidently the main dish— quantities of fried fish, chip potatoes, and hot peas; meanwhile Mr. Borley had been out and now reappeared carrying a crate of bottled beer. The party began to find places at the table while the sorrowful-looking man, whose name was Margesson and whom one would have expected to speak like an archbishop, boomed across the table, quite unsorrowfully and with the zest and accent of an auctioneer: "Ladies and gentlemen, may I remind you that we shall soon be at the mercy of Mrs. Beagle." Here followed a chorus of groans and catcalls. "So I'm not going to keep you from the really serious business of the evening, which is to eat the last decent meal we shall have for a week. Before we begin, though, and speaking as the senior member of this company, —bar Lanvin, who's a permanent resident,—may I offer you a welcome, Mr. Smith, and beg you to take no further notice of that truncated nitwit Tommy Belden, nor of that moon-faced stew-pan, Richard Borley, nor of... " He had an insult for each of them, culminating in the arrival of a fat over-powdered woman with a large smile she bestowed upon everyone from the doorway, whereupon Margesson turned on her and exclaimed: "Now, Miss Donovan, you old bag of bones, don't stand there ogling the men—come and meet our guest, Mr. Smith, commonly called Smithy—"

And so it went on. Not till weeks later, when he had got to know them as human beings, did he realize that they had behaved with extra extravagance that evening in order to put him at his ease, and that the insults were a convention in which they took particular pride—the more horrific and ingenious, the warmer the note of friendliness indicated. A climax came when Margesson, at the end of dinner, rose to make an appeal on behalf of an actor whom they had formerly known and who had fallen on bad times. Margesson's speech began: "Ladies and gentlemen, if such there still are among this depraved and drink-sodden gathering—some of you, even in your cups, may remember Dickie Mason, one of the dirtiest dogs who ever trod the boards of a provincial hippodrome—"

The party lasted till after three in the morning, and was only then dissolved at the energetic request of Mrs. Gregory, who said the neighbours were being disturbed. Towards the end of it, Margesson took Smith aside and said: "Well? Can you stand us?"

Smith answered with a laugh: "I think so. I'm having quite a good time, anyhow."

"The train's at ten tomorrow morning."

"Yes, Paula told me."

"Some people sleep late, that's all."

That seemed another odd remark, but he didn't begin to grasp its significance till later on when several people shook hands or clapped him on the back with the remark: "See you tomorrow, Smithy."

Paula walked with him to the corner of the road. He said: "I'm really glad I came—they're a warm-hearted lot, and it's nice of them to expect me to see them off in the morning."

"I'd better tell you what else they expect. They think you're coming with us—to Rochby and all the other places."

"But—"

"Now don't begin to argue. Maybe I've bungled again—you've only got to say so, and the whole idea's dropped. But there's a job for you if you want it. In fact it's just about a hundred jobs rolled into one— you'll find that out, if you take it on, and if you don't like it or something better turns up, then you're free to go like a shot."

He said quietly: "What did you tell them about me?"

"Just part of the truth. I said you'd been ill, that you were better now, that you were a friend of mine, and that you wanted a job... But all that didn't get it for you—don't worry."

"What did, then?"

144

She laughed in his face. "I may as well go on telling the truth, even if you hate me for it. I think it was probably because they could all see you were such a gentleman."

Afterwards he realized the meaning behind the remark. The other members of the company were NOT gentlemen, nor ladies either, in the restricted sense of the word. They could act the part, successfully—even terrifically; no duke or baronet ever wore an opera cloak or swung a gold-knobbed cane with such superb nonchalance as Mr. Borley—indeed, it is extremely probable that many a duke and baronet never possessed an opera cloak, or swung a gold-knobbed cane at all. And that, of course, was the point. The gentlemen in Salute the Flag lived up to the ninepenny-seat idea of gentlemen; they were much realer than the real thing. So also in speech and accent nobody could approach Paula for aristocratic hauteur: when, in her impersonation of a duchess, she exclaimed to a footman, "Do my bidding, idiot!" the blue blood became almost as translucent in her veins as in those of Mr. Borley when the latter addressed the German officer—"You contemptible hound—you unmitigated cur—you spawn of a degenerate autocracy!"

In private life, so far as members of a second-rate touring company could enjoy any, they tended to keep up the manners and moods of their professional parts, combining them with a loud geniality expressed by a profusion of "old boys" and hearty back-slappings; yet behind all that they well knew the difference between the real and the too real, and how the same difference was apt to be recognized by others. Hence the usefulness of Smith. He had a way with him, despite—or perhaps BECAUSE of—his shyness, diffidence, embarrassments, hesitations. Where Mr. Borley's loud and overconfident "Trust me till the end of the week, old chap" failed to impress a country tradesman, Smith could enter a shop where he wasn't known and ask for what he wanted to be sent to his hotel without even mentioning payment. And where even Mr. Margesson could not, with all his sorrowful glances, persuade a small-town editor to print as news a column of disguised and badly composed puffery, Smith could rewrite the stuff and have the newspapers eager for it.

No doubt it was for somewhat similar reasons that Nicholas Nickleby became a success with the company of Vincent Crummles—except, of course, that Nicholas graduated as an actor. Smith did not aspire to that, but he speedily became almost everything else—advance press agent, scene-painter, bookkeeper, copy-writer, toucher-up of scenes that were either too long or too short or not wholly successful, general handy man, odd-jobber, negotiator, public representative, and private adviser. He was always busy, yet never hurried; always pleasant, yet never effusive; always reserved, yet never disdainful. In short, a perfect gentleman.

There certainly could not have been devised a more likely cure for all that remained of his mental and temperamental difficulties. The constant meetings with strangers, the continual handling of new problems and thinking out of extempore solutions, the travelling from one town to another, the settlement in new lodgings—all combined to break down the pathological part of his shyness; yet shyness still remained, and with it there developed an almost ascetic enjoyment of certain things—of rainy hours on railway platforms with nothing to do but watch the manoeuvres of shunting in a goods yard, of reading the numbers on houses in a strange town late at night, knowing that one of them hid a passing and unimportant destiny. His work also brought him into contact with average citizens of these many provincial towns—the barber, the tobacconist, the stationmaster, the shopkeepers who were given a couple of free seats in exchange for a playbill exhibited in their windows, the parson who sometimes preached a sermon attacking the show as indecent (good publicity if you could get it), sometimes the parson who came himself with his wife and children, but most often the parson who neither attacked nor patronized, but just passed by in the street with a preoccupied air, recognizing the smartly dressed strangers as "theatricals" and therefore in some vaguely opposite but no longer warring camp. One of these clerics, with whom Smith got into conversation, commented that the Church and the theatre were now potential allies, being both sufferers from the same public indifference—"Your leaky roof and my leaky roof are the price paid for the new cathedrals of Mammon." Whereupon he pointed across the street to a new cinema advertising a film which, so it turned out after further conversation, they had both of them recently enjoyed.

Smith saw a good deal of Paula during these busy days and even busier evenings, but somehow their relationship did not seem to progress to anything warmer or more intimate. Outwardly he became just as friendly with a few of the others, especially with young Ponderby, the tweedy youth, whom he grew to like. Ponderby was not much of an actor; his job depended entirely on the possessing of astoundingly conventional good looks. In Salute the Flag all he had was a couple of lines; he rushed into the general's headquarters with the cry, "The enemy are attacking! Give the order to advance!"—whereupon the general, who was a spy in disguise, was supposed to look sinister while Ponderby backed towards the door, delivering his second line as an exit: "Or if you don't, sir, then, by heaven, I will myself!" This was designed to bring a round of applause, and by careful attention to timing and movement Ponderby usually got one. Margesson, who managed the company, was very strict about everyone getting his "round." There was a technique about such things: you stood in the doorway, hand on the door-knob, staring hard and throwing your voice up to the farthest corner of the gallery—if the "round" didn't come, or came too sluggishly, you rattled the door-knob and repeated the final line with greater emphasis.

One Saturday, in the town of Fulverton, Ponderby spent the morning drinking in an attempt to destroy the effect of too much drinking the night before; by mid-afternoon, when he and Smith happened to be alone together in the lodging-house, it was clear that he could perform in the evening only with extreme hazard, if at all. He had done this sort of thing several times before, so Smith neither believed nor disbelieved a story of bad news from home; but he felt some sympathy for the youth, especially as he knew this latest offence would probably cost him his job. Ponderby knew this too, and as the hour approached for the first show he took quantities of aspirin and pick-me-ups, all of which only added to his symptoms of physical illness. By six o'clock he was begging Smith to take over his part, as the only way by which Margesson might be placated; after all, provided the show wasn't interfered with, Margesson might not care—the part was so small, and the clothes would fit too. Smith was reluctant to agree; he didn't feel he would be any good as an actor, even in the least possible part; but then Ponderby wasn't good either, so that argument didn't carry far. And it was undoubtedly true that the part, though small, was structurally important, so that a last-minute cut would be extremely awkward; and Saturday, also, was the best night for Fulverton audiences.

Everything forced him to an eventual consent, subject to Margesson's approval; but he still did not like the idea.

He went to the theatre earlier than usual and found Margesson in the midst of some trouble with scene-shifters; when he said that Ponderby was ill and he himself could take his part, Margesson merely answered in a hurry: "Had too much to drink again, I suppose... All right then—mind you get your round."

He did not have any chance to tell Paula about it, but the news that he was taking Ponderby's part caused little surprise; he was such a handy man, and the part was only two lines—there seemed nothing very remarkable about the arrangement.

He was a trifle nervous as he changed into the uniform of a British second lieutenant, but not more so than he often was at times when people would never guess it. Quite a natural nervousness too; he knew that many actors and public speakers were always like that, it was really abnormal not to be. Something in the look of himself in the mirror struck a half-heard chord in his submerged memory; he did not come on till the middle of the last act, so he had time to smoke cigarettes and try to catch the chord again, but that was stupid; the more he stared at himself in the mirror, the less he could remember anything at all. Then suddenly, with a frightening stab of panic, he asked himself what Ponderby's lines were—he had never thought of memorizing them, because he assumed he knew them so well; he practically knew the whole show by heart, for that matter— they all did. But now, when he sought to speak them to himself, what the devil were they? He tried to visualize that part of the play: the general at his desk, twirling his moustaches and muttering "Hein" under his breath—that was to show he was a spy in disguise; then Ponderby rushing in—"The enemy are attacking! Give the order to advance!" Now why should a second lieutenant tell a general what to do? Never mind— that was part of the play. Anyhow, Ponderby backed across the stage—not too quick, though —give the general time to give some more twirls and look suspicious; then on the exit—"Or if you don't, sir, then, by heaven, I will myself!" That was it; and wait for the round... He said it all over again to himself: "The enemy are attacking—give the order to advance— or, if you don't, sir, then, by heaven, I will myself!" Twenty words— the smallest part in the show. Saying them over a third time, he heard the call-boy's "Ready, sir."

He went out into the wings, standing where he could see the general at his desk. The general (little Tommy made up with comic moustaches) was rifling drawers with a terrific amount of noise (exactly as a spy wouldn't do), glancing through piles of paper in search of a stolen treaty—even if it were there, he was going through them so fast that he couldn't possibly find it; but that again had to be done or nobody would get the point— anything else was what Margesson called "this damsilly West End pansy-stuff where you come on the stage and light a cigarette with your back to the audience and call it acting." Smith stood there, waiting for the cue, which was the word "Hein." He felt a little queer; he was going to do something he had never done before; it would be awful if he did it badly, or didn't get his round; the only comfort was that Ponderby did it pretty badly himself.

Suddenly he heard the general say "Hein." It electrified him, like a word spoken inside his own head; he felt his feet as items of luggage that didn't belong to him as he marshalled them for the forward rush. His first impression was of a dazzling brilliance and of the curious fact that there was no audience at all; then, as he stared to verify this, faces swam out of the darkness towards him: row upon row, stalls, boxes, circle, balcony, all were returning his stare from tens of thousands of eyes—quizzically, he thought at first, as if they were aware that this was the supreme moment of all drama and were anxious to compare his performance with previous ones by Irving, Coquelin, and Forbes-Robertson... but then, with a flash of uneasiness, he saw malevolence too, as if they hated him for not being Irving, even for not being Ponderby. He knew he had to conquer this uneasiness or it would conquer him, just as he knew he had to rush up to the general's desk and say "The enemy are attacking—give the order to advance!" He saw Tommy eyeing him watchfully—that was part of the play, but Tommy's eye held an extra watchfulness, as if he were hating him too—for not being somebody else.

And then a very dreadful thing happened; he began to stammer. It was the old, the tragic stammer—the one that made his face twist and twitch as if he were in a dentist's chair; he stood there, facing the general, facing the audience, facing God, it almost seemed, and all he could do was wrestle with the words until they came, one after the other, each one fighting to the last.

The audience began to titter, and when he crossed the stage to struggle with the rest of the words they were already yelling with laughter. "Or if y-y-you d-d-don't, sir, then, b-b-by G-g-god, I w-w-will m-m-myself!" The laughter rose to a shriek as he still stood there, waiting, trembling, with lips curving grotesquely and hand fumbling at the door; and when he finally rattled at the knob till it broke off and rolled across the stage into the footlights, the whole house burst into hilarious shouting while the lads in the gallery stamped their feet and whistled through two fingers for over a minute.

He got his "round" all right.

He left the stage in a daze, somehow finding himself in the wings, passing faces he knew without a word, yet noting for agonized recollection later that some looked anxious, others puzzled, a few were actually convulsed with laughter. Alone at last in the dressing-room he closed the door, locked it, and for several minutes fought down an ancient resurrected hell of fear, mental darkness, and humiliation. Several knocks came at the door, but he did not answer them. Later, when the wave had passed over and he knew he was not drowned but merely swimming exhausted in an angry sea, he summoned enough energy to change his clothes. By that time the play had reached the final scene in which all the company would later be on the stage—he waited for the cue, "You cannot fire on helpless womankind," followed by the cheers and rough-and-tumble of the rescue party. Back-stage would be deserted now; he unlocked his way into the corridor and escaped through the stage door into an alley by the side of the fire staircase. As he turned the corner he could see a long queue already forming for the second performance, which reminded him that Ponderby's part must be played by someone else in that; Margesson would have to arrange it; anyhow, that was a trifle to worry about, a mere pinhole of trouble compared with the abyss of despair that he himself was facing.

Of course he must leave; they would not wish him to stay; he could offer no explanation, because there was none that would not repeat his humiliation a hundredfold.

Hurrying across Fulverton that night, across the brightly lit Market Street full of shoppers, through the side roads where happy people lived, it seemed to him that someone was always following, footsteps that hastened under dark trees and dodged to avoid street-lamps; an illusion, perhaps, but one that stirred the nag and throb of countless remembered symptoms, till it was not so much the ignominy of what had happened that weighed him down as the awareness of how thinly the skin had grown across the scar, of how near his mind still was to the chaos from which it had barely emerged. He hurried on—eager to pack his bag and be off, away from Fulverton and the troubled self he hoped to leave by the same act of movement; for surely place and self had some deep association, so that he could not now think of Melbury without... and then the renascent fear in his soul took shape; they were STILL trying to get him back to Melbury—they had been trying all the time, while he, falsely confident during those few weeks of respite, had gone about with an increasing boldness until that very night of self-betrayal. And such stupid, unnecessary self-betrayal before a thousand onlookers, among whom was one, perhaps, who did not laugh, but rose from his seat and quietly left the theatre, taking his stand on the pavement where he could watch every exit... Suddenly Smith began to run. They should not get him—never again. He stopped abruptly in the next patch of darkness, and surely enough the footsteps that had been following at a scamper then also stopped abruptly. He ran on again, dodging traffic at a corner and almost colliding with several passers-by. It was man to man, as yet—the enemy were attacking, give the order to advance! He turned into the short cut that led directly to his lodgings—a paved passage-way under a railway viaduct. Then he saw there was a rope stretched across the entrance and a man standing in front of it.

"Sorry, sir—can't get by this way tonight."

"But—I—what's the idea? Why not?"

"Can't be helped, sir—it's the law—one day a year we have to keep it closed, otherwise the railway company loses title."

"But I must go—I'm in a hurry!"

"Now come on, sir, I'm only doing my duty—don't give me no trouble —"

Suddenly he realized that there was more than one enemy; this man was another; there were thousands of them, everywhere; they probably had the district surrounded already...

"Come along, sir, act peaceable—"

"PEACEABLE? Then why are you carrying that gun?"

"GUN? Why, you're off your chump—I've got no gun! D'you mean this pipe?"

But he wasn't taken in by that, any more than by the nonsense about the railway company and its title; he jumped the rope, hurling the fellow aside, and ran along the passage-way; in a couple of minutes he had reached the lodging-house, whereas it would have taken ten by the road.

He had hoped to have the place to himself, knowing that on Saturday nights most landladies did their week-end shopping. But he had forgotten Ponderby, who shouted a slurred greeting from the sitting-room as he passed by to climb the stairs. "Hello, Smithy—get along all right? Knew you would —nothing to it—damn nice of you, though, to help me out..."

He heard Ponderby staggering into the lobby and beginning to follow him upstairs, but the youth was very drunk and made long pauses at each step, continuing to shout meanwhile: "Was Margie wild? I'll bet he would have been but for you. Why don't you come down and have a drink with me—you deserve it... Friend indeed and a friend in need—that's what you are —no, I'M the friend in need and YOU'RE the... oh, well, never could understand the thing properly. What're you doing up there? Not going to bed yet surely? What time is it? Maybe I'D better go to bed, then they'll all know I've been ill... What's that? Can't hear what you say..."

Smith repeated: "No, don't come up, I'm coming down."

"All right, Smithy—I'll go down too and get you a little drink. Must have a little drink —you deserve it."

By this time Smith had packed; he was naturally a tidy person, and having to do so regularly had made him expert and the job almost automatic. As he descended the stairs he felt calmer, readier to do battle with the forces arrayed against him; and that made him feel a little warm towards the weak healthy boy who never did battle at all, but just drank and debauched himself in a bored, zestless way. He turned into the sitting-room, where Ponderby lay sprawled again on the sofa, head buried in the cushions.

"Hello, old boy—was just mixing you a drink when this awful headache came on again. Don't mind me—sit down and give me all the news."

Smith did not sit down, but he took the tumbler, which was almost half full of neat whiskey, poured most of it back into the bottle, and sipped the remainder. He did not usually drink, but he hoped now it might help to steady his nerves, might give him greater calmness for the journey, wherever that was to be.

"Tell me all the news, Smithy. Don't mind me—I've got an awful head, but I'm listening."

Smith said there was no particular news to tell.

"Oh, I don't mean the theatre—damn the theatre—I mean NEWS. Heard the paper-boy in the street an hour ago—shouting something—went out and bought one—there it is— couldn't read it, though—my eyes gave out on me. What's been happening in the world?"

Smith stooped to pick up the paper with momentary excitement; was it possible that already... no, of course not—an hour ago was actually before the thing happened, apart from the time it would take to make a report and get it printed. He glanced at the headlines. "Seems those two fellows have flown across the Atlantic—Alcock and Brown."

"Flown across the Atlantic? That's a damn silly thing to do—but I'll tell you what, it's better than being an actor. Well, drink a toast to 'em, old boy—what d'you say their names are?"

"Alcock and Brown."

"Alcock, Brown, Smith, and Ponderby—drink to the lot of us. Sounds like a lawyer's office—that's the job I used to have—in a lawyer's office. Damn good lawyers, too—wouldn't touch anything dirty. That's why they got so they wouldn't touch me. Rude health like mine in a lawyer's office—out of place, old boy—sheer bad taste —frightens the clients. So one fine day I did a skedaddle from all that messuage. Know what a messuage is? Lawyer's word..."

Smith said he must go, if Ponderby would excuse him.

"GO? Not yet, surely—wait till the others come—don't like to be left alone, Smithy."

"I'm sorry, but I really must go now."

Then Ponderby raised his head and stared.

"Right you are, then... but, good God, what's the matter? Been in a fight or something?"

"I've got to go. Good night, Ponderby."

"Nighty night, Smithy. And don't think I'll ever forget what you've done."

You won't and neither will anyone else, Smith reflected, picking up his bag and hat in the lobby and walking out of the house. Nobody saw him. The night was warm and dark. He wondered why Ponderby had asked if he had been in a fight, and at the first shop window he stopped and tried to catch his reflection in the glass. He smiled—he had forgotten to comb his hair; it showed even under his hat, rumpled as if—well, yes, as if he had been in a fight. That was easy to repair, since he carried a pocket comb, and at the same time he took out his handkerchief to wipe the perspiration from his forehead. Then he did more than smile, he actually laughed, because of the colour of the handkerchief afterwards. He had forgotten to clean off the makeup. All the way across Fulverton, then, he must have been looking like that—if anyone had seen him, but nobody had—until Ponderby. Oh yes, there was the man with the gun—but it had been very dark just there, under the viaduct. He wiped off the makeup and threw the handkerchief over a fence.

He knew they would go to Fulverton Station first of all, especially for the night train to London; but he was not such a fool as to do anything so obvious. There was a station about twelve miles away, on a different line —Crosby Magna it was called; if he walked throughout the night he would be near the place by dawn and could take the first train wherever it went. He did not feel particularly tired; the whiskey had fortified him, and a certain rising exultation as he left the outskirts of Fulverton kept him tramping at a steady three miles an hour. It must be just about the close of the second performance by now; they would be taking curtain calls, then chattering in the dressing-rooms, looking forward to the usual Saturday supper at the lodging-house. A decent crowd; he had been happy with them. He began to look back upon that life with a certain historic detachment; it was all over, and it would have had to be over soon, anyway, for a reason that now, for the first time, he admitted to himself. He had been growing too fond of that girl; gradually but insidiously the feeling had been growing in him, so that soon the only freedom he could have found would have been either away from her or with her altogether; it would soon have become impossible to keep on seeing her continually and

151

meaninglessly in trains, dining-rooms, theatre back-stages: impossible much longer to have suppressed the anxieties he had already begun to feel about all the chance contacts of their daily lives —whether she would be in or out at a certain hour, or would happen to sit next to him here or there, or who the man was who met and talked with her so long after the show. Such things had not mattered to him at first, partly because he had been so humble about himself—why should she bother about him at all, what had he to offer? She loved life, she loved people —be honest about it, she loved men. He had even, at first, experienced a sardonic pleasure in seeing her warm to the chance encounters that fill the spare moments of stage life—his look, as he said good-night to her when he was going home to bed and she to a party somewhere, had often contained the message—Have a good time, you've done all you can for me, the rest I must do myself; so thank you again and good luck.

That was his message to her now, as he walked from Fulverton to Crosby Magna and heard the chime of midnight from a distant clock. But he knew that it could not have been so had he stayed with the company, so that actually his leaving was well timed, an escape from bondage that would soon have become intolerable.

He reached Crosby Magna towards dawn—a small deserted country station on a single line. There was a time-table pasted up from which he discovered that the first train was a local to Fellingham at ten minutes past five. He had over an hour to wait, and spent it leaning against his bag on the station platform. He felt rather drowsy; it was pleasant to rest there, with the sunrise on his face. Presently he realized that a man was staring down at him.

"Waiting for the train, sir?"

"Yes."

"It's due in now. I'll get you a ticket. Where to, sir?"

"Er... Fellingham... single..."

He dragged himself to his feet and followed the man into the small booking-hall.

"Fellingham, there you are, sir. Not travelling with the company this time?"

"WHAT?"

"Couldn't help recognizing you, sir—I was at the theatre in Fulverton last night. Very funny indeed you was, sir—funniest bit in the whole show. Well, here's your train, sir."

He insisted on carrying Smith's bag and choosing a compartment for him, though the train was practically empty. It was, indeed, one of those trains that seem to exist for no reason at all except to wander through the English countryside at hours when no one wants to travel, stopping here and there at places where no one could possibly have any business, especially on a Sunday morning, and all with an air of utter vagrancy, like that of cattle browsing or a woman polishing her nails—a halt here for several minutes, then an interval of movement, even a burst of speed, then a slow-down to hardly a pace at all, and so on. Fellingham was only forty-odd miles from Crosby Magna, but the journey, according to the time-table, would take over two hours. But it was pleasant enough to look out of the window on field and farmstead in the early morning, the lonely roads disappearing into a hazy distance, a stop for the guard to throw out a parcel to a man who stood by a crossing gate waiting for it, long manoeuvres of shunting in and out of sidings to detach various empty wagons. No sound when the train stopped save that of the brakes creaking off the wheels and the breeze rippling the grasses in near-by fields. Whenever he put his head out of the window at a station, another head, red-haired and a boy's, was leaning out three coaches in front, and this somehow began to suggest that he and the boy were alone on the train—final survivors of something or else first pioneers of something else.

Presently the horizon began to show a long, low-lying cloud, but a few further miles revealed it as a line of hills—rather high hills, they looked, but he knew they could not be, because there were no high hills in that part of England.

Of course he would not go all the way to Fellingham; that would make the trail too easy, especially after the porter at Crosby Magna had recognized him—unfortunate, that had been. He would get out at some intermediate station and make his way elsewhere across country.

The train had stopped again by the time the hills became clear—a station called Worling. He thought this would do as well as any other, and was just about to jump down to the platform when his bag flew open, spilling some of the contents on to the compartment floor; by the time he had them repacked the train was off again. But it did not really matter; one place was as good as another.

The train cantered on, like horses now more than cattle, steadily, at a good pace, as if anxious to reach some friendly stable; the track wound more closely into the uplands and soon entered a long shallow valley under a ridge that rose rather steeply at one point into two rounded summits; you could not tell which was the higher, but neither was very high—maybe seven or eight hundred feet, with a saucer-shaped hollow between. Just under the hill the roofs of a village showed amongst the trees, but the train turned capriciously away from it, choosing to stop at a station called Rolyott that was nothing but a shed in the middle of fields. He got out there, handing his ticket to the solitary porter, who stared at it for a moment and then said something about Fellingham being three stations further on; Smith smiled and said that was all right, and as the train moved off again the red-headed boy who was always looking out of the window saw him smiling and smiled back. That made him feel suddenly cheerful. And besides, the air was warm, blended with scents of hay and flowers, and the tree-hidden village looked tempting even at the end of a long road; he set out, walking briskly. A few hundred yards from the station, withdrawn into a hedge so that no one could see it save by search or chance, a broken signpost pointed to the ground, and he had to climb through nettles to decipher its stained and weather-worn letters: "To Beachings Over, 1 Mile."

He walked on, murmuring the name to himself, as he always did with names — Beachings Over, Beachings Over; and then Beachings Over came into view—a group of gray old cottages fronting a stream over which slabs of stone made bridges. There was a square-towered church as well, a public-house called for some undiscoverable reason the "Reindeer"—a ledge in the stream where the water sparkled as it curled over green reeds. And beyond the village rose the sunlit ridge—one hill now quite clearly higher than the other, but only a little higher, and between them that gentle turfy hollow.

153

He crossed one of the stone bridges. A man coming out of a house stared with friendly curiosity and said "Good morning." A fluff of wind blew a line of hollyhocks towards him. An old man was clipping a yew hedge along the vicarage wall. A sheep-dog stirred in the shade and opened a cautious eye as he passed. He felt: This is home; if they will let me stay here, I shall be at peace. He turned off the road by a path towards an open field that climbed steeply. Near at hand was a cottage, with a buxom elderly woman tending the garden. "There'll be a nice view from the top this morning," she said knowingly as he came near. "Five counties they say you can see, on a clear day." He smiled and then she said: "Leave your bag here if you like— it'll be quite safe."

"Good idea... Thanks very much. And could I—perhaps— trouble you for a glass of water?"

"Water if you like, sir, but cider if you prefer."

"Well, yes, indeed, if it's no trouble."

"No trouble at all, sir—I'll just have to go round to the stillage."

"STILLAGE?"

"That's where we keep it, sir, being that cool off the stone, you'll be surprised."

She came back with a pint-sized mug, which he drained gratefully.

"Glad you're enjoying it, sir—it's good cider, that I do say, though I brewed it myself."

He wondered if he should offer to pay her, but she saw his look of hesitation and added with swift tact: "Don't you worry, sir—you're very welcome. Maybe when you've climbed up and down again you'll feel like some cold beef and pickles and a nice raspberry tart—we serve meals, you know, all day on Sundays."

"You get many visitors?"

"Hardly a one, but we're ready for 'em if they come. Gentleman once told me this was the prettiest village in all England."

"Certainly it might be... Well, thank you again—perhaps I will want that meal."

He resumed the climb, feeling glowingly free after the drink and without his bag. The sky was dappled with clouds like sails, the smell of earth and grass rose in a hot sweetness. He walked steadily, stopping only to look back when a chime floated upwards from the church tower; Beachings Over, its gardens and roofs, lay in the fold of the valley as if planted there. He climbed on till the ridge was close at hand, beyond the next field and the next stone wall, the two hills curving against the sky. After a little time he reached the saddle between, and there, hidden till the last moment, lay a pool of blue water, blown into ripples under passing cloud shadows. It looked so cool he took his clothes off and bathed—there in sight of all the five counties, so it amused him to think. Then he lay in the sun till he was dry, feeling the warmth of sun and cider soaking into every nerve. Presently he dressed, found a shady spot under a tree, and closed his eyes.

The sun on his face woke him; it had moved round the sky but was near the horizon and no longer hot. His glance followed the curve of the hill and came to rest on the already graying pool; he was surprised to see a girl there, perched on a jutting rock and paddling her feet. He watched her for a moment, quietly fitting the picture into his mind before recognition came, and with it a curious mounting anger because he suddenly knew why it was he had grown so desperately in love with her; it was because she had made him so, because she followed him about everywhere, because, from the moment of their first meeting, she had never let him go—despite all acting and casual behaviour and false appearances. And she had followed him even to Beachings Over.

Aware that he was watching her, she turned and then came towards him, high-stepping barefoot over the grass.

"Smithy—you're really awake? Why did you run off like that? Were you ill? What's been the matter?... The woman at the cottage said you were here—said you'd left your bag, so you'd have to come down, but I didn't want to wait, and yet I have waited—hours—while you've been asleep..."

"I'm—I'm—sorry."

"For keeping me waiting? It's MY fault—I could have wakened you any time, but you looked so tired and you hadn't shaved—I guessed you'd been out all night somewhere."

"But I'm so terribly sorry—no, not for that—for what happened before then—at the theatre—"

"Oh, THAT? Darling, you shouldn't ever have taken it on, but it didn't matter—got the biggest laugh in the whole show—Margie even said he'd change the part if Ponderby could do it that way, but he was afraid he couldn't. Anyhow, he's going to keep in the bit where the door-knob comes off—that's good for a laugh any time."

"But do they think I did it DELIBERATELY?"

"I told them you did—I swore you fixed the whole thing with Ponderby just for a gag; Ponderby said you had too, I made him—they all thought it was marvellous, but then they think you ARE marvellous, anyhow."

"MARVELLOUS?"

"Well, you know—unpredictable. One of those shy ones who suddenly blaze out and startle everybody and then go shy again. What'll you do next? Maybe fly the Atlantic like those two fellows. Maybe murder somebody or elope with a duchess. It's all part of being a gentleman. You're privileged— like the boys on Boat Race Night."

"Paula—why do you talk like that?"

"Well, it's true, isn't it?" She bent over him. "There's such an indefinable je ne sais quoi about you, darling."

"What did you follow me here for?"

"To bring you back, of course."

"But I'm not coming back."

"Oh, it's only Sunday evening—there's no show-till six tomorrow night in Polesby—you don't have to make up your mind till tomorrow afternoon."

"I'm not coming back. I CAN'T go back. Don't you realize how I felt —"

"I know—don't try to tell me—I saw you on the stage and I was the only person who knew for certain you weren't acting—because I'd seen you like that before, in the shop at Melbury. Remember?"

He said grimly: "It wouldn't be very easy to forget—any more than last night."

"Except that you're not BOUND to go on the stage, ever again, so what does it matter? Whereas at Melbury you were like that all the time—except with me."

"Yes, except with you."

"Maybe there's something about me too—so far as you're concerned."

He moved restlessly. "There was something then, but there's a barrier between us now, compared with how we were in those days."

"There's only this between us, Smithy—I remember when you needed me, and I'm sure I'm not going to hang around when you don't need me any more. But I thought you might need me today—that's why I'm here."

"_I_ feel just the opposite—you were so generous when I DID need you I've hated to feel you could still do things out of pity as you're doing now."

"That's not just the opposite—it's the same."

"It's why I've kept away from you, anyhow, because I CAN do without you, I know I can, I MUST."

"Oh God, don't boast. I can do without you too, for that matter. Let's be independent as hell. Let's each fly in different directions and wonder why for the rest of our lives." She began to pull on her stockings. "Aren't you hungry?"

"Now you mention it."

"Let's go down. The woman at the cottage said she could give us— "

He interrupted, laughing: "I know. Cold beef and pickles and raspberry tart."

"I said we'd have it."

"You're right about that."

He helped her to her feet and they stared about them for a moment.

"Smithy, how DID you manage to find such a heavenly place?"

"As so many things happen—pure chance. My bag flew open as I was going to get out of the train somewhere else. How did you find I was here?"

"Darling, it was so EASY. I asked at Fulverton Station, and they said you hadn't been there, so of course I thought of Crosby Magna—"

"OF COURSE? Why of course?"

"Well, it was pretty obvious you'd think it WASN'T so obvious—and then the porter there remembered you, and the guard remembered you'd walked towards the village, and the woman at the cottage said you were up here staring at the five counties,—it IS five, isn't it?—everybody remembered you, old boy. You aren't terribly good at making people forget you."

"They certainly won't forget my performance last night."

"Back again on the same old subject? I told you they all thought it was marvellous."

"Then why did they think I didn't stay for the second show?"

"I told them it was because you suddenly got scared of how Margie would take it—I said it was just like you, to put on a gag like that and then get scared about it."

"Seems to me you thought of EVERYTHING."

They began the descent amidst the gathering twilight, striding down upon Beachings Over as from the sky. A curl of blue smoke rose from the huddle of roofs, the church bell was ringing for evening service. Something in the calm of that darkening panorama kept them silent till they were within sight of the cottage; then she said: "Oh, by the way —I told the woman you were my husband."

"Why?"

"Because she'd have thought it queer for me to be chasing up a hill after any man who wasn't."

"Is there anything ELSE you've told anybody about me?"

"There isn't yet, Smithy, but there might have to be. I'm always ready."

She took his arm as he unlatched the gate that led through an avenue of hollyhocks to the cottage. It was small and four-square, with windows on either side of the front door; at one side of the porch a board announced "Good Accommodation for Cyclists." The woman who had given him the cider led them smilingly into a room that opened off the flagged lobby; it was evidently the parlour, crowded with old-fashioned furniture, pictures, and photographs. A yellow piano with a fretwork front lined with faded silk occupied most of one wall; an oval mahogany table stood in the centre. The single window was tightly closed, yet the room smelt fresh and pleasant. He opened the piano and struck a few of the yellow keys; the strings twanged almost inaudibly. Inside the closed space of the room they felt embarrassed to begin a conversation, especially while the woman kept chattering in and out as she prepared the table. She told them her name was Mrs. Deventer and that her husband had been a sailor, so badly injured at Jutland, poor man, it was a mercy he died. "But there, there, that's all over now and never no more, as the saying is... You'll take some nice ripe tomatoes with your beef, perhaps, sir? And how about a drop of something to drink?—there's my own cider, but if you'd prefer anything else my girl can run over to the Reindeer and fetch it... 'Tain't far, you know—nothing's very far in the village—that's what I always feel when I go into Chelt'nam —that's our nearest town, you know—I go there oncet a year, or maybe twice

—it's a wonderful place, but my, it does so make you tired walking through all them streets—we ain't got only the one street here, and that's plenty when you're gettin' old..."

She talked and talked, bringing in everything she could think of till the table was crowded with tomatoes, lettuce, cheese, a huge loaf of bread, a pot of tea in case they wanted it, and a jar of chutney, her own special make. At length there could not possibly be anything else to bring in, and she left them reluctantly, with a slow smile from the doorway.

He said: "Well?"

"Well, Smithy?"

"You look thoughtful, that's all."

"Darling, I was just wondering what you had against me."

But the door opened again—Mrs. Deventer bringing in a lighted lamp. "I thought you'd maybe want it. Longest day of the year, round about, but it still gets dark... Maybe you'll be stayin' the night? You've missed the last train either way by now, I suppose you know that. Of course there's rooms at the Reindeer, but mine's as good, I always say, and cheaper too."

The yellow lamplight glowed between their faces after she had gone.

"Possessive woman," he remarked. "MY cider, MY girl, MY chutney, MY rooms."

"Room, she SAID. Didn't you see the notice outside—'Good Accommodation for Cyclists'? But I don't suppose one has to be a cyclist."

He said, after a pause: "I don't know why you should wonder about me like that. How could I have anything against you? Except for the same reason that I couldn't."

"Too subtle, darling, unless you tell me what the reason is."

"I love you."

Her voice leapt to the reply: "Smithy, you DO? You do REALLY? I've loved you ever since I first set eyes on you—as soon as I saw you in that shop I thought—there's my man. Because I'm possessive too—MY man, MY chutney, MY room—all mine." And suddenly she took his hand and leaned down with her cheek close to it. "I could have killed you, though, while you lay on top of that hill, fast asleep. KILLED you... Oh, God, I'm so happy... What's the name of this place?"

"Beachings Over."

"Beachings Over... I'll get US from THAT—for ever. Remember the game you used to play with names?"

Later, in a room so consecrated to cyclism that even the pictures were of groups of pioneer free-wheelers, he asked her if—when he had fully recovered—if he did fully recover, of course—and if he found a job that could support them both—if and when all those things happened—would she marry him?

158

She said she would, of course, but without the delay. "I think it's only two weeks they make you wait."

"But—" He seemed bewildered by her having stolen, as usual, the initiative. Then he said, slowly and with difficulty: "I'm not RIGHT yet. I'm not even as near to it as I thought I was. For half an hour last night I felt the return of everything bad again—black—terrifying. I'm better now, but less confident."

She said she didn't mind, she would look after him, because she had just as much confidence as ever.

"And there's another thing—"

"ANOTHER, Smithy?" She was trying to mock him out of his mood.

"Wouldn't they ask me a lot of questions at the registry office?"

"You mean questions about yourself that you couldn't answer?"

"Yes."

"They might ask you one question _I_ never have—and that is if you've been married before."

"Of course I haven't."

"How can you be certain, old boy, with that awful memory of yours?"

He pondered to himself—yes, how COULD he be certain? He hadn't any logical answer, and yet he felt fairly certain. When people had visited him in those hospitals, relatives of missing men who hoped he might turn out to be someone belonging to them, HE had similar hopes, but only of finding a home, parents—never a wife. Did that prove anything?

She watched the look on his face, then added with a laugh: "Don't worry —I'll take a chance on it if you will."

Eventually it was agreed that they should go to Polesby the next day, announce their plans to the company, and ask for a few weeks' holiday. She was sure Margesson would agree, if they approached him fairly and squarely; he liked both of them, and the slack season was on. They rose early and took a walk to the end of the village, discussing a future of which Beachings Over seemed already to have become a part. "Oh, Smithy, isn't it beautiful? I didn't see it like this yesterday—I was so worried about finding you —but it's just the sort of place I've always dreamed of. I know that's sentimental—but stage people are—they love the sweet little cottage idea, though most of them would be bored to death if they ever got one—mercifully they don't, as a rule—they either die in the poorhouse or save enough to buy a pub on the Brighton Road..."

She chattered on, and soon it was time to walk back to the cottage for Mrs. Deventer's excellent breakfast, pay their bill, and assure her they would return soon for a longer stay. The old lady was delighted, keeping up the farewell greetings all the way down the avenue of hollyhocks to the front gate. By the time they passed the post-office the morning papers were just being unloaded; Smith bought one and scanned the front page during the mile-long tramp to the railway station. Mostly about Brown and Alcock, he told her, summarizing the newly announced details of the first Atlantic flight in history. Not till they were settled in the train did she glance at the paper herself. Then, after a few moments' desultory reading, she looked up with a suddenly changed expression. "SMITHY!"

"What's the matter?"

"I don't want it to come as a shock to you, but there's something here that looks as if—" she hesitated and then gave a short laugh— "as if they can't come up to you... for being crazy."

"Who can't?"

"Brown and Alcock."

"But I don't know what you mean."

"Better read this—and don't let it upset you—probably it's not anything serious."

She handed him the paper, pointing to a small paragraph on an inside page. It was headed "Assault under Viaduct—Fulverton Man Injured," and ran: —

That he was assaulted by an unknown man was the story told to the Fulverton police last night by Thomas Atwill, railway policeman, who was found unconscious under the Marshall Street viaduct at a late hour. Taken to the Cottage Hospital, Atwill stated that he had been on plain-clothes duty to prevent pedestrians from using the footpath under the viaduct, it being necessary to do this for one day each year in order to preserve the company's legal title to the right of way. Shortly after nine o'clock a man endeavoured to break through the temporary barrier erected for this purpose, and when Atwill sought to remonstrate with him, he received a severe blow on the head. Describing his assailant as young, rather tall, and clean-shaven, Atwill said he was a gentleman, not a "rough." The police are investigating the unexplained disappearance of a member of a local theatrical touring company.

He put aside the paper, stared at her for a moment, then let his head fall slowly into his hands. When he looked up he was very pale. The train was stopping at Worling, where a crowd of farm workers waited on the platform. She had only time to say: "Darling, if anyone gets in, don't look like that."

Nobody got in, and his controlled features relaxed.

"Oh, Smithy... you don't remember?"

"I remember jumping over—it wasn't a barrier—just a rope. And if I hit the fellow, it was accidental—a push that made him fall, maybe with his head on the pavement—I didn't look back, I was running." He added, leaning forward with both hands on her knees: "I do want you to know that I'm not a homicidal maniac rushing about committing crimes and then forgetting about them. When I said that last night for half an hour I felt the return of all the bad things, I meant things in my own mind —fears that I had to fight down... but they were in my own mind, and I DID fight them down, I NEVER lost control. I want you to believe that— no matter who else disbelieves it."

"I believe it, Smithy. But there are—as you say—people who wouldn't."

160

"I know that."

"We mustn't go to Polesby."

"_I_ mustn't. YOU can. You're in no danger—on your own." He cried out, with sharp bitterness: "Perhaps you'll stay clear of me after this."

Ignoring that, she said: "Probably the man isn't seriously injured if he recovered consciousness so soon—"

"You don't need to comfort me."

"But it's true—the whole thing'll blow over if he's not badly hurt —and also if we don't go to Polesby. London's a better idea. If we change at Saxham we can get a London train from there. We'll find somewhere to stay—where no one will know who we are. London's the best place for that. We both have enough money to last for a time."

"But what about you—your job? They'll expect you at Polesby tonight. They'll know we're together."

"They'd be fools not to know that, anyway. I swore I'd never come back unless I brought you with me... Darling, don't look so anxious. _I_ believe you. This is just bad luck—it somehow doesn't count..." She took his troubled head in her arms and rocked it gently against her. "I can't help laughing, though, at one thing." She picked up the paper and re-read, crooningly, as to a child: "'Atwill said he was a gentleman, not a rough.' That's you all over, Smithy—I always said so."

They left the train at Saxham, but had just missed the best London train of the day; four hours to wait for the next. The interval was pleasantly spent in strolling about the ancient town. The second London train came in late, and they were told to change again at Santley Junction—"but it all helps," she said, "if anyone were trying to follow us." They reached Santley towards dusk and had to cross a platform crowded with waiting passengers. When the next train came in, also late, it was already so full that only tussling and scrimmaging could make further room; but eventually this was accomplished and they found themselves in a compartment occupied by an uncountable number of shouting children, all in nominal charge of an elderly, shabby, but bright-eyed clergyman who gestured apologies for his own inability to subdue the din. "It's been their great day," he explained, forcing a way for the newcomers. Then he helped them, quite unnecessarily, to put up their bags and parcels on the rack, adding with a smile: "Not hostile —only heedless." As soon as the train re-started the children shouted with renewed abandon, leaning out of the windows, jumping on the seats, breaking into song choruses that were taken up by other children in adjacent compartments until the whole train, nearing London, became one long pandemonium streaking through suburb after suburb, over bridges across blazing highways, through smoke-filled tunnels, past rows of back gardens from which shirt-sleeved householders watering their flowers looked up to wave good-humouredly, alongside commons where lovers did not stir as the sudden crescendo engulfed them. At short range, however, it was harder to ignore, a sheer wall of sound behind which three adults, lips to ear and then ear to lips, could only contrive an intermittent mouthing of words.

"It's their annual outing," said the parson, still feeling some need to apologize. "We aim at discipline but—" He gave a little wrinkled smile.

Smith nodded, and Paula, from the other side, whispered loudly in his ear: "If this bothers you, let's get out at the next station and find another compartment."

"No, no, it's all right."

And later, from the parson: "I hope you don't find their high spirits too exhausting."

"THEY don't, evidently," she answered.

"I know—amazing, isn't it? Don't believe I ever shouted like that when I was a boy. TERRIFIC!"

"Good thing you keep a sense of humour about it."

"Oh yes. I don't mind the row so much, but I'm scared when they lean out like that—I've warned them over and over again but I can't make them listen."

Smith suddenly intervened: "Do you think _I_ could? Perhaps coming from someone else—a stranger?... Now, boys, supposing you stand away from those windows!"

The different voice, pitched over the wall of sound, somehow reached its goal; the swarming clusters turned, sharply disconcerted, nonplussed, ready for rebellion but sensing control; then the different voice continued, releasing them a little: "That's right, sit down—plenty of room for all of us. What about another song?"

From further along the train came the chorus of "Keep the Home Fires Burning"; they joined in it, one by one, a gradual deafening surrender, while the stations flashed by more frequently and the suburbs merged into the slums. She whispered in his ear exultantly: "Smithy, how marvellous! And to think I was afraid they were bothering you!"

The parson was also pleased. "I really am extremely obliged to you, sir."

"Not at all."

"ASTONISHING!"

"Just as much to me, I assure you. I didn't know I could deal with 'em."

"You must have a knack... I haven't any—with children. You're going to London?"

"Yes."

"In a great hurry when you arrive?"

"Not particularly."

"I wonder whether you could spare, then—say five minutes? I always have trouble with them at railway stations, and the Mission's only across the street. If you would..."

"Certainly—if I can. The magic may not work the second time."

"Let's have faith that it will."

At the terminus it was as if the whole train burst open, a human explosion on to the platform, yells and bangings of doors while the parson watched Smith bring gradual order out of the chaos. Then began the slow marshalling of two hundred youngsters into line, their realization that a new personality was in command, and their acceptance of the inevitable—truculent at first, then indifferent, finally quite cheerful. But the operation took considerably more than five minutes; it was over a quarter of an hour before the children had all been escorted through the busy station precincts to a side street whence they could be safely dismissed to their homes.

The parson stood beaming on the pavement. "I really cannot express my gratitude. I hope you haven't been too much delayed."

"Oh no."

"You mean you had no plans for—the evening?"

"Well—er—nothing special."

"Then I wonder—if you REALLY have nothing else to do—it would give me great pleasure if you'd both dine with me—"

It was Paula who answered, in the instant way in which she decided everything: "Why, yes, we'd be glad."

The parson wrinkled another smile and began fumbling his way through a passage running by the side of the Mission building into an unkempt garden; beyond it stood a large ugly soot-black three-story house. He unlocked the front door, admitting them into a lofty hall-way totally unfurnished down to the bare boards of the floor. "I don't think names are at all important," he said, ushering them further into a room, "but mine is Blampied."

"Smith," said Paula.

He offered them chairs, following their glances round the room with a perverse pride. "Isn't this a terrible house? It was built in 1846, when parsons were supposed to live in style. Twenty rooms—I only use five. Kitchen, bathroom, bedroom, this, and my housekeeper's. This is the best. We live in squalor punctuated by small simple meals of excellent quality— onion soup tonight, if you happen to like it."

Meanwhile an elderly gaunt-faced woman was preparing the table, showing neither surprise nor any other emotion at the presence of guests, and needing no instructions from the parson. Presently the three were sitting down before big bowls of the soup; there was nothing else but cheese, he warned them, but they could have more soup if they wanted. It was so good that they did, and asked for it with enthusiasm. Meanwhile the parson chattered on, a cordial, increasingly inquisitive host.

"You two people have much further to go?"

Smith said: "No, not very far."

"You live here in London?"

"Er... yes."

"Don't let me keep you, but don't go till you want to."

She said: "Oh, there's plenty of time." It was as if she were reluctant to leave.

"Yes, the buses and trams run late. I expect you can get to your home that way."

"I—I think so."

"You only THINK so?"

"Matter of fact, we haven't got a home—yet. We've got to look for one."

Smith flashed her a warning glance, but she went on: "I don't suppose it'll be very hard."

The parson's curiosity seemed to become less rather than more as he responded: "If it's the slightest help to you, please stay here for the night. My housekeeper can find you bedding, and there are fifteen rooms to choose from."

"That's awfully kind of you, but—"

"Just as you please, of course. Only I thought your husband looked tired."

"He's not my husband—yet."

The parson smiled. "To be sure... but after all—fifteen rooms? Enough—one would think."

Then suddenly she said: "Maybe, as you've got a sense of humour, you can help us... We want to get married, but it has to be quiet—we don't want anyone to know—"

"Runaway?"

"Yes, that's it... maybe you know of a registry office somewhere near?"

"There's an office nearly across the street, but for sheer quietness, why don't you allow me to marry you in my own church? Hardly anyone ever comes to any of the services— it would be the most unnoticed marriage I could possibly imagine..."

So they were married at St. Clement's, Vale Street, London, N.W., and as they left the church after the ceremony newsboys were racing down the street offering extra editions —"Peace Treaty Signed at Versailles." It was June 28, 1919. The bridegroom bought one of the papers on his way with his bride to their home further along Vale Street—a tall Victorian house that possessed the initial advantage of being owned by a deaf old woman who lived in the basement and offered the higher floors for rent. She had agreed to let them have two big furnished rooms, plus bath and kitchenette, for a pound a week; there was also an oblong walled garden they could share with other tenants, but of course they never did. After several weeks of living in the house they still hadn't said more than "Good morning" and "Good evening" to the people who occupied the floors above and below; and an especially odd thing was that the man who lived above was a policeman.

But they were happy. It was strange, in a way; they had hardly any money and so far no jobs, and they were half scared of every knock on the door, because a daily visit to the newsroom of the free library revealed that the police were still probing what had already attained some small renown as "the Fulverton case." The victim was said to be

164

"still improving," but that began to seem almost ominous, since anything short of recovery showed how seriously he had been hurt; and one morning there was an even worse sound in the news item: "Hospital authorities at Fulverton report no change in the condition of Thomas Atwill, who is still suffering from head injuries as a result of an assault by an unknown man under a railway viaduct three weeks ago."

The unknown man felt sincere remorse over the fate of the innocent Atwill, but even that could not dim the joys of a partnership that was half fun, half fear, so that every falling asleep was like an unspoken prayer for safety and every waking up a miracle of survival. Sometimes they would hear the policeman clumping down the stairs and back again in his heavy boots, and she would run to the window to look out and come back saying—"It's all right, Smithy—it's there—go to sleep." That was a joke between them, because they had once agreed that nothing in the world could be more reassuring than a London policeman, half dressed, going downstairs at midnight to put out an empty milk-bottle on a front doorstep—a symbol that no harm would come, that God was somewhere over the policeman's roof and theirs.

They felt their chief danger might come from a chance recognition in the streets, and for this reason they avoided the better-known parts of London where country visitors might be expected to sight-see; they also kept indoors most of the day, discovering almost with surprise how quickly the time passed and how little the restrictions bothered them, provided they were together. They would do most of their shopping late at night, economy combining then with prudence, for just before closing time in those unfashionable districts the butcher and greengrocer and fishmonger would sell off cheap what was left of their day's supplies. While she was bargaining Smith would often stop to listen to some street-corner orator haranguing the multitude—the multitude consisting, as a rule, of a few apathetic onlookers, working-men with one hand round the bowl of a pipe and the other in a trouser pocket. "The typical English attitude," Blampied commented afterwards, "good-humoured, tolerant, vaguely sceptical— sceptical just as much of the truth as of lies. What a lot it will take to move men like that, but when they DO move—IF they ever move—what a cataclysm!"

They were beginning to feel a friendly intimacy with the parson, all the friendlier because his attitude was such a quaint mixture of particular inquisitiveness and general incuriosity. He could put the most intimate questions—once he asked: "Are you and your wife so united that you could use the same toothbrush?" Yet he never mentioned or fished for information about Smith's background or parentage, until one day, when they were having dinner with him as they had come to do rather often, he suddenly asked: "What shall I say if somebody traces you here and questions me about you?"

They stared at him with such disconcerted blankness that he added: "Didn't you say it was a runaway marriage?"

They knew him so well by then that they did not particularly mind having betrayed themselves by the startled stare; and the fact that his later remark gave them an easy cue for evasion tempted them all the more to tell him nothing but the truth. Paula looked across the table to Smith, caught and exchanged a glance, then began: "Yes, it was certainly runaway, but probably not the kind you're imagining. We aren't likely to be troubled by objecting parents. Mine are both dead, and his are..." She looked again at Smith.

Blampied nodded, as if satisfied, but Smith addressed him with a smile: "There wouldn't be much point in deceiving you, would there?"

"Depends what you want me to do. If you want me to lie about you to others, at least you must tell me the truth about yourself."

"That sounds a rather unusual standpoint—for a clergyman."

"Perhaps I'm a rather unusual clergyman."

"Well, here's an unusual story."

"Good... go ahead."

Smith then spoke briefly of his war injury and resultant lack of memory. He called it a LACK now, not LOSS—"because I don't FEEL any loss. It doesn't really bother me any more—there are days and nights when I never even think about it... but there it is, all the same. Perhaps I ought to have told you when you married us."

"Why?"

"Well, signing my name in the register. Smith may not be the true one."

The parson, sitting at the head of the table, half rose and extended his arms over their shoulders. "But it was YOU I married," he said, "not your names."

"So it doesn't matter?"

"Not a bit. And it's perfectly legal and binding. Is that all you have on your conscience?"

"Not quite all." Encouraged by a further look from Paula, Smith went on to relate the incongruous mishap to Thomas Atwill under the railway viaduct. Blampied listened with increasing interest; once or twice his face twisted into a smile; they were so accustomed to his taking the oddest possible view of things that it did not surprise, although it considerably relieved them when at the end of the recital he began to laugh. "It's the idea of a RAILWAY COMPANY having a right of way that tickles me! Know anything about rights of way?"

This seemed a side issue, but most of Blampied's conversations avoided anything in the direct line of argument. Smith said no, not very much.

"They're trying to close them all over England. You must come with me sometime on one of my crusades. I make a nuisance of myself on village greens every now and again —just by way of a holiday from London. I inform the villagers of their ancient heritage —the commons and the pastures and the paths across the fields that the landlords have stolen and will go on stealing, whenever they get the chance. A clerical predecessor of mine, John Ball by name, made a similar nuisance of himself six hundred years ago or thereabouts—but I think he must have been much more of an oratorical spellbinder." He added, coming back to the point, "So THAT'S why you two children are in hiding? You're afraid that if anything should happen to Thomas Atwill—"

"Oh, he'll get better all right," Paula intervened hastily, "but even when he does it could be troublesome if we were traced because—because —" She looked across the table, adding: "We've told you so much we may as well finish—don't you think so, Smithy?"

Smith said: "I mentioned that the war injury affected my memory. It also —at one time —had other effects. They sent me to Melbury —the big hospital for shell-shock cases. I was on their dangerous list."

"You mean liable to die?"

"Well, no—liable to live—but dangerously."

Again Blampied laughed. "I see. I really begin to see."

They both joined him in laughing, glad to ease their embarrassment by so doing. Then the parson came behind Smith, putting his arm affectionately round the young man's shoulders. "You needn't worry. The reputation of crank and misfit gives me a certain freedom of reply. If, for instance, I'm asked if I know anyone named Smith, and I say I never heard the name before, it'll merely give rise to an extra legend..."

The more they came to know Blampied the more they realized his remarkableness and the less they felt they completely understood him. At their first meeting in the train he had seemed just the timid, unworldly parson of fiction, almost of caricature, bearing his cross in the form of Mission boys he could not control and summer outings he must have loathed. Later he showed himself more perplexingly as a mixture of ascetic and gourmet —only onion soup for dinner, but how good it had to be. Later still, when he described "crusades" that had sometimes led to rough-and-tumble fights on village greens and once at least to his own imprisonment, he almost became the conventionally unconventional "fighting parson." And beyond that, but by no means finally, there was the visionary, the mystic. It was not easy to analyse or estimate the sum-total, and many persons with whom he came into contact had long since given up the task as either hopeless or unprofitable. But one could not meet and talk to him for ten minutes, in any one of his moods, without an impression of stature—mental, moral, psychic, or perhaps some blending of all three. And he had also (as Smith found out when he came to work for him) an astoundingly various collection of intimate friends.

Most of these friends lived abroad, so that occasions for personal meetings were rare; but he corresponded, regularly and voluminously, and it was this task that had lately made him aware of failing eyesight, and so of the need for someone to help him with it. Smith gladly volunteered, and it became a habit that two or three mornings a week Blampied would dictate slowly while the other took down in a longhand that soon developed into a private shorthand, marked by curious abbreviations and a general meaninglessness to the outsider. Afterwards, at his leisure, Smith would rewrite or type the letters in full. They went to most of the corners of the world—a hotelkeeper in Yokohama, a university professor in Idaho, a train conductor on the Orient Express, an Austrian soldier lying wounded in a hospital in Salzburg, an editor in Liverpool, a rubber planter in Johore, a woman head of an advertising agency in Brisbane... these were a few out of the twenty-odd. All, it appeared, were people whom Blampied had met at one time or another. "I used to travel a good deal, before the war put an end to it, and now, I fear, I have neither the zest nor the money to resume. But for a few shillings' worth of stamps each week, I can almost achieve the same object... This morning, for

167

instance, I shall write to M'sieur Gaston Auriac, Rue Henri Quatre, Antananarivo, Madagascar. We met only once—on a steamer between Capetown and Durban, but we talked for long enough to make the discovery of each other. Maybe you were surprised when I asked you whether you and Paula could use the same toothbrush? You see, I have never married, so I don't know whether physical oneness goes as far as that— but I do know that in the realm of mental and spiritual things there can be a similar oneness —the knowledge that yours and mine are no longer yours and mine, but OURS for every possible use. And this awareness, once acknowledged by both parties, lasts for ever. Gaston and I may disagree about this and that, but because our thought processes are in the same world, there's a sense in which we can use each other's minds. We're both impervious to sentimentality and mob optimism, and both of us also, if I may so express it, are accustomed to think proudly... We found that out during our three-hour talk seven years ago, and though we have never met since, we both know that it must still be true, despite all the changes that have taken place in the world about us... Just now, we're in the midst of an argument as to the right way to treat Germany now the war's over. Gaston thinks the Allied armies should have pushed on to Berlin, even at the cost of an extra year of fighting, and then have broken Germany into fragments, acting with ruthless severity on the lines of delenda est Carthago... I, on the other hand, would have offered terms of simply astounding generosity— lifting the blockade the day after the Armistice, forbearing to ask for meaningless and uncollectable reparations, and inviting all the defeated countries into an immediate conference on equal terms to discuss the disarmament and rehabilitation of Europe. As you can imagine, we're enjoying as violent a discussion as the somewhat intermittent mails to Madagascar will permit. But the point is: both of us are still thinking proudly. Gaston is no frenzied sadist wishing to destroy for the sake of destroying; I am no milk-and-water humanitarian yearning over a defeated enemy merely because he is defeated and has been an enemy. Both of us have the same aim in view —the cure of the thousand-year-old European disease; both methods have succeeded at various times throughout history —his, I admit, more often than mine. Either might succeed today. But what will NOT succeed, and what we both know will not succeed, is the unhappy mean between the two —the half-way compromise between sentiment and vengeance—the policy of SAFE men playing for SAFETY." He added, smiling: "So you see, Mr. Smith, why it did not shock me the other day to hear that you had been classed at one time as a dangerous man. All my friends are dangerous men."

Smith came to enjoy the work of transcribing these letters, and sometimes also he helped with Church and Mission activities, especially those for which Blampied had little ability, such as children's organizations. He found that his experience on the train had been no fluke, but the result of an apparently inborn aptitude for handling youngsters. Even the most stubborn, and from the worst slum homes, responded to his instinctive offering of ease and discipline; in fact it was the most stubborn who liked him and whom he liked the most. He began holding classes in the Mission building, classes that did not invade the religious field (which he did not feel either the inclination or the authority to enter), but touched it variously and from neglected angles—classes on civics, on local history, on London and English traditions. He was so happy over all this that it came to him with a sense of retrospective discovery that he must LIKE children—not sentimentally, but with a simple, almost casual affection. "You'd have made a good schoolmaster," Blampied once said, and then, when Smith replied he wasn't sure he'd care to spend all his time with children, the other added: "Exactly. Good schoolmasters don't. Anyhow, you can help to make up for the fact that I'm a bad parson."

"Do you really think you are?"

"Oh yes. Ask anybody round here. People don't take to me. I haven't an ounce of crowd magnetism. And then I'm lazy. Only physically, I think, but then that's the only kind of laziness most people recognize."

"I think you're old enough, if you don't mind my saying so, to be forgiven a certain amount of physical laziness."

"Yes, but I'm not lazy in the forgivable ways. If I went to Lord's to watch the cricket they'd think I was a sweet old clergyman who deserved his afternoon off, but as I'm only lazy enough sometimes to go without a shave —"

Smith laughed, knowing what he meant, for while it could not be said that the parson neglected his professional duties, it was certainly true that he made no effort to make himself either a worldly success or a beloved failure —the two classifications that claim a roughly equal number of adherents among the clergy. Nor, despite the fact that he inclined to High Church fashions, did he join the fanatical brotherhood of those who systematically disobey their bishops; his own disobediences were personal, casual, almost careless—wherefore his bishop disliked him all the more. So did various influential parishioners to whom he refused to toady; while the poor, to whom he also refused to toady, rewarded him with a vast but genial indifference. A few devoted lay workers ran the adjacent Mission, but they were not devoted to HIM, and when they pushed on him such tasks as the supervision of the annual outing it was with the knowledge and hope that he would have a bad time. Nor did they care for his church services, which they thought cold and formal; they realized, correctly, that he was not the kind of cleric to "drag the people in," and from time to time they plotted, more or less openly, to have him supplanted by some energetic slum parson who would unite both Church and Mission into a single buzzing hive. But it is by no means easy to dislodge a parson of the Church of England, and Blampied had suffered no more than a gradual reduction of dues and stipend during his twelve years of office.

He was, in fact, though he hardly realized it because his wants were so few, very close to the poverty line. He wore the shabbiest clothes; he lived on the simplest and cheapest of foods, though always well cooked; he paid cash to tradespeople, but owed large sums to local authorities for taxes and bills of various kinds. About a month after his first meeting with Smith, his housekeeper fell suddenly ill and died within a few days; he was a good deal upset by that, but admitted that it had saved him from having to get rid of her, since he could no longer afford the few weekly shillings for her part-time services. It was then he suggested to Smith and Paula that they should move into the house and live rent-free in return for similar help; they were glad to consent, since their own money was rapidly dwindling.

Out of the unused fifteen they chose two large attic rooms with a view over roof-tops northward as far as Hampstead and Highgate, and it was fun to begin buying the bare necessities of furniture and utensils, searching the Caledonian Market for broken-down chairs that could be repaired and re-upholstered, discarded shop fittings usable as bookshelves, an old school desk that showed mahogany under its coating of ink and dirt. Gradually the rooms became a home, and the entirely vacant floor beneath encouraged a kinship with roofs and sky rather than with the walls and pavements of the streets.

Towards the end of September Blampied received a quarterly payment which he chose to devote to a crusading holiday rather than to paying arrears of his borough council rates; having invited Smith and Paula to join the expedition, he took them for a week into rural Oxfordshire "making trouble wherever we go," as the parson put it, though that was an exaggeration. The question of country footpaths was, he admitted, his King Charles's Head —every man, he added, should have some small matter to which he attaches undue importance, always provided that he realizes the undueness. Realizing it all the time, Blampied would puzzle over ancient maps in bar parlours, inquiring from villagers whether it was still possible to make the diagonal way across the fields from Planter's End to Marsh Hollow, and generally receiving the answer that no one ever did —it was much quicker to go round by the road, and so on. "I reckon you could if you tried, mister, but you'd 'ave a rare time gettin' through them nettles." A few more pints of beer would perhaps elicit the information that "I remember when I was a kid I used to go to school that way, but 'twouldn't be no help now, not with the new school where it is." Yet those, as the parson emphasized, drinking his beer as copiously as the rest, were the paths their forefathers had trod, the secret short cuts across hill and valley, the ways by which the local man could escape or intercept while the armed stranger tramped along the high roads. All of which failed to carry much weight with the Oxfordshire men of 1919, many of whom, as armed strangers, had tramped the high roads of other countries. They obviously regarded the parson as an oddity, but being country people they knew that men, like trees and unlike suburban houses, were never exactly the same, and this idea of unsameness as the pattern of life meant that (as Blampied put it) they didn't think there was anything VERY odd in anyone being a LITTLE odd.

Several times the parson spoke on village greens to small, curious, unenthusiastic audiences, most of whom melted away when he suggested that there and then they should march over the ancient ground, breaking down any barriers that might have been erected during the past century or so; but in one village there was a more active response, due to the fact that the closing of a certain path had been recent and resented. It was then that Blampied showed a certain childlike pugnacity; he clearly derived enormous enjoyment from leading a crowd of perhaps fifty persons, many of them youngsters out for a lark, through Hilltop Farm and up Long Meadow to the gap in the hedge that was now laced with fresh barbed wire. Smith found he could best be useful in preventing the children from destroying crops or tearing their clothes; he thought the whole expedition a trifle silly but pleasingly novel. Actually this particular onslaught had quite an exciting finish; the owner of the property, a certain General Sir Richard Hawkesley Wych-Furlough, suddenly appeared on the scene, backed by a menacing array of servants and gamekeepers. Everything pointed to a battle, but all that finally developed was a long and wordy argument between the General and the parson, culminating in retirement by both sides and a final shout from the General: "What the hell's it got to do with YOU, anyway? You don't live here!"

"And that," as Blampied said afterwards, "from a man who used to be Governor of so many islands he could only visit a few of them once a year —so that any islander might

170

have met his administrative decisions with the same retort—'What's it got to do with YOU? You don't live here!'"

The notion continued to please him as he added: "I was a missionary on one of those islands—till I quarrelled with the bosses. I always quarrel with bosses..."

Gradually Smith and Paula began to piece together Blampied's history. Born of a wealthy family whom he had long ago given up no less emphatically than they had him, he had originally entered the Church as a respectable and sanctioned form of eccentricity for younger sons. Later, even more eccentrically and with a good deal more sincerity, he had served as a missionary in the South Seas until his employers discovered him to be not only heretical, but a bad compiler of reports. After that he had come home to edit a religious magazine, resigning only when plunging circulation led to its bankruptcy. For a time after that he had dabbled in politics, joining the early Fabians, with whom he never quarrelled at all, but from whom he became estranged by a widening gulf of mutual exasperation. "The truth is, Smith," he confessed, "I never could get along with all the Risers-to-Second-That and the On-a-Point-of-Orderers. If I were God, I'd say—Let there be Light. But as I'm not God, I'd rather spend my time plotting for Him in the dark than in holding committee meetings in a man-made blaze of publicity!"

He formed the habit of talking with the two of them for an hour or so most evenings, especially as summer lagged behind and coal began to burn in a million London grates. To roof-dwellers it was a rather dirty but strangely comforting transition—the touch of smoke-laden fog drifting up from the river, the smell of smouldering heaps in parks and gardens, the chill that seemed the perfect answer to a fire, as the fire was to the chill. For London, Blampied claimed, was of all cities in the world the most autumnal —its mellow brickwork harmonizing with fallen leaves and October sunsets, just as the etched grays of November composed themselves with the light and shade of Portland stone. There was a charm, a deathless charm, about a city whose inhabitants went about muttering, "The nights are drawing in," as if it were a spell to invoke the vast, sprawling creature-comfort of winter. Indeed no phrase, he once said, better expressed the feeling of curtained enclosure, of almost stupefying cosiness, that blankets London throughout the dark months—a sort of spiritual central heating, warm and sometimes weepy, but not depressing—a Dickensian, never a Proustian fug.

Those were the happy days when Smith began to write. As most real writers do, he wrote because he had something to say, not because of any specific ambition to be a writer. He turned out countless articles and sketches that gave him pleasure only because they contained a germ of what was in his mind; but he was never fully satisfied with them himself and consequently never more than slightly disappointed when editors promptly returned them. He did not grasp that, because he was a person of no importance, nobody wanted to read his opinions at all. Presently, by sheer accident, he wrote something that fitted a formula; it was promptly accepted and—even more important for him at the time—paid for.

After he had worked all morning he would often set out in the afternoon with Paula on a planless excursion decided by some chance-met bus; or sometimes they would tramp haphazardly first to the left, then to the right, mile after mile, searching for books or furniture in old, gas-lit shops, and returning late at night through the narrow defiles of

171

the City. They liked the City, the City with a capital C, and especially at dusk, when all the tea-shops filled with men, a curious democracy within a plutocracy— silk-hatted stockbrokers buying twopenny cups while at the same table two-pounds-a-week clerks drank similar cups and talked of wireless or motor bicycles or their suburban back gardens. And afterwards, as Paula took his arm on the pavement outside, they would be caught in the human current sweeping along Old Broad Street in a single eastward stream, then crossing Liverpool Street like a flood tide into the vast station delta. He loved to see those people, so purposeful and yet so gentle, so free and yet so disciplined, hurrying towards the little moving boxes that would carry them home to secret suburbs —secret because they were so unknown to one another, so that a bus shuttling all day between Putney and Homerton gave one a mystical curiosity about all the people in Homerton who had never seen Putney, and all the people in Putney for whom Homerton was as strange as —perhaps stranger than—Paris or New York. There was something fantastic, too, in that morning and evening migration, huger in man-miles than any movement of the hordes of Tamerlane, something that might well be incomprehensible to the urban masses of the future, schooled to garden cities and decentralization. But there could never be such romance as in the pull of steam through the Bishopsgate tunnels, or faces that stared in friendly indifference as trains raced parallel out of Waterloo.

He wrote of such things, and he wrote as he saw—a little naïvely, as if things had never been seen before—like the line drawings of a child, with something of the same piercing simplicity. It probably helped him, as Blampied said, to have forgotten so much about himself, because into that absence came an awareness far beyond the personal reach—the idea of the past as something to be apprehended in vision rather than explored in memory. He wrote, too, of the countryside as he had seen it: of the men in the pubs with their red faces shy over mugs of beer —old couples outside their cottages on summer evenings, silent and close, yet in that silence and closeness telling all there is in the world —a pedlar unlatching a gate with slow steps towards a lonely house — farm workers at midday, asleep under trees—a little road over the hill, curving here and there for no reason at all... scene after scene, as a child turns pages in a loved picture book, yet behind the apocalyptic wonderment of it all there was something to which talks with Blampied had added shape and quality—the vision of a new England rooted far back in the old, drawing its strength from a thousand years instead of its weaknesses from a hundred.

"Follow that vision," Blampied once said. "Follow it wherever it leads. Think it out. Write it down. I'd say PREACH it if the word hadn't been debased by so many of my own profession."

"I couldn't preach, anyhow. No more public appearances for me after the last one."

"But preaching doesn't need a pulpit. All it needs is what you have —a faith."

"Is yours the same faith?"

"You have your vision of England, I have mine of the world—but your England will fit into my world." He added, after a pause: "Does that sound arrogant? Maybe. We mustn't be afraid of a secret arrogance. After all, we are spies of God, mapping out territory lost to the enemy when faith was lost." His eyes twinkled as he touched his collar. "It isn't

THIS, you know, that makes me say so. Religion's only one of the things that can die without faith. Take another, for the sake of something you may feel I'm more impartial about—take the League of Nations. It's sickening now of that deadliest of modern diseases—popular approval without private faith; it will die because it demanded a crusade and we gave it a press campaign, because it's worth our passion and we deluge it with votes of confidence and acts of indifference. It might have sprung alive out of the soul of a saint; it could only be stillborn out of a clause in a treaty. It should have been preached until we were all aflame with it; instead of which it's been flattered and fawned upon till most of us are already bored with it. Sometimes I've even thought we should have given it ritual—a gesture to be made whenever the name's mentioned, like the sign of the Cross for the faithful, or—for the faithless—blowing out the match after the second man's cigarette." As if reminded by that he pulled out his pipe and began to fill it as he continued: "This is a good moment to say how much I hope you'll stay with me here—both of you. That is, if you're happy."

"We're very happy. But I have to think of how to make a living."

"Life's more important than a living. So many people who make a living are making death, not life. Don't ever join them. They're the grave-diggers of our civilization—the safe men, the compromisers, the money-makers, the muddlers-through. Politics is full of them, so is business, so is the Church. They're popular, successful—some of them work hard, others are slack, but all of them can tell a good story. Never were such charming grave-diggers in the world's history—and part of their charm is that they don't know what they are, just as they don't know what WE are, either. They set us down as cranks, oddities, social outsiders, harmless freaks who can't be lured by riches or placated by compliments. But a time may come when we, the dangerous men, shall either be killed or made kings—because a time may also come when it won't be enough to love England as a tired business man loves a nap after lunch. We may be called upon to love her as the Irish love Ireland—darkly, bitterly, and with a hatred for some who have loved her less and themselves more."

After another of their talks he told Smith of a friend of his in Liverpool, editor of a provincial paper with a small but influential circulation. Apparently Blampied, unknown to Smith, had sent some of his literary work for this man to see; and now had come a request to see not only more of the work, but the writer of it. "So I hope you'll pay him a visit, because whatever project he has in mind, or even if he hasn't one at all, I know you'll like him personally."

"Another dangerous man?" Smith queried.

Blampied nodded with an answering smile.

Smith was eager to go as soon as possible; after further communication an appointment was made for just after Christmas. Paula and he spent the intervening week in a glow of anticipation, culminating in a Christmas dinner in their own attic room, with Blampied as a guest. They decorated the place like children and found him like a third child in his own enjoyment of the meal and the occasion. Later in the evening he gave them, to their complete astonishment, an almost professional display of conjuring tricks; after which Paula offered some of her stage impersonations, including one of a very prim Victorian wife trying to convey to her equally prim Victorian husband the fact that she rather thought she was going to have a child. Towards midnight, when Blampied had drunk a last toast with them and gone down to his rooms below, they sat on the hearth-rug in the firelight happily reviewing the events of the evening, and presently Smith remarked that her impersonation of the Victorian wife was new to him—he didn't remember her ever doing it on the stage, but he thought it would have gone very well if she had.

"But it wasn't written then," she answered. "I write all my own sketches —I always did —and I wrote this one last night when you were downstairs talking to Blampied. I suppose it was on my mind—the subject, I mean—because I'm in the same position, except that I'm not going to be prim about it."

He took her into his arms quietly, sexlessly, as they sat before the fire. Those were the happy hours.

The next day, as if their happiness were not enough, Blampied brought them news of another kind. It was now many weeks since they had last seen any mention of the Fulverton case, and though they felt easier about it they still opened newspapers with a qualm. But that morning Blampied had been searching old papers for something he wished to trace and by sheer accident had come across something else. "It seems that your Thomas Atwill left hospital more than a month ago, and though of course that doesn't mean the case is closed, I daresay the news will be a load off your mind."

It so definitely was that the idea occurred to them to celebrate by doing things they had been nervous of for so long—a regular evening out. They asked Blampied to join them, but he excused himself on the score of work; before they left the house, however, he shook hands with Smith and wished him a pleasant trip, for it had been arranged that he should leave that night for Liverpool. Even though it would only be for a few days, the impending separation added spice to the evening. They went first to the Holborn Empire to see Little Tich, then for supper to an Italian restaurant in Soho. When they emerged, still with a couple of hours until train time, he saw a hansom cab swinging along Coventry Street, temptingly out of place on a cold December night, but for that very reason he waved to it, telling the man to take them anywhere, just for the ride. Under the windy sky the blaze of Christmas still sparkled in the shops as they drove away, jingling north and west along Regent Street, through Hanover Square and past Selfridge's to Baker Street, with ghosts of Londoners stepping out of their tall houses ("And if I mistake not, my dear Watson, here is our client just arriving"), bidding them godspeed into the future; and because they both had faith in that future they were drenched in a sort of wild ecstasy, and had the cabby drive them round and round Regent's Park while they talked and laughed and whistled to the parrots every time they passed the Zoo.

Those were the happy moments.

Later, on the platform at Euston, walking up and down beside the train, she said she wished she were going with him, though she knew they couldn't afford it, the little money he was beginning to make by writing wasn't nearly enough for such unnecessary jaunts. "I know that, darling, but I still wish I were going with you, and if you were just to say the word, like the crazy man you are, I'd rush to the booking-office and buy a ticket—which would be stupid. I don't really mean it, Smithy—I'm only joking, of course. But I'm part of you—I'll only be half alive while you're away— we belong to the same world, as Blampied says about his friends—"

"I know that too. There's something RIGHT about us—about our being together here. And Blampied wants us to stay."

"I'd like to stay too. I love that old ugly house."

"So do I. And d'you know, I don't WANT to remember anything now— anything I've ever forgotten. It would be so—so unimportant. My life began with you, and my future goes on with you—there's nothing else, Paula."

"Oh, what a lovely thing to tell me! And by the way, HE said he hoped you wouldn't remember."

"Blampied?"

"Yes. He's devoted to you."

"I should be proud to think so, because I'm equally devoted to him." He kissed her laughingly. "Must we spend these last few seconds talking of someone else?"

"But he isn't altogether someone else. He's part of us—part of our happiness—don't you feel that?"

"Darling, I do—and I also love you!"

"I love you too. ALWAYS."

"The whistle's going—I'd better get inside. Good-bye, Paula."

"Good-bye, old boy."

"That's the first time you've said 'old boy' for weeks!"

"I know, I'm dropping it. Now I'm not a touring-company actress I don't have to talk like one. I can impersonate anybody, you know—even the wife of a writer on a secret errand to an editor in Liverpool..." The train began to move. "Oh, DARLING—come back soon!"

"I will! Good-bye!"

He reached Liverpool in the early morning. It was raining, and in hurrying across a slippery street he stumbled and fell.

PART FIVE

Rainier began to tell me most of this during the drive back from Melbury that night; a few minor details, obtained afterwards from other sources, I have since fitted in. We drove to his Club, because Mrs. Rainier was at Stourton; after perfunctory greetings to a few members in the lobby he ordered drinks to be sent up to the suite he usually lived in when Kenmore was not in use.

He had talked rapidly during the car journey, but now, in quieter surroundings, he seemed to accept more calmly the fact that there was much to tell that he could at last quite easily recall. Once, when I thought he was growing tired and might remember more if he rested for a while, he brushed the suggestion aside. "You see, I want to tell you all I can in case I ever forget it again, and if I do, you must remind me—you MUST — understand?" I promised, and he continued: "Not that I think I shall— it's too clear in my mind ever to be lost again. I could find Blampied's old house in Vale Street now if I tried—Number 73, I think it was— or maybe 75—that much I HAVE forgotten, but I suppose I can't expect memory to come back without the normal wear-and-tear of years. Or can I? Has it been in a sort of cold storage, with every detail kept fresh?"

We laughed, glad of an excuse to do so, and I said it raised an interesting point which I wasn't expert enough to decide. He then resumed: "Because I actually FEEL as if it all happened only the other day, instead of twenty years ago. That house of Blampied's, for instance—it had four dreadful bay windows, one on each side of the front door and two others immediately above in the room that wasn't occupied—the attics hadn't got any bay windows. There was a pretty grim sort of basement, too, where the housekeeper lived—she didn't have to, she chose it because she was crazy enough to like it. She was a queer woman altogether—God knows where Blampied picked her up or how long she'd been with him, but he cried when she died, and looked after her cat—which was also a queer animal, an enormous tabby—spent most of its life sleeping, probably because of its weight—it had won a prize as the biggest cat north of the Thames." He added, smiling: "I daresay you think I'm inventing this —that there aren't prizes for big cats. But some newspaper ran a competition as a stunt—two first prizes, for North and South London —and Blampied's housekeeper's cat won one of them."

No, I thought—you're not inventing; you're just enjoying yourself rather indiscriminately, as a child frolics in the sand when he first reaches the seashore; I could see how, in the first flush of recollection, the mere placement of the past, the assembling of details one after the other, was giving him an intense pleasure, and one by no means discountenanced by his use of words like "grim" and "dreadful."

He went on like that for some time, going back over his story, picking out details here and there for random intricate examination; and carefully avoiding the issue that was foremost in my thoughts. Then, once again, I saw that we had talked till dawn and well past it, for there was already a pale edge to the window. I switched off his bedroom light and pulled the curtains; far below us the early morning trams were curving along the Embankment. We watched the scene for a moment; then he touched my arm affectionately. "Time for an adjournment, I think. I know what's in your mind, it's in mine, too, but it's too big to grasp—I'm collecting the small things first. You've been good to listen to me. What have we on Monday?"

My thoughts were so far away I could not give an immediate answer, though of course I knew. He laughed at my hesitation, saying he hoped I should not lose my memory just because he had regained his. By then I had remembered and could tell him: "Anglo-American Cement—ten-thirty at the Cannon Street Hotel." To which he replied, almost gaily: "The perfect closure to all our conversation..."

"Don't you want me for anything tomorrow?"

"No, I'll sleep most of the day... at least I hope so... Good night."

If this is a difficult story to tell, it may be pleaded in partial defence that the human mind is a difficult territory to explore, and that the world it inhabits does not always fit snugly into any other world. I must admit that I found the fitting a hard one as, some thirty-six hours later, I watched the sunlight stream through stained-glass windows to dazzle the faces of Anglo-American Cement shareholders. From the report afterwards sent out with the dividend I find that Rainier spoke as follows:—

"You will be glad to know that our sales have continued to increase throughout the year, after a somewhat slow beginning, and that prospects of continued improvement are encouraging. The government's national defence preparations during the September crisis of last year led to additional consumption of cement throughout the country, and this, at prices we were able to obtain, resulted in generally satisfactory business. During the year we opened a new plant at Nottingham which we expect to enhance production very considerably during the coming year. Your directors are constantly watchful for any opportunities of further economies, either by technical developments or by the absorption of competing companies, and with these aims in view, it is proposed, in addition to the usual dividend of 10 per cent, to issue new shares at forty-two shillings and sixpence in the proportion of one to five held by existing shareholders." (Loud applause.)

We had had no chance for private conversation on our way to the meeting, for the secretary of the company had driven with us; and afterwards there was a directors' hotel lunch that did not disperse until almost three o'clock. As I went to retrieve our hats at the cloak-room I overheard comments on how Rainier had been in grand form, looking so much better; wonderful year it had been; wonderful the way he'd pulled the Anglo-American out of its earlier doldrums—remember when the shares were down to five bob?—nice packet anyone could have made who'd helped himself in those days— well, maybe Rainier did, why not?—after all, he'd had faith in himself, faith in the business, faith in the country—that's what was wanted, pity more people didn't have it.

Later, as we were driving away, I repeated the compliments to Rainier, thinking they might please him. He shook his head sombrely. "Don't call it faith. I haven't had FAITH in anything for years. That artist fellow, Kitty's young man, told me that when he was drunk—and he was right. Faith is something deeper, more passionate, less derisive, more tranquil than anything I've ever felt in board-rooms and offices—that's why peace won't come to me now... God, I'm tired."

"Why don't you go home and rest?"

He stared at me ironically. "So simple, isn't it? Just go home and rest. Like a child... Or like an old man. The trouble is, I'm neither. Or else both." He suddenly patted my arm. "Sorry—don't take any notice of my bad temper."

"I don't think you're bad-tempered."

"By the way," he said smiling, "I've just thought of something— it's a queer coincidence, don't you think?—two of my best friends I first met quite accidentally on trains... Blampied and yourself..."

"I'm pleased you should class me with him."

"Why not? He talked to me—you listen to me—even when I want to talk all night. That's another thing I ought to apologize for— "

"Not at all—in fact if it helps you now to go on talking— to continue the recollections —"

"I don't think I've much more to say, unless there's anything you'd particularly like to know?"

There were many things I wanted to know, but for the present I felt I could only mention one of them. "Those articles you wrote, some of which were published—"

"Yes?"

"What papers did they appear in?"

"The Northern Evening Post took two or three—the worst. The others —don't know what happened to them. Maybe they fell in the gutter when the car hit me."

"You were carrying them—THEN?"

"Yes, I was on my way to see the editor."

"A pity you hadn't taken copies."

"It was before the days I bothered about carbon paper. You see, I never behaved like a full-dress author. I used Blampied's typewriter because he had one, but I didn't card-index anything or call the room where I worked a study or self-consciously burn any midnight oil. Matter of fact, I was in bed by ten on most nights, and I wrote if and when I felt like it. I never thought of the word 'inspiration' as having anything to do with me —it was a continual vision of life that mattered more than words in print, but if I did get into print I had more ambition to be alive for half a day in a local paper than to be embalmed for ever between covers on a library shelf."

"All the same, though, those articles might have been collected in book form."

"Blampied thought of that, and Paula and I once made a choice of what we thought were the best—but I wasn't very keen on the idea, and it certainly wasn't likely any publisher would have been either. I remember it chiefly because the evening we were choosing them Blampied came in and found us huddled together on the floor with the typed pages surrounding us. He asked, 'What are you two planning—the book or your future?'— and Paula laughed and answered 'Both.'"

We had entered Palace Yard, passing the saluting policeman and a swarm of newsboys carrying posters about Hitler. As we left the car a few seconds later Rainier added: "It's odd to reflect, isn't it, that at that very moment a few hundred miles away a man whom we had never heard of was also planning a book—and our future."

178

We crossed the pavement and entered the Gothic doorway; the House, as always, seemed restful, almost soporific, on a summer afternoon.

"And you've never written anything like those articles since?" I queried, after a pause.

"I've been too busy, Sir Hawk, as the lady called you, and possibly also my prose style isn't what it used to be. I did write one book, though— or perhaps Sherlock would have called it a monograph—the title was Constructive Monetary Policy and an International Cartel—I hope you've never heard of it."

I said I had not only heard of it but read it.

"Then I hope you didn't buy it when it first came out, because I came across it the other day on a barrow in the Farringdon Road, marked 'Choice' and going for fourpence."

I smiled, recognizing the familiar self-ridicule by which he worked himself out of his moods. We walked on through cool corridors to the Terrace and found a table. As nearly always, a breeze blew over the parapet, bringing tangs of the sea and of wharves, a London mixture that added the right flavour to tea and buttered toast and the special edition of the Evening Standard. More bother about Danzig; Hitler had made another speech. Some Members came along, stopped at our table to exchange a few words of greeting; one, of them, seeing the headlines, exclaimed: "Why don't they let him have it, then maybe we'll all get some peace?"—but another retorted indignantly: "My dear fellow, we CAN'T let him have any more, that's just the point, we've GOT to make a stand—eh, Rainier?" Rainier said: "We've got to have peace and we've got to make a stand—that's exactly the policy of the government." They passed on, uncertain whether he had been serious or cynical (and that uncertainty, now I come to think of it, was part of the reason why he hadn't climbed the higher rungs of the Parliamentary ladder).

He looked so suddenly exhausted after they had gone that I asked if he had been able to sleep at all during the previous day and night.

"Not much. A few hours yesterday morning after you left. The rest of the day I devoted to an investigation."

"Oh?"

"I went to Vale Street to look for Blampied's old house. It's disappeared —been pulled down to make room for one of those huge municipal housing schemes. All that part of London seems to be changed—and it's certainly no loss, except in memories. I couldn't even find anybody who REMEMBERED Blampied."

"That's not very surprising."

"Why not?" He stared at me sharply, then added: "D'you mean you don't believe he ever existed?"

"Oh, he existed all right. But he died such a long time ago."

"When?"

"In 1920."

"Good God! Within a year—of—of my—leaving— like that."

"Not only within a year. Within a month. JANUARY 1920."

"How do you know all this?"

"I also spent part of yesterday investigating. I searched the obituaries in newspaper files and found this." I handed him a sheet of paper on which I had copied out the following from the Daily Gazette of January 17, 1920: —

We regret to announce the death at the age of seventy-four of the Reverend John Sylvester Blampied, for many years Rector of St. Clement's Church, Vale Street, North London. Pneumonia following a chill ended a career that had often attracted public attention—particularly in connection with the preservation of ancient footpaths, a cause of which Mr. Blampied had been a valiant if sometimes tempestuous champion. His death took place in Liverpool, and funeral services will be held at St. Clement's on Friday.

Rainier stared at the paragraph long enough to read it several times, then handed it back. His face was very pale. "LIVERPOOL? What was he doing there?"

"It doesn't say."

"I—I think I can guess. He'd gone to look for me."

"We don't KNOW that."

"But isn't it probable?"

"It's—it's possible. But you couldn't help it. You couldn't help finding out who you were."

"I can't help comparing what I found with what I lost!"

"You didn't lose permanently. You've got it all back now."

"But too late." He waved his arm with sudden comprehensive emphasis. "ISN'T it too late? I'm down to ask a question in the House shortly, but not THAT question, yet it's the only one worth asking or answering... isn't EVERYTHING too late? I should have stayed in that London attic. There were things to do in those days if one had vision to do them, but now there's neither time nor vision, but only this whiff of putrefying too-lateness. It was almost too late even then, except that by a sort of miracle there came a gap in long-gathering clouds—an incredibly last chance—a golden shaft along which England might have climbed back to glory."

"Less lyrically, you mean you'd like to set the clock back?"

"Yes, set it back, and set it right, and then wind it up, because it's been running down ever since Englishmen were more interested in the price of things on the market than what they could grow in their own gardens."

"I see. A back-to-the-land movement?"

"Back anywhere away from the unrealness of counting able-bodied men as a national burden just because they're listed as unemployed, and figures in bank ledgers as assets just because they're supposed to represent riches. Back anywhere from the mood in

180

which poor men beg me for jobs in Rainier factories and rich men for tips about Rainier shares."

"All the same, though—and you've often said it yourself— the Rainier firm gives steady employment to thousands—"

"I know, I know. But I know too that the way that made Rainiers rich was the opposite of the way to make England strong."

"Yet if war comes, won't the riches of Rainier have been of some benefit? After all, the new steelworks you were able to build two years ago, and the mass-production motor plant—"

"True—and what a desolate irony! But only HALF true, because strength is only half in tanks and steel. The other half is faith, wisdom —"

A House servant approached and said something in his ear; he answered, consulting his watch: "Oh yes. I'll come at once." Then he added to me: "It's time for that question."

We left the table and walked through the Smoking Room to the Lobby; then we separated, he to enter the Chamber, I to watch and listen from the Strangers' Gallery.

Again, as earlier at the Cement meeting, I was in no mood for correct secretarial concentration; from where I sat the main thing that impressed me was his strained pallor on rising to speak; in the green-yellow glow that came on as dusk fell his face took on a curious transparency, as if some secret hidden self were flooding outwards and upwards. But that, I knew, was a mere trick of artificial light; the House of Commons illumination flatters in such a way, often gilding with spirituality a scene which is not, in itself, VERY remarkable—a few Members going through the formality which would later entitle them to boast of having "raised the matter in the House," than which, except for writing letters to The Times, fortunate generations of Englishmen were never called upon to do more. That afternoon the benches were thinly populated, nothing important was expected, and I find from newspaper reports that the following took place:—

Mr. Charles Rainier (Conservative: West Lythamshire) asked whether a consignment of trade catalogues dispatched by a business firm in his constituency had been confiscated by the port authorities at Balos Blanca, and whether this was not contrary to Section 19 of the recent Trade Convention signed at Amazillo.

The Right Honourable Sir George Smith-Jordan (Conservative: Houghley), replying for the Government, said he had been informed by His Majesty's Consul at Balos Blanca that the reported confiscation had been only partial and temporary, affecting a certain section of the catalogues about which there appeared to have been some linguistic misunderstanding, and that the greater part of the consignment had since been delivered to the addressees. As to whether the action of the port authorities had or had not been an infringement of any clause of the Amazillo Trade Convention, he was not in a position to say until further information had been received.

Mr. Jack Wells (Labour: Mawlington) asked whether, having regard to the general unsatisfactoriness of the incident, His Majesty's Government would consider the omission of Balos Blanca from the scheduled list of ports of call during the proposed Good-Will Tour of the British Trade Delegation in 1940.

The Right Honourable Sir George Smith-Jordan: No, sir.

Immediately after that, Rainier picked up his papers and walked out, leaving the Mother of Parliaments to struggle along with barely more than a quorum till after the dinner hour. Meanwhile I left the Gallery, in which a small crowd of provincial and foreign visitors had been defiantly concealing their disappointment at the proceedings below, and met him in the Lobby; he was gossiping with strangers, but behind the façade of casualness I saw how haggard he looked, his face restlessly twitching in and out of smiles. Seeing me approach he made a sign for me to wait while he detached himself from the crowd—they were constituents, he explained later, and constituents had to be humoured, especially when one's majority had been only twelve last time. "They're so proud because they heard me ask about that catalogue business—they have a touching belief that a question in Parliament pulls invisible wires, sets invisible forces in motion, works invisible miracles all over the world."

Passing through the Smoking Room again on the way to the Terrace we saw the name "McAlister" on the notice-board that announced current speakers; Rainier smiled and said that was fine—McAlister always gave one a chance to stroll for half an hour with the certainty of not missing anything. "By the way, I'm dining at the Historians' Club, so I don't think I'll need you for the rest of the evening."

"Are you down to speak?"

"I'm not on the programme, but I daresay I'll be asked."

"You don't have to go if you'd rather not. I can make up some excuse."

"What's the idea—encouraging me to shirk?"

"I thought—perhaps—you might be feeling rather exhausted."

"Not a bit of it NOW. I'm game for more than a speech at a Club dinner. You'd be surprised if you knew what's in my mind."

We stepped into the cool evening air and began walking towards Westminster Bridge. He had given me a cue to say what I had been planning most of the day.

"My advice would be to put the whole thing OUT of your mind, now that it's happened at last, and there isn't a gap any longer. You ought to be satisfied."

"SATISFIED?" He swung round on me. "When you say that I wonder if— if you quite realize—what it all amounts to?"

"Oh yes, I do. It means that so far as there was ever anything abnormal in your life, you're now completely cured."

We came near the Bridge, a blaze of illumination from lines of trams, and in that light I saw such anguish in his eyes that I could only repeat, with an emphasis that somehow drained away as the words were spoken: "Utterly and completely cured."

"You don't REALLY think that's all it amounts to? You must know there's only one thing that matters—only one thing left for me to do."

"And that is?"

"I must find her."

So there it was squarely before us, the issue that had of course been in my mind, that I had done a pathetic best to make him shirk by conscientiously shirking it myself. We walked a little way in silence.

"After all these years," I said at length, "it doesn't seem very likely."

"I must try."

"It was up to her, surely, to look for you—yet apparently she never did."

"Maybe. Maybe not. I don't care. And besides—there's my son. She was going to have a child."

"But even a return of memory can't prove it was a boy."

He smiled. "No, but I hope so. I've always wanted a boy. He'd be eighteen now. I must find him... both of them."

"And if by chance—not that I think there IS much chance— but just for the sake of argument—if you SHOULD happen to succeed, what then?"

He answered with a certain impregnable simplicity: "Then I should be happy again."

"Possibly, but apart from your own personal happiness... Look here, why not think it over—not now—but later—calmly— when you're alone?"

"I'm calm now, and it doesn't particularly help me to be alone when I think. I was thinking it over very clearly all the time I was asking that question in the House."

"Yes, I could see you were—but that doesn't meet my point, which is that you haven't—you can't have—reckoned with all the complications—"

"COMPLICATIONS? You'll be telling me next I ought to consult old Truslove!"

"Actually I wasn't thinking of legal complications at all, though they doubtless exist. It's other kinds you'd find most disagreeable— newspaper publicity, gossip and scandal that wouldn't do you any good politically."

"I think I've had enough good done to me politically."

"And then of course there's your wife. Whatever your private feelings are, and of course it's none of my business, you ought at least to consider HER position."

"Anything I ought to do now is nothing compared with what I ought to have done before."

"But that's in the past—IRREVOCABLE."

"No, not if she and I can find each other again."

"It seems to me we're talking about different persons."

"Oh, I see."

We walked on for another spell of silence. Then I said: "But you don't even know that the... the other woman's ALIVE?"

He was silent for a while. "DO you?" I pressed.

"No, that's true." Then suddenly: "But if she is, and I can find her, then nothing on earth will stop me—neither publicity, nor politics, nor... " He turned to me abruptly. "I don't want to be dramatic. Let's leave that to the journalists who'll have the job of making a nine days' wonder of it."

"Maybe they won't. Maybe they'll have more important news, the way events are going."

As we turned into the Smoking Room the board showed that McAlister was still speaking. A group of Members at one of the tables greeted Rainier chaffingly and asked him to join them; as if relieved to be rid of the argument he gave me a nod of friendly farewell and sat down with them, completely master of himself so far as voice and manner were concerned. But I heard one of them say, just as I was entering the corridor: "You look pretty washed-out, Rainier—what's the matter? Hitler getting on your nerves?"

I went back to my rooms in Bedford Square and spent the evening with the latest editions of the papers. But I could not keep my mind on the fast-developing European crisis; my thoughts were full of Rainier and his story; I mused upon his whole life as I now knew it: childhood at Stourton, with the despotic father and adored mother; schooldays; then the war, the hospitals, the brief unmemoried idyll; then the return to the routine struggle that had brought him wealth, power, and a measure of fame. I could not but feel his personal drama near to me as I turned on the radio for the larger drama of our times, for that too had reached a moment of desperate retrospect.

About midnight I strolled into Tottenham Court Road and watched the crowd pouring out of theatres and restaurants; when I returned there was a letter pushed under the door. It was from Rainier, enclosing another letter. He wrote:—

I said I would let you see that last note Kitty wrote me; here it is, and whatever it means to you, to me, re-reading it just now, it meant as much more as you can possibly imagine. Yrs. C. R.

The letter from Kitty, dated September 30, 1929, was as follows: —

MY DEAR CHARLES,

I'm writing this in a hurry, but after thinking things out as slowly and carefully as even you could—in fact I've been gathering together many thoughts I began to have the moment we left the Jungfraujoch last April, in the train and on the boat, and then again off and on ever since, and especially in the restaurant tonight—Dearest, it wasn't the weather or the altitude or the stock market—it was our own hearts sinking a little, and I'm going to face that frankly, because I doubt if you ever would or could. I can't marry you, Charles dear—that's what it amounts to. We've had marvellous times, we'd still go on having them, we have so much in common, the same way of seeing things, the same kind of craziness (though you keep yours in check more than I do)—you could make me perfectly happy if only I were selfish enough not to care or stupid enough not to

184

notice that at some point in the final argument you waver and turn away. So here's my decision—No, darling, while it's still not quite too late; and here are my plans—I'm leaving London immediately, I'll have gone before you read this—I shall probably join Jill (wherever she is, Luxor, I think)—not tragically, but in a mood to see what fun I can find —and I usually can. I'm sending this by special messenger because I want it to reach you before you go to the office, so that you won't send out those invitations and then have to cancel them—as for selling short to amuse me, it wouldn't amuse me, I'm afraid, but if you think it would amuse you, why don't you do it? Dear Charles, I want you to be happy, to be amused, to do things because you desire them, not because you're urged or tempted; I wish we could be and do all we talked of on the mountain, but the fact is, I'm not the one for you, though God knows the mistake was excusable for both of us, because I'm NEARLY the one—I claim that much and it's something to go on being proud of. But "nearly" isn't enough for a lifetime —it would be too hard to strain after the hidden difference. And there's something else that may sound utterly absurd, but let me say it —sometimes, especially when we've been closest, I've had a curious feeling that I REMIND YOU OF SOMEONE ELSE—someone you may have met or may yet meet—because with that strange memory of yours, the tenses get mixed up—or don't they? But Charles, because I AM so nearly the one, and because I love you more than anyone I shall ever marry, will you forgive me for this upset and stay friends?—K.

I went to his City office the following morning and waited till after ten o'clock (he usually arrived at nine); then I rang up his Club and was told he had left very early, giving no forwarding address. It was a day of such important engagements that I went over to the Club immediately, hoping to find out more than they would tell me over the telephone.

The porter, who knew me, said he had left about six, by car.

"Hanson was with him then?"

"No, sir, he drove alone. It wasn't his usual car—quite a small one, a brown two-seater."

"But he hasn't got a two-seater."

"Well, he went away in one—that's all I can tell you, sir. I think it was an Austin, but I'm not sure."

"And he left no message for me?"

"No, sir—no message for anybody, except that he'd be away till he got back. That was his phrase. He seemed in a very cheerful mood. I thought maybe he had some good news, but it don't look like it from today's papers."

"Well, I expect I'll hear from him—it's all right." I went away as if I thought it really was, because I was anxious not to start gossip at the Club. Then I went back to the City office and pretended the mystery was cleared up—he'd had to go away for a few days on an important political errand; I telephoned to cancel all his appointments for the day, giving the same story, except that to those in the political world I made out it was a business errand. There were certain advantages in belonging to two worlds. I wondered if I should hear from him, by either wire or telephone, as the day proceeded, but no message came, and in the late afternoon I drove to Stourton. There were several cars outside the main entrance, but none was a brown two-seater; I hadn't really expected it. Woburn met me on the threshold. "What are YOU doing here?" he greeted me, as if he owned the place.

"What are YOU doing here, for that matter? Still on the catalogue?"

"No, I've finished that and several more since. I'm just a guest."

"Well, that's very nice."

"There's going to be a big party this week-end."

There was, and that was what I had come about. "Where's Mrs. Rainier?"

"On the terrace—dispensing cocktails and small talk with her usual glassy proficiency. Just a local crowd—they'll go soon."

"Let's join them."

I realized then, as soon as I saw her in the distance, how keenly my sympathies had been enlisted for a woman whose glassiest proficiency could hardly help her much in the situation that was now so rapidly developing. As we shook hands she seemed to me rather like a pathetic tight-rope walker doing her tricks in confident unawareness that the rope was about to be cut.

The crowd were mostly neighbours whom I had met before, but there was one fresh face—Sir William Somebody, whom I knew to be a retired diplomat who lived on his pension in a farmhouse rented from the Rainiers. Mrs. Rainier introduced me with the remark that perhaps, having just driven from London, I could give him the latest news. "Sir William thinks the situation's far worse than people realize."

I passed on what news there was; then a girl called Cynthia exclaimed: "We mustn't miss the wireless bulletin. Hasn't he been making another speech today?" (It had come to the point where an unrelated "he" could only refer to Hitler.)

"Just words, nothing but words," someone else muttered.

"Better than actions, anyhow."

Mrs. Rainier intervened lazily: "Oh, I'm not so sure of that as I used to be. I mean, when you're waiting for something to happen, and rather dreading it..." She went on: "Have you ever been going somewhere with a crowd and you're certain it's the wrong road and you tell them, but they won't listen, so you just have to plod along in what you know is the wrong direction till somebody more important gets the same idea?"

"A parable, darling. Please interpret."

She seemed embarrassed by being the focus of attention—which was unusual of her. "No, thanks, Cynthia. That's been enough words for ME." She laughed and came round with the cocktail-shaker, refilling the glasses, including her own.

Sir William resumed: "Well, if he DOES march into Poland, we shall fight." Then suddenly he pointed to the great avenue of elms for which Stourton was famous. "Look at those trees—planted two centuries ago, deliberately, by someone who thought of a

186

time when someone else would see them like this. Who could do such a thing today?" Nobody informed him, and after a pause to deposit an olive stone in an ash-tray he went on: "The most we do is to bury things under foundation-stones so that future civilizations can dig into our ruins and wonder."

We all laughed, because after a few drinks what can one do but laugh; then in ones and twos the party dispersed and drove away in its cars. I went to the library and turned on the radio for the news bulletin; Hitler's speech had been just another threat to march. Somehow one didn't believe he would; there had been crises before, ending up in a deal; so that one had the half-cynical suspicion that both sides were secretly arranging another deal and that the wordy warfare was just shadow-boxing, face-saving, anything but a prelude to the guns. While I was listening Sheldon entered to announce that dinner would be almost immediately, and that Mrs. Rainier had said "not dress."

"Good—since I haven't brought anything."

"I think Mrs. Rainier anticipated that."

"Very thoughtful of her."

"You left Mr. Rainier in the City?"

"Er... yes."

"Then you'll be going back in the morning?"

"I expect so."

He nodded and went to the door, then turned and asked: "What's going to happen, do you think?"

"Can't tell yet, but it looks pretty serious."

He said, still standing in the doorway: "I mean what's going to happen to Mr. Rainier?"

He went on, facing my stare: "You said he's in the City."

"I didn't say that. I said I left him there."

"Don't you know where he is now?"

"No."

"Isn't that rather peculiar?"

"Many things are peculiar, Sheldon."

"Are you worried about him?... You must excuse me, I have a special reason for asking."

"I'm sure you have. It might even be the same reason I have for not answering."

He came back into the room. "Mr. Harrison... has he gone away to look for somebody?"

"I really don't think I can discuss—" Then something in his glance made me add: "But supposing he had—then what?"

187

He smiled his slow slanting smile. "Then you don't need to worry."

"I didn't say I was worrying at all. But why don't I need to?"

"Because he won't succeed in finding the person he's looking for."

"How do you know?"

"Because he never has succeeded."

He left me then, and a few minutes later the dinner-gong sounded. When I joined Mrs. Rainier in the dining-room, with Sheldon standing at the sideboard, I had a feeling they had been exchanging glances if not words about me, but I could not say much during dinner, on account of Woburn's presence. As if by tacit agreement we left him most of the talking, which he kept up very agreeably throughout the meal—he was really a very adaptable young man, you would have thought him born and bred at Stourton, except that most of those who had been were so much less smoothly articulate. I was wondering how I could shake him off afterwards, but Mrs. Rainier did it for me, saying outright that she expected I had some business to talk over, so if Woburn would excuse us...

"Do you mind if we have a fire?" she asked, as soon as we were alone in the drawing-room. I helped her to remove the heavy screen, saying something about the night being cold for the eve of September.

"It isn't that," she answered, kneeling on the hearth-rug. "But it makes a more cheerful background when so many uncheerful things are happening."

Looking at her then, I realized for the first time how much more she was than merely vivacious and attractive; her face had a beauty that poured into it from within—a secret, serene radiance. She went on, stooping to the fire: "You've saved me the trouble of calling at the office tomorrow —I wanted to ask about something."

"Good job you didn't, because I'm not sure Mr. Rainier will be there."

"Oh? He's gone away somewhere?"

"Yes." I remembered him saying she was never surprised at any of his movements. "And as I don't know when exactly he'll be coming back, I was wondering about the week-end plans."

"The political situation's so serious I doubt if we'd have had the party anyway. Yes, let's cancel it."

"That's what I was going to suggest."

"Nice of you, but why didn't you telephone?" She added hastily: "Not that I'm not pleased to see you—I always am—but it gave you the journey."

"Oh, I didn't mind. I'm equally pleased to see YOU."

She laughed. "Now we've had the exchange of compliments—"

She didn't know what else to say, I could see that; and after a pause I resumed: "What was it you wanted to ask about if you had called at the office?"

"Oh yes, maybe you can tell me just as well. Why did you and Charles drive out to Melbury the other night?"

The sheer unexpectedness of the question nonplussed me for a moment. In the meantime she went on: "And don't blame Hanson—he wasn't to know he'd overheard such a tremendous secret!" She was laughing.

"Oh, not—er—exactly a secret."

"Well, a mystery."

I said to gain time: "And you were going to pay a special visit just to ask that?"

"Yes, indeed—I've been terribly curious ever since I heard about it."

"Then it's my turn to say why didn't you telephone?"

"Perhaps because I wanted to see your faces when I asked you—it's so much harder to hide something that way!" She laughed again. "Won't you let me in on the puzzle? Melbury's such an odd place for anyone to make a trip to."

It suddenly occurred to me that she had to know, and now was the chance to tell her. I said: "Mr. Rainier was once in a hospital at Melbury."

In the blaze of fresh firelight I could see the laughter drain away from her face and a sudden pallor enter it; but in another second she was smiling again.

"Well, it seems a queer reason for driving somewhere in pouring rain in the middle of the night. For that matter Charles was at other hospitals too —he was pretty badly hurt in the war, you know. It even affected his memory for a time. I never knew quite how much you had gathered about all that—" She was striving to seem very casual.

"Just the main facts, that's all."

"He told you them himself?"

"Yes."

The smile remained as if fixed to her face. "Oh, I'm so glad, because it shows how close you must have been to him as a friend. He doesn't often talk about it to anybody. And to me he NEVER talks about it."

"Never?"

"No, never. Isn't that strange? But then he's so little with me— and mostly we have business or politics to talk about. Our marriage is a very happy one, but it's never been —well, CLOSE is perhaps the word. We've never even had a close quarrel."

"But you love him?"

"Well, what do you think? I adore him—most women do. Haven't you noticed that? All his life he could always have had any pretty woman he wanted."

"So it isn't surprising that he GOT the pretty woman he wanted."

"More compliments?... Oh, but you should have seen the girl he was engaged to when I first became his secretary. I WAS his secretary—you knew that too, I suppose? She was much prettier than me, AND younger. Kitty, her name was. She married somebody else and died—I can't think why —I mean why she married somebody else, not why she died—she died of malaria—I suppose there's no reason at all for that, except mosquitoes. I think they'd have been very happy—she and Charles, I mean, not the mosquitoes—but she'd have tried to make him give up the business. I know that, because she told me."

I could catch a note of hysteria subdued behind her forced facetiousness; I said, as calmly as I could: "You knew her well, then?"

"Only by talking to her while she used to wait in the office for Charles."

"Tell me—if it isn't impertinent to ask—were you also in love with him then?"

She laughed. "Of course. Right from the first moment I set eyes on him... But that didn't make me jealous of Kitty—only a bit envious, perhaps. I wonder how it would have worked out—Charles without all the business and politics. Of course he found out later I was the one to help him in that, and so I have—I've done my best to give him everything he wants—success—his ambitions... and yet sometimes lately I've thought... well, like my parable."

"Parable?"

"Cynthia called it that during cocktails, don't you remember? About going somewhere with someone and having doubts about it being the right road, but there's nothing you can do but plod along until the other person begins to doubt. And then, of course, if you admit that you had doubts all the time, as likely as not he turns on you and says—well, why didn't you warn me?"

"Well, why didn't you?"

"Because he wouldn't have taken any notice if I had. In fact he might not even have married me—and I WANTED him to marry me. After Kitty died he threw himself into business more than ever—which gave me my chance —oh, I admit I was quite designing about it. So was he. He found how good I was—what a valuable merger it would be. He was always clever about mergers..."

"Did that entirely satisfy you?"

"No, but I thought it might lead to something that would—to the REAL closeness. But it's hard to get close when so many things are in the way... May I have a light?" She was reaching for a cigarette on the side table and I could see that her hand was trembling. She added, as I held the match: "Do you want a drink in exchange?"

"I think I'd rather wait till later."

"Later? Well, how long do you expect to sit up and talk parables?"

I said then: "Mrs. Rainier, I think I'd better tell you more about the visit to Melbury."

"Oh yes, the mystery—do PLEASE tell me everything! What did you find there?"

190

She was smiling as I began to tell her, and the smile grew faint as I proceeded, then appeared again in time for the end. I told her all that was important for her to know— the fact of his earlier marriage, his life during those brief months immediately afterwards, and how that life had come to an abrupt finish. I did not try to make it easier for her by a gingerly approach to the problem, or by minimizing its complexities. And I told her how he had reacted to the recent return of memory—his first excitement, then his calmer determination and bitter regret for the years between. Finally I told her that though it seemed to me highly unlikely that after two decades he would succeed in tracing someone who hadn't apparently succeeded in the much easier task of tracing him during the same interval, and though the gap of years gave legal as well as every other kind of sanction to what had happened since, she must be prepared for the faint possibility; and that if it happened the publicity would be neither pleasant for her nor helpful to his position.

"He must know that too."

"Yes, but in his present mood he doesn't care."

"Oh, HE DOESN'T CARE?" She said that so softly, so gently, still smiling. I tried to think of something to express the wave of sympathy that overcame me; in the end I could only give her my silence. Presently she touched my hand and said: "Thank you for telling me all this."

"I must say you take it very well."

"Did you expect me to make a scene?"

"No, but... when I try to imagine your feelings..."

"I don't feel anything yet, at least not much, but I keep on thinking of what you said— that HE DOESN'T CARE!"

"I know it's terrible, but—"

"Oh, no, it's WONDERFUL! He'd throw over everything—his future —his ambitions— EVERYTHING—if he could find her!"

"In his present mood he thinks so."

"Don't keep saying 'in his present mood.' Maybe his present mood is himself, and all the other moods were false... How do we know?"

"There's one thing we do know—that people are remembered as they were last seen— and twenty years is a long time."

She turned to me with brightly shining eyes.

"How sad that is, and how true."

"And from your point of view—how fortunate."

"Oh no, no—I wish she were still as he remembers her. I wish there WERE such a miracle. If all of us could go back twenty years—how different the world would be! I want him to be happy, I always have... Now will you have your drink?"

"If you will too."

She went over to the table and mixed them; I could see she was glad of something to do. Stooping over the glasses she continued: "I suppose he told you a great deal more than you've told me?"

"Only details."

"Ah, but the details—those are what I want to hear. Did he remember things very clearly?"

"Yes."

"Places and people?"

"Yes."

"Tell me some of them."

I hesitated, again catching the note of hysteria in her voice; she added: "It doesn't hurt me—as much as you think. Tell me some of them... You say he met her first at Melbury?"

"Yes—on that first Armistice Day."

"And they were married in London?"

"Yes."

"Where did he propose to her? Did he tell you that?"

"A village in the country somewhere—I think it was called Beachings Over."

"Beachings Over... an odd name."

"England is full of them."

"I know—like Nether Wallop and Shallow Bowells..." She turned round with my drink. "And war coming to them all again. Do you think there's still a chance of avoiding it?"

"There's always a chance of postponing it."

"No—we've had enough of that."

"I think so too."

"But we're not ready yet, are we?"

"We're terribly unready. We missed our ways years ago and found a wide, comfortable road, fine for sleep-walkers, but it had the major drawback of wandering just anywhere, at random."

"Charles always thought that, but as a rich man it wasn't easy for him to say so. Being rich tied his hands and stopped his mouth and took up his time —so that the wasted years wasted him too..."

"I think he's begun to realize that."

"Yes, he's sure of something at last... Another drink?"

"No, thanks."

A long pause. "There's nothing we can do about it now, is there?"

"Are you talking about—er—the country—or— er—"

"Both, in a way."

"I think one can make up for lost time, but one can't salvage it. That's why HIS quest is so hopeless."

Her voice softened. "So you think that's where he's gone—to look for her?"

"It's possible... But to look for her as she WAS, and that's impossible."

The hysteria touched her voice again. "Tell me another detail—no matter how small or trivial—please tell me—"

"I think you're needlessly upsetting yourself."

"No, it isn't upsetting—it's—it's almost helping me in a way—tell me something—"

"I'd rather not, and besides, it's hard to think—"

"Oh, but you said he talked all night and you've only talked for an hour so far. There must be hundreds of things—names of places or incidents that happened here or there— or how she looked..."

"Well... let me see..."

"How DID she look? Did he remember her well?"

"He seemed to, though he never described her exactly—but he did say—I believe he said when they first met she was wearing a little fur hat like a fez... Or no, I may have mixed things up—that was Kitty when she stepped out of the train at Interlaken."

"Interlaken?"

"They had a holiday there—he and Kitty."

"I know. And SHE was wearing a little fur hat like a fez? Or the other one? Or both, maybe—but wouldn't that be rather improbable?"

"Yes, of course. I'm sorry—it was like me to choose a detail I'd get confused over."

She put her hand in mine. "It doesn't matter. You've been very kind. I wish I'd known you better—and earlier. Thank you again."

"You understand that I'm anxious to help BOTH of you?"

"Yes, I understand. But I don't know how you can."

"Anyhow, there's a sort of chilly comfort in thinking how unimportant all one's personal affairs are these days."

She got up and began walking to the door. "Yes, but when that sort of comfort has chilled one quite thoroughly, the warmth comes—the feeling that nothing matters EXCEPT personal feelings... the what-if-the-world-should-end-tonight mood."

We shook hands at the doorway, and there she added, smiling: "Perhaps our world IS ending tonight..."

* * * * *

I stayed in the drawing-room a little while after she had gone; then I thought it would be only civil to find Woburn. He was in the library, listening to the radio. "Still nothing definite. You know, if there's a war, I want to get in the Air Force." We had another drink and talked for about an hour before going upstairs.

I had asked Sheldon to call me at seven; he did so, bringing in a cup of tea. "I thought you'd wish to know the news—it just came over the wireless." Then he told me.

I got up hurriedly. It was a perfect late-summer morning, cool and fresh, with a haze of mist over the hills. Woburn had brought a small radio into the breakfast room; we hardly exchanged a greeting, but sat in front of the instrument, listening as the first reports came through. Presently Mrs. Rainier entered, stood in the doorway to hear a few sentences, then joined us with the same kind of whispered perfunctory good-morning. The bulletin ended with a promise of more news soon, then merged into music.

That was how we had breakfast on that first morning of the second war —to the beat of a dance band and with the sunlight streaming through the windows of Stourton.

After breakfast we heard the news repeated, and found the strain almost intolerable. We strayed about the gardens, the three of us, then came back to the radio again; this time there were a few extra items, reports of half the world's grim awakening.

The newspapers came, but they were already old—printed hours before.

I telephoned the City office, and had to wait twenty minutes before the line was clear.

Then Woburn, after wandering restlessly in and out of rooms, said he would take a long walk. I think he would have liked either Mrs. Rainier or myself or both of us to suggest accompanying him, but we stayed each other with a glance. "He's a nice boy," she said, when he had gone.

"Yes, very."

"Does Charles like him?"

"Yes, I think so."

"I always hoped he would. I feel we've almost adopted him, in one sense."

"I sometimes think he feels that too."

"I'd like him to feel that... I once had a child, a boy, but he died..."

"I never knew that."

"Charles would have made a good father, don't you think?"

"Yes... he must have been terribly disappointed."

"What will Woburn do now?"

"He said he'd join the Air Force."

She moved restlessly to the radio, where the music had suddenly stopped. Another news item: the Germans had crossed the Polish frontiers at many places; the war machine was already clanking into gear.

"I can't stand this—I half wish now we'd gone with him for the walk. Don't leave me alone here—you don't have to return to the City, do you?"

"No, not yet, anyhow. I just rang up the office. They haven't had any news or message."

"Oh... let's go somewhere then. I'll drive you. There's nothing else to do —we'll go mad if we sit over the radio all day."

We took her car, which was an open sports Bentley, and set out. The Stourton parkland had never looked more wonderful; it was as if it had the mood to spread its beauty as a last temptation to remain at peace, or, failing that, as a last spendthrift offering to a thankless world. We passed quickly, then threaded the winding gravel roads over the estate to an exit I had not known of before—it opened on to the road to Faringdon. Through the still misty morning we raced westward and northward; but at Lechlade the sun was bright and the clock showed ten minutes past ten. A few miles beyond Burford the country rolled into uplands, and presently we left the main road altogether, slowing for tree-hidden corners and streams that crossed the lanes in wide sandy shallows, till at last in the distance we saw a rim of green against the blue.

"Perhaps it will be a simpler England after the war," was one of the things she said.

"You're already thinking of AFTER the war?"

"Of course. The NEXT Armistice Day, whenever it comes."

"It'll be a different England, that's very certain. Not so rich, and not so snobbish—but maybe we can do without some of the riches and all the snobbery."

She nodded: "Maybe we can do without Stourton—and Bentleys."

"And two-for-one bonus issues."

"And guinea biographies like the one somebody once wrote about Charles's father."

"And parties for His Excellency to meet the winners of the Ladies' Doubles."

She laughed. "And champagne when you've already had enough champagne."

"How CAN we be so absurd—on a day like this?"

"Maybe it isn't so absurd."

"Where are you taking me?"

"Oh, just somewhere in England, as the war bulletins may say one of these days."

We drove on, mile after mile, till at a turn of the road the hills ahead of us sharpened into a ridge and at the same turn also there was a signpost which made me cry out, with a sudden catch of breath: "Did you see THAT?"

"I know. I wanted to come here."

"But—you shouldn't—it's only torturing yourself— "

"No, no. I promise I won't be upset—see, I'm quite calm."

"But all this probing of the past—"

"That's where the future will take us, maybe—back to the past. A simpler England. Old England."

And then we came upon the gray cottages fronting the stream, the square-towered church, the ledge in the stream where the water sparkled. We parked our car by the church and walked along the street. A postman late on his morning rounds stared with friendly curiosity at us and the car, then said "Good morning." A fluff of wind blew tall hollyhocks towards us. Somebody was clipping a hedge; an old dog loitered into a fresh patch of shade. Little things—but I shall remember them long after much else has been forgotten.

There seemed no special significance anywhere, no sign that a war had begun.

But as we neared the post-office I caught sight of something that to me was most significant of all—a small brown two-seater car. I walked over to it; a man saw me examining the licence. "If you're looking for the tall gentleman," he came over to say, "I think he took a walk up the hill."

I turned to Mrs. Rainier. "CHARLES?" was all she whispered.

"Might be. It meets the Club porter's description and it was hired from a London firm."

We turned off the main road by a path crossing an open field towards the hill; as we were climbing the chime of three quarters came up to us, blown faint by the breeze. The slope was too steep for much talk, but when we came within a few yards of the ridge she halted to gain breath, gazing down over the village.

"Looks as if it has never changed."

"I don't suppose it has, much, in a thousand years."

"That makes twenty seem only yesterday."

"If we meet him, what are you going to say?"

"I don't know. I can't know—before I see him."

"He'll wonder why on earth we've come HERE, of all places."

"Then we'll ask him why on earth HE'S here. Perhaps we'll both have to pretend we came to look at the five counties."

196

She resumed the climb, and in another moment we could see that the summit dipped again to a further summit, perhaps higher, and that in the hollow between lay a little pond. There was a man lying beside it with arms outstretched, as if he had flung himself there after the climb. He did not move as we approached, but presently we saw smoke curling from a cigarette between his fingers.

"He's not asleep," I said. "He's just resting."

I saw her eyes and the way her lips trembled; something suddenly occurred to me. "By the way, how did you know there were *five* counties?"

But she didn't answer; already she was rushing down the slope. He saw her in time to rise to his feet; she stopped then, several yards away, and for a few seconds both were staring at each other, hard and still and silent. Then he whispered something I couldn't hear; but I knew in a flash that the gap was closed, that the random years were at an end, that the past and the future would join. She knew this too, for she ran into his arms calling out: "Oh, Smithy—Smithy—it may not be too late!"

CPSIA information can be obtained at www.ICGtesting.com
Printed in the USA
BVOW09s0752211015

423453BV00004B/34/P